THE IMPERFECTS

THE IMPERFECTS

AMY MEYERSON

THORNDIKE PRESS
A part of Gale, a Cengage Company

LIBRARY OF CONGRESS CIP DATA ON FILE.
CATALOGUING IN PUBLICATION FOR THIS BOOK
IS AVAILABLE FROM THE LIBRARY OF CONGRESS

ISBN-13: 978-1-4328-8321-8 (hardcover alk. paper)

Published by arrangement with Harlequin Books S.A.

Printed in Mexico
Print Number: 01   Print Year: 2020

For my son, I promise to tell you all the stories I know and to help you discover the ones I don't.

"O Diamond! Diamond! Thou little knowest the mischief done!"

— SIR ISAAC NEWTON

VII

"O Diamond! Diamond! Thou little
knowest the mischief done."

— SIR ISAAC NEWTON

VIENNA, 1918

She keeps a journal to forget as much as to remember. She writes to remember the taste of Istvan's mouth, the rumble of his laughter. To memorialize the vows they made to each other, which were real even if they were not before God. She writes to forget how it ended in violence. To banish the memory of escaping with the children, leaving him alone to fight a surging mob.

Her words are fast and jumbled. They aren't meant to be reread, to document the end of an era, the fall of an empire, the collapse of a romance. They are for her, right now, in these early-morning hours when everyone else in the palace is asleep, so her thoughts drift to Istvan and the child inside her.

She stumbles midsentence at the sound of footsteps approaching her chamber. Her first thought is that the men with guns are back. Heart pounding, she clutches the journal to her chest. Light trickles in from the hall as the toe of a boot inches into her bedroom. She clings to the journal as though her memories of Istvan will protect her. This is it, she thinks. The men with guns will get her this time.

A slender figure enters her room, his face backlit by the pale light from the hall, shadowing his features. As he approaches, he motions for her to stay quiet.

"We must go." His German is eloquent. Aristocratic. Familiar. "We must leave now."

He steps closer and she sees the outline of his ears, the way they stick out like a child's.

"Your Imperial Majesty?" Her body relaxes, then tightens with a new discomfort. He's a gentle man, this emperor. Faithful to the crown and his wife. Still, he shouldn't be in her bedroom.

She rests her journal on the bed and stands too quickly, having to sit back down. By now, she should be used to the swell of her stomach, the way abrupt movements spark pains in her pelvis, but every morning she experiences it anew, the secret that she won't be able to hide much longer.

The emperor's face always surprises her. His sad eyes. The thick mustache he looks too young to grow. He looks impossibly young now as he rests his hand on her shoulder. The contact startles her, and he pulls away like he might catch something. He knows. Of course he knows. The empress must have told him. Just yesterday, she'd stood when the empress appeared in the nursery, and her skirt caught the contour of her round stomach. She watched as the truth landed on the empress's face. The look of horror that she was with child and unwed. Of betrayal.

"The car is waiting. We must leave now." He motions for her to hurry.

After she follows him into the hall, she realizes she's only wearing a nightgown and has left her journal on the bed.

She turns back toward the room. "I need a coat."

"Take mine." He lifts the black jacket from his shoulders and wraps it around her, the wool thick and heavy. He signals for her to walk ahead of him down the dimly lit hall.

"The children," she says as they pass the nursery.

He nudges her to keep walking. Fear animates her limbs, propelling her forward.

The halls of the palace are eerily silent. They have been this way since she arrived. The sentries have returned to Hungary, the palace gendarmes have dispersed in Vienna. The Life Guards, despite the lifelong oaths of loyalty they took, have abandoned their posts. The footmen, the chambermaids, the doorkeepers, all gone. Cadets have taken their place, fewer than there were before and younger. Two of these young men wait at the door to the courtyard. Another four stand at the bottom of the stairs where the emperor's personal car is waiting. She's never ridden in it before.

The sky is brightening with dawn, blanketed in mist that makes the gray stone courtyard look like a painting, slightly blurred, romantic. The emperor descends the stairs, and she follows as though sleepwalking.

A cadet opens the car door, ready to assist her into the backseat. The driver stares ahead like he is as mechanical as the engine. She walks up to the car, but the emperor stops a few paces back. She looks at him and realizes that she's expected to leave alone.

"Please, no," she begs. It's becoming clear. The family does not need to leave, not yet. Only her. She pleads, refusing the cadet's hand. Please, don't make her leave. The children, she loves them. They need her.

The cadet looks uncertainly at the emperor, who shakes his head, indicating that he shouldn't force her into the car.

12

These days, she fatigues easily. Chasing the children around the nursery or strolling beneath the pergolas of the Privy Gardens leaves her body too tired for sleep. Her refusal to get into the car ends quickly. She reaches for the cadet's hand. He stares at her, this fresh-faced boy, and she knows what he's thinking. What will become of her? To this she adds, what will become of the child inside her?

Once she's seated, the cadet shuts the door and steps away. Before the driver turns over the engine, the emperor approaches the open-air car. Only the damp, cool morning separates her from the emperor. He hesitates, and she remembers she is still wearing his coat. She begins to take it off.

"Keep it," he says.

She wraps it tightly around herself.

"Do you have somewhere to go?"

"I have a cousin." She has not seen her cousin in five years, not since she got the job at the palace. He is her only family, this cousin. He will take her in because she will not give him a choice.

In the time they've been outside, the sky has lightened to peach along the horizon. It has that promise of a new day, but she is not hopeful for this day or the one that follows. She knows she will not see the children

13

again. They will assume she abandoned them like everyone else did. She stares at the emperor's conflicted face and knows he will not reconsider. After all, this was not his decision. It was the empress's. He may rule the crumbling empire, but in this task, he is just the messenger.

With rushed movements, he reaches into his right pocket and lurches toward her, clutching something bulky.

"Take this," he says, leaning into the car and burrowing his hand into the pocket of his coat that she still wears.

She does not see what he gives her, only feels its weight. It's heavy. Metal. Cumbersome against her thigh. He steps back, and the driver starts the engine. The car bounces down the gravel road to the eastern gate. She glances back. The trees lining the drive create a tunnel with the emperor at the end, waiting in front of his sprawling yellow palace. He does not wave. He does not turn away. She watches him until the palace disappears from sight. Only then does she reach into the pocket to discover what he's given her.

PART ONE

ONE

The email hits the Millers' in-box at 4:07 p.m., Eastern Standard Time, with news that Helen Auerbach has died. Ashley, the eldest of Helen's three grandchildren, is shuttling her kids between school and extracurricular activities — soccer for her nine-year-old son, ballet for her eleven-year-old daughter. She hates how gendered their hobbies are. Why can't Tyler dance? Lydia kick balls? When she poses such questions, both children look slightly embarrassed for her, like she has mustard on the tip of her nose. Between school drop-offs and pickups, team practices and music lessons, her husband Ryan's dry cleaning, grocery shopping, and volunteering at the animal shelter, Ashley eats one to two meals a day in her car. Mustard on her nose is always a possibility.

Minutes before the email arrives, Ashley is daydreaming about that restorative hour where she will have the house to herself, her children ensconced in their predictable hobbies, her husband still at work in Manhattan, the dinner she's bought at the farmers' market, but will tell her family she's cooked, wrapped in tin foil on the kitchen counter. She'll pour a glass of wine and draw a bath. Ashley has never been the type of person who's needed alone time. In fact, she's always been somewhat afraid of it. She's never been a worrier, either. Lately, a bath here or a walk there has become a necessary escape from constantly having to pretend that everything is fine. During that peaceful, reprieving hour, she'll breathe, reminding herself that it's still too early to know what will happen to her husband.

From the backseat of her SUV, Ashley hears her daughter shriek and looks up in time to spot her son's fist let go of a tuft of Lydia's hair. Then another scream, this time from her son, followed by, "Mom! Lydia punched me." Ashley would never admit it, but she admires how Tyler always starts it yet always manages to position himself as the injured party. It's a quality he shares with his father. Ashley thinks it will suit him well in life until she remembers her husband's current situation.

"Tyler, leave your sister alone," she snaps, making eye contact with her dejected son through the rearview mirror before immediately feeling guilty. She isn't a yeller, at least not with her children. As she starts to apologize, her cell phone chimes. Her eyes drift toward the console where her phone rests in the cup holder. She squints to read the notification through the cracks cobwebbing her screen thanks to a drop months before.

Helen is dead.

That can't be right. She lifts the phone and there it is, the subject of a new email, announcing her grandmother's death.

"Mom!" Tyler's voice echoes with urgency. Ashley looks up from her phone as her SUV glides toward the sedan still idling at the red light. She slams the brakes, but not before her bumper crunches into the car ahead of hers.

Deborah Miller — not Debbie or Deb or Debra but a trisyllabic Deb-or-ah — is being pricked by dozens of needles minutes before she learns that her mother has passed. Chester, her acupuncturist-recently-turned-lover, pulls each needle out with a flourish that sends chills to every part of Deborah's body. She waits for him to take her on the table from behind, but the whole session has been dishearteningly professional, and she starts to wonder if she invented their romance. Deborah ran into Chester while she was on a blind date with a recent divorcé that hadn't been going well. Quickly falling into the maternal role, she asked the divorcé about his new bachelor pad, his new beard, his new sports car, tuning out his answers as she swore to herself she would never in a million years be set up again. As her date rambled about his morning running routine — another *new* — Deborah spotted a man seated alone at the bar. His ponytail cascaded down the back of his suede sports coat. Desiring a glimpse of his face, she peered into the mirror behind the bar. She'd never seen Chester without his white acupuncturist coat. Suddenly, it hit her just how beautiful he was. He looked up and held her gaze through the mirror, as if he was finally seeing her, too. She mouthed, *Help me,* and he smiled devilishly before walking over to her table.

That night they hadn't even made it out of the parking lot, so strong was their desire for each other. Now, three weeks and several romantic encounters later, he leaves her naked on the acupuncture table, not even a wandering finger as he reports that he'll see her in the reception area. When she emerges, fully clothed, he tells her it will be seventy-five dollars. Deborah hesitates, causing him to say the full price again. Seventy-five dollars. He smiles while he waits for her to pay, no devilishness about it. Deborah hands over her credit card, stunned, bruised, and hoping beyond all hope that her card won't be maxed out. As Chester turns away to run her card, her phone buzzes. Helen is dead.

Helen is dead?

Almost every day of her sixty-five years, Deborah has dreaded her mother's death. As a child, when it was just Helen and Deborah, she woke each morning in a panic — *What if mom is dead?* — until she heard her mother rummaging in the kitchen downstairs. As Deborah grew older and Helen's body never suffered the smallest of scares — not a benign lump, a broken bone, a treatable form of cancer — Deborah feared it would catch up to her mother all at once. One day, Helen would be dead. But she hadn't expected that day to be today, not while she is fretting about her credit limit and Chester's indifference toward her. Before she knows it, she's crying. Chester eyes her, annoyed, and she wants to shout, *Get over yourself. This has nothing to do with you.* Only it does have *something* to do with him because she wants him to hold her and instead he's holding a receipt for her to sign, his irritation palpable. This makes her cry harder, over her mother who should not have died today, over the loss of the best lay she's had in years, over the fact that on top of everything else, she's going to have to find a new acupuncturist.

Jake, the middle Miller child, receives the email a few minutes after he is supposed to be back from his lunch break. He eats the same thing during every shift: a carne asada burrito from the taco stand across the street from the Trader Joe's where he works. Rico, who works the register, always charges Jake for a taco instead of burrito, provided Jake shares his joint with him. Jake is happy to comply. As often as he indulges, Jake never smokes alone. It's a line he's drawn that he believes keeps him on the right side of having a problem. Recently, he's traded the joint for a cannabis-oil vape pen. His girlfriend, Kristi, was insistent. If he wants to continue smoking daily — more like hourly, not that he corrects her — he has to give up the fresh bud for something easier on his lungs. At least she hasn't tried to make him quit.

"What's this shit?" Rico asks when Jake

hands him the pen, twisting it between his fingers.

"The key to domestic bliss," Jake says, grabbing the pen and taking an unsatisfying pull from its metal mouthpiece. The high is good, but the oil tastes like pennies and he can't feel the smoke as he holds it in his lungs. Maybe Kristi is trying to get him to quit, after all.

A few minutes later, Jake is waiting at the crosswalk for the light to change, pleasantly high, enjoying the final moments of natural light before he retreats into the fluorescent belly of Trader Joe's.

"Jake?"

In his current state, it takes him a moment to recognize the man standing beside him at the light. It's the cinematographer from the film Jake wrote years ago. Tim or Todd or something like that.

"Hey . . . man," Jake says, hoping the guy won't realize that Jake can't remember his name. "It's been forever."

"You're telling me. What have you been up to? Working on anything new?" Ted Sullivan, Jake remembers suddenly, who won a Spirit Award for Jake's film. Last Jake heard he was shooting a new Marvel movie.

"Just this and that," Jake says, and Ted nods eagerly until he notices Jake's Hawai-

23

ian shirt. Even without his nametag, it's obviously a Trader Joe's uniform.

"Cool." Ted draws out the word before falling silent. Jake prays for the light to change as cars continue to race down Hyperion Avenue.

Conversations such as these notwithstanding, Jake enjoys working at Trader Joe's. The register is his favorite. He loves talking to everyone who passes through his lane, learning how to spatchcock a chicken or about the mystical benefits of organic pomegranate seeds. In the past, he would have viewed the customers as potential characters — the cheery newlywed who buys sunflowers each morning, the waifish actress who slips a bag of jalapeno cheese crisps on the counter, the elderly man who pays in bills that have been folded into origami cats — but Jake barely thinks about writing anymore. Only at times like these, when he runs into someone from his past or when his older sister, Ashley, the only family member besides Helen who still speaks to him, carefully asks him if it's time to try writing again. Kristi never pressures him, despite his failure to fulfill the promise he'd had of the up-and-coming screenwriter when they'd met.

Kristi. Her name hits him with a pang of

guilt when he remembers what she told him this morning. Well, not told him so much as barked at him, "I'm pregnant, you idiot," before leaving for the veterinary clinic where she works as a technician. He'd only been teasing when he'd found her huddled over the toilet and asked if she'd one too many chardonnays. How was he supposed to know she was puking for more natural reasons? After she left, he returned to bed, staring at the crack along their ceiling. He and Kristi have been together for two years and have never talked about having kids, even though they are at the age where every couple either has kids or has at least discussed it. Every couple except Jake and Kristi, so obvious is the impossibility of their raising a child together.

The light finally changes and Ted waves goodbye as he steps into the crosswalk. Jake remains on the curb, letting Ted get a comfortable distance ahead, as he tries to relax his spiraling mind. Reality is ruining his high.

As he steps into the crosswalk, his phone buzzes.

Helen is dead.

He freezes in the middle of the road,

25

rereading those three words blazing on his screen. *Helen is dead.* They become a strange configuration of curved lines and circles that he cannot decipher. Helen is dead? He spoke to her last week. She'd called him from the hardware store to ask if there was any difference between generic triple-A batteries and Energizer. She often called him with questions that she could have asked the clerk or the waiter or the librarian but preferred to ask Jake.

One horn wails, then another. Jake's eyes drift toward the line of drivers, waving for him to move. Someone shouts, "Get out of the way, asshole."

Holding his phone, Jake jogs to the parking lot, head foggy and mind on loop.

Helen is dead?

The email the Millers receive is from Beck, who, at thirty-five, is Helen's youngest grandchild. Not Rebecca or Becky or Becca, except to her grandmother, but a curt, efficient *Beck* that suits her personality. She's the only Miller that still lives in Philadelphia, the closest to Helen, the next of kin. At least, she *was* the closest to Helen until a few days ago, when she arrived at Helen's house on Edgehill Road to find the front door ajar. It was supposed to start snowing

26

again, and Beck had wanted to make sure that Helen's fridge was stocked. Right away, she knew something was wrong. Helen was standing in the middle of her spare living room, ranting to herself in German. Helen never spoke German. She'd renounced the language when she immigrated to America.

Alarmed, Beck placed the bag of groceries on the coffee table and tiptoed over to her grandmother, who stared vacantly into the fireplace. When Beck lived in this house as a teenager, her grandmother would light a fire every time it snowed. Beck and Helen would bundle on the couch, watching reruns of *Murder She Wrote* and adding logs to the fire. A few years later, when Beck went to college, the chimney cracked and was deemed structurally unsound. The fireplace hadn't been lit in decades.

Beck touched Helen's shoulder, alarmed at how frail it was.

"Helen? You okay?"

Helen didn't react, just kept muttering to herself in German. Beck listened for familiar words. She just heard a string of harsh inflections, one syllable repeated like a chant: *brush, brush, brush* with a slight roll of the *r*.

Helen had always been remarkably lucid, recounting spots along the Danube where

27

she swam as a child and annual visits to the Wiener Staatsoper because her father loved the opera. She'd recall legal cases Beck had worked on better than Beck did, conversations about warehouse parties that Beck had been to in high school, parties she couldn't believe she'd detailed to Helen. Before that day, Helen had never appeared remotely senile.

"Helen," Beck said louder. She debated calling her Grandma. The Millers rarely called Helen Grandma. They never called Deborah Mom, and both were fitting. Helen was more than a grandmother; Deborah was less than a mom.

Helen turned toward Beck, eyes unfocused, white hair loose around her weathered face. Helen always painted her cheeks red, her lips fuchsia, always dressed in slacks and a blouse, even on days when she wasn't expecting to see anyone. Yet here she was: face bare, body cloaked in a pink bathrobe, feet disappearing inside plush slippers.

"You." Helen approached Beck, standing close enough that Beck could smell the staleness of her breath. "You took it. My *brrrush.*"

"Shh," Beck whispered. "It's okay. I brought lunch from the deli."

"What'd you do with it?" Helen demanded

28

in her faint accent.

"It's right there." Beck pointed to the grocery bag on the coffee table.

Helen grabbed the bag, throwing the food on the floor.

"Stop that!" Beck bent down to pick up the sandwiches.

"It's not there. Where'd you put it?"

"Please, Helen. Let's sit down. I'll get you a glass of water." She tried to guide Helen toward the couch, but the old woman was surprisingly strong and Beck didn't want to hurt her.

"*Diebin!*" Helen shouted. "You thief."

"Helen, you're scaring me."

"I want you out."

"You're being absurd." Beck dropped to the couch, the old cushions giving with her weight, metal springs digging into her thighs.

"Absurd? For not wanting a thief in my house? My own flesh and blood, who steals from me?"

"Steals from you? I brought you liverwurst, on rye. What kind of thief brings lunch?"

Helen crossed her arms against her chest. "You've been a cheater since high school." Helen's gaze raked over Beck. "And all those tattoos, like some sort of criminal."

29

Beck looked at the faded robin on her right forearm, the pyramid on her left, *focus* in block letters on the underside of her wrist. Helen had always been intrigued by her tattoos, asking Beck to tell her why a bell jar was so important she had to graft it onto her ankle. Although Helen went to schul on high holidays and lit candles every Sabbath, she didn't have the same stance on tattoos that most European Jews her age did.

Helen opened the front door, letting in a blast of cold air. "Get out of my house."

Beck's body tensed as she remained seated. They were at an impasse, one Beck didn't understand.

Finally, when it was clear Beck wouldn't budge, Helen began to shout that word over and over again — *brrrush, brrrush* — until Beck started to worry that a neighbor might call the cops, might take Helen away, deciding a woman in her nineties — none of the Millers was certain how old Helen was — shouldn't be living alone.

Beck stood and smoothed her jeans. "You win. I'll go."

She fought for Helen's flushed cheek, giving her a gentle peck before she left. As she waited on the curb for her Lyft, she kicked at a hard, blackened pile of snow. Periodically she turned toward the house, wishing the curtains weren't drawn so she could see inside. When the car pulled up, Beck hopped into the backseat, unable to hold back the tears any longer.

Beck wasn't sure what to do. When she got home, she looked up the German word from Helen's feverish outburst — *brush,* which Google informed her was spelled *brosche.* Brooch. Right away, the story came together for Beck. For unclear reasons, Helen thought Beck had taken some brooch she'd misplaced or possibly hadn't owned for years. Beck tried to remember any notable jewelry Helen had owned. She wore clip-on earrings, a thin, gold chain around her neck. No brooch.

"Maybe it's time to put her in a home," Ashley, the eldest and wealthiest Miller sibling, had suggested when Beck called. That was always Ashley's first impulse, to throw money at a problem.

"Absolutely not. Helen would rather die than be put in a home."

"It's not up to her."

"It's not up to you, either."

It *was* up to Ashley, ultimately. Ashley would pay for the home, and with the checkbook came the final say. Everything Ashley would have selected, somewhere

31

near her in Westchester with nutritionists and higher thread counts than any sheets Helen had ever slept on, would have been the opposite of what Helen would have wanted. It was why, of the Miller children, Ashley was the least close to their grandmother — not because she was the oldest and had lived the shortest period of time with Helen, but because they never understood each other. Helen liked a modest life; Ashley had run as fast as she could from it.

"Don't take it out on me. I'm worried about her, too," Ashley said.

Beck knew the appropriate response was to apologize, but it was easy for Ashley, two states away in New York, to worry.

"We're not sending her to a home."

"Do you want me to come down?" Ashley asked. "No, wait, Ty has his last indoor soccer tournament of the season this weekend. I could drive down Sunday, once it's over. I'd probably only be able to stay until nine or so. I have to get the kids to school in the morning."

Ashley did have a husband, perfectly capable of cheering from the stands and buttering toast, but Ryan was never the type to make the bed or bag lunches, even before they had children. Beck liked Ryan. Although a large man, he was unimposing, happy to follow along with whatever activities the Millers had planned, so long as it didn't interfere with college football.

"Maybe I can see if the kids can do a sleepover next weekend."

"Ash, it's fine." Beck waited for Ashley to fight her on this.

"Well, let me know if there's anything I can do."

Disappointed, Beck briefly considered calling Deborah, who lived an hour away in New Hope, but decided not to. If anyone knew how to make a bad situation worse, it was her mother. It did not even occur to her to call Jake, all the way on the west coast, despite his closeness with Helen. Once again, Beck was left alone to take care of their grandmother.

Beck repeatedly called Helen, trying to explain the misunderstanding, to get her grandmother to realize she would never steal from her. Each time, Helen would hang up on Beck or, if she was feeling indulgent, call Beck a *diebin* — a thief — which sounded crueler in German than it did in English. Beck wanted to confide in her ex-boyfriend, Tom, a partner at the firm where Beck worked as a paralegal. If they'd still been together, he would have stroked her hair as he told her to give Helen a little space. Soon enough, she'd realize her mistake. But Tom had dumped Beck a few weeks ago. Now, instead of finding excuses to walk by his office, she hibernates in her cubicle. This is exactly what she's doing when she gets the phone call about Helen.

At 2:36 p.m., Beck receives a call from a 610 number she doesn't recognize. She intends to silence her phone, then hesitates, intuition compelling her to answer.

"Becca, is that you?" a vaguely familiar voice asks. Becca. Only Helen calls her Becca.

"Who's this?" Beck asks more firmly than she intends. She hasn't been sleeping well since Tom left.

"Becca, it's Esther." When the name doesn't immediately register, Esther adds, "Helen's neighbor."

"Oh, hi, Esther." Beck is too confused to intuit where the conversation is headed. Her finger traces the robin tattooed onto her forearm, its red crest fading to orange. "Did Helen ask you to call me?"

The typing of the other paralegals reverberates in Beck's ears as Esther breathes into the receiver.

"Esther?" Beck asks, worry creeping in. "What's going on?"

34

"Helen didn't show up for our bridge game yesterday. Or our walk this morning. I went by her house, but she isn't answering."

And with those swift words, with the panic in Esther's voice, the fight with Helen fades away.

"I'll be right over." Beck puts on her coat before she's even hung up the phone.

Beck peeks over the top of her cubicle toward Tom's office. His light is on, and she dashes in the opposite direction toward the HR office, knocking on the frame of Karen's open door.

Karen looks up when she finds Beck standing there, clearly rattled. She's a no-nonsense middle-aged woman with a heavy South Philly accent — *wudder* not water, *beg-el* instead of bagel, *tal* never towel — and the look of pity Karen casts at Beck is so out of character it makes Beck even more uncomfortable around Karen than she's already been feeling. After they broke up, Tom had insisted they inform Karen that they'd decided to amicably part ways when it was obvious that Beck had been dumped.

"Something's happening with my grand-mother," Beck says, her voice catching.

"Go," Karen responds without hesitation.

Beck nods and hurries out into the cold, damp afternoon.

35

■ ■ ■ ■

"Helen," Beck calls as she knocks on Helen's door. She and Esther stand on the porch shaded by an oak tree that helps keep Helen's house cool in summer and outright cold on this mid-March afternoon. A strong gust of wind pounds their sides. "Helen, are you there?" The curtains are drawn in the living room. The porch light is on, despite the brightness of the afternoon. "Helen," Beck shouts over the roaring wind.

Beck digs through her purse until she locates her keys. Using her hip, she pushes open the door, warped from years of hot summers with no air-conditioning. As soon as they are inside, she sees that it isn't just the swollen wood that has caused the door to stick. A pile of mail blocks the door, and Helen's living room has been trashed, as if a robber had ripped it apart.

"Oh, dear," Esther says when she sees the mess.

"Helen," Beck calls as she runs upstairs, pausing when she arrives at Helen's closed bedroom door. Despite having lived in the house for seven years, Beck has only been in Helen's room a handful of times. Helen locked the door every time she left, even when she was only headed down the hall to her sewing room, the key dangling from a gold chain around her neck. Today, the room is unlocked, which means one thing: Helen is inside.

Beck cracks open the door.

"Helen, are you there?" When there's no answer she opens the door wider, momentarily relieved to find the bedroom smelling, as the house always does, of cigarettes, floral perfume, and mildew. Then she notices the mound beneath the bed's pink comforter.

Helen's eyes are shut. Her long white hair, woven into pigtail braids, falls to either side of her unmoving shoulders. During the day, Helen twists those braids into a crown around her head. In high school, when Beck's hair was longer, Helen would fashion it in the same style, only Beck would wind glow sticks in her crown before running off to a warehouse party with her friends. Helen would shake her head, telling Beck she looked radioactive.

Beck sits on the bed beside her grandmother, shaking her lightly. "Helen?"

Helen's stiff body rocks when Beck touches her, causing Beck to bolt to the other side of the room. She thuds into the right side of the dresser, and there's a clatter as something that was lodged behind it falls to the floor. Beck bends down to retrieve a bejeweled flower brooch. It's surprisingly heavy, about the length of her palm. A large shield-shaped yellow crystal hangs beneath a V of smaller dark green crystals. Some of the clear rhinestones on the studded petals and sepals that surround the flower are missing, leaving empty circles of white metal in their place. An orchid, Beck thinks. Of course. *Brosche.*

Oh, Helen. It was right here this whole time.

A gasp echoes from the doorway, and Beck turns to find Esther standing at the threshold of Helen's bedroom, hand over her mouth. Beck slips the brooch into her blazer pocket where it's bulky against her hip. "Call 9-1-1."

Beck remains at Helen's side, stroking her grandmother's cheek until the paramedics, the police, then the medical examiner arrive. She answers the police officers' questions in a daze, relieved when it's over quickly. Afterward, Beck sits alone in Esther's living room, waiting for Esther to return from the kitchen with a tray of cookies Beck won't eat, a pot of tea she won't drink. Beck reaches for her cell phone and taps the mail icon. She types her sister's name into the address line, her mother's, debates for a moment, then adds her brother's, too. Of course he should be on this email. He's close to Helen, or as close as he can be, given he lives 2,500 miles away. Still, it's hard for Beck to voluntarily include him.

The time on Beck's phone reads 4:07 p.m. In the subject line, she types: Helen is dead. This is indelicate, she realizes. Every other subject she considers — News About Helen, Bad News About Helen, News or simply Helen — feels misleading, so she sticks with Helen is dead. In the body of the email she explains: Sorry to have to tell you like this. I just found her at the house. I'll be in touch when I know more.

Beck hits Send and rests the phone in her lap. A few hours ago her most pressing concern was avoiding Tom on the way to the bathroom. Helen would have said there's nothing like a death to get you to stop wallowing over some unworthy man.

Outside, the ambulance pulls away from the curb, taking her grandmother away. Its lights aren't flashing. Its siren has no reason to be on. The weight of the brooch in her blazer pocket tugs at the side seam. Beck pulls it out and fingers the sharp tips of the leaves, the rough holes where the rhinestones have fallen out. Why hadn't Beck fought harder to make Helen understand

39

that she would never steal from her? Helen died of natural causes. Still, Beck can't help but think that her grandmother might still be alive if Helen had never lost the orchid brooch.

TWO

Once the ambulance is gone, Esther sits on the couch in her apartment beside Beck. Her living room is almost identical to Helen's, same layout, same parquet floors. She hesitates, then hands Beck an envelope with Helen's will.

"A few months before we moved my mom —" Esther's voice cracks. Joyce, Esther's mother, had been Helen's longtime neighbor. A few years ago, Esther and her brother relocated Joyce to Brith Shalom House. Then, rather than put the house on the market, Esther elected to move back. Beck remembers, last fall, Helen telling her that Joyce had passed.

"I was sorry to hear about Joyce," Beck says, taking the envelope.

Esther rubs her arms to ward off the chill of her mother's death. "I took her and Helen to the library. There was this website, with form wills. I was both their witnesses."

Her voice falters again, and Beck wonders why Esther has chosen this moment to give her the will, until Esther adds, "Instructions for the funeral are in there, too. I'm not sure if you're aware, with Jewish funerals, everything needs to be done right away." Even though Esther says this delicately, her words sting. Does Esther really think Beck knows that little about Judaism? Sure, she wasn't bat mitzvahed; she doesn't know how to bless wine or the dead, but she knows the dead must be buried quickly.

Before Beck can get too offended, Esther hugs her, clinging like she's sending Beck off to war.

"You were her favorite," Esther whispers, and Beck thanks her, not knowing what else to say.

Beck returns to Helen's house and stares at the disarray consuming the living room, unsure where to begin. She assembles the pillows on the couch and sits down, not quite ready to confront the mail, the magazines tossed about the living room. How many times has she sat on this couch, talking to Helen with a candor Beck didn't have with many people? Other nights, too, when they didn't talk, just played hand after hand of gin rummy or watched episodes of *Perry Mason*. Helen was her best friend, Beck realizes. The moment she cleans the house, the moment she heads to her apartment, her best friend will be gone.

It takes her hours to muster the courage to clean the mess and call a car home.

Sorry I didn't return your calls, she writes to her family once she's returned to her apartment. Each Miller has called and texted and called again. It's been a long day. Helen's with a shomer (not sure I'm spelling that correctly) at the funeral home. Beck can't bring herself to write "Helen's body." She isn't religious. She isn't even spiritual, but she'd like to believe that part of Helen will bear witness to the funeral she meticulously planned. Helen wanted everything according to tradition. Technically, she should be buried tomorrow. I can't arrange everything that soon, and she can't be buried on a Saturday, so we'll have to wait until Sunday. Is that enough time for everyone to get here? I'm thinking we will sit shiva for three days? Up to you how long you want to stay. Beck knows the hostility they will read into this. Part of her craves it. None of them had to find their grandmother's rigor-mortised body. None of them had been accused of being a *diebin*.

Breathe, she tells herself. It isn't their fault that she wasn't here for Helen at the end.

Also, I'm attaching a copy of the will. As

43

executor, it's my responsibility. Beck knows the smug tone they will read into this, too.

As you can see, the will is straightforward, Beck continues. Helen left Deborah the house and the rest of the estate to Jake, Ashley, and me; although I'm not sure what else there is besides the house. She didn't have a bank account or retirement fund. Helen famously didn't trust the bank. "Like my undergarments, I keep my money close," she'd once told a horrified Beck and Jake. I'll need everyone to sign an agreement while they're in town, so I can file the probate paperwork and settle Helen's estate. These words are too formal for family, too official for Helen's memory, but Beck writes as the executor, not as the bereaved. Still, she adds, I hope everyone can make it. I know Helen would want you here.

Beck was confused and a little offended to see that Helen had left the house to Deborah. Deborah, who at seventeen had left as quickly as she could. Deborah, who had forsaken her children in that home. Deborah, who out of obligation saw Helen once every few months, whereas Beck visited her weekly out of a genuine desire to spend time together. Deborah, who would mortgage the house into foreclosure.

Otherwise, there were few surprises in the

44

will. What money Helen had tucked away in coffee cans in the kitchen and potpourri satchels in the spare bedroom and envelopes beneath her bed was to be divided evenly among Beck, Ashley, and Jake. It was all standard other than one exception Helen had written into Article IV: *My yellow diamond brooch goes to Becca.*

Beck finds her blazer and locates Helen's brooch in the pocket. The brooch is too heavy to pin to her T-shirt, so Beck holds the orchid to her chest, staring at the large crystal in the mirror above her dresser. Tarnished and abused, the brooch can't be particularly valuable. It's costume jewelry just gaudy enough to be hip. Although if Beck had tried to explain to Helen why the missing rhinestones made it cooler, Helen would have shaken her head, saying young people were idiots. Still, this brooch meant something to Helen, and she wanted Beck to have it. At least, she *had* wanted Beck to have it when she'd drafted her will. Then she'd accused Beck of stealing her own inheritance.

Ashley is wrapping the leftovers from dinner when her phone chimes with Beck's second email. She wonders whether Ryan knows she lies about cooking the dinners that are clearly professionally made, whether he notices that there are never dirty baking sheets or pans. Of course he doesn't notice. He's too busy with his own secrets to notice anything that's going on with her. *Relax,* she futilely reminds herself. Anger won't help. She puts the chicken thighs in the fridge and reaches for her phone.

Burial will be Sunday . . . Shiva for three days . . . I know Helen would want you here. At the sink, Ashley stares onto her dark backyard. Would Helen have wanted her at the shiva? She and Helen have never been close, not like Beck and Jake were with Helen, not even like Deborah was in her own way. Ashley was seventeen when they moved in with Helen, both eyes toward life after high school, beyond the reach of the Miller family. In turn, Helen didn't try to protect or mother her the way she did Beck and Jake.

An arm wraps around her waist, jarring Ashley out of her thoughts. A set of lips kiss her cheek. Ashley recoils, then feels guilty. Action and reaction, disgust, then pity — it pretty much captures her entire relationship with her husband these days.

Ryan pretends not to notice. He lets go of her, walking over to the island.

"Kids are asleep," he says, leaning against

46

the granite countertop. "They're still a little spooked."

This is the children's first death outside of school pets and television. Ryan was raised Protestant but only felt strongly about a Christmas tree and an Easter ham, never church or the afterlife. Even after Googling it, Ashley still isn't clear how, as a Jew, she is supposed to feel about the afterlife, so they didn't tell the children that Helen was in a better place. Instead, they explained that Helen was very old and had lived a full life. Even as she'd said this, Ashley had questioned whether it was true. Helen was from Vienna. Sometime during WWII, she'd come to the US alone. She'd married, had Deborah, then her husband had died. And after that . . . she'd crafted wedding dresses and skirt suits for women much richer than she was. She'd been a steady presence in the decaying house on Edgehill Road. Ashley wasn't sure any of that constituted a full life.

"You okay?" Ryan asks Ashley, pointing to her neck. She rubs it absentmindedly, remembering the car accident. Not even an accident, a tap so light it hadn't scratched either car. Still, the other driver, an older man, had insisted on calling the police. It consumed most of the afternoon. Tyler had

47

missed soccer practice; Lydia, rehearsal for the spring recital. Both children were confused and scared, even before Ashley told them about Helen.

"I'm fine," Ashley says coolly, hungry for a fight. She closes the dishwasher and stares at her husband. She hates that she recoils from his touch. She is still attracted to him, yet she can't shake her anger. Anger over what he's done. Anger that it broke him. Anger that he exposed that brokenness to her and now, despite his handsome face, despite how much she wants to want him, all she sees is a weak man before her. A weak man who is going to be fired, possibly worse.

Ryan works as in-house counsel for an international chemical company in charge of its patent applications. Due to the amount of patents they need to file, it's common practice to hire outside patent lawyers to do the extra work. Instead of hiring multiple part-time attorneys as was policy, Ryan hired one attorney. His friend Gordon, a DUI lawyer in Las Vegas. Gordon had no business completing the patent applications, but he was broke and he was Ryan's best friend. So Ryan corrected Gordon's mistakes, submitted the applications on his behalf and fed him more work. Then it just became easier for Ryan to complete the applications himself, and, since he was doing the work, adding extra hours to his already consuming job, it didn't seem fair that Gordon was being paid for Ryan's time. They arrived at an arrangement where Ryan's company paid Gordon, then Gordon returned a percentage of the money to Ryan. Ashley didn't know the details, how long it had been going on, how much money Ryan had made off his *side job*. Recently, the company had initiated a random internal audit and discovered the unsanctioned arrangement Ryan had set up with one DUI lawyer in Las Vegas.

"What's going on with the audit? Any updates?" Ashley knows he won't tell her. He only revealed the arrangement to her because she'd found him huddled on the bathroom floor beside the toilet, rocking himself and muttering incoherently about how he'd trusted Gordon and now he was going to get fired. It had taken two glasses of Scotch to get him back to sleep. In the morning, he immediately began downplaying the story he'd told her. Ashley had seen the fear in his eyes, the desperation in his quaking body, as he said, "I've ruined everything." She trusted that memory more than her husband's reassurances that everything was fine.

"It's just an internal audit," he says. "Please. We've been over this."

"Have you talked to Gordon?"

"I don't want to get into it."

"I have a right to know. This doesn't just affect you."

Ryan walks over and takes her in his arms. She doesn't push him away. She doesn't hug him back, either. "It's sweet of you to worry. I overreacted. It's just some paperwork that needs explaining — I'll sort it out."

"Would it help if I went back to work?" She tries to say this casually, but her voice betrays her. Ashley was the one who had wanted to quit. Even though she loved her team, her clients, she knew with that first bout of nausea that she didn't want to balance a family and career. For the first few years, when Lydia was little, then Tyler followed, she loved spending full days at the park, the zoo, children's museums. When they got older and started school, they didn't need her as much, and her responsibilities quickly became less maternal, more domestic. Ashley had always hated doing laundry, cooking, had never had a domestic bone in her slender body.

"You already have a job," Ryan says, kissing the top of her head. "The hardest job in the world." He gives her a final squeeze before walking out of the kitchen.

They weren't always like this. When she and Ryan first met, she was making more money than he was, and one of the things that drew her to him was that he wasn't intimidated by her success. Instead, he supported her, stocking her fridge when she was on a deadline so she wouldn't have to think about feeding herself, leaving her little love notes or drawings when he left for work before she did. Gradually, the idea of caring for her took over so much that now he saw it as an affront to his responsibilities as a husband when she mentioned returning to work. It grew out of his love for her, for the children, but it made her dependent on him in ways she didn't like, even before she'd found him curled up on their bathroom floor.

Ashley checks Beck's email again. Burial will be Sunday . . . Shiva for three days. Ashley and Ryan have already agreed that she will drive down for the day and go alone to the funeral, but she writes, I'll stay through the shiva. Let Ryan figure out what to do with the kids while she's in Philadelphia for a few days. Let him see just how hard the hardest job in the world is.

■ ■ ■ ■

The chime from her phone startles Deborah awake. Momentarily, she isn't certain where she is. The dream was so real she hadn't realized she was sleeping. She'd drifted to childhood, to a vacation she and Helen had taken when Deborah was twelve. Helen had pulled her old Chevy out of the driveway, and they took I-95 to Portland. Deborah could feel the wind on her face as she stuck her head out the window before her mother told her she wasn't a dog, to get back in the car. It was stifling with the windows closed, and to distract herself Deborah turned on the radio. Helen quickly turned it off. It became a game — at least Deborah found it fun — turning on the radio every few minutes before her mother clicked it off again, until Helen snapped, "I'm trying to concentrate."

They drove the rest of the way to Maine in silence.

In the hotel room, Deborah had sulked. Helen ignored her, standing before the mirror, coating her lips in the bright pink lipstick she continued to wear for the next fifty years. "Tomorrow, we'll drive up to Bar Harbor where we'll eat lobster. We can go fishing, if you'd like."

"I hate fishing," Deborah claimed, even though she'd never been fishing before.

Helen put down the lipstick and stared intently at her daughter. "This is a privilege, you know. Not everyone lives the kind of life where they can go on vacation."

"I never asked to go on vacation with you." She waited for Helen to take the bait, for them to fight, because Deborah *did* want to be on vacation with Helen; she just wanted her mother to take her to Atlantic City where they could go on rides on the boardwalk. She wanted cotton candy, not lobster.

"Should we turn around and go home, then?"

"No," Deborah pouted.

"Good," Helen said, closing her lipstick. "Because I'd really like to go whale watching. I've never seen a whale."

The room is almost dark. As her eyes adjust, Deborah recognizes the shape of her mattress on the floor, the couch separating the two-burner stove and refrigerator from the rest of the studio. It all comes flooding back to her — the vacation in Maine; the word *privilege,* which became one of Helen's favorite English words, a reminder to her daughter of all the privilege that was stripped from her in Austria; Helen's death just that afternoon.

Deborah turns on a light and stumbles into the kitchen for something to eat. It was bright out when she'd fallen asleep. She'd only meant to shut her eyes. Now, it's ten thirty and she's famished. There's one large pot and an array of hot sauces in her fridge. She puts the pot on the stove to warm the remains of the lentil stew she'd made earlier that week, only to discover that there isn't enough left to heat up. She'd kill for a burger, but it's been six months since she last cheated on her vegan diet, and she is determined to make it to a year. Or seven months at least. Her phone chimes again, and she reads Beck's email.

Helen left her the house on Edgehill Road? And they were going to sit shiva? Was this some sort of twisted punishment from beyond, insisting that all the Millers gather for three days? She finds a spoon and begins to eat the remnants of the cold stew. The texture of the clumpy yellow mash makes her queasy. She throws the spoon back in the pot, feeling even more nauseous as she realizes this is Helen's attempt at reconciling them.

"Oh, Mom," Deborah says to the globs sticking to the sides of the pot. She rarely called Helen Mom, and she relishes it now. *Mom.* This house is a privilege, even if she'd sworn after high school that she'd never go back. But she'd already moved back with her children after Kenny left. Maybe she was always destined to return to the house on Edgehill Road.

She emails her children to tell them she'll be there. She does not mention her inheritance. She doesn't open the will attached to Beck's email, either.

As Jake unlocks the door to his apartment, a haziness lingers from the pot he smoked that afternoon. Somehow he made it through his shift at Trader Joe's, although he couldn't have named a single characteristic about anyone who had been through his checkout line, not even the person who had yelled at him for double-charging his credit card. The only things he could focus on were that Kristi was pregnant and Helen was dead. At some point, while he distributed samples of edamame hummus on garlic pita chips, those facts became aligned, as though one life was exchanged for another. Suddenly, Jake couldn't imagine anything he needed more than to have the baby.

In his kitchen, he sets down the bag of

groceries to prepare chicken cacciatore — the only dish he knows how to make from scratch — and flowers he bought for full price rather than salvaging from the throwaway pile. Lilies, Kristi's favorite. The blooms have just opened. They'll last for days.

By the time Kristi's key turns the lock on the front door, the apartment is warm from the oven and rich with the aroma of spicy tomatoes and peppers.

"Chicken cacciatore," she calls. "You must be feeling like a real jerk."

"Words can't begin to describe." He hands her the bouquet of magenta lilies. She takes the flowers, offering him her cheek in place of her lips. He gives her an exaggerated kiss, mashing his lips against her skin until she laughs.

Kristi sighs as she throws her tote bag over one of their mismatched dining chairs and opens the cabinet to find a vase for the lilies. Jake can usually tell by her mood if they put a dog down, if they performed a risky surgery that was unsuccessful. Today, between the pregnancy and her spat with Jake that morning, Kristi has other reasons to be somber and fatigued. Kristi has never met Helen, but she knows how close Jake was to his grandmother. When he tells Kristi about

Helen, she will stroke his hair and tell him everything will be all right. She will instantly forgive him. Although Jake sees Helen's death and his baby's life as inextricably linked, he doesn't want to use Helen to make Kristi forgive him. So, for now, he doesn't tell Kristi about his grandmother's death.

Instead, he asks, "How long have you known?" watching her trim the lily stems.

"A week or so." She fills the vase with a few inches of water and arranges the lilies. He knows it's important not to act hurt that she hasn't told him until now. "I know we can't afford to, but I want to have the baby."

Again, Jake plays it cool even though his heart is pounding. Does she assume he'll to try to talk her out of it? Was he the type of guy to talk a girl out of it? Could they have a baby in their one-bedroom apartment? What else could they do? It's not like they could afford a bigger apartment. Should they get married? And what would Kristi's parents think? Jake lives in perpetual fear of the Zhangs, who, although perfectly fluent in English, speak to each other in Cantonese when he is around, almost certainly commenting on their disapproval of their daughter's choice in partner. He hates how thoughts of the baby end in fear of Kristi's parents.

"Did you hear me?" she asks, and Jake looks up at her. "I'm going to keep it."

"Okay," he says even though he means, *Of course we're going to keep it.* Helen is dead and Kristi is pregnant. There was never any doubt they were going to keep it.

"Jesus, Jake, it's not like I said I feel like Indian instead of pizza. You can't just say *okay.*" She disappears down the hall into their bedroom, pulling the door shut behind her.

Jake sits alone in the kitchen, dismayed. He's screwed up so many things in his life — his writing career, his closeness with Beck, his spacious, rent-stabilized apartment, his two previous relationships. Somehow, he's been with Kristi for two years and hasn't ruined it. Yet.

Jake walks down the hall, stopping at the closed plywood door.

"Kris," he calls, trying to amass words that might make her feel better.

Before he can say anything, his phone buzzes, and he reaches into his back pocket.

"What?" Jake says as he reads Beck's email. Deborah gets the house? *Deborah?* "This can't be right." Jake opens the will attached to the email. In Article III, it couldn't be clearer: Helen left the house on Edgehill to Deborah. Jake leans against the wall, banging his head on the plaster.

Kris throws open the door, offering a concerned look. "What happened?"

"It's Helen," Jake says. "She's . . . she's dead." He's not ready to tell her about the house, to hear her rational explanation for why Helen would have left it to Deborah.

Kristi burrows into Jake's chest. "Oh, Jake."

He holds her tighter, relieved that she's momentarily forgiven him for failing to show enthusiasm about her pregnancy. "I'm sorry I'm so bad at this. I can't wait to have a baby with you. From the moment you told me, it's been the only thing I've wanted. I don't know why it's so hard for me to tell you that."

"I've had a week to process this." She gazes up at him and he kisses the crown of her head. "You've only had a few hours. I shouldn't have jumped down your throat."

Jake laughs. "If that's you jumping down someone's throat, I'd hate to see your version of blind rage."

Kristi slaps him lightly on the arm. "It's a horrible sight, so I'd recommend staying in line, mister." The smile falls from her face. "Can we really do this?"

"People raise children on less all the time." The look on Kristi's face is dubious. "I'll pick up some extra shifts. Or I can start bartending again, do two jobs for a while."

"But when will you write?" After all this time, she's still worried about his career.

Jake runs his hand through her silky hair. "Let's just be excited for now. There's lots of time to worry later."

In general, Jake knows his ethos of "enjoy now, worry later" is not an effective worldview. As Kristi hugs him tighter, he realizes, for the moment, it's the right perspective.

"The funeral's on Sunday. Will you come with me?"

"Jake, we can't afford one plane ticket, much less two. You go. Your family needs you."

Kristi has only met Ashley and her kids when they visited last spring. She hasn't met the other Millers. She doesn't understand that they don't need him at all. Still, she's right. Jake hasn't seen Beck or Deborah in six years. This is something he needs to do alone.

So the Millers will be united again. The four of them. Together, for the first time since Jake ruined everything in Park City.

THREE

When Jake Miller's movie premiered at Sundance six years ago, he decided to fly the Miller women to Park City: Beck, Ashley, even Helen, although he knew she wouldn't attend. Helen had never been on an airplane and hadn't been to the movies in at least a decade. "I'll just fall asleep," Helen had told him. "And that's an awful lot of money to spend on a nap." Then she'd added, "Invite Deborah," and Jake promised he would. Deborah had surprised him by saying yes, then surprised him even more by making it to the airport without any car accidents or lost licenses or unexplained disappearances. Then again, Jake should have known that an all-expenses-paid trip to a film festival wasn't something Deborah would have missed.

The Millers knew little about Jake's movie other than it was called *My Summer of Women* and was about the summer a

61

twenty-one-year-old boy came of age in a house of women. If the Millers had known anything about storytelling, they would have realized that no man writes such a story unless it's based on personal experience. But they didn't think *a twenty-one-year-old boy* meant Jake, or that *a house of women* meant them. They didn't look up the trailer online or read the script. Well, Beck had asked to see the script. Jake avoided sending it to her. Looking back on it, Jake knew what he was doing. Even if he'd told himself it was nerves — the desire to remain infallible in the eyes of his younger sister — if he was completely honest with himself, he knew the film was about them, that it was funny at their expense. What he didn't foresee was that it was a ticking bomb, about to upend everything.

Beck was in her second year of law school, subsisting off instant ramen and boxed wine. On the flight, she sat in business class beside her mother, clinking champagne glasses as they toasted Jake, the family artiste, soon to make theirs a household name. Ashley was flying from New York, also sipping champagne on a business-class ticket purchased by Jake, enjoying a respite from her three-year-old son and five-year-old daughter, a break that made her feel guilty but not so guilty that she didn't ask the flight attendant for a second glass of bubbly.

The Miller women met in Salt Lake City where a driver took them to that small, usually quiet town in the mountains. When they arrived at the hotel, Jake was doing an interview and had left a note saying he would meet them at the premiere. They opened the bottle of champagne welcoming them to Sundance and modeled their clothing options like they were college girls. Deborah even let Ashley put makeup on her, and she marveled at how much younger her skin appeared, lacquered and blushed. While Beck opted for her standard look of thick black eyeliner and crimson lips, she agreed to wear one of Ashley's black dresses and a pair of heels rather than the jeans and vintage sweater jacket she'd selected for the premiere. Jake had told them to be casual, but nothing about this was casual. So they dressed the part of the family in the film, over-the-top and ridiculous without even knowing it.

Jake sat between the Miller women in the second row of the theater. When the opening credits cast his name in thick black letters, Deborah squeezed his knee. Beck elbowed him approvingly from the other side, and Ashley reached over Beck to ruff le Jake's hair. Jake felt his cheeks warm at the unusual bounty of affection.

From the first scene he realized just how willfully ignorant he'd been. Deborah was the first to notice. The opening credits dissolved, and an approximation of her filled the screen, pacing a front porch that looked suspiciously like the porch at Edgehill Road. The actress wore just enough makeup to look haggard, draped in a long gray sweater and bangles. Deborah ran her hand through her short, purple-red tousled hair, stopping when the actress ran her hand through her short, purple-red tousled hair after she realized she'd locked her keys in the house. Ashley stifled a laugh, and Beck shot Jake a wary look.

The film took place in the late '90s and detailed the summer after the protagonist Josh's junior year of college. Instead of doing an internship or something that would ease the transition into his looming post-college life, he'd returned home to work at the local hardware store, as he had every summer since he was sixteen and his family had moved into their grandmother's house. Now he was twenty-one and could drink at the local bar, which was where he ran into their neighbor, a sultry divorcée. She spent the summer teaching him to understand women's bodies, even as he failed to understand the minds of those in his own home: his disheveled mother, who was always in and out of their lives, in and out of jobs, in and out of doomed relationships; his disturbed and brilliant sister, who had been expelled from high school for breaking into the principal's office to change her grades; his grandmother, who pretended not to see the money his mother took from her purse, the empty beer cans his sister hid at the bottom of the trash bin; and his older sister, who lived in New York with her oafish fiancé and only made a brief appearance at the end of the film.

The Miller women grew stiffer as the film continued. Meanwhile, the audience laughed, inching their bodies toward the screen, entirely engrossed.

Toward the end of the summer, the mother was hospitalized following a mishap at a catering event that had almost cost her her arm. Instead of a limb, the accident had cost her her future earnings, as she had no health insurance. From the divorcée, Josh had learned how to ask women what they needed, how to listen to their desires. In the end he did hear the women around him, their pain and their loneliness, which he couldn't fix, but could try to understand.

The film ended the night before Josh went back to school, with a barbecue at the family house. Josh had used the money he'd made that summer, an unrealistic sum from part-time hours at a hardware store, to anonymously pay off his mother's medical bills. His family wrongly assumed the support came from their absentee father, penance for abandoning them for the open road. Josh's silence was his final sacrifice, his noble understanding that he was better off not taking credit. In the final scene, three generations of his family laughed as their mother served them ears of corn with her one good hand, her cast a sign that she was staying put, at least until her bones reset.

When the film was over, the crowd applauded, and Jake stood to thank them, keenly aware of the women beside him who weren't applauding, who looked as though they'd seen a ghost.

The Miller women remained seated once everyone else left the theater. After walking out with some producers, Jake returned to retrieve them. The delight faded from his face as he realized he couldn't keep pretending this was just a movie.

"Nancy Bloom?" his mother howled. "You *slept* with Nancy Bloom?"

"That's your takeaway?" Beck barked at her mother. "Who gives a fuck about Nancy Bloom?" And then to Jake, "The stuff with grades? The beer?" Jake looked confused, and she tapped her head like he was brainless. "Were you trying to completely humiliate me?"

At the time, Beck wasn't considering the possibility that her law school adversary might do a little digging and realize that Jake's movie was more fact than fiction. She wasn't thinking about how she'd chosen to leave her high school expulsion off her law school application. At the time, she was focused solely on the impossible betrayal that her brother had taken her most vulnerable moments and used them to garner a few laughs.

"It was just a movie." Jake shrugged, doing his best to look innocent.

"That —" Beck pointed at the dark screen "— was character assassination."

Jake was blocking the aisle, so Beck shoved him as she stormed toward the lobby.

"I'm glad Helen wasn't here to see this," Deborah said as she swept past Jake. "And you could have been a little easier on Beck."

Jake and Ashley watched her leave, dumbfounded, since the film had undoubtedly been the hardest on Deborah. People saw what they wanted to see in others' images of themselves, Ashley reasoned. Sure, it stung when the crowd had laughed at Ashley's character's attempts to eschew her middle-class Philadelphia roots. Even she had to laugh when an exaggerated version of Ryan drunkenly bounced off a taxi, unhurt. It was funny, and Ashley could take a joke.

Sound trickled in from the lobby where people were milling, waiting for the shuttle to take them to the after-party. Ashley studied her brother's troubled face. Wrinkles were starting to form at the corners of his eyes, white hair at his temples. He still had a boyish look to him, but his looks weren't aging as elegantly as they might.

"It was a beautiful film," Ashley told her brother. "But you never should have made it."

"I didn't realize," he said. "I knew it was about me. I didn't realize it was about them, too."

Ashley wanted push back; he *had* to realize. How could he not? In his stunned expression, she could see that, like always, Jake Miller had been so focused on what he wanted that he'd blinded himself from the destruction his self-absorption caused. All of the characterizations in the film had been accurate, all except that of Jake/Josh, the family savior.

Ashley wove her arm through her brother's and escorted him out of the theater. "I've got twenty-four hours with no children and no husband — I don't intend to waste it."

Jake laughed as they stepped into the bustling lobby where everyone wanted to talk to him. Ashley stood at his side, agreeing with all the middle-aged men in faded jeans and leather boots that Jake was brilliant, that no one deserved this more than him. And no one did.

By the time they got back to the hotel suite, Deborah and Beck were gone.

With everything set for the funeral, Beck doesn't know what to do with herself until Sunday. She should take the day off; only, if she does, she'll sit in her apartment reflecting on Helen's death, on the brooch, on the mat by her front door emptied of Tom's shoes, on all the other ways he's disappeared from the apartment — his bag of softball gear by the couch, his clothes intermingling with hers in the hamper — and the ways he's remained. The furniture he purchased and left for Beck; the mail that's addressed to him, mail she sneaks into his office when she knows he's at court or a deposition; the rent, which he's paid his share of through the end of their lease in October. She hadn't wanted Tom to pay the bulk of their rent when they'd been living together and certainly doesn't want him to continue paying it now that he's gone. But she can't afford to pay it by herself, nor to move, so she chooses to see it as reparation for his cowardice.

She doesn't want to spend the day wallowing, so she puts on her blazer and black jeans, buttons up her vintage wool coat, winds her scarf around her neck, and locks her apartment. As she's stepping onto her stoop, something catches in her chest, and she rushes back inside. On her nightstand, she locates the brooch and pins it to her lapel. Its presence on her plaid coat calms her, like a black ribbon to commemorate Helen.

At just before nine, the office is only half-full. The light in Tom's office is off, and Beck swiftly passes, settling into her cubicle and rousing her monitor to life.

Karen from HR taps on the partition wall, eyeing Beck's shelves, absent of family pictures, of framed aspirational quotes, of postcards from faraway friends. "How's your grandmother doing?"

"She passed," Beck says, her attention focused on her screen. If she sees the expression on Karen's face, she'll lose it. "I'm just going to finish up the Cunningham brief, then I'll need to take the first half of next week off."

"Oh, Beck." Karen bends down and awkwardly wraps her arms around Beck and her desk chair. "Don't worry about the brief. Someone else can do it."

"It's easier if I get it done."

Karen continues to stoop beside Beck, rubbing her shoulder. Normally it would make Beck uncomfortable. Today, it's nice having someone comfort her, particularly someone she doesn't know very well. Karen's eyes drift to Beck's coat and the brooch. Beck fingers it self-consciously.

"It was my grandmother's."

"It's exquisite." Karen leans close enough that Beck can see dandruff clinging to her middle part. "Do you mind if I —" She motions toward the orchid. Beck shifts in her seat, watching as Karen lifts her lapel to investigate the brooch. "It looks like it's from the '40s or '50s." Karen reaches into her pocket for her cell phone and turns the flashlight on. When the light catches the crystal, Karen gasps.

"It's just an old piece of costume jewelry," Beck says.

"I don't know." Karen's fingers outline the air around the bedazzled petals. "Those diamonds look real. And the large stone, the fire when I shined the light on it, you don't get

71

that kind of rainbow effect off quartz or glass."

Beck half listens as Karen, in her thick Philly accent, explains dispersion, the way light refracts off the facets of a stone. Citrine — a type of yellow quartz typically used in midcentury costume jewelry — has very low dispersion, so it won't cast colors the way stones with high dispersion will.

"My guess is it's a peridot." Karen sucks in her breath. "It's more yellow than green, so it's not as valuable as a darker peridot. Still, the clarity is high, especially for a stone that big."

Beck can hear Helen chuckling. Such a fuss over a piece of junk jewelry.

Karen stops talking. She turns the flashlight on her phone off and stands. "I come from a family of jewelers. I didn't mean to overstep."

Beck tries not to laugh. "No, it's just — if you knew my grandmother, you'd know this was fake. She didn't have . . . She wasn't the type . . ." Beck feels desperate to tell this near stranger what kind of woman her grandmother was. Someone who saved bones to make broth. Someone who got shoes resoled and stitched up worn clothing. Someone far too pragmatic and unsentimental to hold on to a valuable piece of jewelry.

Karen reaches for a Post-it pad on Beck's desk and scribbles an address onto it. "I'm no expert, but I'd say you're wearing a new car on your jacket." A Kia or Tesla? Beck wants to joke, but Karen looks so serious as she holds the Post-it out to Beck. "Ask for Leo. And if he tries to tell you it's in bad condition tell him I said to stop being an asshole."

In the elevator, once Beck is finished with the brief, she holds out the lapel of her jacket so she can see the orchid. In the fluorescent light, the yellow stone is dull, and Beck doesn't understand what caused Karen's outburst. Karen probably *did* notice something reflected in the stone — her own imagination refracting, splintering into the hundreds of fantasies people have about family heirlooms.

The elevator opens in the lobby, and she buttons her coat to brave the cold afternoon. As she swirls through the revolving doors to the street, she reaches for her scarf in her pocket. When she weaves it around her neck, she peers down at her lapel. Sunlight hits the orchid, and a rainbow explodes from the yellow crystal. Beck doesn't gasp so much as lose her breath at the sudden, impossible beauty of the stone against her coat. She scans the sidewalks to see if anyone else has noticed, but the pedestrians continue unperturbed. Quickly unclasping the brooch, she buries it in her purse and clutches her bag against her side as she heads toward the bus stop to return to her apartment. She should go to Orphan's Court to begin the probate paperwork. Even more than the phone call with the rabbi and the conversation with the medical examiner, the paperwork is the first real step in saying goodbye to Helen. She isn't ready for that yet.

Beck waits at the corner for the bus, stuffing her free hand in her pocket. Her fingers graze the Post-it. *Romano Brothers Jewelers, 714 Sansom Street.* At the bottom of her purse she finds the orchid brooch and stares between it and the address on Sansom.

Beck snaps a photo of the brooch and sends it to the only jewelry expert she knows, a former client from the firm, Viktor. Just inherited this, she explains. My coworker thinks it might be valuable. You can't tell in the photo, the stone (maybe a peridot?) sparkles in the light. What do you think?

"This is ridiculous," she says as she hits Send and continues to wait for the bus. Almost immediately, her phone chimes, and she's surprised Viktor has responded so quickly. It's Jake, forwarding his flight information as if he expects one of them to be waiting curbside. She's been so focused on the arrangements for Helen's funeral she hasn't fully accepted that she's going to have to see Jake again. And not just see him but spend three days with him, confined in the house on Edgehill Road.

The bus pulls up, and as Beck is about to mount the steps, her phone dings again. It's Viktor.

Come see me at once.

Gemstones aren't rocks to Viktor. They aren't a commodity, the promise of eternal love, a marker of social status. They are millions of years of history, he's told Beck. First, as carbon in the mantle, then as discoveries among the rubble of the earth's crust, and finally as physical evidence of the many lives that touched each stone. If anyone will know whether Helen's brooch is valuable, it's Viktor.

Beck met Viktor when he was in need of legal assistance. As soon as they began working together, they developed an instant kinship. Trained as a jewelry maker and gemologist, Viktor worked as a designer at Tiffany's, until his employer discovered his side gig, the one that bought him the penthouse apartment on Rittenhouse Square. Beck didn't know you could make real fake jewelry. As it turned out, in the jewelry industry, knockoff rings could indeed hold real diamonds and still be counterfeit if they were a trademark in-fringement. *What was wrong with it?* Viktor had argued, and Beck had agreed. They were his designs, unique, if similar, to the ones he'd sketched for Tiffany's. The top of the box did not say Tiffany & Co., even if the color had a striking resemblance to *the* little blue box. Beck liked that Viktor aimed to make Tiffany-esque engagement rings more affordable, and Viktor liked that Beck worked with an unrivaled passion to prove his business was lawful.

As instructed, Beck walks directly to Viktor's building on Rittenhouse Square. When she arrives, she stares up at the opaque windows that reach toward the sky. She was here once before, a year ago, for a thank-you brunch he held for Beck and Tom, who had been lead attorney on Vik-tor's case. The judge had ruled that Viktor's ring boxes were not a color trademark infringement, saving him from having to pay Tiffany's damages. He got to keep the money he made, so long as he agreed to stop making his rings. At their celebratory brunch, Viktor had served champagne along with eggs royale — eggs Benedict, Beck discovered, with lox in place of ham — and the three glasses went straight to her head. She tried to hide it as Viktor walked Tom and her to the elevator. Alone in the small marble elevator, Beck glanced over at Tom to see if the champagne had affected him, too. It was the first case they'd worked together, and they'd never spoken about anything else. They'd certainly never had any charged energy between them. In that contained space, Tom had looked thirstily at Beck before reaching over to kiss her. Beck was too surprised to kiss him back. He pulled away sheepishly. Apologies ensued — it was inappropriate, he was so sorry, he shouldn't have done that — until she kissed him, as much to silence him as to rediscover the pressure of his lips.

Beck continues to stare at the dark windows, realizing that she will have to ride in that elevator again.

When Viktor opens the door, he looks younger than a year ago, closer to sixty than seventy-one. He wears a fitted black cashmere turtleneck, his white hair slicked back, his signature diamond ring adorning his pinky finger.

"Ms. Miller," Viktor says, waving her inside. Beck lets Viktor take her coat and hang it on the coatrack in the entryway.

"If I didn't know better, I'd think you have some secret antiaging potion. You don't, do you?"

Viktor laughs. "Peace of mind, my dear. Thanks to you."

Beck was the one to discover that Viktor's jewelry boxes shone green in direct light and thus were not Tiffany blue but turquoise, a color so common it could not be trademarked. The case had helped to ensure Viktor's solvency as well as Tom's track to partner. It did little for Beck, other than allowing her to stick it to "the man" — she had nothing against Tiffany's in particular, just the fact that they were a corporate entity that profited off women's desire to feel loved — and to receive a gift certificate from the firm to her choice of Stephen Starr's restaurants.

Beck follows Viktor into his living room, lined with shelves of old hardback books, where he offers her a flute of bubbly. Beck remembers the champagne last time she was at Viktor's apartment and declines. Viktor helps himself to a glass and sits in the regal leather chair across from hers.

"So, let's see this mystery brooch," he says, crossing his legs.

Beck finds the orchid brooch at the bottom of her purse. When she gives it to Viktor, he stares at it for longer than she would have expected. He shifts his hand so the stone dances in the light. While his expression remains impassive, Beck detects a spark in his eyes as the brooch shimmers in his palm.

On the coffee table, Viktor locates a loupe and lifts it to his right eye as he leans toward the orchid brooch. It's a tiny noise, almost imperceptible, but Beck hears it: Viktor's cough as he surveys the large yellow stone.

"This was your grandmother's?" Viktor finally asks, his eye still burrowed into the loupe.

"Is it antique?"

Viktor returns the loupe to the coffee table. He holds the orchid to his cashmere sweater. "It's a fur clip. Custom job."

A fur clip? The only thing Beck can imagine less than her grandmother owning a valuable piece of jewelry is clipping it to a mink stole. *Oh, Helen. This must really be amusing you now.*

Viktor flips the brooch over, pointing to a stamp along a ring of metal circling the girdle of the yellow stone. It reads *950.* "Platinum. During the war, platinum wasn't available to jewelers, so this is definitely postwar." Beside *950,* the letters *SJ* are engraved. "That's what's called a maker's mark, like a jeweler's logo. I don't recognize this one, though. It's not one of the big houses." He flips the brooch back over and draws a circle in the air above the petals. "This type of pavé was popular in the '50s. My guess is it was fabricated in '54, '55." His finger traces the large yellow-green stone at the center, which Beck is starting to suspect is indeed a peridot, and smiles outright. "Here's where things get interesting. Given the era, this should be a brilliant cut. Instead, it's a double rose cut, which went out of fashion in the early 1900s. Unheard of in midcentury jewelry." His face grows even more youthful as he tries not to giggle.

"Is it a peridot?" Beck isn't certain she pronounced the name of the stone correctly. Given Viktor's expression, she assumes she's butchered it.

"Beck," he says excitedly. "This is a diamond."

Beck knows nothing about diamonds. She's always preferred turquoise to emeralds, silver to gold. Still, she knows that Ashley's sizable diamond is three carats, a mere pebble compared to the rock in Viktor's hand.

"A diamond? But it's so big."

"I know." They stare at the large yellow diamond, glittering with lush color.

Suddenly, Beck feels dizzy. Helen's most valuable belonging, other than the house on

Edgehill Road, is a decades-old television set. How could Helen have owned a diamond like this? Not owned . . . possessed.

"Let's not get ahead of ourselves," Viktor cautions.

He rests the brooch on the glass coffee table and disappears into the kitchen. Beck hears a faucet flow, then Viktor returns with a cup of soapy water, a travel-size toothbrush, a pink cloth, and a small metal tool.

"Do you mind?"

Beck shakes her head, and Viktor deftly lifts each prong away from the yellow stone. He flips the brooch over and the stone tumbles from the finding onto the pink cloth in his left hand. The stone is domed on both sides and shaped like a shield, about the size of a robin's egg. Viktor dips the toothbrush into the soapy water and begins scrubbing the faceted yellow stone. It grows noticeably less cloudy, if still a bit dull.

Viktor taps the tweed couch beside his chair and Beck moves closer. She leans toward him as he holds the diamond up to the light. One side juts out asymmetrically. "See how it's lopsided here?" He runs his finger along the uneven side to the table of the diamond. "And how the faceting doesn't optimize the stone's dispersion? That tells me it was cut for size, not fire. Those kinds of cuts —" he whistles "— were popular in the sixteenth and seventeenth centuries."

"So you're saying this is an old diamond?"

"Not just old. Historic." With this, he hands the cloth and stone to Beck, then hops up to scan his wall-to-wall bookshelves.

Beck stares at the enormous yellow diamond, waiting for Helen's face to appear in it, to roll her eyes and say, *Please, you always knew I had my secrets.* Beck knew that Helen had stories she'd never shared. Stories about what happened to her family in Vienna during the Holocaust, why she traveled to the US alone. These were an untold past, one that Beck assumed held too much pain for Helen to revisit. This stone, though, it bears secrets, ones Beck can't begin to imagine.

Viktor plops into the chair with two books and an electronic scale. One book is gray canvas. The other has a glossy dust jacket and is titled *Historic Diamonds.*

Together, Beck and Viktor count the sides of the shield-shaped diamond — nine — and weigh it on the electronic scale — 137.27.

"Is that carats?" Beck asks, astounded. Viktor nods, reaching for the gray canvas book. He opens it to a chart of famous yellow diamonds. Beck and Viktor scan the carat weights of the diamonds until they reach the fifth largest on the chart — the Florentine Diamond. Its carat weight is noted at 137.27, the same as Viktor's scale. It's listed as nine-sided.

"Oh, my . . . This is . . . Wow." Viktor tries to piece together a sentence. It's the most excited Beck has ever seen him. His foot taps erratically; his face erupts into a smile as he puts his arm around Beck and pulls her to him, laughing.

"What's the Florentine Diamond?" Beck asks.

Viktor lets go of Beck and flips through the glossy book until he stops on a black-and-white photograph of a massive four-tiered hatpin that looks more like a chandelier pendant than a piece of jewelry. Each of the top three tiers is comprised of several round stones surrounding larger square and circular stones. At the bottom, the largest stone dangles from the pin, surrounded by tiny stones that look like lace. The gem hanging from the bottom is more or less the same shape as the yellow diamond resting on Viktor's scale. Beneath the photograph, a caption reads *Florentine Diamond as hatpin. Last known setting. Photograph c. 1870–1900.* Beneath the photograph there is another image of the diamond. Its description says *The Florentine was a 137.27-ct, nine-sided fancy yellow 126-facet double rose cut. This is a replica. The real diamond was lost to history.*

"What kind of hat could support a pin like that?" Beck asks.

"A crown. I don't know how the royals didn't snap their necks, with all the gemstones they wore on their heads."

Beck studies the photograph of the hatpin with its arcs of small round stones and larger square ones at the center. "Are those all diamonds?"

Viktor nods. "Worth a pretty penny, too. There must be at least a hundred of them in that hatpin, each a few carats. It belonged to the Habsburgs until the fall of the empire. After that —" Viktor waves his hand as if disappearing the piece of jewelry into thin air.

"The Habsburgs? Like Franz Ferdinand?" Beck searches the crevices of her brain for any other information on the Austro-Hungarian royal family. She took European history in college, then promptly never thought about the subject again.

Viktor shakes his head. "Franz Ferdinand is the only Habsburg most folks have heard of because his assassination started WWI, but he was never emperor, so the Florentine didn't belong to him. It belonged to his older brother, Emperor Franz Joseph, who put it in a necklace for his wife, Sisi, not that it made her love him." Viktor flips the book around to read the paragraph beneath the photograph's caption. "It seems that Sisi was the last person to wear it. She was assassinated by an Italian anarchist. After that, the Habsburgs thought the diamond was cursed, so no one wanted to wear it. They fashioned it into this hatpin and put it on display at the Kunsthistorisches Museum in Vienna. When Franz Joseph died, his great-nephew Karl inherited the throne, briefly. Two years after his ascension, WWI ended, and the monarchy was overturned. Before Karl fled with his family, he had one of his advisers take the crown jewels from the treasury and the Florentine from the Kunsthistorisches Museum to send ahead to Switzerland. Only, when the royal family arrived abroad, the Florentine wasn't with the other jewels. It hasn't been seen since."

Beck points to the yellow diamond, suddenly afraid to touch it. "Until now? You think that's the Florentine Diamond?"

"It's possible that this has been cut down from a larger stone, but it has the exact weight of the Florentine. Plus, as the chart shows, there are only four known yellow diamonds in the world that are larger than 137.27 carats — the Incomparable, the Oppenheimer, the De Beers, the Red Cross — and they're all accounted for."

"So unless someone has, what, mined a huge yellow diamond and kept it a secret for centuries, this has to be the Florentine?"

"I'm surprised it hasn't been recut. Usually if diamonds have been missing —" Beck notices that Viktor doesn't say *stolen* "— they're recut so they can't be identified. Your grandmother must have been pretty attached to this diamond if she didn't cut it. Instead, she hid it in a midcentury brooch."

Beck's attention shifts between the photo of the hatpin and the orchid brooch sitting on Viktor's table. The orchid brooch, with its tiny pavéd stones, looks so different than the tiered hatpin, with its chunky round and square diamonds. It's difficult to believe they had held the same stone. But that was the idea.

Viktor studies Beck, and she realizes she's frowning. "This is good news. This diamond is going to make you very rich."

"If it's legally mine."

Viktor shrugs. "There are people who don't care about that sort of thing. But we're getting ahead of ourselves. We need to get it graded."

"Graded?"

While Viktor finds a box for the diamond, he explains that before they can establish that the diamond is the Florentine, they must send it to the International Gemology Society to verify that it is in fact a diamond. After testing it, IGS will issue a colored diamond grading report, detailing the growth features, the clarity characterizations, and the measurements of the diamond.

"Is it safe, sending it to them?"

"They are the best in the world. I'll deliver it to their offices myself. And everything's anonymous, so even when they confirm it's real, they won't know whom they are confirming it for."

Beck's phone buzzes. It's Ashley. Can you make sure there's food at the house on Sunday? You know how I get if I haven't eaten. She includes an emoji of a monster, as though that makes her text cute. Ashley has a way of texting like everyone is her employee. Although she has a surprising number of employees for someone who doesn't work — babysitters, a dog walker, a trainer, a housecleaning service — Beck isn't one of them.

It's a shiva, Beck writes. There's no such thing as a Jewish event without food.

Great! Let me know if there's anything I can do to help, Ashley responds. Momentarily, Beck feels bad for being uncharitable toward her sister, then remembers that there's nothing for Ashley to do; Beck has already taken care of everything.

The time on her phone says 3:30 p.m. "I've got to get to court to file the paperwork."

Viktor holds the brooch out to her, hollow at the center where the yellow diamond once sat. "There are a few carats of emeralds here. Diamonds, too. You can always sell them and melt the platinum down. And some unsolicited advice, it's probably best not to list the brooch as an asset of the estate. Just until we're clear what we're dealing with."

Beck knows what Viktor is really saying. If it's listed as an asset, there's a record of it. Taxes will be due, steep taxes, and she will have to sell. Before she can sell, she will have to prove it's legally hers. For now, until she's certain of its value, it's just a sentimental heirloom, a worthless piece of costume jewelry that no one will fight her for.

Beck hesitates as they walk toward the front door. "How rich will this diamond make me?"

Viktor purses his lips, calculating in his head. "The diamond is worth about three million. If we can confirm it's the Florentine, I'd suspect you could get ten for it."

Beck coughs at more money than she's ever envisioned, more money than she owes in worthless law school loans and the remaining credit card debt her mother racked up in her name when she was a teenager.

"Ten million?" Beck manages to whisper.

"With diamonds like that, it's the history, the lineage, that gives it most of its value. It's one thing to have a diamond that is 137 carats — it's another thing to have a 137-carat diamond that belonged to Marie Antoinette and Napoleon." Viktor explains that Marie Antoinette, a Lorraine-Habsburg herself, wore it on her wedding day. Napoleon's second wife, also of Austrian royal decent, held on to it during her brief tenure as the French empress.

In the elevator, Beck forgets about how Tom had kissed her in that small marble-and-mirror interior. The rush of so much money lasts a few floors until she feels nauseous. She's positive the grading report will prove the diamond is the Florentine. She's also fairly certain that Helen knew this wasn't a piece of cheap costume jewelry, that when she'd called it her *yellow diamond brooch* in her will, it's because it *was* a yellow diamond brooch. So why hadn't Helen sold it and elevated herself from her modest circumstances? There were plenty of people who didn't care about things like good faith or proof of lawful ownership. Why would she have kept something so valuable? And if Helen knew how much it was worth, far more than the house or any savings under her mattress, why had Helen left it exclusively to Beck?

When the doors open to Viktor's lobby, Beck can't get her legs to move. The exception written into Article IV. *My yellow diamond brooch.* She'd sent the will to her family.

She grabs her phone and skims through their short, almost callous responses to her email. No one mentioned the yellow diamond brooch in the will. Her body relaxes. Of course they didn't notice. That would require an attention to detail none of the other Millers has. Besides, they have no reason to suspect that anything in the will is unusual, that with those four small words — *my yellow diamond brooch* — Helen left Beck a fortune.

"Going up?" a man asks as he steps into

the elevator. She shakes her head and darts out. As she steps onto Eighteenth Street, Beck nods at the doorman, who looks at her suspiciously, or maybe that's just her imagination. Beck feels guilty, and she knows that guilt isn't over something she's done but something she's about to do.

When she meets her family at the cemetery, she won't tell them about Helen's brooch. It isn't about money. The brooch was Helen's secret. In leaving it to Beck, she's passed its secrecy on to Beck, too.

FOUR

Deborah can't believe she's late. Sure, her internal clock runs about ten minutes behind the time on her cell phone, but how can anyone be late to her own mother's funeral?

When she races up the snow-covered hill to the plot, the looks on her children's faces convey that they are not surprised by their mother's tardiness.

The rabbi stumbles when she sees Deborah huffing and puffing before she continues to read in Hebrew. Her voice is soft and rhythmic. Although the words sound like gibberish to Deborah, they are comforting. Of course Helen would have requested a female rabbi. She'd always insisted her doctors were women, her dentist, her hairdresser. If she could have found female gravediggers, she'd have wanted them, too.

"You're late," Beck whispers, her eyes steady on the rabbi.

"I got lost."

"How do you get lost in Bala Cynwyd?" Beck hisses.

"You're being rude," Ashley says to Beck and Deborah, even though, other than the rabbi, there is no one there to take offense. Helen had specified that she wanted her funeral graveside, for family. Deborah knows that the only family Helen had were the Millers. She never learned precisely what happened to Helen's parents and brother, only that they hadn't survived the Holocaust. Although she's heard countless stories of her grandmother Flora, who would take Helen to the cinema, her brother, Martin, and father, Lieb, who would ride the Ferris wheel with her, Helen never told Deborah the stories of their deaths. And Deborah had never met her father's family. He died in Korea when she was two. Whatever family he had, as far as Deborah knew, Helen had never met them, either.

Deborah rubs a crystal in her coat pocket, trying to center herself as the rabbi recites the Mourner's Kaddish. Despite being only a few miles from her childhood home, she really did get lost. How was she supposed to know there were two Laurel Hill Cemeteries? As she listens to the rabbi, Deborah realizes, subconsciously, she was late on purpose. So much easier to arrive once the ceremony already started, once she could avoid an uncomfortable reunion with her children.

Beck can feel Deborah's manic energy, so she steps away from her. She just walked up to Beck and stood beside her as though they were allies. Even though Beck is the least distant from Deborah, that doesn't make them close. They talk maybe once a month, usually about Helen. Beck can count on one hand the times she's seen her mother in the past year. She continues to inch away from Deborah, but any farther and she'll be standing right beside Jake. She doesn't want to be allies with him, either.

Icy wind slaps Jake's face as he listens to the rabbi. Was March in Philadelphia always this cold? He's been on the west coast too long and doesn't own a proper winter coat, so he stands graveside, hugging his jean jacket to his body. Jake's eyes sting from a sleepless night on the red-eye. His flight landed at six thirty that morning, and he'd taken a cab to Edgehill Road. He'd wanted to see the house one last time as Helen's. It looked exactly as he remembered, as though he could skip up the walkway to the porch and find Helen in her wool slacks, sipping brandy on the couch inside. Jake sat on the steps, feeling the warmth of the morning sun through the biting cold. It was going to be tougher than he anticipated, seeing Beck, seeing Deborah.

He was first to the cemetery, and fortunately Ashley was next to arrive. He hugged her before asking, "Isn't there something we can do about the house?"

"Like what?" Ashley looked tired, not like Jake did from the red-eye, but a prolonged fatigue that had turned her skin sallow.

"We can't let Deborah have it."

"Why not?"

"Because of everything she put us through."

"That was years ago." Ashley had only lived on Edgehill Road for one year. She wasn't around when Deborah's weeklong retreats turned into months-long disappearances. She didn't witness how it had changed Beck, made her withdrawn until their once bubbly younger sister became defensive and secretive. "It's just an old house."

"You know she's going to sell, first chance she gets," Jake said, trying a different approach.

"If it goes to us, we'll just sell, too." And then Ashley being Ashley asked him, "Do

95

you need money?"

Before Jake could tell her this wasn't about money, Beck stepped out of the back of a blue sedan. She walked toward them like she was debating turning around and jumping into her Lyft.

Beck hugged Ashley deeply, as siblings should. She hesitated, then hugged Jake, too. He tried to hold her closer and longer, but she pulled away almost immediately.

When Jake broached the topic of the house with Beck, she was distracted, her eyes everywhere except Jake.

"Leave it alone," she warned. He didn't know if she meant the house or their relationship.

"It doesn't make you mad that it's going to Deborah?"

Beck turned to him, and he'd preferred when she wouldn't meet his eye. "You don't even live here."

While Jake knew he should let it go, he couldn't help himself.

"But to Deborah?"

"You know nothing about their relationship," Beck said, walking away to greet the rabbi.

Now, Jake watches his sister twitch with anger and doesn't understand. How can Beck be this angry and not want to fight for

96

the house? How can Deborah get the house, *their* house, when she couldn't even bother to show up on time to Helen's funeral?

Ashley and Deborah turn toward Jake, and he realizes it's his turn to sprinkle dirt on Helen's casket. Jake's surprised Helen would have wanted a funeral. Helen always said that spending money on the dead was like watering plastic plants. No, Helen was more the type to say, *Burn my body and throw the ashes out with the trash.* This thought paralyzes him. How could he think this? Helen would never burn her body.

The soil is cold and gritty against his palm. He takes the biggest handful he can and lets it slip through his fingers into the open grave below. Jake only knows the outline of Helen's family's story, but he knows that if her family didn't return from the camps, they didn't get pine boxes lowered into the ground.

Ashley is the last one to throw dirt on her grandmother's casket. She takes a small handful and tosses it as quickly as possible into the grave. She's starting to regret staying for three nights, for leaving the kids home with Ryan. If Lydia and Tyler were here, the Millers would have a reason to remain civil. Deep breaths. She didn't get sucked into their drama when she was a teenager; she will not get sucked in now. She has enough of her own real, life-changing issues to worry about.

Once the ceremony is over, Beck follows Deborah to her VW Rabbit — the Red Rabbit as her mother has taken to calling it — while Jake and Ashley walk in the opposite direction toward Ashley's SUV. Beck's phone buzzes, and she stops to check a text from Viktor. Grading is complete. Should be getting the diamond and report within the hour.

Already? Beck writes. The grading report was supposed to take a week, even with Viktor's connections.

It's not every day the lab gets a 137-carat yellow diamond. Beck notices that he doesn't call it the Florentine.

Deborah waits by the Red Rabbit for Beck to catch up. While Beck cannot imagine her mother in any other car, she also can't believe the old beast is still running. The maroon paint has rusted and oxidized. The leather piping along the seats has chipped off, but the car is still in one piece.

"I need to go do something for work," Beck says. "Just real fast."

"You're serious?" Deborah asks. "It's Sunday. And the day of your grandmother's funeral."

Beck finds her keys and takes the one to

Helen's house off the ring, holding it out to her mother. Deborah shakes her head and dangles her keys. "I already have one."

"I'll just be an hour. I have to drop something off."

Deborah unlocks the passenger door and opens it for Beck. "I'll drive you."

"No, it's fine. Really. You should be there in case any of Helen's friends come. It's your house now." Beck reaches into her purse for the agreement she's drafted, acknowledging that they have all read and accepted the terms of the will. The Millers need to sign it before she can release the assets of the estate, before the brooch is officially hers, before the house is officially Deborah's. "I need you to get Jake and Ash to sign this."

"What is it?" Deborah asks without reaching for it. Beck knows she's feeding Deborah to the lions, but Deborah deserves this. If she's going to keep the house, she will have to endure the opposition and anger that comes with it. It's just an added bonus that this frees Beck from having to get her siblings to sign the agreement, from the morally dubious territory of not mentioning the brooch to them.

"It's just a formality, acknowledging we're all aware of the distribution of assets in the will. Once everyone signs and I get the short certificate, I can start distributing the assets." The legal jargon is intended to bore Deborah into compliance, and she looks dumbfounded. "It means you can get the house."

Deborah takes the paper. "They don't want me to have it."

Beck isn't used to seeing her mother look this defeated. "Helen did."

Deborah shuts the passenger door and walks to the driver's side of the car. "I still don't think it's right, them making you work today."

"I'll let them know you think that."

"We'll see you in an hour," Deborah tells more than asks Beck. The Red Rabbit coughs as Deborah turns the key in the ignition. She watches her daughter's slender figure grow smaller in the rearview mirror.

Deborah hadn't meant to foist her parenting obligations onto Helen. After Kenny left, that period of her life is a blur. The months she spent searching for Kenny. The self-betterment conventions that it took her years to realize were a scam. The cross-country trips with men who never became boyfriends. The ideas that never became businesses. She could never explain any of it to her children. Helen had never asked

100

for an explanation. When Deborah returned, she welcomed her home without so much as admonishing, *You're a mother. Mothers don't leave their children.* Deborah was also a daughter. As a daughter, she'd left, too.

Viktor is waiting for Beck with his signature glass of champagne. His face falls when he notices the black ribbon pinned to her sweater.

"You're just coming from the funeral. I'm so sorry. I didn't realize."

She shrugs and takes one of the flutes from Viktor. "Please tell me we're celebrating."

Viktor giggles, unable to contain his excitement. She follows him into the living room where a glossy pamphlet from IGS — the International Gemology Society — rests beside the box with Helen's yellow diamond.

When she opens the report, a sketch of Helen's yellow diamond stares back at her. Numbers and descriptions fill the report: the diamond's dimensions and proportions, its polish, its color grade and clarity characteristics, its inclusions and UV fluorescence, which Viktor explains is the color that it emits under a UV light. In the comments section, the gemologist listed the uniqueness of the cut, the number of facets, a heart-shaped feathering along the girdle.

Viktor points to the drawing of the diamond with a marking of the heart inside. "That's a tiny crack within the diamond. Probably why your grandmother didn't have it cut. If someone tried to cut it, it may have cleaved the diamond and ruined it."

Viktor keeps calling it *the diamond*, not *the Florentine*. The grading report says nothing about the Florentine Diamond, either.

"So it's not the Florentine?" Beck asks, disappointed.

"IGS doesn't identify diamonds. It only grades them," Viktor explains.

"What's the difference?"

"A grading report tells you about the characteristics of the diamond, not its provenance."

Beck follows Viktor into the dining room where two plates of food hide beneath porcelain lids. The brunches, his help with her grandmother's diamond, these aren't acts of generosity and gratitude alone. Despite his penthouse with a view of Rittenhouse Square, his curated library and bottles of expensive bubbly, Viktor is lonely. She vows to visit him more often.

As Viktor seats himself at the head of the table, he says, "The characteristics are what enable you to identify a stone. Most diamonds aren't perfect. They have feathers, like the heart-shaped one in your diamond, and other inclusions. Flaws that make them unique. That's how you identify diamonds — through their imperfections. The grading report tells you what makes your diamond unique, not whether those unique characteristics are those of the Florentine." Viktor lifts the lids from their plates to reveal almost perfect plates of eggs royale. "It's the Florentine. You just have to prove it."

When the Millers return from the cemetery, someone has covered all the mirrors. Esther, Deborah assumes, who is already in the dining room, spreading trays from Hymie's across the table.

It catches Deborah's breath to see those platters of rugelach, corned beef, and lox. The knishes, laid out on one of her childhood plates, choke her up more than the burial at the cemetery. Little about the house has changed since Deborah was a child — not the ivy-trimmed plates, not the oak table Helen bought at a garage sale that was too big for the modest dining room. Only a newer television in the corner and rose carpeting on the stairs, which Helen had installed after Beck had slipped and needed stitches.

Deborah looks around the familiar living room, calculating how long it's been since she's seen Helen. A swell of guilt rises as she realizes it's been a month, that she often went longer than that without seeing her mother.

A hand reaches toward Deborah's. Fingers interlace hers, nails manicured and pink, a sizable diamond sliding down the ring finger. Ashley is the most attractive of her children. Or the highlighted hair, expensive clothing, and facials have made her so. She's become the least Miller. Then again, Ashley is not a Miller anymore. She's a Johnson, stripping herself not just of her maiden name but of the resentments that come with it. Ashley has no interest in fighting Deborah for the house. She has no intention of making Deborah feel worse. That's not necessarily the same thing as forgiveness, though.

Esther orders them to take off their shoes, and Jake leans over Ashley as she unzips her boots. "Who's the boss lady?" he asks.

"You don't remember Esther?" Ashley whispers back. "Her mom was Helen's best friend? She lives next door." Jake remembers Nancy Bloom, from around the corner. He doesn't remember Esther or her mother from next door. Jake dips his hands into the bowl of tepid water that Esther holds toward him. As he shakes off the droplets, he sees it as a shot, a close-up. The dining room, covered in platters of food, his mother and sister holding hands, the tension and sadness in the room, Beck's palpable absence — it's all so cinematic. Maybe Jake will write a film about this shiva, about Helen. A film to honor his grandmother's passing, nothing like *My Summer of Women.* It sends a jolt of excitement through him, having an idea for a movie.

The Millers squish together on the couch as Esther takes the chair beside them, smacking her lips as she eats a plate of rugelach. The dry heat from the buzzing radiator makes the room stuffy. The Millers don't have an appetite, despite Esther asking them every few minutes if they are hungry. When she's finished her plate, she announces that she will be at her house if they need anything.

As she's leaving, Deborah asks her, "What are we supposed to do now?"

"Remember Helen." Esther shuts the door behind her as she leaves.

Jake stares at the platters of food in the dining room. "Do you think anyone else is coming?"

"No," Ashley says, an uncharacteristic heaviness to her voice.

"Of course other people are coming," Deborah protests. All of Helen's old neighborhood friends are dead, even Esther's mother, but people have always liked Helen.

The Millers sit in silence, waiting for the other people to arrive, waiting for someone to begin to remember Helen. When no one does, Deborah announces that she's hungry. She wonders how much thinner she'd be if she didn't eat out of discomfort. She wonders if that thinness would make her as happy as the corned beef sandwich she assembles on her plate.

"So much for veganism," Ashley quips. She means this to be funny, but it's not the right setting for sarcasm. "Sorry."

Deborah shrugs. "Helen never let food go to waste. I'm honoring her." She settles into the armchair Esther has left vacant. Suddenly, she can't eat. "Helen used to roast a chicken on Mondays. Then Tuesdays she'd make chicken salad with whatever scraps she could get off the carcass and on Wednesdays we'd have chicken soup. Not even the bones went to waste."

"We know," Jake says. "We lived here, too."

Ashley shoots Jake a chiding look. Judging from the bruised expression on Deborah's face, he may have gone too far. Unlike Ashley, he has no intention of apologizing.

"I don't understand why Beck isn't here," Jake says, fidgeting.

"She had to do something for work." Deborah rests the untouched sandwich on the table.

"Her grandmother dies, and they can't even give her the weekend off?" Ashley remembers all those weekends Ryan supposedly couldn't get off, all those soccer tournaments and Disney movies he missed, the vacation to Los Angeles he had to cancel. He was at work, but not because his company demanded it. Ashley laughs in disbelief. Was she always this gullible or only once her husband started lying to her?

Ashley's face has always been expressive, like a mood ring darkening from blue to black at the first sign of distress. Jake monitors his sister and understands, as Ashley does, that Beck is not at work. Even though he has no idea where she is, he should have known that if the timing of Beck's work task seemed too convenient, it's because it was.

Deborah can feel the shift in the room, the static air building entropy. Before it unleashes and they band together against Beck, Deborah finds the agreement Beck gave her.

"We need to sign this," she tells Ashley and Jake as she puts the document on the coffee table. "So Beck can settle the will."

"You mean so you can get the house," Jake says.

"She was my mother, Jake." Deborah keeps

her tone even. "I know you don't understand our relationship, but —"

"You're right, I don't. I don't understand, after everything you did to us, to Helen, why she would leave our house to you. She must not have been in her right mind. In fact, how do we know you didn't do something sneaky to trick her into leaving it to you?"

"Jake, come on," Ashley cautions.

Deborah remains steadfast. "I don't have to justify Helen's decisions to you."

"Well, I'm not signing that." Jake leans back and crosses his arms against his chest. He knows he's acting like a child. His posture dares his sister and mother to call him out on it.

Ashley and Deborah exchange looks, and Deborah is grateful that at least one of her children doesn't hate her, at least not outright, anyway.

"Why do you have to make this harder than it already is?" Deborah asks.

Jake leans forward, his face cloaked in mock surprise. "I'm the one who makes things harder? You're serious? That's rich. Really, that's —" Jake stops midsentence when he hears a knock, then turns to see the unlocked door creak open. A tall, clean-shaven man in his thirties bows his head as he steps into the living room.

"Is Beck here?" he asks. "I'm Tom."

They've all heard of Tom. Helen had told Jake and Deborah he was a stable fellow. Consistent, which Beck needed more in a partner than someone who was interesting or fun to be around. For her part, Beck had told Ashley that Tom was smart, intriguingly strait-laced. Beck didn't know that someone so buttoned-up could be so right for her until, one day, Beck reported that she was wrong. Tom wasn't right for her at all.

"Did Beck invite you?" Ashley asks warily.

"You're a lawyer, right?" Jake lifts the agreement from the table and holds it toward him. "Maybe you can help us sort out some details from Helen's will before we sign this?"

"Jake," Ashley starts, "we should wait until Beck gets back —" but Tom's already walking toward the couch, arm outstretched to take the agreement from Jake.

FIVE

Beck startles when she walks into Helen's house and finds her family huddled around the coffee table with Tom. Deborah cryptically peers over at her youngest daughter, while the expressions on the others' faces are clearer: Ashley is furious, Jake betrayed, Tom disappointed. Tom? Why is he sitting with her family, communing like old friends planning a bank robbery?

"I didn't invite you," Beck says by way of greeting to her ex-boyfriend. And then she sees it, opened on the computer resting between them. Helen's will. They must have noticed the exception in Article IV. Instinctively, she clutches her purse as though one of them may try to snatch the diamond from her.

Beck surveys her family, her siblings who do not look as elated as they should at the prospect of their inheritance. Then she remembers: they don't know the diamond's worth. They're upset because Beck is keeping a secret.

Tom stands. "I just wanted to pay my respects."

Beck thinks he's going to leave so the Millers can engage in the fight that is imminent. Instead, he walks up to Beck, and she prays that he both will and will not touch her. His hand rests in the air an inch from her shoulder, a terrible compromise between her desires.

"Can we talk?" He motions her toward the porch.

Outside, it's cold enough to see her breath and Beck exhales fast plumes as she tries to control her emotions. That terrible compromise continues, as Beck wants to scream at Tom — *What the hell are you doing here?* — and wants him to pull her to his chest, to stroke her hair as she clings to him.

Before she can do anything, Tom holds his arms up in protest. "I wasn't trying to butt in."

"Seriously, I never asked you to come."

"You didn't have to. I know how close you were with Helen."

"We aren't friends, Tom. If you haven't noticed, I go out of my way to avoid you at work."

"I've noticed."

"Then why would you think I'd want you here?"

"I still care about you. Even if it didn't work out between us."

"You have a funny way of showing it, conspiring with my family."

"Beck." He reaches for her. She shakes her head, and he digs his hands into the front pockets of his khaki pants. He isn't wearing a jacket, and he shivers visibly. Beck knows he won't admit that he's cold, that he'll stay outside as long as she wants him to. "They were screaming at each other. I didn't know what to do."

"You could have left, minded your own business."

Tom gives her a funny look as though the suggestion is preposterous. "When I told them who I was they asked me to look at the Receipt, Release, Refunding, and Indemnification Agreement you gave them." Of course Tom calls it by its full name. He's always finding subtle ways to flaunt his expertise, only it's never bothered her before. "I looked at the will to explain to your brother that he really didn't have a case for contesting your mother's ownership of the house." Tom sways from foot to foot to keep warm. "Why didn't you tell your family about the brooch?"

Tom is a good lawyer, scrupulous, with loyalty to the law, not to her. He knows that a brooch listed as having a yellow diamond should be appraised before the assets are distributed. He knows her family could dispute the will, arguing that Helen didn't understand the value of what she'd left to Beck, or worse, they could claim that Beck had undue influence.

"Because it's nothing," she tells him. He looks skeptical. "You know why." And he does. Tom knows all about Jake's movie, about the credit cards Deborah took out in Beck's name, the months when she had no idea if her mother was coming home, let alone still alive. He knows about Beck's complicated feelings toward Ashley, who left the minute she could, only wishing to be closer to Beck once she had kids and decided that family was important.

"You should have told them. As executor, it was your duty."

"You're serious? My duty?" Beck stares at Tom until he looks away, uncomfortable, and she understands that they could never be together, not really. They are both governed by a steadfast sense of right and wrong, but Beck's, however fallible, is her own, while Tom's is based on the law, comprised of rules in place of morals to follow. "Just because I told you a few stories about my family doesn't mean you know what's going on here." The anger radiates from her core, raising her body temperature despite the afternoon's chill. She feels overwhelmed by all the things she wants to shout at him, the more pressing fight with her family waiting in the living room. So she just says, "Go," pleased that she's managed to stay calm, that she didn't give him the satisfaction of discounting her as irrational.

Tom looks at his watch. He once told Beck that he wears a watch so he can stare at it at opportune times.

"I've got to get home and finish up some work before the week starts." She wonders if he remembers that he's revealed this move to her. "I'll call you later?"

Hands burrowed in his pockets, Tom heads down the pathway toward his parked car. He won't call and she doesn't want him to, only now she's left to feel rejected when her phone doesn't ring.

Tom offers her a wave and a reconciliatory smile before pulling away from the curb. As Beck watches his car drive away, she realizes he feels guilty for breaking up with her.

Beck can locate the precise moment in

January when their relationship was over, even though it took Tom another month to move out. Lying in bed, with Beck's cheek against his smooth chest, Tom had mentioned an upcoming business trip to Los Angeles.

"Your brother lives there?" he'd asked, knowing that Jake did. "Do you want to come with me?"

Tom considered family a necessity, like a house or a car or a comfortable pair of loafers. He called his parents every Sunday, saw his brother every few weeks. It didn't matter that the only thing they had to talk about was the Eagles — you saw family regardless of whether you enjoyed spending time with them. In fact, one of the things he loved most about Beck was how much she treasured her time with Helen. One thing he couldn't understand was the fact that she'd once been close to Jake, too, only they hadn't spoken in half a decade.

Beck made up some excuse about being busy with work, and he continued to stroke her hair, eventually asking, "What happened between you two?"

Like a fool, she'd wanted him to understand. So she told him everything, starting with high school.

The thing no one ever understands about

Beck in high school is that she was happy. Sure, when she stopped to think about her father, a wave of hurt would rise; when she envisioned her mother at some ashram in Vermont, a burst of anger; when confronted with the image of her siblings recreating themselves at college, a torrent of jealousy. But she'd developed a tightknit group of friends at Lower Merion, closer and more loyal than she'd had at her previous school. She liked the goulash and roasted chicken Helen made for her. She was much happier, she emphasized to Tom, than anyone recognized. Almost twenty years later, that fact remains important to her.

So why did she do it? It wasn't about the grades — that's another detail she emphasizes. It was about Mr. O'Neal, her eleventh-grade English teacher. His smugness. His skeeviness. His completely unwarranted antipathy toward her. The worst part was, she'd been excited to enroll in his class. He assigned *The Bluest Eye*, *Slaughterhouse-Five*, *The Lone Ranger and Tonto Fistfight in Heaven*. He wore jeans instead of Dockers and would curse so long as it was out of enthusiasm.

From the first day, he formed an instant dislike of Beck. Sure, she'd walked in with a nose ring and blue hair woven into buns,

116

her pierced belly button exposed beneath her tank top, her first tattoo — the Venus symbol — already visible on her lower back. But she'd done all the summer reading and got a 10/10 on the pop quiz that first day. She always raised her hand, never spoke out of turn. Still, Mr. O'Neal would rarely call on her and, when he did, he would nod vacantly at her careful comments, always quick to move on to the next student, praising whatever Reid Taylor or Jon Rubens or one of the other jocks said, usually a regurgitation of Beck's ideas in less precise terms. And worse, he gave her a C on everything she wrote.

Beck had never gotten a C, had never been average at anything. When she tried to talk to Mr. O'Neal about her grades, she'd left his classroom in tears.

"Maybe if you spent more time on your arguments and less time desecrating your body, you'd see a reflection in your grades." Beck followed his eyes down her small bust to the charm dangling from her belly button. His gaze remained on her bare stomach until he sucked in his breath, shook his head, and walked away.

She didn't dare tell anyone what he said and started wearing bulky sweatshirts to all her classes. Still, the Cs continued, with comments in the margins like, *Seriously? Are you kidding me? Is this for real?* She knew her work was sound, understood in some abstract way that his comment about her body had been inappropriate, but he'd embarrassed her and made her doubt herself. Soon, that doubt spread into her other classes where she was afraid to speak, afraid to submit the assignments she'd completed, afraid to go to school at all.

It took two weeks of absences for the school to call Helen.

Looking back on it, Beck had wanted to get caught. She was sixteen. She didn't know how to talk to anyone about how pathetic and exposed her English teacher made her feel. And the grand irony is that Beck spent those two weeks studying at the library. Her friends thought she was skipping school to be with an older guy they'd met at a party, but the only older guy she spent her days with was the librarian, who talked to her about Virginia Woolf and Douglas Adams, never noticing her exposed midriff, her wild blue hair.

When two weeks had passed, Beck returned home from the library, acting as though she'd been at school, to find Helen waiting on the couch, disconsolate. To Beck's surprise, Helen didn't yell or make her feel guilty. Rather, she'd said, "Explain it to me, Becca. Tell me why a girl as smart as you would want to skip school."

After a lot of deflecting, Beck finally told her about Mr. O'Neal, the doubt he inspired, the homework she'd completed during her absence. She left out his comment on her appearance. It was still too embarrassing to say aloud.

The next day, in the principal's office, Helen dropped the pile of work Beck had completed over the last two weeks on the principal's desk and asked Beck to wait in the hall. Beck never learned what Helen had said to her principal behind that closed door. When it opened, the principal looked ashamed and defeated; Helen, ferocious and beautiful. The principal told Beck that the absences would not be reflected on her record, but it was up to the teachers whether they wanted to give her credit for the assignments. Given the circumstances, he assured her they would. Beck didn't know what circumstances he meant, but Helen cautioned Beck to thank him for his decision.

That would have been that if not for Mr. O'Neal, the only teacher who refused to accept her outstanding work. Beck spent the rest of the year sitting in the corner of the room, head down, body cloaked in a hoodie, counting the minutes until class was over. Every once in a while, when they spoke of the treatment of Hester Prynne or Offred, she found herself raising her hand. Mr. O'Neal cast her the same slow nod whenever she spoke, an expression on his face that she couldn't decipher but made her deeply uncomfortable.

It wasn't about the C he gave her for the year, how that grade might affect her chances of getting into college. That wasn't why she broke into the principal's office and logged on to his computer. Mr. O'Neal made her feel small and had gotten away with it.

She might have gotten away with it, too, if she'd just changed her grade. Once she was logged into the system, she couldn't help herself. She searched all of Mr. O'Neal's grades and saw that he'd given Reid Taylor, Jon Rubens, and the other jocks A-range grades while most of the girls received Bs and Cs. Callie Morgan, who had braces and pimples and still looked like she was in middle school, received an A, but Olivia Thomas, a cheerleader who wore low-cut tops and also happened to be number two in their class, got a B. Lizzie Meyers, the bustiest girl in their grade, who was by no means a genius but hardworking, got a C-. The pattern continued across Mr. O'Neal's other classes. She counted twelve girls, including herself, who received grades she knew were lower than they deserved. Eleven other girls, who must have felt as exposed and vulnerable as Beck did. It provoked a rage in Beck that made her sloppy. If she'd just changed her grade, from a C to a B, no one would have noticed. Instead, Beck gave them all As. And she still may have gotten away with it, if Lizzie Meyers wasn't quite so conscientious and hadn't thanked Mr. O'Neal for rewarding her hard work. That made him curious, so he did a little digging, which led to Beck's expulsion.

Before Tom, she'd never told anyone what Mr. O'Neal had said to her. Not Helen, who despite winning that early battle against the principal had lost the war when it came to Beck's status at the high school. Not her other boyfriends, who didn't even know she'd been kicked out of school. Not Jake, who had returned home for the summer and spent countless nights with her on the porch, smoking pot and assuring Beck that everything would turn out okay. Before Tom, Beck couldn't bring herself to explain the way Mr. O'Neal's eyes had lingered on her body, like he was both aroused and disgusted, like he was so much better than she was.

At first, Tom had hugged her close, but his arms slackened as she explained her decision to leave the expulsion, a senior year homeschooled, off her law school application. He held his breath as she told him that she would have gotten away with that, too, if it weren't for Jake's movie, or for Molly Stanton, Beck's main competitor for editor of the school's law review. Maybe if Beck hadn't had such open disdain for Molly, who had a position waiting for her at her father's firm, Molly wouldn't have looked into Beck's past after seeing Jake's movie. Maybe she wouldn't have alerted the deans about Beck's expulsion, and Beck would now be a fifth-year, partner-track lawyer rather than a paralegal.

"So you don't regret it?" Tom had asked.

If she'd had her guard up, Beck would have said yes, would have given him the party line, remorse and shame, a speech that might have been appealing to the law school, the Bar's Character and Fitness Committee. Instead, she told him the truth.

"I don't regret any of it. Mr. O'Neal was a lecherous creep who should have been fired. And Molly Stanton was an entitled daddy's girl who should have accepted that

I was a better student than she was. I didn't have anything handed to me. I worked hard. I know I should feel guilty, but I don't. I still feel mistreated."

After that, Tom nodded for too long, then rolled over and pretended to fall asleep. Beck listened to the forced rise and fall of his breath, struggling to say something that might help him understand. She knew in that moment their relationship was over.

A month later, when he stood in the entryway with his suitcases, she wanted to be angry with him. Instead, she was crushed; she'd finally opened up to someone, and it had resulted in her being alone once again.

After Tom's BMW turns right off Edgehill Road, Beck watches the empty street, taking a brief respite on the porch. A moment to collect herself and decide what to say to her family. She finds the black jewelry box in her purse, and when she opens it, the diamond sparkles in the sunlight. Under no circumstances will she tell them about the Florentine Diamond. Dollar signs will flash in Ashley's eyes, even though Ashley is the only Miller who does not need the money. A movie will build in Jake's brain, one that exploits Helen and her private life. Pain will quake in Deborah's limbs as she realizes the house was a distraction from the estate's true gem.

She considers lying to them — *You know Helen, it was just a piece of junk jewelry she thought I might wear. I totally forgot about it* — but Ashley has always been able to see through her lies. If she shares the diamond with them, she will have to sell, and Beck has decided that, like Helen, she will keep the diamond buried in her drawer, a sentimental gift, a brooch priceless with family lore, not a historic diamond.

Beck snaps the box shut and drops it in her purse. It's decided, then. Beck will waltz inside as though she's hidden nothing. She will reset the diamond in the brooch and it will return to a piece of costume jewelry her grandmother kept in her dresser. Besides, it's not the diamond Beck is after. It's the stories it holds.

When Beck reenters the living room, there's a moment of charged silence as her family waits like a room full of predators with no prey.

Finally, Ashley grabs the computer and waves it toward Beck. "Anything you forgot to tell us?"

"Careful," Jake warns, taking the laptop from his sister. Ashley's attention shifts briefly to her brother, expecting him to cower. "Some of us can't afford to just buy another computer."

"What?" Beck says casually. "You mean the brooch?"

"Yes, Beck, I mean the brooch. What did she call it?"

Jake reads from the computer screen, " 'My yellow diamond brooch.' "

" 'My yellow diamond brooch,' " Ashley repeats.

Beck laughs, feeling alarmingly calm. A sixth sense, the Miller sense, where she can predict everything her family will do. This is going to be easier than she anticipated. "What? You think it was worth money or something? It's a piece of costume jewelry I found in her dresser."

"Can I see it?" Deborah asks. "I don't remember Helen wearing a brooch."

"It's at my apartment," Beck lies.

"How convenient." Jake returns the laptop to his messenger bag. "Your boyfriend told us that the way Helen listed it, we still have to split the estate evenly. You get to keep the brooch, but you have to pay us two-thirds of what it's worth out of your share of the money she left us."

Beck flinches. "He's not my boyfriend. But sure, I'll give you twenty dollars for the brooch. That's about how much it's worth. In fact, if you're so hard up —" Beck digs her wallet out of her purse and finds a ten-dollar bill. She balls it up and throws it at her brother. "That's all I have. I'll get you another ten next time I go to the MAC machine."

"You're being ridiculous," Jake says.

"You don't get to tell me how I'm being."

"You're both being ridiculous," Ashley announces, hands on hips as though Beck and Jake are Lydia and Tyler.

Deborah mimics Ashley's pose and says, "Why don't we take a step back." Her children turn to her, teeth bared, and she sits down in the armchair, bizarrely proud of the three humans she created, able to defend themselves.

Beck forces a laugh. "Honestly, it slipped my mind. It's just some rhinestone thing."

"Why would she call it a diamond?" Jake asks.

"Really, Jake. I didn't take *you* for the gold digger," Beck says, casting a cool glance at her sister.

"What the hell is that supposed to mean?" Ashley says over her brother, who asks, "Jesus, Beck, can you be honest for, like, a second?"

"Like you, the paragon of honesty?"

126

"When have I been dishonest?" Part of Jake wants a candid answer.

"Right, your problem is you confuse divulging other people's secrets with honesty."

"Oh, this old sob story again. Look, I fucked up, all right? At some point you're going to have to get some new material."

"Why? You haven't." Beck doesn't actually know what's going on with her brother's career, only that since *My Summer of Women,* he hasn't made another movie.

"Come on, Beck," Ashley says, noticing the hurt on Jake's face. She, too, doesn't know what's going on with Jake's career, if he's writing or has given it up, but she knows his fight with Beck has something to do with the fact that he hasn't worked as a screenwriter again. "Let's stay focused on what's going on here. Why didn't you mention the brooch?"

"Did you ever think I didn't want to hurt your feelings? *Sorry, Ash, Helen liked me best.* Excuse me for not wanting to rub that in your face."

"Oh, that's such bullshit."

"Don't confuse spending the most time with Helen as her liking you best," Jake says.

"This really isn't the time or place for all this," Deborah says, crossing her arms and curling into the chair. "This is Helen's shiva."

"Do *not* take the position of the morally superior," Ashley snaps.

"When did you become so bossy?" Deborah asks.

"She's always been bossy," Beck says.

"Always," Jake agrees. Only, when Beck turns to look at him, it isn't out of solidarity.

From there, Jake isn't sure what he says, which of the other Miller women calls him a traitor. He doesn't know when they turn their attention from him to each other.

"Beck Miller," Ashley chants, "protector of other people's feelings. Beck Miller, the considerate and noble. Like any of that could go on your tombstone."

Beck mimics the same singsong. "Ashley Miller, the reliable. Ashley Miller, the caretaker. Like that could go on yours."

"Girls, let's —" Deborah begins, but her daughters scowl at her.

"I'm sorry I have a family, Beck, that I can't drop everything because you're having another crisis."

"When have I ever asked you for help?"

"That's true. You don't. You just hold it against us when we can't magically read your mind and behave exactly how you want."

"I'm the one who expects everyone to cater to *me?"*

"Are you calling me self-centered?"

"I don't need to — it's plastered across your Botoxed face."

"So now you're better than me because you make yourself ugly instead of attractive?"

Beck runs her hand through her dyed black hair and hugs her tattooed arms to her chest. Even before her cosmetic alterations, Ashley was the prettier one, but the laws of sisterhood have always commanded that neither utter this truth.

"I'd really like to see the brooch," Deborah chimes in. She doesn't actually care about seeing the brooch. She believes Beck didn't want to hurt her siblings' feelings, especially over a piece of junk jewelry. But she doesn't like the bruised look on Beck's face. The only thing she can think to do is divert attention from it.

"Why?" Jake asks. "You already took the house — now you want to take the brooch, too?"

"I didn't take anything. Helen left it to me," Deborah says, already regretting that she's reinserted herself into their argument.

"Just like Helen left the brooch to me," Beck says.

"You know we can contest the will? We can get the court to evaluate it," Ashley says.

"Look who's suddenly become the family litigator," Beck snipes. "What, because your husband is a lawyer you suddenly are, too?"

"And because you were kicked out of law school you're suddenly the family magistrate?" Ashley counters.

Jake watches as their shouting gets louder. It's straight out of a scene from *My Summer of Women.* He loses himself in the cadence of their argument until everyone grows silent. Esther and three white-haired women stand frozen in the entryway, holding casserole dishes. Jake reaches out to take the casseroles before the women drop them.

Soon the Millers have to be respectful because the living room is full of old Jewish women and two men from the neighborhood, the younger family from next door who shared a porch with Helen. Despite the covered mirrors, the washed hands, the casserole dishes, this is not a typical shiva. Everyone is laughing and talking over each other. While the Millers have retreated to opposite corners of the room, their shoulders relax as they listen to the stories the visitors share.

At sundown, the house grows quiet again when the guests leave. The presence of the Millers' fight lingers. They flop heavily on the couch, too tired to speak. No one is going to apologize. Deborah turns on the television and clicks through the five channels Helen gets, evening news on the networks and a children's show on PBS, before turning off the television.

Beck glances at her phone. It's almost seven. No message from Tom, not that she'd really expected him to call.

Beck stands. "I'm going to call it a night."

"You're leaving?" Jake and Deborah say in unison.

Ashley shakes her head in disbelief. "Sure, run away."

"It's been a long day. We're all tired. I'll see you in the morning, okay?" Beck walks toward the front door.

"Beck," Ashley calls. "Is it really just a piece of junk jewelry?"

From the couch, Jake, Deborah, and Ashley stare at Beck, their faces animated with hope. As Beck holds their hungry gazes, she feels the weight of her family.

She feels the weight of her standoff with Jake, his incessant desire for forgiveness. While he often sends her texts, referencing inside jokes from their childhood and remembers to send her a birthday card each September, he's never outright apologized for his characterization of her in his movie. She can tell that he still doesn't understand why she felt so betrayed.

She feels the weight of her frustration toward her mother for abandoning them, for taking out two credit cards in Beck's name, which, nineteen years later, Beck is still paying off. For her mother's scheming. Before the catering and dog walking, there was the cake business, the tarot cards, the salad dressing company, the zodiac jewelry, the diet pills. Trying and quitting had been her full-time job. It consumed more of Deborah's attention than her own children.

She feels the weight of her fraught relationship with Ashley, who disappeared for college, then marriage, then motherhood, only visiting Philadelphia once she had Lydia and Tyler. Every time they visit, Ashley puts on a performance — the perfect housewife, the perfect mom. How can Beck really know her sister when Ashley doesn't know herself?

Mostly, Beck feels the insurmountable weight of Helen's death, the weight of everything she didn't know about her grandmother, the weight of the Florentine Diamond in her bag. Beck scans her open purse and sees the black box. Their fighting will continue until she tells them about the diamond. It will continue after she tells them, too. Fights where they say things they can't unsay. Fights where they all become greedy, petty caricatures of themselves.

Her gaze shifts between the black box and her family. Even if the brooch is rightfully Beck's, the past it represents does not belong to her alone.

Beck takes the diamond out of its box and places it on the coffee table. In the muted light of Helen's musty living room, the diamond looks more brown than yellow. As she pushes it toward them, it catches the glow of the lamp and jumps with color. Her family gasps, aware that, ugly or not, something hallowed has been placed before them.

"This was in the brooch," she begins.

The Millers spend three restless days and nights in the house on Edgehill Road; even Beck, who never returns to her apartment. She finds some clothes from high school in the spare bedroom, sifting through camo pants and striped mini-tees until she unearths black pants that Helen must have made her, pants she's probably never worn. Guests filter in and out, bringing food and flowers as condolences, even though mourners are not supposed to accept flowers during the shiva.

When one of Helen's former clients offers the Millers lilies, Jake thinks of Kristi. He hasn't told his family about the baby. They will lecture him on how he's not ready, by which Ashley will mean kids are expensive and Beck will mean there should be some law against him procreating. None of their opinions matter, only Kristi's. He is ready. Sure, it wasn't planned. True, they make less than thirty dollars an hour combined. And they have no idea what they'll do about child care. But the parenting, the love, the family — he's more than ready.

He texts Kristi. I miss you and our little one. It's weird, missing someone who hasn't been born yet.

At night, once the guests have left, the Millers discuss Helen and the diamond. Beck is honest with them about the grading report, about Viktor's estimation that the diamond is worth ten million dollars. The diamond is upstairs, hidden. Only Beck knows its location. The Millers agree to this arrangement because they know Beck is more civil when she feels in control.

"I don't understand how she could have had this," Ashley says, flipping through the IGS grading report. "One hundred and thirty-seven carats? Do you know how big that is?"

"How long do you think she's had it?" Jake stares at the brooch, the tiny clear and green stones, which Beck says are diamonds and emeralds. Even with the Florentine Diamond removed from the brooch, it's the most valuable thing he's ever held. The money it's worth won't solve all his and Kristi's problems, but it would create a cushion, one that might ease Kristi's panic over the costs of having a baby.

Ashley takes the brooch from Jake, running her finger in the empty setting at the center of the orchid. "I mean, how could it be a diamond?"

Deborah leans over Ashley's shoulder to inspect the brooch. "It's a cattleya orchid." None of her children are surprised that she knows what type of flower it is.

"Viktor thinks it's from the mid-'50s."

"Who's Viktor?" Deborah says, squinting suspiciously at Beck.

"A former client," Beck says to her mother. "A friend. Don't look at me like that, he's old. Don't look at me like *that,* either. You're not his type."

As far as Deborah knows, she has not looked at Beck one way or another.

"Unless Helen has paperwork for it, there's really no way to know when or how she got it." Beck grabs the brooch from Ashley and shows them the symbol *SJ* on the back. "This is the maker's mark, so if we can figure out who made it, we can start to piece together a paper trail. Viktor didn't recognize the brand, and I'm not sure how we'd go about locating them. There've been so many tiny jewelry companies over the years, it's like finding a needle in a haystack."

"So was finding the Florentine Diamond, right?" Ashley smiles.

"*If* the yellow diamond is the Florentine, it's been missing since 1918. Helen wasn't alive then, so it must have passed through at least one other person's hands."

"Why did you say *if* it's the Florentine?" Jake asks.

"It's the Florentine," Beck says.

"So why *if*?" Jake prods.

"Because the Florentine isn't like the Hope Diamond. We know it's the Hope Diamond because it's never gone missing. We can trace its ownership. The Florentine's been missing since it disappeared out of the museum in Vienna a century ago. *If* it's the Florentine, there's no official record of what happened between Austria in 1918 and when Helen wrote it into her will. So, you either need to build a paper trail, which is beyond doubtful, or you need to prove it's the Florentine through characteristics of the diamond itself, kind of like scars or tattoos, something that makes the Florentine different from any other 137-carat diamond." Beck is careful not to say, *I need to prove.* She's careful not to say *we,* either.

"Are there a lot of 137-carat diamonds?" Deborah asks.

"As far as gemology experts know, there's only one."

"So then it is the Florentine Diamond," Deborah presses.

"We still have to prove it," Beck says, annoyed.

"Did Helen steal it?" Jake asks, a scene building in Jake's head: Helen, in a beret, slips a pearl-handled pistol on the counter of a jewelry store and tells the shopgirl, *Be a doll and get me the diamond, won't you?*

The Millers stare soberly at Jake. Helen the jewelry robber might make a great character, but Helen the thief does not.

"Is there another explanation?"

"There has to be," Beck says.

"One hundred and thirty-seven carats." Ashley stares into the empty setting at the center of the brooch. "That's, like, really big, like can't wear on your finger big."

"Is it possible that Helen brought the diamond over during the war?" Jake tugs at the fuzz on his chin. He's never been able to grow enough facial hair to have a goatee or proper sideburns, much less a beard. "Helen's Austrian. So's the Florentine. That can't be a coincidence."

The Florentine is not Austrian, Beck thinks. It was mined in India, then eventually landed with the Medicis in Florence — hence the name — before Charles of Lorraine brought it to Austria upon his marriage to Maria Theresa von Habsburg.

Instead, she says, "Of course it can be a coincidence. That's the definition of a coincidence."

"Besides," Deborah says, "how would a poor Jewish girl have gotten her hands on the largest diamond from the Austrian Empire?"

Jake shrugs. "Stranger things have happened."

Beck knows he's right, only she doesn't want Jake, with his Hollywood imagination, to be the one to figure out the mystery of how Helen got the diamond.

"If Helen didn't bring over the diamond, someone else must have," Jake says.

"One hundred and thirty-seven carats — that's, like, seven times the size of Kim Kardashian's ring."

"Ashley! We get it. It's a big diamond."

"Don't snap at me," Ashley says to Beck, giddy but sulking.

"You're a broken record. Yes, it's massive.

Can we move on?"

Jake feels his patience waning. "Move on to what? The fact that you still don't think you have to share it with us?"

"I *don't* have to share it with you," Beck counters.

As Deborah tries to follow her children's conversation, her mind keeps drifting to childhood, those weeks where they didn't have enough money for meat, the outdated skirts Helen made her wear, patched and re-hemmed. Did her mother have the diamond then? If so, why didn't she sell it? Their lives could have been so different; their relationship, too, if Helen had hawked the diamond.

"Why'd you bother telling us if you aren't planning to share it?" Ashley asks, knowing that Beck will share. Even if it gets ugly, she will not get to keep a ten-million-dollar diamond while Jake and Ashley split Helen's old sofa and teacup collection.

"Because I thought you deserved to know that Helen was keeping a secret."

"How considerate of you," Jake says.

"You're really not planning on sharing with us?" Ashley's voice grows louder, and the cycle begins anew, the Miller-style blowout where they cast cruel but true criticisms at each other, injuries none of them remembers minutes later when they are calm again. They make no progress, not in the fighting, not in negotiating Beck's inheritance, and not in solving Helen's secrets, either.

Over those three days, Ashley cannot help googling the Florentine Diamond. She emails Jake articles she finds on gemhunters .com and jewelrymysteries.net: "The Florentine Diamond: The World's Most Famous Diamond You've Never Heard of . . . and for Good Reason," and "The Jewelry World's Greatest Mystery." The articles offer theories on who may have stolen the Florentine: an untrustworthy adviser, a crooked servant, a Nazi who hid it in a mine in Salzburg, an American soldier who found the diamond buried in that mine, a Habsburg descendant who passed it covertly from generation to generation. Any of these sound promising? Ashley writes to her brother.

Who knows? Maybe the Habsburg descendant? It's the simplest explanation. Those are usually right.

Look — Ashley sends Jake an article on Marie Antoinette — the Florentine belonged to Marie Antoinette. She wore it on her wedding day! I can't believe I held something that

140

Marie Antoinette wore.

In return, Jake sends her an article, "The Curse of the Florentine Diamond." This writer says the diamond cursed everyone who wore it. Maybe it will curse Beck for being selfish.

Maybe she'll be beheaded like Marie Antoinette. After Ashley hits Send, she realizes her comment isn't funny.

Then Jake writes, Or maybe she'll be killed by an Italian anarchist like Sisi. (She was the last Habsburg to wear the diamond.)

Jake's own poor humor does not quell Ashley's guilt. Are we right? Helen did leave it to her.

Helen always assumed the best of Beck, Jake responds. If she left it to Beck, it's because she thought Beck would do the right thing.

It's worth a lot of money, Ashley writes. Jake must be thinking about money. Beck must be, too. Certainly, Deborah is. Despite the questions it raises about Helen, it's impossible not to fantasize about ten million dollars.

I still don't understand how Helen had this. What Jake means is, *Why didn't we know more about our grandmother?*

She told us the things she wanted us to know, Ashley writes, feeling bad for how little she'd wanted to know about Helen before.

By Tuesday afternoon, there are no more visitors. As the light around them fades, the Millers sit in Helen's living room, ready for their final night together to be over. The family who shares a porch with Helen has made them one last meal, shepherd's pie, which Esther cuts and leaves on plates for the Millers.

"You all did a good job," Esther says as she's leaving. "Most families don't make it through the shiva without old resentments rising up." The Millers can't tell if she's joking. Esther smiles at them, genuinely.

"Well," Ashley says once Esther has disappeared down the sidewalk, "I read that we're supposed to end the shiva with a drink. I know I could use one."

She searches the kitchen cabinets, finding only brandy. Ashley pours each of them a glass.

"L'chaim." She raises her glass. The Millers repeat the toast, clinking their cups.

Ashley makes a face as she struggles to swallow her drink. "It tastes like cooking brandy."

Jake downs his in one shot and laughs. "Beck, remember when we used to sneak mugs of this?"

Beck smiles. "Just as bad now as it was then."

"Tastes fine to me," Deborah says, finishing her glass and pouring another.

With each glass of brandy, the Millers cringe less until the brandy almost tastes good. As the amber liquid hits her tongue with its caramel sweetness, Beck imagines the next morning when they return to their separate lives. Will they be better for this time together? Families closer than the Millers have irreconcilably disbanded over will disputes, forever estranged and angry. If they fight over the diamond, there will be lawsuits and mediators and years of legal battles. It would never end. It would define their lives. It would ruin them all, more than they are already ruined. It would be the opposite of what Helen had wanted.

Beck puts her half-full glass on the table and races upstairs to find the diamond hidden inside a pair of rainbow tube socks in the back of her old closet. She unfolds the socks, and the diamond falls into her hand. It catches the light and fragments of rainbow shine. Beck hears Helen's voice, her accent burnishing each word: *This is the right thing to do.*

"I know," Beck says to the diamond. "But

it won't be easy."

And she knows what Helen would say. *Nothing right ever is.*

The Millers stop whispering when Beck reappears downstairs, watching her with a mix of suspicion and eagerness.

"Look," she says, putting the diamond on the table between them. It catches their breath again, just how unfathomably large it is. "I don't want to keep fighting." What she means to say is *I'm sorry,* but it isn't in her blood to reconcile with an apology.

"And we do?" The frustration rises in Jake like bile.

Beck shakes her head. She's already regretting what she's about to say. On a legal pad, she writes, *Family Settlement Agreement.* "Forget the will. We'll draft a new agreement where we all split the diamond. Deborah, too."

"What?" Jake and Ashley say at once.

"No way," Jake adds. He jostles his leg, trying to remain calm.

"That's my deal, 25 percent for each of us, take it or leave it."

"Why should we split with Deborah?" Ashley asks.

"We shouldn't," Jake says.

Deborah doesn't look at her children as they argue her fate, stung by Ashley and

144

Jake's dismissal, which pales beneath the pride she feels for Beck. She stares at the words Beck has written on the lined yellow paper: *Family. Settlement. Agreement.*

"This is a family heirloom," Beck argues. "Deborah is part of this family. We split evenly or not at all."

Jake can feel his nails digging into his palms, thirsty for blood. "What about the house? We should split that evenly, too."

Deborah is about to interject when Ashley frowns at Jake. "Just let her have the house, Jake."

Deborah watches her eldest children communicate without words. Jake glares at Ashley, who holds his stare.

Jake is the first to look away. "Please don't bankrupt the house."

Deborah is about to protest that she would never, but she cannot make this promise. Instead, she says, "I'll do my best to take care of it."

Beck finishes drafting the agreement and drops it on the table for them to read. "Once we sign this, we're relinquishing our right to dispute the will. This agreement states an even split." She looks at her family. "There's one condition. We don't sell the diamond unless everyone agrees."

The Millers nod, their skin tingling at the

thought of so much money. For Ashley, it's the sensation of diving into a perfectly cool pool on a hot day, the relief of a safety net. For Jake, it's the dizziness he felt when his agent called to tell him he sold *My Summer of Women.* For Deborah, it is like listening to a foreign language, a series of sweet sounds she doesn't understand. These emotions, the fantasies that blossom in their wake, are short-lived. Beck isn't finished.

"And we don't sell until we find out how Helen had this diamond."

"Do you think we'll be able to find out?" Ashley asks.

"I don't know," Beck admits. "We should try to find out quickly, though. It makes me nervous, having something so valuable and not knowing if it's legally ours. If the wrong people find out about it, we could lose it like that —" She snaps her fingers.

The Millers commit their promise to paper. They will find out how the diamond came to be Helen's. They will begin researching immediately. Pen poised above Beck's makeshift agreement, Jake sees the power of this as a camera shot, but he shakes it away. He's already written that movie, the one where the Millers learn to forgive each other, and it ruined everything. He won't write that movie again. Instead, if they can discover how Helen had the diamond, he'll write that script. It isn't the movie he initially pictured; it's better. Whatever secrets this large yellow stone holds of Helen's, it's the story he needs to tell. He's certain of it.

"I still don't understand how Helen had this," Ashley says, signing her name beneath her brother's. "It literally makes zero sense."

Beck usually hates when people say *literally* — they almost always mean it figuratively. Today, she agrees with her sister. It makes less than zero sense, less sense even than voluntarily splitting the diamond with her family. It's counterintuitive. Illogical. Yet here on the table between them, the diamond sits, heavy with stories it can never tell. With truths they may never be able to find. Still, they sign their names on the Family Settlement Agreement, vowing to each other that they are going to try.

■ ■ ■ ■

PART TWO

■ ■ ■ ■

Part Two

Six

Beck's low heels click on the marble floor as she crosses the lobby of Federalist Bank. While the Millers have agreed that the local, family-run chain is the perfect place to keep the diamond, Beck can't fight a mounting sense of dread as she follows the manager through a series of steel doors into the vault. Helen hid her money in coffee cans and potpourri satchels across the drawers and shelves of the house on Edgehill Road. She set the Florentine in a brooch that she kept in her dresser. Even if this *is* the safest place to store the diamond, Helen would never have entrusted it to a bank.

They stop inside a windowless room lined with floor-to-ceiling safe-deposit boxes. The manager puts her key into one of the locks on the box Beck has paid for, indicating to Beck to insert her key into the other keyhole.

"Just put it back when you're done and

ring the bell." She points to the button on the wall and slips her set of keys into her pocket. Before she walks out, she adds, "And remember the two copies of the key I gave you are the only ones. We don't keep a copy here. So, don't lose them." The heavy door thuds shut behind her.

Beck tosses her raincoat onto the table and rests the safe-deposit box on the counter. From her bag, she unearths the black box with the diamond. The brooch is tucked into her nightstand at home. Although valuable, it's not so valuable that it needs to be harbored inside a bank. Beck flips open the lid. Inside, the Florentine Diamond shines a rich yellow against the black velvet interior. She shifts it so the color jumps, shards of rainbow flashing. The safe-deposit box rests open on the counter, its dull gray interior so bleak compared to the green and blue light that sparks from the diamond. *This is the safest place for the diamond,* Beck reminds herself. Here, the Florentine will become just another unknown treasure in a vault.

As Beck walks out of the lobby into the chilly afternoon, she emails her family: All set! They are all set. This is the arrangement they've agreed upon. Still, Beck can't shake the feeling that she's betraying Helen by leaving the diamond at Federalist Bank.

Ashley receives Beck's email as she's walking into the lobby of Bartley's Auction House in midtown Manhattan. All set!

Momentarily, Ashley reconsiders whether she's doing the right thing. She's told no one about her meeting at Bartley's, not even Ryan. It feels good keeping a secret from him. Not good exactly. Vindicating. It doesn't feel good keeping a secret from the Millers, but Beck is not all set. She isn't thinking far enough ahead. Eventually, they'll have to sell the diamond, and when they do, Ashley doesn't want them to be desperate.

When the elevator opens on the tenth floor, Georgina is waiting in the lobby, arms wide. "Ash." Georgina kisses her on both cheeks. "You haven't aged a day."

While Ashley managed to lose the baby weight, to find a shade of dirty blond that looks real, to smooth her skin with a dermatological arsenal just shy of plastic surgery, her age is beginning to show. Her blue eyes have turned gray, the once-taut skin of her neck now hangs loose, and her earlobes sag from years of heavy earrings. Georgina, on the other hand, with her shiny dark hair and toned olive arms, really does look like she's still twenty-seven.

Ashley smiles, unable to tell Georgina that she looks the same, too.

In the aughts, Ashley and Georgina had been part of a circle of female twentysomething professionals in Manhattan. They met monthly for drinks, to network, to lament the daily advances of their male coworkers and bosses, and to confess the less overt ways their female superiors tormented them. The group disbanded organically as many of the twentysomething professionals became thirtysomething mothers and wives. Georgina hadn't married or shifted to part-time employment; instead, she'd climbed the ladder at Bartley's until she landed as a jewelry specialist.

Georgina threads her arm through Ashley's as they walk across the lobby, covered in Annie Leibovitz photographs and Andy Warhol prints, into what looks like a high-end jewelry store. Glass cases line the walls, filled with glittering gemstones. Georgina unlocks one case and pulls out a sapphire-and-diamond bracelet, clasping it around Ashley's wrist. "This belonged to Grace Kelly."

Ashley marvels at the delicate bracelet.

"Such a shame, really. The bracelet is so

expensive that whoever buys it will wear it once, maybe twice a year. It will spend the rest of its life in a vault."

The Florentine might live its life in a vault, too, but it won't be the one in Federalist Bank.

Georgina sighs as she returns it to the case. "You wanted to talk about a family heirloom you inherited?" The disinterest in Georgina's voice is palpable — old acquaintances must materialize all the time to talk to her about some modest family jewel. Ashley feels giddy as she anticipates shocking Georgina.

Another tall, thin jewelry specialist helps a couple, gazing into a case across the room. In the corners, two large men pretend not to watch them.

"Is there somewhere private we can talk?"

"That's probably a good idea," Georgina says, amused.

Ashley follows her down a hall to an office with a view of midtown. It's one of those deceptively sunny late-March days where it looks like it should be warmer outside than it actually is. A Steichen photo hangs on one wall, a Hockney painting on the other. Ashley doesn't need to ask if they are real.

"One of the perks of the job, we can borrow pieces before they're auctioned off. So,

155

tell me about the diamond you want to sell. Do you have it with you?"

"No, but I have this." Ashley finds a copy of the IGS grading report in her bag and passes it to Georgina. During the shiva, she'd snapped a quick photo of it while Beck was distracted. "The diamond was set in a '50s brooch." On her phone, Ashley flips through some photographs until she locates one of the orchid with its signature stone missing. As she shows Georgina the image, fractured by the shards of her broken screen, she curses at herself for not getting her phone fixed. "My sister seems to think it's —"

"The Florentine Diamond," Georgina says, reading the numbers on the grading report. She glances briefly at the photograph of the orchid before her eyes return to the page. "Have you shown this to anyone else?"

"My family's seen it, and my sister has this gemologist who got the report for us."

Georgina keeps reading, then places the report facedown on her desk. "Ashley, you can't be showing this to me. To anyone."

"Why not?"

"You know why."

"It's worth ten million dollars." Ashley forces a smile, her heart racing.

"This isn't an issue of value. No reputable

house is going to represent you."

Ashley feels queasy, like she's both famished and going to be sick. Georgina's face softens, and Ashley realizes that she isn't hiding her anxiety half as well as she hopes.

"Look, off the record, that diamond has been missing since 1918. There might be a completely legitimate explanation for how your grandmother had it, but when it goes public that it's resurfaced, a lot of people are going to come looking for it. You need to have your ducks in a row before showing that to anyone else. My advice? Talk to a lawyer, and start doing some digging." Georgina's nails click against her glass desk, and Ashley realizes that the diamond makes her nervous, too.

"You aren't going to tell anyone, are you?" Ashley wishes she'd phrased her question differently, that her words didn't have the uptick of apprehension at the end.

"There's nothing to tell. You came in looking to sell a stone, and it didn't satisfy our requirements. End of story." Georgina smiles as she stands. Ashley knows that smile, its smug satisfaction. Even if there's nothing to tell, Georgina is logging this for her unwritten memoir, *Confessions of a Bartley's Jewelry Expert.*

As Ashley follows Georgina down the hall,

she tries to remember any real conversation they've ever had. She knows Georgina grew up on the Upper East Side but can't remember what her parents do, if she has any siblings, if Georgina's even met Ryan.

Georgina presses the button for the elevator, and kisses both of Ashley's cheeks goodbye. "It's great to see you. We have to get a drink on the books."

"Absolutely." Ashley hears the defeat in her voice.

As soon as the elevator doors close, she flops against the mirror. Why did she think this was a good idea, coming to see Georgina, presenting the Florentine Diamond like she expected a gold star? At least Georgina won't tell anyone, Ashley thinks, then she isn't so sure. In the mirror, the elevator's fluorescent lights magnify the deep purple under her eyes. She appears not just tired but haggard. As she looks away, Ashley has a striking suspicion that she's totally fucked up.

Jake has always worked best with a routine. It's how he finished *My Summer of Women* in mere months. It's why he hasn't finished any script since, because he never fell into a pattern. So, he sets his alarm for eight each morning. He measures coffee grounds for a pot, pours twelve ounces into a to-go cup for Kristi, and settles at their kitchen table for his morning writing session before work.

"I could get used to this," Kristi says when she appears in the kitchen in her pink scrubs, grabbing the coffee and offering Jake a quick peck goodbye. Jake wonders whether she means the coffee or the writing, or maybe both.

Jake has also always found that a good script comes easily. The outline writes itself. The scenes pour out of him like he's the medium that manifests the world, fully realized. So it makes him light-headed when, on the first page, the cursor blinks after *INT.* and no location follows. Interior, what? Where is Helen? At the house on Edgehill Road? The apartment where she grew up in Vienna? Was that apartment big or small? And where is the Florentine Diamond? Is this even the story of Helen finding the diamond? Of something else entirely?

The coffee cup beside his computer is drained. Still, he hasn't written a word. He wanders into the living room and opens the drawer in the side table where he stores his stash. Since returning from the east coast, Jake has decided to stop smoking pot. He wants to be present for Kristi's pregnancy, the baby. Throwing away the pen was easy, but the five joints he keeps in the side table — well, that would be an affront to his former self, and he doesn't want to quit that way. Only three joints remain and he brings one to his nose, the sweet, earthy aromas almost giving him a contact high.

The end of the rolling paper hisses as it catches fire. Jake leans back and shuts his eyes, savoring the rare treat of smoking alone. Of course he's stuck. With *My Summer of Women,* he already knew how the story unfolded. Now, he knows nothing, not how Helen got the diamond, not how the diamond arrived in America, not even how Helen got to America. He knows it was by boat, but he's never heard the story of how she ended up here alone or what happened to her family. How can he tell a story if he doesn't have a beginning or an end?

As he bikes to work, Jake feels shamed by the hours he's wasted when Kristi thinks he's being productive. Unfailingly, she believes in him. Unquestionably, he doesn't deserve it.

Stocking usually helps clear his mind, so he asks if he can be on the floor instead of the register. Jake falls into a rhythm as he balances bags of avocados on top of each other. His thoughts return to Kristi, her unwarranted faith in him despite his not having finished a script the entire time they've been together. His mind drifts to the last script he tried to write, in the spring, when Kristi's parents had stopped in LA on their way home from China. Over king crabs at the banquet hall they frequented in Alhambra, Kristi's mother showed them a picture of her childhood house in Guangzhou. The Zhangs hoped to buy back her family's home, which they'd been driven out of before she fled the country. Kristi's mother told the story of her escape, first swimming the Shenzhen Bay to Hong Kong, then traveling to an aunt's house in San Jose. Jake saw it clearly, the film of her life, shifting between the contemporary story of reclaiming her childhood home, the past narratives of her idyllic childhood, and the traumas of the Cultural Revolution.

Throughout their visit, Jake couldn't stop thinking about the film. It would be epic. It would be moving. It would reignite his career. While the Zhangs stayed at his apartment with Kristi, he spent the night on Rico's couch outlining the first act. He knew he needed to do some hefty research, but he wanted to sketch Mrs. Zhang's story before he forgot the way she'd described it. Later that week, once the Zhangs returned to the Bay Area and Jake returned to his apartment, he couldn't wait to tell Kristi about the script.

"Your mom's story is really compelling." He hesitated, braving a look at Kristi, who stood before the bathroom mirror, hair woven into a towel atop her head, grazing her lashes with a mascara wand. "It would make a great movie."

Kristi turned away from the mirror. "Tell me you aren't thinking what I think you're thinking."

Jake picked at his cuticle. "I'm not thinking anything."

"Seriously, Jake. My mom's private. I'm surprised she told you. It means she trusts you." The next unspoken line hung in the air: *Don't break that trust.*

"I was just saying it would be a good movie, is all."

Kristi laughed and resumed her communion with the mirror, rubbing rouge across her cheekbones. "Imagine you, Jake Miller, writing that movie? Social media would eat you alive."

Later that night, when they returned from whatever bar they'd gone to, Jake waited until Kristi fell asleep, then found the partial outline on his computer. He moved it to his Bad Ideas folder where so many other unfinished scripts had gone to die.

As Jake restocks the herbs, he thinks of Kristi's mom trusting him with her story. Helen hadn't trusted him with hers. How could he write about her, if she didn't want him to know her past?

His phone chimes and he sees Beck's email. All set!

How could they be all set about anything?

During his lunch break, Jake isn't intending to tell Rico about the Florentine Diamond. He doesn't even plan to tell Kristi. He doesn't want to get her hopes up about the money from the diamond until he's certain it belongs to the Millers.

Only, when Rico takes the joint from Jake and says, "I'm sorry about your gran. How you doing with it all?" Jake doesn't know how to explain to Rico how he's feeling. Rico, who can detail his mother's asylum process with such precision that Jake tried briefly, ill-fatedly, to write a script about it. Rico, who sees his sisters and brother and cousins at his abuela's house each week. Rico, who is his best friend, but what does that really mean? They smoke joints and meet at bars to watch basketball. God, when did pot become such an incredible downer?

Jake doesn't want to be sad, so he forces a laugh and tells Rico, "I've got a killer story for you," and Rico's eyes spark as he passes Jake the joint. "Have you ever heard of the Florentine Diamond?"

From there the storyteller emerges in Jake. Rico laughs, not believing a word. Jake doesn't mind. In fact, he's relieved; it makes him clearer about his script. The script won't be believable until he understands what drives the narrative, how Helen got the diamond, why she kept it.

"Don't you have to be back at work at two?" Rico asks.

Jake checks his phone and sees that it's two twenty. He stomps out the joint and waves goodbye to his friend. As he runs through the outdoor dining area, he notices a man with greasy black hair, wearing a leather jacket and eating alone. At the time, Jake notes only that, on this perfect seventy-five-degree day, the guy must be sweating his balls off in his leather jacket.

Deborah has moved so many times she has it down to a science. She knows the exact proportions of the Red Rabbit, that all of her clothes and kitchenware will fit in the trunk. She knows to move the passenger seat forward so she can fit her white rocking chair in the backseat, to double knot the mattress to the roof so it won't blow off on

I-95. The rocking chair is the only possession that made the move from her and Kenny's first apartment in Fairmount where she nursed Ashley, to the house in Mt. Airy where she nursed the others, to the house on Edgehill Road where it's now returning. She wishes she could call Chester for help. His 4Runner would come in handy, as would his body, but Chester hasn't called her all week, not since he left her naked on his acupuncture table. So, she leaves the furniture that doesn't fit in the Red Rabbit in her studio and makes her way back to her childhood home. She already knows her landlord won't give her the deposit back.

Before unpacking her car, Deborah lights a bundle of sage and sets her intention to fill the house with positivity. She begins in the kitchen and fans the smoke through the living room and out the front door. It's not Helen's energy she's trying to erase but all the fights they've had in this house. Once she's satisfied with the energy downstairs, she sages the three bedrooms upstairs and settles at the dining room table to read her tarot cards. When she pulls the Six of Wands, the Star, and the Knight of Swords, all upright, she knows she's ready to move in.

She unloads the kitchenware into the

drawers and cupboards and sets the rocking chair in the living room, but her clothing is a different matter. Helen's bedroom is the biggest. It has the most light. Deborah has already decided she will stay there, but when she goes to put her clothing in the dresser, it is packed with her mother's garments. The sage may have carried the lingering presence of their arguments out of the house but it's done nothing about the dresses Helen sewed, still hanging in the closet.

She calls Beck with the pretense of dinner. "Please," she begs when Beck hesitates, "I could use a little company." Whatever Beck interprets in her mother's desperation, she tells Deborah she'll come over early next week.

When Beck arrives for dinner, she can't hide her shock over how Deborah has altered Helen's home. The house on Edgehill Road has always been the same. Built in the '20s, the row houses were Tudor style with stone columns and brick facades beneath stuccoed second floors and gabled roofs. Helen raised Deborah in the second bedroom, which became Beck and Ashley's room when the Millers lived with Helen after their father left. Jake was forced to camp out in the third bedroom, Helen's office, where women from the Main Line would stand on a box as Helen measured the hems of their dresses. Jake didn't like sharing a room with all that taffeta. He hated having to roll up his mattress each morning, reminded that the room where he slept wasn't his. When Ashley left for college, Jake bribed Beck to switch rooms with him. He promised to teach her how to drive and to bring her to upperclassmen parties, but Beck would have swapped for nothing. She loved the shadows the bolts of lace made across the walls, the peppery smell of freshly cut fabric, the colorful threads she'd find on her sweaters throughout the day. She was all too happy to roll the mattress up each morning, to know, should their circumstances change, she could move that easily.

Now, all the cream-colored walls have been painted lavish colors. The house's natural scent of floral perfume and cigarettes has been buried beneath the aromas of curry powder, hot peppers, and sage.

"I added some color," Deborah confesses when she finds Beck staring at the teal walls of the living room.

Beck turns to her mother, ready to lash out, only Deborah is visibly nervous, eager for her daughter's approval. Moving here must be more complicated for Deborah than Beck understands.

So, Beck fights the urge to tell her mother she's ruined their house and instead lies. "It's perfect."

Deborah sighs, clearly relieved.

After dinner, Beck follows her mother through the peach hall into Helen's now mint-colored bedroom, cloaked in piles of Deborah's clothes. The closet door is closed, and Beck realizes that her mother hasn't opened it yet.

The closet is the only part of the house that still smells like Helen. The scent of mothballs, cigarettes, and floral perfume has intensified after being trapped in the windowless space. The clothes rack is brimming with bright pantsuits, wool slacks, collared blouses. Above Helen's clothing, cardboard boxes are stacked neatly. Below, a row of orthopedic beige shoes.

They begin with the clothes, creating two piles, one to keep and one to give away. At first, everything ends up in the keep pile, but what are they going to do with the plaid pants Helen made, the silk blouses, the wool blazer that does not complement either of their styles?

"Maybe we can box them up and put

them in the guest room closet?" Beck suggests.

The shoes are a different matter. Helen was not a cobbler. They swiftly bag them and toss them in the giveaway pile.

"What are in those boxes?" Beck points to the ones above the empty clothes rack.

Deborah shrugs and reaches for the first box. It's filled with ledgers from before Beck was born, shorthand for services she only partially understands. *DR* must mean dress, but what is *MG*? Everything is priced lower than Beck would have expected for tailored clothes, even in 1962.

"I guess this is why we never had meat more than once a week," Deborah says, flipping through the ledgers.

When they've read through Helen's records, Beck and Deborah return the box to the shelf and reach for another. The next one is filled with photographs of women they do not recognize, a few actions shots where Helen is taking their measurements. In one photo, Helen stands beside a bride at a reception hall. Helen's cheeks look artificially blushed, her blue dress impossibly sapphire.

They pull down the third box, anticipating more relics of Helen's seamstress career. Deborah hopes she's hiding her disappointment from her daughter. This was what Helen kept in her closet, photographs of strangers' weddings?

Beck emits a sharp breath when she opens the third box. A tattered doll, wearing a blue dress with an apron, rests on top of two photo albums. Disproportionately large, aquamarine-blue eyes stare back at her. The doll's nose and the mouth are small, giving it an otherworldly look. Its shoulder-length hair is brown and coarse. The doll's head and limbs are made of peach porcelain, browned in spots where grubby hands must have held it. "Was this yours?"

Deborah shakes her head. With its large red cheeks and distorted features, the doll would have given her nightmares as a child. "I've never seen it before." After a pause, she adds, "Do you think it was Helen's?"

"Who else's could it be?" Beck turns the doll over, inspecting it. She lifts the dress, and on the cushioned body a faint red stamp reads *Made in Austria.*

"She must have brought it from Vienna," Deborah says as she takes the doll from her daughter and hugs it to her chest. The porcelain limbs, while dirt-stained, are free of chips or cracks. A slip of the finger, a grip too loose, and the doll would have shattered. Instead, it had survived the careless-

170

ness of youth, the voyage to another life.

Deborah maintains a firm grip on the doll as Beck pulls out the two photo albums. They sit on Helen's bed, flipping through the first album. It's filled with several Miller milestones: Beck's kindergarten graduation, Jake's first guitar recital, Ashley's My Little Pony–themed birthday, Jake's and Ashley's high school graduations, Beck's college graduation party celebrated in the living room downstairs.

In one photograph, they are in the backyard of the house in Mt. Airy. Jake looks to be about eleven, frizzy curls blossoming into his signature style. Ashley must have been twelve, but looks several years older. Beck smiles, her oversized adult teeth having recently grown in, a piece of watermelon dangling from her right hand. Beside her, the picture is torn, ragged at the edges, and retaped so that Deborah stands beside her children. Their father's hand is the only part of him that remains in the photograph. It grips their mother's shoulder, disembodied.

Deborah laughs. It is the perfect gesture to describe Helen. Seemingly harsh; fundamentally protective.

"I'm keeping this." Deborah rests the doll on the bed as she peels the plastic sheet back to remove the picture.

171

Like the first album, the photographs in the second book are chronological, beginning with black-and-white images from before Deborah was born. Deborah has seen some of the photographs of her grandmother Flora, her grandfather Leib, her uncle Martin, their family's stall in the Fleischmarkt. Shots of them picnicking along the Danube and visiting the Vienna Woods where Leib could recite the Latin name for every plant they encountered. Whether these were the actual names or something he made up to awe his children, Helen never knew or cared.

"You can't tell from these photos," Deborah tells her daughter, "but your great-grandmother Flora had the most glorious red hair."

"And Helen never learned what happened to her family?" Beck asks, staring at a shot of Flora, Leib, Martin, and Helen in what looks to be their modest living room.

Deborah shakes her head. "Her brother and dad were sent to Dachau, so they probably died there. I don't think she ever learned what happened to her mother. When the Holocaust Museum opened in the '90s, I remember her looking, but she didn't find any information on her." Deborah stares at the photograph in her daughter's hand. "I wish I'd known them. My father, too. Sometimes I wonder how my life would be different if he hadn't died, if he'd come back from Korea."

Deborah was only three months old when Joseph Klein was deployed, then two years old when he died. Helen rarely talked about him, never took Deborah to visit his grave, always changed the subject when Deborah begged for stories about her father similar to the ones Helen told about her family in Vienna. She'd explain that she'd only known him for a few months before they married, that he was almost as much of a stranger to her as he was to Deborah. "Your father died a hero. That's more than most people can say," Helen would tell her. "I wish we'd both gotten to know him better." Rarely one for physical displays of emotion, Helen's eyes would well, which made young Deborah feel a complicated mix of remorse and longing. It pained her mother to discuss the future they'd lost, but it made Deborah wish she could know more about her father. Ultimately, the loss of Joseph Klein was another thing that distanced Helen and Deborah when it could have brought them closer.

Deborah sniffles, and Beck feels something akin to guilt that she doesn't know the loneliness of her mother's childhood, but the feeling quickly calcifies. Her mother doesn't know the loneliness of Beck's youth, either.

Deborah feels something shift in Beck, the evening at risk of falling apart. Though the details were different, she'd repeated the pattern between her and Helen with her own children, separating herself from them to avoid confronting what was missing in their lives. "You know I have lots of regrets," she begins, "about how I was after your father left. I . . . I should never have . . . I should have been there for you and your siblings."

Beck cannot look at her mother. Although she's been waiting for a more eloquent version of this apology, her mother's timing is predictably terrible.

Beck continues flipping through the album, reaching a few photos of Helen holding a baby. Even as an infant, Deborah's high forehead and square jaw were evident.

Deborah surveys her daughter instead of the photographs in the album. Is there anything she can say that will make Beck forgive her? Anything that will justify her mistakes? Not justify; make them human instead of monstrous.

"Who is this?"

Deborah turns her attention to a black-

and-white photograph of a man she doesn't recognize, sitting in the living room downstairs, Deborah propped on his knee.

"Is that your father?" Beck peels back the plastic sheet and holds the photo close to her face. There's an obvious resemblance between Deborah and this man, same long slender noses, same high foreheads, square jawlines, wide-set eyes. "It can't be. He's got to be, like, fifty. He would have been too old for Korea. Maybe he's your grandfather? Did you ever meet your father's family?"

"No. They were in the Midwest or something." Deborah leans over her daughter's shoulder and feels her stomach drop. She has no memory of this moment, yet she feels an innate yearning as she looks at this unfamiliar man.

"Um, Deborah?"

Deborah follows her daughter's finger to another photograph of the man, this one from a dark restaurant. Helen is seated beside him in a booth, his arm around her bare shoulders. Two champagne coupes rest on the table. A banner in the background reads *Happy New Year, 1955.* Helen wears her hair up, accentuating her sweetheart neckline beneath a fur stole. On the right side of Helen's stole, the orchid brooch clings to the fur.

In 1955, Deborah's father was dead. In 1955, Deborah was the daughter of a widow. In the photograph, a band is visible on the man's ring finger but Helen's fingers are bare.

They flip through more photographs from Atlantic City and Fairmount Park of Helen and the man. Some where Deborah is nestled between them. Others where they only have eyes for each other.

In first grade, Deborah's class had been assigned family trees. When she asked her mother for help, Helen had grown furious. "What kind of assignment is this? Prying into students' lives." At the time, Deborah thought her mother's reaction was because of the trauma of her family's deaths during the Holocaust, of her war-hero husband killed in Korea, the inappropriateness of making a first grader parade that kind of tragedy before her classmates. If these photographs have anything to say about it, Helen may have being hiding another secret unsuitable for the first grade.

Deborah shuts the album. "That's enough for one night."

"Can I make you some tea?" Beck asks as she stands from the bed.

"I'm fine." Deborah struggles to smile.

"This has just been . . . a lot."

As Beck walks out with the album tucked under her arm, Deborah calls to her. "Can you leave the album?"

Beck rests the album on the dresser where she found the orchid brooch. She doesn't want *this* to be the story of the Florentine or her grandfather's identity. Yet, this photograph from New Year's Eve is invaluable. It means Helen has had the diamond since at least 1955. As she says good-night to her mother, she wonders how many other secrets lay dormant in Helen's bedroom, how many truths the Millers will be able to uncover about their grandmother.

SEVEN

Two weeks have passed since Helen's shiva, and already strange things are beginning to happen. Things that can only be explained by the presence of the Florentine Diamond. Ashley is the first to notice. Since she's returned from Philadelphia, she's started swimming again, a ritual from her childless days in the city. It's less expensive than therapy and more effective. Right now, Ashley needs an inexpensive outlet for her anger toward Ryan. Despite his continued insistence that he'll sort through the misunderstanding with his company, nothing will vanquish the memory of Ryan cowering in the corner of their bathroom, his anxiety as he told Ashley he'd ruined everything.

As she pulls into the YWCA parking lot, a dark sedan turns in behind her.

An hour and a half later, Ashley's hair is wet from the shower, her muscles fatigued and head cleared by the swim. It's drizzling, and Ashley dashes toward her car, past the dark sedan parked in one of the handicap spots. It doesn't have a disabled placard. The driver is a dapper middle-aged white man. He looks up from the newspaper he's reading and flashes a neighborly smile at Ashley that makes her think he's waiting for his wife to finish her aerobics class.

Ashley heads straight from the pool to the library, eating her premade salad when she's stopped at red lights. She takes massive bites, unable to shovel the food into her ravenous body quickly enough. It's one of those moments when the car gives her a false sense of privacy. It does not have tinted windows. Everyone around her can see her behaving like a pig. Embarrassed, she glances into the rearview mirror and sees the dark sedan stopped at the light behind her. The man is good-looking in the way she often finds attractive, the tall, dark, and handsome type. The way Ryan is good-looking. For the first time since she found him on the bathroom floor, she feels a pulse of desire for her husband.

Ashley turns the stereo up as she navigates the familiar streets toward the library. When she steers her car into the underground parking lot, the sedan rolls down the tunnel behind her. The man is alone in the car. No wife in spandex. Why was he parked outside the Y if he wasn't there to pick someone up? Maybe he was waiting out the rain? It's a bit odd. Then again, people are odd. She shrugs it off as she heads up to the library.

In addition to the pool, Ashley has started visiting the local library each afternoon. After her disastrous meeting with Georgina, Ashley shifted her efforts from trying to sell the diamond to trying to prove that it's legally hers. Only problem is Ashley had no idea how to begin researching Helen's past. She'd wandered into the library, looking for a dummy's guide to ancestry, and instead found Clara, the head librarian.

Clara is not a researcher but an avid recreational user of ancestry.com. She's traced her own family back to the Vikings and enthusiastically offered her support when Ashley asked her about genealogical resources. Clara showed Ashley how to use ancestry.com. Together, they located the most recently available census from 1940, where they were pleased to discover that Helen was boarding on Monument Street in Philadelphia. Ashley hadn't realized that in 1940 Helen was already living in the US, only fourteen years old, which made her ninety-two when she passed in March. She'd assumed her grandmother was closer to one hundred.

From there, Clara helped Ashley make a family tree, which she called the Miller Family Tree, even though no one on it was a Miller other than Deborah, Beck, and Jake, not even Helen. Not even Ashley Johnson. After Ashley added the Millers and Helen, she included Ryan, her children. While she was unable to locate Helen's birth certificate or her great-grandparents' marriage license, she knew Helen's family's names enough to fill them on the tree: Flora, Leib, and Martin Auerbach. To add more ancestors, she needed more information.

Deborah quickly became defensive when Ashley asked for Flora's maiden name.

"I don't know what you want me to say," she said. "I know she taught Helen how to sew and had bright red hair, but Helen never told me her maiden name."

"Do you know when she died?"

"Don't you think if I had that kind of information I would have told you? Helen's dad and brother were shipped to Dachau, but she never found out what happened to Flora."

"What about your father?" Ashley asked. When she'd typed "Joseph Klein" into the database, over 70,000 hits had popped up.

She limited the search to military records, but no casualty or service records appeared for Joseph Klein in Korea.

"Leave it alone," Deborah cautioned.

"Helen must have told you something that might help me find him. Where was he deployed? When was he born? Where was he from?"

"I said to leave it be." Deborah's voice had an unusual curtness to it.

When Ashley reported their mother's strange behavior to Beck, Beck explained the photographs they found in Helen's closet, the man who looked like Deborah but was too old to have fought in Korea.

"So Joseph Klein isn't our grandfather?" Ashley asked her sister.

"I'm not sure there *was* a Joseph Klein, at least not one that Helen knew. I did some digging and didn't find anything."

Momentarily, Ashley felt guilty for being so forceful with their mother. Then she realized that it barely took any investigating to know something was amiss with Helen's story. For years, Deborah must not have asked about her father.

The tree looked anemic with just the Auerbachs, the Millers, and the Johnsons on it, but Ashley had run out of extended family to explore. Well, more Millers could have been added. It would have been easy to find her father Kenny's family, but she refused to indulge that curiosity. So she saved the Miller Family Tree with just those eleven names, fearing she'd never locate more family.

Today, as Ashley approaches the reference desk, Clara motions for Ashley to hurry. "I've been waiting for you all morning. You'll never guess what I found."

As Ashley leans over Clara's shoulder, she feels a flurry of anticipation. Clara smells like white musk. She wears a dress with book graphics on it. She's unlike Ashley's other friends, which makes Ashley like her even more.

Clara clicks on a link to the *New York, Passenger and Crew Lists, 1820–1957* and a record for Helen Auerbach pops up on the manifest from the SS *President Harding,* sailing from Hamburg to New York on April 23, 1939.

Halfway down the page, *Helen Auerbach* is listed on the manifest. Fourteen years old; Occupation: pupil; Able to read and write: German; Country of birth: Germany; City: Vienna; Race or people: Hebrew.

"Why does it say Vienna is in Germany?"

"Austria was annexed into Germany before the war, so in 1939, Austria wasn't its own country," Clara explains. "I had to look it up, too."

Ashley runs her finger down the list of six names beneath Helen's on the first page of the manifest. Their names and ages are unique, but beneath *pupil,* beneath *German,* beneath *Vienna* and *Hebrew,* the six rows say the same thing: *DO.*

"*DO* means ditto," Clara says, squinting to make out the letters. Ashley feels a sting of disappointment that she didn't intuit this on her own. She scrolls farther across the manifest. "Huh." Clara's finger grazes the columns on the screen. Helen's passage was paid for by a Mr. Irvin Goldstein. He is also listed as the *FR* — friend — Helen was joining in the United States, on Cyprus Street in Philadelphia. Again, the six slots beneath Helen's *FR* and the final destination read *DO.* "Do you know him, Irvin Goldstein?"

Ashley shakes her head. "Never heard of him. So, he paid for all their passages? And they all were going to live with him? I thought she lived on Monument Street?"

"Maybe Irvin Goldstein had some sort of arrangement set up," Clara says distractedly as she continues to sort through the manifest. Suddenly, she clenches Ashley's forearm. "Look —"

The manifest list continues, the acronym

184

DO bleeding down the page. Clara and Ashley count forty-three more names, fifty in total, all traveling with Mr. Irvin Goldstein.

Clara's pointer drifts down the age column for the fifty names allocated to Mr. Goldstein. "They're all children."

"Helen was the oldest," Ashley realizes when she skims the children's ages and sees a fourteen in Helen's age column.

"So this Irvin Goldstein," Clara says. "He sponsors fifty Jewish kids to come to the US?"

"Have you ever heard of that before?"

"I've never heard of anything like it," Clara says, typing furiously. "Wowzers." On Google, Clara finds a list of articles from the *New York Times,* the *Philadelphia Inquirer,* the *Philadelphia Jewish Exponent,* the *Philadelphia Record,* the *Jewish Times:* "50 Children Refugees Arrive from Vienna." "Philadelphia Lawyer and Wife Travel to Vienna to Rescue 50 Jewish Children." "Young Refugees Make Good Americans."

Ashley has no idea if this has anything to do with the diamond. Regardless, it's significant. Helen never told the Millers that she was part of a fleet of children brought to the US. There must have been a reason why.

Ashley's phone buzzes. A text from Lydia. Can we get ice cream on the way home?

185

She's conflicted about her eleven-year-old having a phone. Ryan bought it for her while Ashley was in Philadelphia, a transparent attempt to win over their daughter, an obvious indication that he's about to torpedo her life.

Ashley checks the time and realizes she's supposed to pick her children up in fifteen minutes.

"I should go," Ashley says abruptly.

"Let me just print the records and the articles for you."

The printer squeaks as it churns out the SS *President Harding*'s manifest, the articles on Mr. Goldstein and the fifty children. Ashley reaches into her wallet to pay the ten cents for each copy, but Clara waves her away. "It's on the house."

Ashley rushes toward the elevator, cursing at herself for being late. Although punctuality has never been her strong suit, she's always careful to be waiting outside the school before the children are let out. In the parking lot, Ashley walks so quickly she almost doesn't notice the sedan parked in the handicap spot, that same handsome man half-obscured by his paper.

The following day, when Ashley sees the same model of navy car at the grocery store, it sends a chill down her spine. Is this man following her? It's just a dark Buick, she tells herself; there are probably hundreds, thousands, of dark Buicks in Westchester. As she walks past the car, she sees that same handsome, nondescript man behind the wheel. Then, at the drive-through at the bank, the Buick pulls into the parking lot as she's withdrawing money.

When the Buick pulls up to the curb outside her children's school, her body seizes. The man is definitely following her. Only he isn't trying to hide. He wants her to know he's trailing her. He wants her to be afraid. On the drive home, the children prattle on about their day. Tyler's in hysterics over the music teacher, who farted during class, then pretended it was his recorder. Lydia insists that that didn't happen, to which Tyler proceeds to make fake farting noises, Lydia begging, "Mom, make him stop."

Ashley isn't listening. Her full attention is on the car in the rearview mirror, taking each turn she does, patient and lurking.

"Mom?" Lydia says. "You just passed our house."

Ashley laughs like it was the product of daydreaming. She turns around. The sedan pulls over but doesn't turn back with her. When they get to the house, Ashley tells the kids, "Run ahead. I'll be in in a minute."

She waits in the driveway, watching the rearview mirror. After a few minutes, the sedan rolls past her driveway, then speeds off.

It's no longer a hunch. Ashley finds her phone and texts her siblings: I'm being followed.

She tries to determine why anyone would be following her and can only come up with one answer — the Florentine Diamond.

Jake gets Ashley's text while he's walking to the gym down the street from the Trader Joe's where he works. Since he's gotten back from the east coast, he's decided not only to stop smoking weed but also to get in shape. Rather, he's decided he should probably get his heart rate up a few times a week and his biceps prepared for the weight of a newborn.

Before he can respond or even process Ashley's text, he receives another from Beck, then Ashley, a conversation unfolding without him.

What do you mean you're being followed?

I mean there's a big guy in car following me.

Why would he be following you?

Why u think? Ashley texts an emoji of a diamond.

How would anyone know about the diamond?

Three dots appear on Ashley's side of the text chain, then disappear. Jake puts his phone in his back pocket and walks into the gym, deciding Beck is right. No one could possibly know about the diamond. Even if Ashley told a friend, like Jake did, no one would believe them, not yet. Not until they know how Helen had the diamond, why she kept it.

As Jake plods along on the elliptical, he ruminates on motivation, the essential element of story. Why would Helen have kept a diamond worth ten million dollars? Why was it so important to her? Cigarette smoke wafts into the cardio room through the open window that leads to the street. He finds the smell strangely calming.

"Somebody needs to tell that asshole to take it down the block," the buff, older man on the machine beside Jake says to him. His scalloped muscles rouse a deep shame in Jake, whose biceps never pop, not even when he flexes them.

Jake peers onto the street and sees a greasy-haired man leaning against the meter outside, taking steady drags from a cigarette. He's wearing a leather jacket. *The* leather jacket from the taco stand when Jake told Rico about the Florentine Diamond. Jake's left foot slips, and he catches himself just before his head hits the elliptical's console.

"You okay?" the man on the machine next to him asks. Jake rights himself and nods, pedaling faster. He checks the street again. The man takes a final drag of his cigarette before grinding it out with his steel-toed boot, so inappropriate for the warming weather. He gets in his car and speeds away. Jake's heart starts pounding too quickly for the modest exertion of his legs.

Later, during his afternoon shift, Jake dishes out plates of baked fish, wondering about the man. Was it a coincidence? Silver Lake is the kind of neighborhood where you run into the same people everywhere. He often sees the scallop-muscled man from the gym at Trader Joe's and the sports bar where he and Rico watch the Clippers. Besides, the guy in the leather jacket couldn't have heard Jake and Rico's conversation. They were in the parking lot behind the Dumpster. He would have needed superhuman hearing. Jake shakes his head and laughs at himself. He's glad he's quitting smoking pot. It's making him lose his judgment.

With each passing day that Jake doesn't see the man again, he grows more convinced that Ashley, too, is being paranoid. It's uncharacteristic of her, but since they found the diamond, she's been on edge. He opts not to engage when she reports that the navy Buick is at the farmers' market, the nail salon, the animal shelter.

Jake doesn't expect to see the man in the leather jacket again, not outside the gym, not at Trader Joe's, certainly not at Palermo Ristorante where he takes Kristi on a date. Kristi has always been a voracious eater. Since announcing her pregnancy, her appetite has both doubled and diminished. Everything besides carbs makes her nauseous. Kristi only wants pizza and pasta, not the fancy stuff that the neighborhood has in abundance, but the old-fashioned Italian American food they both grew up on.

Palermo is so pitch-perfect it's almost a set. Red leather booths. Dim chandeliers. Laminated menus. All the garlic bread you can eat and waiters with thick Italian accents. Kristi and Jake are finishing their salad course when the man in the leather jacket sits down at a booth in the back. Jake chokes on a piece of iceberg lettuce, coughing so hard that Kristi rushes to his side of the table and starts hitting his back.

"You okay?"

"Who knew salad eating was an extreme sport," Jake jokes, once he's caught his breath. The man pretends not to see Jake, infinitely interested in the laminated menu. It's definitely him. Ashley wasn't being paranoid. She's being followed. So is he.

Kristi is too absorbed in her salad to notice the panic across Jake's face as he signals to the waiter. She stops eating when he asks for the check.

"Kris, we gotta go."

"What are you talking about?" Garlic bread dangles from her mouth. "We haven't even gotten our entrées."

"We'll eat them at home. Trust me, we have to leave now."

Kristi begins to put on her jean jacket. As they're leaving, he braves one final look at the man in the corner, who smiles at him. It's a friendly smile, *too* friendly, and Jake walks more assertively toward the door, his hand on Kristi's back.

"Did you make sure they gave us extra garlic bread?" she asks as he nudges her onto Vermont Avenue.

Once they get into the car, Kristi insists, "What's going on? Jake? Tell me right now what's going on."

Jake rubs the steering wheel as he decides what to tell Kristi. "Helen. She left us a brooch that might have had a valuable in it. This guy that came into the restaurant, he thinks I have it."

"What are you talking about?"

"Beck found it hidden behind Helen's dresser. It's called the Florentine Diamond. It was part of the Austrian crown jewels. When the empire fell, it disappeared. It's worth, like, ten million dollars, and that guy thinks I have it."

"Back up. You found a brooch worth ten million dollars and you didn't tell me?"

"We're not sure it's ours. We don't know how Helen had it."

"That's not the point. How long has this guy been following you?"

"I don't know, a week or two. Someone's following Ashley, too. This is so messed up. I don't know what I'm going to do."

"You're going to call the police," she says like it's obvious.

"I can't. No one can know we have the diamond."

"Why not?"

"Because it might not legally be ours."

"So now you're dealing in the black market? Jesus, Jake."

"I didn't want to worry you."

"That makes me feel so much better. What a relief that you didn't want me to know someone is stalking you because he thinks we have a ten-million-dollar diamond. Jake, if we're going to do this, you can't keep secrets from me."

"What do you mean *if*?"

He grows progressively more worried as Kristi turns away and stares out the window, letting the *if* linger. He really was trying to protect her. And he didn't want to get her hopes up about the money, not until he was certain it was theirs.

When they park outside their apartment building, Kristi asks, "You don't have the diamond, do you?"

"It's in a bank in Philadelphia."

"Well, then," she says, unbuckling her seat belt. "If you don't have it and you can't get it, he's no threat to us." Her tone says something else entirely.

"Why would he think you have the diamond? How could he even know about it?" Beck asks when Jake FaceTimes his sisters that night.

Ashley tries to keep her face impassive while inside she's cursing herself for that nincompoop visit to Georgina's office. Her insults have taken on the maturity of her children. She is a nimrod, a fart face, a dumb butt — Tyler's favorite aspersion. About two hours after their meeting, once Ashley was back in Westchester, safely ensconced in her bubble bath, she remembered the copy of the IGS report she left on Georgina's desk. She'd convinced herself that Georgina had shredded it. That was the responsible thing to do. As she listens to Jake's story, she's not so sure. How could she have trusted Georgina?

"Well," Jake begins, "I may have told Rico about it."

What? Ashley and Beck say at once in distinct tones: Ashley is excited; Beck is furious. Neither knows who Rico is, not that it matters.

"You're such an idiot," Beck adds.

"Don't yell at me, I was just shooting the shit with a friend."

"And you couldn't think of anything else to talk about except the one thing you were supposed to keep secret?"

"Look, I know I fucked up. Please don't yell at me."

They watch Beck do laps around her

195

kitchen as she says over and over again, "I never should have told you about the diamond."

"Beck, I'm scared. Kristi's pregnant. If anything happens to her —"

"Kristi's pregnant?" Ashley asks.

"Yeah, it's still, like, ten weeks, but —"

"You're going to be a father?" Beck cannot hide her disdain.

"That's typically what having a baby entails," Jake snaps back. "I don't know what to do." It's unclear if he's referring to the man who follows him or the prospect of being a father.

Beck stops pacing. "You need to stop talking about the diamond." Beck clicks off before her siblings have a chance to respond.

Ashley makes eye contact with Jake through the screen. His hair is disheveled and his skin is sallow like he hasn't slept in days.

"Do you and Kris want to come stay with us?"

Jake shakes his head. "Kris can't miss work."

"You can always call the police." Ashley knows how preposterous this would sound to the police, especially if Jake doesn't mention the diamond, probably more so if he does.

196

"I didn't know it would turn into this. If anything happened to you and the kids because I ran my mouth, I don't know what I'd do."

Ashley feels a pang of guilt. Even though Jake told his friend, it's much more likely that this has something to do with Georgina, who has access to the entire jewelry world. The whole thing is so illogical that it makes a strange sort of sense — men following the Millers because Ashley showed Georgina the IGS grading report. It's just a matter of time before they start following Beck, before they do more than trail them in dark sedans.

"Just promise me you'll be safe? And, Jake," Ashley says before they hang up. "You're going to make a good dad."

Ashley stares out into her dark backyard, the sound of Sports Center trickling from the living room where Ryan is watching television. She hasn't told Ryan about the man who follows her, the diamond, Georgina. There's still a subtle thrill to keeping secrets from him. More so, it's become routine, and she wonders if this is how the dissolution of a marriage starts, not with secrets but with distance.

Although she doesn't discuss it with her siblings, Beck is worried that someone is coming for her, too, and soon. It keeps her up at night, makes her restless, her body on guard for the slightest commotion. A motorcycle bellows in the distance, the sound growing louder as it approaches her block, then quiets. Is it right outside her stoop? Is someone spying on her? She remains awake until the first rays of sunlight pierce her blinds. It takes her another hour to muster the courage to peek outside. A motorcycle is parked outside her stoop, the driver nowhere to be seen.

She's late to the office, then completes her work in a daze. She does not remember sending one of the partners the brief she finishes. Mechanically, she highlights pertinent sections of a deposition for a first-year lawyer with less experience than she has and twice her salary. The hours pass and Beck's fear magnifies, all the more so because nothing has happened yet.

When she meets her friend Dea for a drink that night, every bar stool could hold a spy. A man in a flannel shirt sits next to her, pretending not to look at her. When he offers to buy her a drink, she relaxes. He's just some dude at a bar hoping for something she's not prepared to offer, something that has nothing to do with a historic diamond. She turns him down, despite Dea nudging her that he's cute, more her type than Tom.

Two glasses of wine later, she leaves the bar alone, checking at every corner to make sure no one is following her. The evening is tepid, and the streets are predictably empty this time of night. She falls asleep, inoculated by the wine, until a few hours later, when she darts awake. She can't remember what she was dreaming, only that it involved handcuffs around her wrists. She reaches for her phone, positive she'll have an alert from the *New York Times* or Apple news: "Diamond Missing for 100 Years Has Returned." Of course, when she checks her phone, there are no news updates, just a text from Dea: Next time, I'm not letting you go home alone! And another from Ashley: This guy's still following me. She's not prepared to deal with either of them, so she turns off her phone and tries futilely to fall back asleep.

The only thing Beck can think to do is get ahead of it. And the only way she can get ahead of it is to find out everything she can about Helen.

At work, she begins with the passenger manifests from the SS *President Harding* that Ashley sent, the newspaper articles on the heroism of an everyday Jewish couple who traveled to Vienna in 1939 when no Americans traveled to Nazi Germany, particularly not Jewish Americans. They used expired visas the US government had agreed to allocate to the kids and brought the fifty children back with them to Philadelphia. In these articles, the children are a unit. Cute and grateful, without names or families perishing at home. Beck knows that one of these children is Helen, one of the families is the Auerbachs, but she learns nothing about them from the fluff pieces of old periodicals.

Somehow, the Florentine Diamond traveled from the museum in Vienna to the brooch lodged behind Helen's dresser. She begins with the brooch, which is hidden in her nightstand. Viktor said it was midcentury. By New Year's Eve, 1955, Helen was wearing it with her mystery man, which means the latest it could have been fabricated was 1954. If she didn't get the brooch made, she likely acquired it soon thereafter. Beck can picture the soft curves of the *S* and the *J* on the back of the brooch, the signature of the company that crafted it.

From her desk, Beck texts Viktor: What are the chances of finding the maker's mark on the back of the brooch?

While she waits for him to respond, she

searches legal databases for information on the Habsburgs and their crown jewels. She downloads a newspaper article from 1924 in the *Hawera Star* about a baron who was arrested after attempting to illegally sell Austrian crown jewels. A court case in the '80s where a would-be Habsburg heir was suing the youngest child of the last emperor for what crown jewels remained. Neither matter turns up in the database search again, not in the papers nor the court records. Still, the Florentine Diamond was one of the Habsburgs' prime stones. There must be a record of it somewhere. She just has to keep looking.

Later that afternoon, Viktor texts back, Highly unlikely. It requires finding the right trademark guide from the right year. But I always relish a challenge. Want me to look into it?

Please. Beck wants to compensate him for his time, but Viktor doesn't need money. And when you find it, I'll cook you dinner at your own peril.

I never took you for a Suzy Homemaker, he writes back.

After work, Beck heads to the Central Branch of the Free Library, where she locates an entire shelf on the Habsburgs. One book catches her eye, *The Death of an*

Empire, a day-by-day account of the last moments of the Habsburgs' reign, of an empire that for centuries seemed too vast to fall. Somewhere in those day-by-day accounts, there has to be mention of the crown jewels the royal family took from treasury, some sales they made in exile. Possibly, this book might include an essential detail to uncover the provenance of the diamond.

During her lunch breaks, she reads the book, careful to check the surrounding tables at Liberty Place to assure no one is watching her. The first thing she discovers is that while the empire may have collapsed, Karl never abdicated the throne. Even on his deathbed in Portugal in 1922, he held a crucifix to his lips as he told his wife, Zita, that he was dying so the empire could live again. While Karl was the last recognized emperor of Austria, his son Otto went on to be the unofficial king. As she reads about Otto's involvement in the creation of the European Union, Beck is struck by the frequency of one name that does not end with Habsburg, Kurt Winkler. He was one of Otto's closest friends, an excessive drinker who quit the bottle after Otto commanded his abstinence as Winkler's emperor. What's crazier than a twenty-year-old man pronouncing himself emperor of his friend was that it worked. Winkler never took another sip. Instead, he devoted his life to documenting the history of the exiled royal family.

Kurt Winkler's name appears in the footnotes and indexes of Habsburg photos attributed to his private collections. Quotes are taken from his books, *Die ungekrönten Habsburger* and *Das Vermächtnis des großen Imperiums,* which Google translates into something like *The Uncrowned Habsburgs* and *The Legacy of the Great Empire.* His collection also includes interviews with the last empress, Zita, where she discussed her family's financial struggles in exile. What if Zita mentioned the illicit sale of the Florentine Diamond in one of her interviews? What if Zita told Winkler how the Habsburgs lost the diamond? Beck needs to get her hands on these books.

But the library doesn't have Winkler's books. When she checks Amazon, the website offers copies in German, each for several hundred dollars.

While Beck waits for one of the lawyers to get back to her on research she's collected for him — a second-year who speaks to Beck like she may be hard of hearing — she googles Kurt Winkler. German floods her screen. When she asks Google to translate, the fourth link is to a newspaper obituary. It includes details Beck already knows about Winkler, that he was the official biographer to the Habsburgs, friends with Otto, plus a few details that she didn't know. He had two children, a daughter who died young, a son and wife who survived him. The obituary is ten years old. Beck looks up his wife, Marietta, who has also passed. His son, Peter Winkler, is still alive and owns a gallery on Schlüsselamtsgasse in Krems an der Donau. The gallery's website includes an email address. Peter might know what happened to his father's Habsburg collection. Without overthinking it, she opens her email and begins typing.

Dear Mr. Winkler,
I am an Austrian history enthusiast who recently came across your father's name in my research of the fall of the Habsburgs. The biographies I've read give the impression that your father was in possession of the Habsburgs' private collection of memorabilia. I think there might be something in his collection that could help with my research. I'm wondering if it might be on public display somewhere, or if I can access it remotely?

Thank you for your time and consideration.

Sincerely,
Beck Miller

The email is intentionally vague. Beck's not sure what she's looking for nor how direct to be with a stranger in her desire to locate information about a diamond that's been missing for a century. She doesn't even know if Peter Winkler speaks English.

"Hello? Earth to Beck?" Beck jumps when she finds the second-year lawyer knocking on her cubicle wall. She quickly hits Send and the email disappears. He drops the research she gave him on her desk. "This isn't right. I asked for precedent on investor and shareholder rights."

Beck skims the case briefings. "That's what this is."

Flustered, he grabs the paperwork and scurries away. All the new lawyers know that Beck has two years of law school under her belt. Her knowledge and expertise should make them like working with her, but she's the least popular paralegal with the greener lawyers. While she tries to hide it, she enjoys putting them in their place. It's one of the few pleasures she derives from her job.

■ ■ ■ ■

Beck intends to tell her mother about the men who are tailing Jake and Ashley, how she's worried she might be being followed, too. She promises her siblings she will. Even if neither of them wants to talk directly to Deborah, they still don't want her to unknowingly be in danger. Over another curried lentil stew at the now colorful house on Edgehill Road, Beck asks Deborah if she's noticed anyone unusual lurking around the house, bracing herself for a frantic response.

"Like who?" Deborah asks vacantly.

"No one," Beck says.

Deborah shrugs, scooping another helping of bright yellow mush.

She's better off not knowing, Beck texts her siblings. I'll keep an eye on her.

She adds checking in with her mother to her list of daily responsibilities.

Deborah has her own ghosts following her as she relocates her business from New Hope to Bala Cynwyd. She cannot escape an altered image of her childhood, of her younger self, bouncing on that man's knee. How happy they looked together. How much like father and daughter.

Relocating Deborah's business makes it

sound like a greater feat than it actually is. There's nothing to move beyond leashes and mixing bowls. She never legally registered her business or even had a website. It's a figurative move, symbolic, one that allows her to take on clients closer to her new home.

Deborah's dog-walking service blossoms overnight, but her vegan catering company isn't as popular in Bala Cynwyd as it was in New Hope. Deborah has four dogs she walks each morning, four others in the afternoon. Each day, after dropping the dogs at their homes, she returns to the house on Edgehill Road and soaks her bloated feet in warm water. She watches Helen's old television with the photo album resting open on the coffee table. During commercial breaks, she inspects the photograph of Helen and the man on New Year's Eve, looking for clues. Helen's dress, the stole, the dimly lit dining room — it's all unfamiliar. In 1955, Deborah was not yet three. Who was staying with her while her mother dined with this man? She doesn't remember any babysitters, not a single night where Helen had left her. Often, as a teenager, she wished her mother would go out, that she would date, have a life beyond the walls of their row home. If she'd had her own life, maybe she wouldn't have been so invested in Deborah's.

Deborah closes the album, unable to look at that photograph anymore. It never occurred to her that Helen was lying about her father. It's just a photograph, a scarce resemblance, but there are no photographs of Helen on her wedding day. No portraits of a soldier in uniform. No dog tags. No Purple Heart or any other recognition of a life lost in battle, nothing to corroborate the past as Helen had presented it to Deborah. When Helen spoke about Joseph Klein, she always reminded Deborah, *How many people can say their father died a hero?* It was romantic, brave, patriotic. A fantasy, one that now seemed to highlight all the qualities her real father must have lacked.

EIGHT

Since seeing the man in the leather jacket at Palermo, there's been an edge to Jake and Kristi's interactions. Kristi doesn't kiss Jake goodbye before she leaves for work. When she returns at the end of the day, she asks what Jake's brought home for dinner without pressing him for anecdotes from Trader Joe's. Normally, she loves his stories about the actors who come in wearing stage makeup, about the man who buys an entire shopping cart full of pita chips, the balloons Jake gifts to rowdy children. She still lets him rub her feet when they watch television, but her sighs are resigned, as though his touch feels good against her will.

At work, Jake restocks vegetables, distracted by Kristi's terse goodbye again that morning. She never answered his question — *What do you mean* if *we're going to do this?* — and it continues to linger in their apartment. He's already bought her lilies and cooked chicken cacciatore. Now, he needs to do something bigger. Maybe he should buy her a promise ring, a prelude to the bigger ring he can buy when they sell the Florentine Diamond.

It happens in a flash. A black leather jacket in his periphery and then it's gone. Jake drops two bags of Meyer lemons on the floor and begins following the jacket.

The man turns down frozen foods, bends around to the next aisle. Jake trails him, peeking down each lane until he finds the man surveying bottles of pinot noir. When Jake storms toward him, the man looks up with a smile and begins to say, "Maybe you can help me —" but Jake grabs him by the lapels and pushes him into shelves of red wine. Bottles clank against each other. Several fall to the ground.

"All right, who do you work for?" Jake gets close enough to the man to smell his hair gel. "Why the fuck are you following me?"

The man raises his hands in protest. "I've never seen you before."

Jake pushes him farther into the shelves. More bottles shatter on the ground. "Who hired you?"

"I don't know what you're talking about." He flinches like Jake is about to punch him. "Please. I think you're confused."

Jake doesn't even realize what's happened until he feels someone lift him by the stomach and throw him to the ground, away from the man now hunched over, a puddle of wine spreading around him. Jake's knuckles sting. He opens and closes his fist, checking to see if his fingers are broken, realizing that he must have punched the man.

"What the fuck, Jake?" Randy, the manager, says as he runs over and blocks Jake's path. "Chill."

Suddenly, Jake becomes aware of his surroundings, the crowd of horrified customers. Two of his coworkers help the man up from the floor.

"He just attacked me out of nowhere," the man says as he follows Jake's coworkers toward the front of the store.

Jake wants to chase after him and shout to cut the bullshit innocent act but Randy is practically carrying him into the back. Once they're in Randy's office, he warns Jake to stay put while he goes to check on the customer Jake punched. "If you move from that chair, I'm calling the police."

Jake drums his thumbs against the arms of the chair, growing increasingly impatient as he waits for Randy. The sounds of the store trickle into the office as Trader Joe's resumes its afternoon rush — the carts' wheels against the linoleum floor, the faint shitty music, the bustle.

Eventually Randy returns and tosses Jake a bag of peas. "For your hand."

The icy bag stings as Jake rests it on his raw hand. Jake has never been in a fight before. He's never felt the softness of flesh against his knuckles, the tingling that radiates through his fingers.

Randy plops into his office chair across the desk from Jake. "He's not going to press charges." Randy shakes his head, relieved.

"*Him* press charges? He's been following me for the last two weeks."

"He says he's never seen you before."

"That's bullshit. He was at the gym. And Palermo. And Mixto." As Jake lists his evidence, he hears how preposterous this sounds. The gym? Two restaurants? Now the local grocery store? "He's been following me all over the neighborhood?" It comes out as a question rather than a statement.

"I know you've been dealing with some family stuff lately —" How does Randy know about Kristi? Jake's only told his sisters, not even Rico. When he sees the expression on Randy's face — those doe eyes people give you when they say, *I'm sorry for your loss,* without conviction — Jake realizes he means Helen. "But you can't go assaulting customers."

Jake starts to stand. "I'll find him. I'll apologize. I'll explain that it was a misunderstanding."

Randy gestures for Jake to stop. "I'd strongly advise against that. You got off lucky." Jake sits back down. "Just go home, all right?"

"Are you firing me?"

"Jesus, Jake, you just attacked a customer and broke, like, twenty bottles of wine."

"I'll pay for the wine."

Randy shakes his head. "You're late for work, everyone else's hour lunch break is somehow an hour and a half for you, and don't even try to claim you aren't stoned all the time."

"You're serious?"

"I'm going to have to ask you not to come into the store. Otherwise, we'll have to get the authorities involved."

"Look, I'm sorry, okay? You're right. My grandmother's death, it's been way harder on me than I imagined. We're finding out all this stuff we never knew about her, and it's got me spiraling. I'll take some time. I'll clear my head. I promise nothing like this will ever happen again."

"My hands are tied here."

The men eye each other for a few moments until Randy looks away. Jake has won nothing in this stare-down. He nods resignedly and heads out of the office.

Randy stops him. "Can you go out the back? And please, don't talk to anyone in the parking lot."

Jake walks out the back in a daze. A heat wave hit earlier in the week, and the oppressive temperatures make his limbs heavy. As he cuts through the parking lot, Manuel, who guides the traffic, watches him warily. Trisha also gives him that sideways eye as she pushes a row of shopping carts toward the store. As he walks past the cheese shop, the sushi restaurant, the gelato place, he feels everyone staring at him, disappointed and disgusted.

In his dark, cool apartment, Jake can finally breathe. He takes off his damp Hawaiian shirt uniform and sits barechested in his reclining chair, staring at the water stains on the ceiling. What the hell just happened? Did he really just assault some random guy? He was certain he was being followed. He tries to determine what made him so sure. Of course, the Millers. He laughs, although it isn't funny. He used to be able to regard them as an outside observer would, but he's lost his critical eye. Ashley has always jumped to conclusions.

Beck has always been quick to anger. Jake, he again realizes, has always managed to fuck a good thing up.

The moment Kristi walks in the door, she notices Jake's hand.

"What happened?" she asks as she inspects his swollen knuckles. They are bruised and raw, but they didn't crack open. "Can you bend it?" Jake bends his fingers a third of the way. Kristi walks into the kitchen. "You need to ice it."

While he waits for her to return, he reaches for his shirt, dangling from the chair, then remembers it's his work uniform. He tosses it across the room, wondering if they'll take the cost of it out of his final paycheck.

He flinches when she puts the ice on his knuckles.

"I don't think it's broken," Kristi says.

Jake means to tell her that he punched someone. He plans to be honest, to banish the *if* with a confession and the promise of how he's going to make up for it.

"Someone slammed my hand in the freezer door," Jake hears himself lying. "I'm sorry, Kris. I'm sorry I didn't tell you about the diamond. I should have. It's just — all that money, the way it could change our lives. I didn't want to get your hopes up

215

until I knew for sure. I was wrong about that guy at Palermo. He wasn't following us. I saw him today. He's just some dude from the neighborhood."

It isn't a total admission, but it's a start. He waits for Kristi to ask follow-up questions, so he can tell her the more damning parts of his day.

Kristi laughs. "Of course he wasn't following you."

"You weren't scared?"

"I was scared because you were. I never thought you were actually being followed because of some diamond." She continues to laugh as she walks into the kitchen, then returns to the living room, disappointed. "Did you forget dinner?"

He tries to find the best way of telling her he lost his job. "I, um —"

"Never mind," she interjects. "I'm dying for pad see ew, anyway. Five minutes?" She trots down the hall to change out of her scrubs.

Jake listens to the hum of the fridge, replaying their conversation. Why didn't he tell Kristi about getting fired? It's not something he can hide from her. He needs to confess now before his lie gets bigger.

When she reappears in the living room, her skin is glowing, and she looks so calm, so pretty, so normal. "You ready?" she asks, tossing him a T-shirt.

He tugs the shirt over his head and follows her out of the apartment without another word.

Unlike Jake, Ashley's sightings of the Buick are not coincidental. Each day, the dapper man is at the Y, the library, school pickups, ATM stops, and the dry cleaner's. Each day, he continues to trail her, same car, same menacing distance. Why hasn't he approached her? What's he waiting for?

At the library, Clara runs toward Ashley waving a book titled *My Grandmother and the Other 49 Children,* which they ordered via inter-library loan. "It's mostly about her grandmother Irma, but look —" Clara flips to the final pages of the hardback. Her finger scans a list of names with short biographies until she lands on Helen Auerbach's. Momentarily, Ashley forgets about the man in the parking lot.

Helen Auerbach stayed in Philadelphia after the Goldsteins rescued her, buying a house in Bala Cynwyd where she lived with her daughter. Helen started a tailoring business, which she continues to run to this day.

Some of the biographies for the other children detail reunions with parents who obtained visas or survived camps, families who were displaced in Cuba and England during the war. Helen's paragraph, like the other shorter paragraphs, says nothing about her family from Vienna.

The glee falls from Clara's face. "That must have made it harder, that the other children reunited with their families."

"Can I borrow this?" Ashley asks.

"That's generally what people do with library books," Clara teases.

"Thank you, Clara," Ashley says more earnestly than she's intended.

"Are you all right?" Clara asks her.

Ashley imagines telling Clara about the diamond, the man who is after her, even Ryan's situation at work. She knows Clara will believe her, that she'll probably have sound advice about confronting the man, about confronting Ryan, too, but she created this mess by confiding in Georgina, and she isn't sure she's ready to trust anyone else just yet.

Ashley forces a smile. "Just a bit overwhelmed."

"Well, prepare to be more overwhelmed," Clara says, flipping to the photographs in the center of the book. One of them is of

Helen sitting on a blanket beside a woman. The caption reads, *Helen Auerbach, picnicking with her mother.*

Ashley turns to Clara. "How did the writer have this?"

"I don't know." Clara flips to the back flap where the author's bio reads, *Cheryl Appelbaum lives in Larchmont, NY, with her husband and their border collie, Yosef.* "I checked the white pages. She's still listed there."

Ashley walks to her car, hugging the book to her chest. She's never been much of a reader but this must be what people mean when they say a book was written just for them. Ashley pauses when she realizes she's breezed past the handicap spot where the sedan is usually parked. Today, the car isn't there. It isn't at the elementary school when she picks up Tyler and Lydia, either.

After three days, she stops checking the rearview as she drives between the Y and the library. She emails Cheryl Appelbaum to see if they can meet for coffee and is unfazed when Cheryl writes back, saying that she's in Europe for the next few weeks. There's no rush, now that no one is following her. She can meet with Cheryl in a month, in two. Time, as far as the Florentine Diamond is concerned, feels vast. Wide open. She wafts between her daily routine, feeling a sense of freedom that she knows can't last — and it doesn't.

On the fourth day, Ashley gets a knock on her front door.

Lydia and Tyler are in the kitchen, eating cereal, while Ryan is upstairs, getting dressed for work. Ashley assumes it's her neighbor Marion, who drops off their paper when it's mistakenly delivered to her porch. When Ashley opens the door, three men stand outside in nearly identical dark suits, with closely cropped hair and politician good looks. She almost doesn't recognize the man who's been following her, he's so similar to the men beside him. Then he smiles and she remembers his smile, his clear brown eyes.

Even before he asks, "Is your husband home?" Ashley understands that this has nothing to do with the diamond.

Ashley tries to act normal as she drives the children to school, but she's seen enough *CSI* and *Law & Order* to know, more or less, who the men were. Did Ryan break the law? Are they here to arrest him? Is she an unknowing accomplice? Will they take her house? Oh, God, will they take the children?

Her children keep calling to her from the

backseat.

"Mom, I'm starving."

"I didn't get to finish my cereal."

"Why'd you rush us out?"

"What's going on? Why couldn't we finish breakfast?"

She pulls into the drive-through at McDonald's. After they've eaten, she drops them off at school like it's any other day. Tyler bounds out of the car, but Lydia remains in the backseat, eyeing her mother through the rearview mirror.

"Who were those men?"

"Just some people your dad works with." Ashley's tone is too upbeat. It makes her daughter squint even harder.

"Is Dad okay?"

"Honey, you're going to be late for homeroom." Ashley shoos her out of the car. Lydia shakes her head, making it clear she doesn't believe her mother, and throws her backpack exaggeratedly over one shoulder as she gets out.

Ashley drives straight home, forsaking the dry cleaning in the trunk, the animal shelter where she's expected at ten. She waits in the car, spying on her house until the Buick pulls out of the driveway. How did she not notice it was an unmarked police car?

On the couch, Ryan sits with his tie loose,

his top button undone.

"The police?" Ashley says. "What the hell were the police doing here?"

Ryan does not look at his wife. "FBI actually."

"The FBI? Why would the *FBI* be at our house?" When her husband remains comatose, Ashley raises her voice. "Ryan, what's going on?"

Ryan hands Ashley a letter, the Department of Justice's seal at the top.

"Work called. They're shipping my things. I'm not even allowed in the building."

Ashley skims the brief letter. A form letter, yet the threat it conveys is anything but routine. "The FBI is investigating you for fraud? And money laundering? You said it was a *paperwork* issue."

"I didn't realize it was illegal."

"Ryan, you're a lawyer."

"A patent lawyer."

"So that's going to be your argument to the judge? Sorry, Your Honor, I didn't realize what I did was against the law?"

"I only got paid for work I did. It wasn't stealing."

"That's not what the DOJ seems to think. How much, Ryan? How much did you steal from your company?"

"I can't do this right now." He walks

222

toward the stairs, but Ashley darts in front of him, poking her finger into his chest.

"You do *not* get to walk away."

He brushes her to the side and mounts the stairs with Ashley trailing close behind, the letter still dangling from her hand.

"It says here they're going to indict you. Are you going to jail? What did you do to our family?"

He turns, matches her furious gaze with his own. "What did *I* do to our family? Oh, I don't know, put bread on the table for the last decade. I did what I thought was right. I didn't know it was illegal. I didn't think I would get caught." He storms up the last few stairs and slams the door behind him.

"Everyone always gets caught," Ashley shouts.

She sits on the top stair and lets the letter fall beside her. She tries to pinpoint a moment when she should have known. All those Saturdays where he went to the office, evenings where he had to work late. It had started about two years ago. At first, she'd thought he might be having an affair, but he often returned home hungry for sex. He never showered first nor smelled of foreign perfume. While he bought her flowers at random intervals — earrings, massages, gifts that signified guilt — nothing in his behavior suggested it was guilt over another woman. Had she wanted those gifts so badly that she'd ignored the obvious signs of a man atoning? Was part of this her fault?

No, she decides as she rereads the letter. She never asked Ryan to be the breadwinner, not permanently. He'd wanted this family arrangement. This lie.

All Jake and Ashley say is that they are no longer being followed. The men are gone, no more cause for concern. Beck isn't sure what to make of their dismissiveness. Their fear had been so convincing it had infected her, too.

It's now late April, five weeks since Beck found the diamond. Five weeks since Helen died. Five weeks where they have panicked and calmed. The following Monday, Beck settles into her cubicle with a renewed sense of purpose. She reads a Supreme Court decision, losing herself in the minutiae of work. She still plans to follow up with Peter Winkler, who hasn't responded to her email, but the pressure is off. No one is looking for the diamond.

An hour later, the receptionist pops her head into Beck's cubicle. "Someone in the front to see you."

Beck follows her through the maze of partition walls to the front desk. A man in a Phillies baseball cap looks up when Beck enters the lobby. She's never seen him before. He stands and bows his head bashfully as he holds out an envelope.

Beck can feel the receptionist eyeing her. She doesn't turn to look, trying her best to walk calmly to her desk. Her knees wobble, her heart races. She wonders if her coworkers notice. She wonders if Tom notices, too, but she keeps her gaze straight ahead as she walks past his office. Whatever is inside the envelope, she knows it has to do with the Florentine Diamond.

When she unfolds the letter, she sees an insignia for a law firm she doesn't know, a Taylor, Washington, and Weiner out of New York. Her eyes skim the page until they focus on three capital letters in the middle paragraph: IGS.

We've procured a copy of the International Gemology Society's (IGS) colored diamond grading report from a reputable third party that wishes to remain anonymous.

A third party? What third party? The only other people who know about the diamond — as far as Beck realizes — are Viktor and

Jake's stoner friend. Could Viktor have told someone? He does have a history in the unsavory corners of the jewelry world, but Viktor has been a friend to her. While his actions toward Tiffany's may have been less than ethical, they weren't illegal and only harmed a company too rich and too powerful for its own good. No, Viktor would never turn on her.

But how could Jake's stoner friend have had the wherewithal to broker a black market deal? That seems equally unlikely. So, who else is left? Maybe someone at IGS? Viktor had said it was anonymous, but the gemologists who graded the diamond owe the Millers nothing.

The letter continues.

The colored diamond grading report issued by the IGS confirms that the diamond in your possession is the Florentine Diamond. The weight, dimensions, and cut of the diamond listed on the IGS report are identical to those of the Florentine Diamond. Additionally, the report noted a feathering "roughly in the shape of a heart," which matches multiple descriptions of the Florentine.

Taylor, Washington, and Weiner, Esq., are writing on behalf of the Italian government.

The Italian government is not interested in determining how the Florentine Diamond came into Ms. Helen Auerbach's possession; it is only relieved that after a period of ninety-nine years, the precious Medici heirloom has resurfaced.

Medici heirloom? She remembers, vaguely, that Francis of Lorraine inherited the diamond when he became the Duke of Tuscany after the last male Medici died without an heir. Frances of Lorraine subsequently married into the Habsburg line and brought the Florentine to Austria. Sure, at one time the diamond had been a Medici heirloom. Why would the Italian government think it belonged to Italy now?

As she keeps reading, her question is answered.

Given the value of the Florentine Diamond, both monetarily and culturally, the Italian government is prepared to offer $500,000 for its return. Such an exchange would negate the need to initiate legal proceedings.

The Italian government isn't positive it belongs to them, either. Otherwise, they would have initiated those formal legal proceedings. They wouldn't be trying to buy her off. One thing is certain, though. After one hundred years, the Florentine Diamond has resurfaced.

NINE

"The Italian government," Jake says as he answers Beck and Ashley's FaceTime call. His sisters sit, stone-faced, on the couch at Edgehill Road. "Why would it belong to the Italians?"

"It's complicated," Beck says. "Austria owed reparations to the Allies at the end of WWI, which included returning some Medici heirlooms to Italy. Basically, if the Austrians had had the Florentine Diamond at the end of WWI, it's unclear whether they would've had to give it back to the Italians. So, if the diamond isn't ours, it might be an Italian heirloom, not an Austrian one."

Ashley picks at her nails while Jake stares into space. Beck doesn't bother explaining the peace treaty and stipulations for Austria returning heirlooms to Italy; she's already lost them.

Lydia and Tyler tumble downstairs, chasing each other around the couch. Deborah barrels after them, two steps at a time, wearing Helen's pink comforter as a cape. Beck is about to tell Deborah that Helen's bedding isn't a toy, until she sees the pleasure across the children's faces as their grandmother lumbers toward them.

"Guys, inside voices — we're trying to have a serious conversation here," Ashley shouts as they race back upstairs, their buoyant laughter lingering after they've disappeared.

"So what do we do now?" Jake asks.

"Nothing," Beck says to Jake. "It's an empty threat. If they had a sound case, they'd be approaching us through proper legal channels."

"It's not a threat," Ashley says. "It's an offer, and I think we should take it." Beck startles. "What? It's a good offer."

"It's an offer," Jake says, circling back and forth across his living room. A modest sum relative to the diamond's worth. His cut would be about as much as he made when he sold *My Summer of Women.* Hollywood money if not historic diamond money. Still, it was enough for a new apartment, enough that he wouldn't have to get another day job while he finished his script. Enough that he wouldn't have to tell Kristi he'd been fired, either.

"You're serious?" Beck shifts her attention between her siblings. "Sure, let's do that. While we're at it, let's just forget about Helen and the fifty children. I mean, why should we care when the Italians are offering us *five hundred thousand dollars.*"

"No one's forgetting anything. I'm going to see Sal Frankel next week," Jake says. Sal Frankel is one of six still living from the fifty children. Kristi found him in an article about an assisted living home near LA.

"You're being dramatic," Ashley says, rolling her eyes. "Besides, even if we sell the diamond, we still have the brooch. We can keep that and not have to hide a multimillion-dollar diamond."

"We made a deal. No sale until we know how Helen had the diamond. As far as I can tell, we haven't gotten very far on that," Beck says.

"You made that deal," Ashley argues. "Like usual, you decided and didn't let us have a say."

"I'm with Ash on this. The last few weeks, looking over my shoulder all the time — it's been hell," Jake adds.

"It doesn't make you pause, for a second, to wonder how the Italians know, why they aren't offering more? If you'd stop thinking about money for one minute, you'd see that something isn't right. How do they even know about the diamond?"

"It was me," Ashley blurts, and before she has time to consider what she's saying, the story about Georgina and Bartley's comes spilling out.

"You did *what*?" Beck says.

"Ash . . ." Jake shakes his head, and it's bizarre to hear disappointment coming from him.

Ashley fights back tears. She'd told Beck she was coming down to strategize their next step, but the truth is that she had to get away from Ryan and the damning FBI letter. Ashley couldn't spend another moment with her husband without wanting to throw something at him.

As her siblings stare at her with disgust and disbelief, she wants to care about the diamond. She wants to care about Helen's past. She *does* care, but right now, all she can think about is Ryan's investigation. They need to hire a lawyer, but most of their money can't be used for representation or anything else, because it was stolen from Ryan's company. Now, here's money that isn't connected to Ryan, money that could keep her husband from prison, assuming he deserves to be saved.

"I just — Georgina's an old friend and I

232

knew you two didn't want to think about selling. I wasn't even trying to sell it. I just wanted to have a plan in case we found ourselves in a situation where we had to sell quickly."

"Well, congratulations. It looks like we're there, thanks to you."

"I was trying to help."

"You're unbelievable." Beck inches away from her sister. "What's your cut even matter to you — $125,000? Isn't that your shoe allowance for the year?" Ashley shoots Beck a cautionary look, which her sister ignores. "What, you need a new Mercedes, and Ryan won't buy it for you, is that it? Or maybe you need a facelift to keep up with the other moms?"

"Beck —" Deborah calls, but it's too late. Beck looks up to see her mother and the kids frozen on the stairs. Tyler sprints upstairs. Lydia follows him.

"Thanks a lot," Ashley says before taking the carpeted stairs two at a time.

Jake monitors Beck through the screen.

"What, taking notes for your next script? Hope I performed well for you."

"Sometimes you're such an asshole." He hangs up.

Beck turns to look at Deborah, who plops down on the couch beside her and drapes the comforter over her shoulders. "We're all assholes sometimes," Deborah says. "It's called being family."

After he hangs up, Jake still feels agitated. Normally, he would pack a bowl and smoke the agitation away. Today, Jake shuts his eyes and tries to meditate, which he's read can be an effective alternative to a substance-induced calm. He counts his breaths in and out, but the irritation persists. How could Ashley have gone behind their backs, to Bartley's no less? Why does she only ever care about money? And why does Beck always have to be so defensive, so mean? For the first time, Jake doesn't regret making *My Summer of Women*.

"Hey, babe," Kristi says as she sits beside him on the couch. Kristi has taken to wearing sweats whenever possible — there's something inexplicably sexy about those gray pants — so he's surprised to see her dressed in jeans and a calico blouse. She reaches for his right hand. His knuckles are no longer swollen and have shifted from purple to yellow. "It's healing nicely. Does it still hurt?"

Jake clenches his fist. "Only when I do this."

"Then don't do that." Kristi laughs. Since

Jake punched the man in the leather jacket, things with Kristi have shifted back to normal, and the way she laughs now, the ways she kisses him goodbye each morning, it feels so right that he almost believes he *did* get his hand stuck in the freezer. Then, after she leaves for work, he remembers he has no reason to leave the house except to buy dinner from a grocery store that is not Trader Joe's. If Kristi realizes that the pre-made foods are from Gelson's, she doesn't investigate.

"So," Kristi asks. "How'd it go with Beck and Ash? Are you going to sell the diamond to the Italians?"

Since Jake told Kristi about the diamond, he's filled her in on the Family Settlement Agreement, the story he's piecing together about Helen's journey to America. Confiding in Kristi is so much better than navigating this alone. She asks questions he doesn't consider, about the families of the children who came over, the property listed on the ship's manifest — whether it included the diamond — the family that Helen boarded with before she started her own. Kristi was the one who thought to look up the surviving fifty children and had convinced Jake to set up a visit with Mr. Frankel, to see if he remembers Helen.

"Ash and I want to sell, but Beck is being a jerk." While Jake is an enthusiastic curser, he can never swear in front of Kristi. Even calling his sister a jerk makes her flinch. He launches into the details of their phone call, how Ashley had visited Bartley's, how Beck immediately went into beast mode. "I know it isn't millions, but the money — it would be a big help." Not a help, a necessity.

"Is that what Helen would have wanted?"

"She'd want to make our lives easier if she could." Kristi raises her eyebrows, compelling Jake to be honest. "No, Helen would never submit to a threat," he admits.

"And you still don't know why she never sold?" Kristi squeezes Jake's arm. "Beck doesn't do a good job of showing it, but she's trying to respect Helen's wishes. If she's cruel sometimes, just remember she's hurting." Without meeting Beck, Kristi understands her better than Jake does. "Why are you looking at me like that?"

Jake realizes he's making his dumbstruck, puppy-love face at her. It happens involuntarily with Kristi. Often. "You just have this way of making everything seem so reasonable — even my sister."

"It *is* reasonable. Some people have a hard time asking for help. It's important to understand things from someone else's

236

perspective." Jake thinks of Kristi's job as a veterinary technician, how she rationalizes her boss's rudeness because he regularly has to administer death, and that kind of emotional trauma would weigh on anyone.

"I'm being a dummy," he says, a statement she never contradicts. "How was work?"

"It was good. We were able to finance surgery for that dog, Curly. You should have seen the look on the little girl's face when we told her the good news." Instinctively, Kristi cradles her nonexistent belly.

Kristi has to work one Saturday a month. Today was that day, Jake realizes. It's odd that she's home before noon.

"They let you go early?" Jake notices the strain on Kristi's face, and he reaches for one of her feet to caress it in the way she likes. "Don't get me wrong, I'm glad to have you home."

Kristi pulls her foot away. "You forgot."

"Forgot what?" As soon as he asks, he remembers. Week fourteen, their second prenatal visit. She'd put it on their joint calendar, which he never checks. He hops off the couch and trots down the hall. "I can be ready in five minutes."

"You have to remember these things, Jake." The disappointment in her voice

237

makes him weak. "I can't do this alone."

He trades his ratty T-shirt for a button-down. It smells musty, but it will have to do.

Jake returns to the living room and sits on the couch beside her.

"You aren't alone," he says. "I just got distracted. All this stuff with my family, I'm letting it consume me. That's why I want to sell. I want to be here. Present, with you and the baby." He realizes he's holding her hand as if he's about to ask for it. "Marry me."

"What?" Her surprise is more extreme than he expects.

"Marry me."

She pulls her hand from his. "Jake, it's no big deal about the doctor's appointment. You don't have to propose to make up for it. I just don't want you to forget again."

"I'm not trying to make up for anything. I'm proposing because I want to marry you." Something inside him sours. "You don't want to marry me."

She looks at him like he's the idiot he generally is. "I do. But not like this. Not when we're late for our checkup and you've got a ketchup stain on your shirt." Jake looks down at a crusty red spot just below his right nipple. He starts to take off the shirt, but she stops him. "Come on, I don't want to be late."

As they are locking up the apartment Kristi says to him, "Ask me again, for real. You don't have to get a ring. Maybe some roses? Or balloons? Make it special. And, Jake? Ashley's always generous with money. If she's pushing to take the offer, there must be something going on. Some reason she needs it."

She's right. Ashley always offers to help out. Jake feels a pang of guilt as he realizes he has no idea what's going on with his sister.

Beck and Lydia wait in line at the Franklin Institute to enter the two-story replica of the human heart. Lydia knows all sorts of facts about the human body: the heart beats one hundred thousand times a day; 8 percent of your body weight is your blood. She begged Beck to bring her, only now she crosses her arms tightly against her chest as though Beck has dragged her here.

As they approach the red staircase into the model heart, Beck says, "I shouldn't have said those things about your mom."

Lydia shrugs.

"It's no excuse, but you know how siblings are. We say things to each other that we

239

don't really mean."

Lydia looks at Beck with disbelief. "Tyler means everything he says to me."

"He doesn't."

"He does. But he's a moron, so I don't care." A steady beat surrounds them as they ascend the stairs.

"Well, I'm a moron, too. And I didn't mean anything I said about your mom."

Lydia nods, deciding whether or not to believe her. Beck has always had a particular fondness for Lydia, who is serious and pensive like Beck was as a child. In the five and a half months since Beck last saw her at Thanksgiving, Lydia has grown at least two inches and lost her baby fat. She has Ashley's naturally dark hair, Ryan's olive skin, and is well on her way to becoming a knockout.

Soon enough, the tension in Lydia's posture disappears, and she's tugging Beck up the stairs, following the flow of blood into the heart.

The halls are narrow and Beck feels claustrophobic as they pass the right atrium. While Lydia has forgiven her, Beck cannot forgive herself. Why does she go to that place of intense anger so quickly? It's never an effective way of communicating. It's cruel and makes her seem unreasonable.

Plus, she knows Ashley has been uncharacteristically invested in finding out about Helen. It doesn't make sense that she would want to sell, to give up so quickly.

The synthesized heartbeat echoes around them, its tempo too fast for comfort. Lydia races ahead, squealing, "We're in the right ventricle!"

Beck dashes after her, remembering how her own father chased her through these very hallways. Every Saturday morning, he would take her to the Franklin Institute to see the heart, the Academy of Natural Science to see the dinosaurs, Reading Terminal where they would wait in line for buttery soft pretzels. These outings were their ritual, just the two of them, something she took for granted until they abruptly ended.

Beck was twelve when her father disappeared, only a year older than Lydia is now. She'll never forget the day the bus dropped her off and she'd skipped up the pathway to their Victorian home, knowing her father would be back from his work trip with a gift for her. When she walked into the kitchen, her mother was talking hurriedly on the phone. Her father's briefcase wasn't beside the table, and neither were his black luggage, his overcoat. When Deborah spotted Beck, she froze, and Beck's first thought was, *Dad is dead.* "He will be, when I find him," Deborah had said. By the time Jake got home from band practice, Ashley from field hockey, Deborah had told Beck details she wished she could unlearn about the various women Kenny met on his work trips. In the past he'd never lied to Deborah about where he went, just whom he met there. Only this time he wasn't in Detroit for a quarterly meeting, like he'd told her. He'd been fired the month before. Their bank accounts had been drained. She'd called every airline. None of them had a record for Kenny Miller out of Philadelphia.

Beck and Lydia scale the right ventricle up to the main pulmonary artery. The narrow pink halls make Beck feel faint. When she and her father had walked these same pink halls, did he know he was leaving?

"Did you like it?" Beck manages to ask Lydia once they are outside the heart, back in the museum.

"It was amazing," Lydia says with child-like wonder. And as if she can read Beck's mind, as if something about the heart makes girls think of their fathers, Lydia adds, "I wish my dad were here."

Why *isn't* Ryan here? The Johnsons come to Philadelphia twice a year, staying at the

Ritz on Broad Street, where they can walk to Old City to visit Independence Hall and Elfreth's Alley. This is the first time the kids and Ashley have visited without Ryan, have opted to stay on Edgehill Road instead of a hotel.

"I'm sure he does, too." This isn't the right thing to say, Beck realizes as soon as Lydia's eyes fill with tears.

"I think my dad's in some sort of trouble."

"What makes you say that?" Beck scans the room for Ashley, who ventured to a separate part of the museum with Tyler and Deborah.

"One night I couldn't sleep, so I went into my parents' room. They didn't see me. They were in the bathroom and Dad kept saying, 'I screwed up.' They've been fighting a lot, but they always stop when they see me."

"Have you asked your mom about it?" Beck wonders whether their fighting has something to do with why Ashley wants to sell the diamond.

"She just changes the subject. And she's been acting really happy. Too happy."

Beck pulls Lydia in for a hug. It had taken her months to realize her father was never coming back. At first everyone had told her, "He's just going through something. He'll be back soon. Your father would never leave

243

you." Then her thirteenth birthday passed with no card, and she knew that if he didn't remember to send a present, he wasn't thinking about her at all. She wished that someone had been honest with her.

"They'll sort it out," Beck promises, releasing her niece. "Your parents wouldn't want you to worry."

The words don't feel like a lie. Ryan is not Kenny.

Later that evening, after Lydia and Tyler are asleep, Beck opens a bottle of pinot noir. Deborah, sensing the tension between her daughters, tells Beck, "I'll take mine up-stairs."

Her uncharacteristic intuitiveness surprises Beck. Maybe it isn't uncharacteristic. Maybe Beck has been too hard on her, on all of them.

Ashley is lounging on the couch when Beck cautiously enters the living room. She sits up as Beck hands her a wineglass, which Beck interprets as an invitation to join her.

Ashley takes a long glug. "I needed that."

"Ash . . . what I said earlier. It wasn't right. I know you care about Helen. Really, I was just heated. You know how I get. I didn't mean it."

"Is that an apology?"

"I'm sorry." Why is it so hard for Beck to say this, even when she *is* sorry, even when she knows that Ashley is going through something with Ryan? "I really am sorry."

Ashley continues drinking her wine, and Beck doesn't force her to accept the apology. Eventually, Ashley leans back and rests her legs on Beck.

"Are you worried about the Italians?" Ashley asks.

"No. They won't disappear, but they don't have a case and they can't force us to sell."

"What if they go public?"

"It's as much in their interest to keep this quiet as ours." Beck takes a large sip of wine. "Lydia said something to me this afternoon. She heard you and Ryan fighting." Ashley darts up, and Beck knows it's true — Ryan is in trouble. "She's worried."

Ashley buries her head in her hands, shoulders convulsing. Beck patiently strokes her sister's silky blond hair, keeping an eye on the staircase in hopes no one will wander down.

Eventually, Ashley's breath steadies and she looks up, red-eyed, at her sister. "Ryan's boss put him in charge of patent applications, and I guess they had more than their team could handle, so they had to farm out some of the work. For whatever reason, it

245

was supposed to be split up between several lawyers, but Ryan channeled it all to his friend Gordon."

"His best man?"

"You know he only got into law school because his last name was on one of the buildings. He couldn't handle the work, so Ryan started doing it himself and pretending Gordon was doing it. I guess Gordon's going through a divorce and is strapped, so Ryan didn't want to fire him. Since Ry was doing all the work, it didn't really seem fair that Gordon was being paid for Ryan's work." Ashley laughs cruelly. "*Fair.* That's actually what Ryan said."

"Fair and legal aren't always the same thing." Beck guesses what's coming — the crimes of fraud, tax evasion, and money laundering if they put the payments in a bank — but she lets her sister finish telling her what happened.

"Gordon paid taxes on all the money before splitting it with Ryan. Well, not really splitting. Ryan took, like, 85 percent. I still don't really understand why it was illegal."

Beck could explain to her sister that Ryan was essentially being paid double for his work since he was a full-time employee. Instead, she asks, "How'd they get caught?"

"Some sort of routine internal investigation where they saw that all the work was going to one lawyer instead of multiple. Ryan hasn't been able to reach Gordon in months. I assume Gordon must have said something to Ry's company. The FBI showed up at our house last week. Ry's meeting with a lawyer this weekend." Ashley twists her engagement ring around her finger. Her diamond is clearer than the Florentine, a brilliant round that makes Ashley's ring look like so many others. "The FBI gave Ryan some kind of letter."

"A target letter," Beck says, and Ashley nods. Beck doesn't blame Ryan for what he did. She's witnessed enough mistakes — her own included — to know that people shouldn't be judged for what they do as much as why they do it. And Beck doesn't know why Ryan did it. They didn't need money, so it must have been about something else. That's what makes Beck feel for Ashley; her husband knew something was wrong and tried to fix it with money.

The target letter is a courtesy or a scare tactic. Either way, it's bad. Ryan needs to give back the money before he's indicted. That might not save him from a jail sentence, depending on how much he's stolen, but the law looks kinder on those who repent. While Beck has so much advice for

Ashley, right now Ashley doesn't need a lawyer. She needs her sister.

"He got fired obviously. We haven't told the kids."

Ashley tells Beck how, for the last week since the agents showed up, Ryan has put on a suit and pretended to go to work. Ashley has no idea where he would go. She made a point of staying away from the house, lingering in the locker room after her swim, reading magazines at the library when Clara had to help other patrons. She didn't ask her husband what he did all day and he didn't offer, not until she was lying in bed, her husband on a pile of blankets on the floor, and he'd said, "You and the kids should get away for a while."

"Why? What are you planning?"

"Can you stop with the accusations? I'm trying to fix this."

Ashley sat up in bed and looked down at her husband, supine on the floor. "How are you going to fix this? You were fired. You're probably going to get arrested. Tell me how exactly you can fix any of this?"

"I'm not going to get arrested, okay? I'm meeting with a lawyer."

"I hope he's not a DUI lawyer from Vegas." Momentarily, she felt guilty when she saw her barb landed.

248

"I'll know more after I talk to the lawyer. The major thing for now is that we're going to have to pay back the money to my company."

"How much?"

"Let me worry about that."

"Ryan, tell me right now how much you owe."

Ryan stared at the ceiling. "Five hundred thousand, give or take."

"*Five hundred thousand* dollars? You're serious? You stole half a million?"

"I know it looks bad. If we cut back our expenditures and —"

"You think canceling cable and your whiskey club is going to cover this?"

"If we sell the house —"

"Sell the house? This isn't just *your* house. I worked for years to help save for a mortgage. I gave up my career . . . I never wanted to quit . . . and now you want to sell the house?"

"You didn't want to quit?" Ryan laughed cruelly. "You can be mad at me for this thing with the FBI, but don't go rewriting history."

He's right, of course, even though he's in no position to be right about anything. "I'm not selling the house. I'd rather divorce you first."

As soon as she said it, she wished she could spool the words back in. It was out there now. This might break them.

"Please, just take the kids for a few days while I talk to the lawyer, okay?"

"I don't know where you expect us to go, seeing as we don't have any money."

The next afternoon, when Beck had called about the Italians, it seemed fated.

Beck pours Ashley more wine. $500,000. The exact amount the Italians had offered. Of course Ashley wanted to sell.

"I don't know what I'm going to do," Ashley says.

"What *we'll* do," Beck corrects her sister.

Deborah sits on the top stair, out of view, listening to their exchange and cursing her daughter for inheriting her taste in unworthy men. She didn't mean to snoop, but she heard their voices through the radiator in Helen's bedroom and knew it was serious. So she tiptoed into the hall. It wasn't nosiness. It was protectiveness, a maternal instinct. And once she started to hear Ashley's story, she couldn't not listen.

Deborah leans back, and the stair creaks beneath her. The conversation grows silent. Deborah waits a minute, hopeful that her daughters will continue talking. When their silence persists, she downs the rest of her wine and trudges downstairs as though in search of more pinot.

In the living room, both daughters study her, trying to determine what she's heard.

"What? Did someone else die?" It's a terrible joke, but it has the desired effect. Her daughters shake their heads, dismayed.

Deborah sits in the rocking chair beside the couch, holding out her glass for Beck to pour her more wine. She can't remember the last time she was this tired. It's a good kind of tired, the exhaustion of racing after children. She races after dogs all the time, but children are different. You have to earn their love. Deborah hopes she's earned their love this weekend. She told the children about their astrological signs and taught them how to tie knots that would confound their friends. She hopes she's earning Ashley's love now by pretending she doesn't know about Ryan. She hopes this is enough for Ashley to let her see the kids again.

Beck turns on the television, stopping on a *Friends* rerun. She was never a fan, but it's the perfect show for them to pretend to watch.

At the commercial, Beck asks Ashley, "When are you going to see the woman who wrote the book on the fifty children?"

"Cheryl Appelbaum? Day after tomorrow.

That's why we have to leave in the morning. She's finally back from *Europe.*" Ashley wishes she could jet off to Europe for a month.

"Cheryl *Appelbaum*?" Deborah asks.

"You know her?" Beck and Ashley say simultaneously.

"Not a Cheryl, but I know an Irma and Hetty Appelbaum. They used to visit from New York when I was a kid." Beck turns off the television and both daughters sit up, eager for more. "What?"

Ashley tiptoes upstairs, returning with the library's dog-eared copy of *My Grandmother and the Other 49 Children.* She tosses the book in Deborah's lap and plops onto the couch beside her sister.

Deborah flips through the pages. "Irma's granddaughter wrote this?" She stops on a picture of two girls posing on the deck of a boat and reads the caption: *Helen Auerbach and my grandmother aboard the SS* President Harding. Helen has one arm slung protectively around Irma's shoulders, the other hugging a doll. Although in better condition, it is the same doll from Helen's box. "What is this? Did Irma and Helen come over together?"

Ashley turns to Beck. "You didn't tell her about the fifty children?"

"What are the fifty children?" Deborah asks. Beck and Ashley glance at each other, deciding what they should tell her.

"Helen was part of a group of kids that was chosen for US visas. A lawyer here in Philadelphia brought them over."

Deborah stares at the back cover of the book where black-and-white images of Irma overlay each other.

"Let's back up," Ashley says. "You've met Irma Appelbaum?"

Deborah nods. "And her daughter, Hetty. She was a few years older than I was. We used to walk down to the five-and-ten. Hetty taught me how to steal."

Deborah can still remember the look on Helen's face when they got caught, furious and confused. "Why must you steal?" Helen had asked, pulling Deborah out of the shop by the back of her neck. "Is there anything I haven't given you?" Deborah was only seven. She knew vaguely that she was doing something wrong, but Hetty told her it was fun, a conquest with the slightest tinge of danger. She hadn't even wanted the Hershey bar she'd slipped into her pocket.

"I always wondered if she and Irma knew each other in Vienna, but I never thought about them coming over together." The smile falls from Deborah's face. "There's so

253

much she didn't tell me."

"She didn't tell us, either," Ashley says. Beck shoots her a look that says she shouldn't compare the secrets Helen kept from them to those she kept from Deborah.

"Why wouldn't she tell me? Not just Irma. I asked her. As a kid, I wanted to know about my father. She'd say he died a hero, and that was that. How could she have kept so much from me?"

Beck and Ashley peer over at each other, unsure how to react. The real question is, why hadn't Deborah kept pressing Helen? Joseph Klein, the war hero — it was such a thin lie.

"We can find him now," Beck suggests.

"How? I don't even know his name."

Well, I guess you should just give up then, Beck thinks. She knows her mother's hurting, but it's so frustrating, her passiveness, the way she'd rather feel injured than have agency.

Before Beck says as much, Ashley asks, "Did you check your birth certificate? Your father's name would be on it."

"I have no idea where it could be."

Ashley reaches over to squeeze her mother's arm. "We can search for it online, if you want?"

Beck watches her sister, mystified. Why

does her sister's empathy surprise her? And how would she have acted if she were in her mother's position? It's not like Beck went looking for her own father. Instead, she told herself that she hated him, that he wasn't worth finding. Maybe she's more like her mother than she realizes.

Ashley scoots closer to Beck and motions for Deborah to sit beside them on the couch. "What do you say? Should we see if a copy of your birth certificate is available?" Ashley opens ancestry.com on her phone and angles it toward Deborah. "Just type in your name."

Deborah hesitates, staring at the search bar on Ashley's screen. A strange calm washes over Ashley as she waits for her mother to say yes. It centers her, this patience, something she's lost in recent months with Ryan and her children. Right now, there's no rush. Her mother can take all the time she needs.

Deborah doesn't want to type her name into a website, to have records appear, to access her father's identity that easily. Right now, however unrealistic, there's still denial. Maybe the man from Helen's photo album wasn't her father. Maybe her mother hadn't lied to her for her entire life.

As her daughters watch her, waiting, she

knows she needs to do this for them. So she types her name into the search bar.

They hold their breath as they wait for the search engine to work its magic. Within moments, hundreds of records appear for Deborah Auerbach. Ashley refines the search until the top hits are documents on the purchase and sale of the house in Mt. Airy, Deborah's high school yearbook photo, her marriage certificate. Ashley scrolls through, but there is no birth certificate for their mother.

"I guess birth certificates for living people wouldn't be on here," Beck eventually says. "With privacy laws and all."

Her daughters monitor Deborah, gauging her reaction. Suddenly, she feels an inexplicable urge to laugh. So much tension, so much buildup, and for what? Helen is dead. She'll never be able to explain why she lied to Deborah. The married man in the photographs is surely dead, too. What exactly are they hoping to learn? She starts laughing so hard her eyes water.

Beck and Ashley exchange worried looks that their mother is finally coming unhinged. But her laughter, saturated in ironic disbelief, isn't irrational. It's relief, Beck realizes. She, too, feels relieved that they did not find their grandfather so swiftly.

"We can order a replacement birth certificate from the state?" Ashley offers, uncertain what's so funny.

"It's that simple?" Deborah asks, trying to control her laughter.

"Let's order you that birth certificate," Ashley says. She fills out the online request. "It should be here in one to two weeks."

A stitch forms in Deborah's side. She grows light-headed. As her laughter quiets, her daughters continue to watch her expectantly. A new tension builds. Never gifted with words, Deborah understands that she must thank her daughters for this, must acknowledge that Helen was not the only mother who kept things hidden from her children.

"I hope you know, everything after your father left, I never meant for any of it to happen." Deborah doesn't know how to explain everything she should have done differently, those weeks where she was out of state with some man whose name she can't remember or at some retreat that has probably gone bankrupt. She can't tell them what she was running from or toward because she doesn't know herself. She just knows that she should have been there for her children and wasn't. She has no one else to blame, not even their father. "I have

257

no excuse."

Ashley shifts her attention from her mother to her sister. The evening is dangerously close to imploding, and neither Beck nor Deborah knows how to put the peace before their own feelings.

When Ashley begins to speak, she doesn't know what she's going to say. She only knows that she needs to take control of the conversation before it turns into an argument. "Do you want to come with us tomorrow?" she asks Deborah. "To Westchester? We'll talk to Cheryl Appelbaum together. It could be helpful, since you've met Irma."

Deborah shrugs, feigning indifference. "Sure, if you think it might help."

"Sounds like a great idea," Beck says. Ashley turns to her, grateful, and Beck realizes she, too, is capable of more than her family assumes. They all are. Maybe the fighting grows out of their limited expectations for each other. If they try to be more generous, if they try to believe in each other, maybe the Millers can be another kind of family, one not so quick to anger. One that forgives rather than holds grudges.

TEN

Two days later, Ashley pulls into Cheryl Appelbaum's circular driveway, looking up at her Victorian mansion. It reminds Ashley of the Millers' former house in Mt. Airy. She hasn't thought about that home in years. Ashley wonders if her mother sees the resemblance. She's never considered what it must have been like for her mother to lose the house after her father betrayed them. Now Ashley can imagine it all too readily. Ryan's lawyer offered him few options. He must plead guilty before he's indicted. He must return the money he owes his company. Even if Ashley helped save for the house, like Deborah, she has little say in what will happen to it.

"Must be a lot easier to write a book when you have all this waiting for you," Deborah says, shaking her head.

"How do you know the book didn't buy this house?" Ashley asks, causing Deborah to scoff as she steps out of the car into the muggy afternoon. Spring has somehow already come and gone. By mid-May, it feels like summer.

As Ashley follows her mother up the path, she thinks about the money she'd stowed away for her dream of a forever home. Even before she met Ryan, she'd been steadily setting aside a quarter of her paycheck. She hadn't been waiting for a man to come along and buy it for her. So how has she gotten here, at the whim of her husband's bad decisions? It's her house, too. She can fight for it. She can do what she'd always done: work and save. She can get a job and regain control of her family's future.

When Cheryl opens the door, she's younger than Deborah anticipated, no more than forty with dark hair falling straight around her shoulders. Dressed lavishly in a silk blouse and trousers, a string of pearls lining her neck, her outfit is out of Helen's closet.

"Please, come in," she says warmly. "I've set up tea in the living room." As they follow her into a cool, dark room with oak panels lining the walls, she chatters about her month-long sojourn to the Amalfi Coast. "We rent a house somewhere different each year. Last year, it was the French

Riviera, and the year before that we got a flat in London —" She continues to rattle off places Deborah has never been, and Deborah has no idea why her mother would have confided in a woman like this.

They sit on a settee across from Cheryl, waiting as she pours them each a cup of tea. "I'm so glad you found me. Helen was one of my favorites. But I'm sure you could have guessed that." Deborah and Ashley cannot venture a guess. Helen would have said this woman was so full of shit you could smell her from a mile away.

Cheryl sips her tea, oblivious to the perplexed stares her visitors offer her. "This book has been an incredible reunion. You're the sixth family that's reached out to me since it was published. One family contacted me to say my book helped with their grief. That's the highest compliment you can get from a reader." Cheryl stares at them expectantly.

"Your book has been very helpful to us, too," Ashley begins, sensing the woman's desire for a compliment. "Helen died two months ago."

Cheryl's face shifts to genuine regret. "I'm sorry I didn't get to see her again."

Ashley reaches for her cup and rests it in

her lap. "When was the last time you saw her?"

"Let's see . . ." Cheryl's eyes flit toward the ceiling. "The hardcover came out in 2009, so it must have been 2007 or 2008."

"Did she come here, to visit?" Deborah asks, creating patterns with the honey across the surface of her tea.

"I went to see her a few times in Philadelphia. She gave me some photographs and paperwork for the book." Cheryl reaches down and produces a pink box, mining through it until she finds a photograph they don't recognize of Helen and Flora sitting outside a café. "Here she is with her mother."

"Flora," Deborah asserts more forcefully than she intends. In this oak room, with this pink box filled with items Helen never showed her and this woman whom she does not like but knows Helen confided in, she's feeling more than a little defensive.

"That's right." Cheryl continues to dig through the box until she finds a German passport for Helen, which she hands to Deborah. In the photograph, Helen wears a white bow in her ear-length hair and a checkered dress with a lace collar. Her smile exposes a lifelong gap between her two front teeth. The passport was issued in 1939 and stamped twice with the Nazi eagle emblem. Helen was fourteen, although she looks younger.

Deborah gasps as she notices Helen's name on the passport, *Helen Sara Auerbach,* written in childish cursive. *Sara.*

Deborah had wanted to name her first-born Sara, had gotten as far as calling her Sara Miller during her first day of life while she was still in the hospital. When Sara was just thirteen hours old, Deborah, sweaty, tired, and proud of her body for producing a child, held her daughter toward Helen. Helen cooed at the baby, nuzzling her nose against the child's splotchy skin.

"Hold on to that smell," Helen said to Deborah as she handed the baby back. "It goes away so quickly."

"This is Sara, no *h,*" Deborah said, stroking the fuzz on the baby's head.

Helen shuddered. *"S-A-R-A?"*

Deborah didn't understand her mother's expression, so she nodded.

"No." Tears welled in Helen's eyes. "You cannot call her Sara. Did I teach you nothing?"

Deborah laughed nervously until Helen started to cry. At that moment, Kenny came in and took Sara from Deborah's shaking arms.

"Anything but Sara," Helen had whispered as she left.

When Dr. Feldman came to check on Deborah, she told the obstetrician the strange story of her mom's reaction. Dr. Feldman's grandmother had survived the Holocaust. Her name was Charlotte Ella Weisz — the Nazis had called her Charlotte Sara Weisz. It was the middle name they designated to Jewish girls whose first names did not immediately register as Jewish. The men were called Israel.

Deborah was dumbfounded. As she looked at the crusted-shut eyes of her newborn, she imagined what that would be like, the rest of Helen's life, having to see her granddaughter and think *S-a-r-a.*

When it was time to sign for the birth certificate, Deborah named her firstborn Ashley.

Now, Deborah hands the passport to Ashley. She never told Ashley about her intended name, but the Nazi insignia inked onto Helen's identification card is horrifying enough, even without knowing about Sara.

"I didn't get to use the passport in the book," Cheryl apologizes, studying Deborah's and Ashley's stunned faces. "You haven't seen this before?"

"No," Ashley says, returning the passport to the table.

"Sometimes it's easier," Cheryl says, "telling your story to people who are not family."

"Irma told you her story," Deborah presses. "You knew everything."

"My grandmother got to tell it as a happy story. Relatively happy, anyway. Her parents and brother came over later that year, from Italy. They found an apartment in the Bronx. I can see how Helen might not want to talk about it, if the rest of her family didn't make it over."

Make it over, like they were playing Red Rover. Sometimes, Ashley thinks, euphemisms are worse than the blunt truth.

Cheryl continues to mine the box and shows them two photographs of Helen and Irma. They have already seen one from the cover of Cheryl's book, on the deck of the SS *President Harding.* In the other, Helen and Irma sit on the steps of a white porch, an American flag hanging above them. Again, Helen has one arm gripping Irma close, the other clutching her doll closer. "That's from Camp Shalom where they stayed temporarily until the Goldsteins could find more permanent housing for them." In the photo, Irma smiles as she leans into Helen, who does not return the expression. Helen doesn't look sullen exactly, or unhappy, just serious. Stricken. "They were the last two girls left at Camp Shalom after the other kids were sent to live with families, so they looked after each other. Helen was like a big sister to my grandmother."

Ashley remembers the anecdote from Cheryl's book, how Helen was the last to leave the camp.

"She was older than the other kids. So it was harder to find a home for her. Plus, the Goldsteins found her . . . How can I put this delicately —" Cheryl looks conflicted as she chooses her words carefully.

"Helen could be a handful," Ashley acknowledges. Of course Helen could be a handful. Look at everything she'd endured, a lifetime of guilt at surviving when her family didn't. Instinctively, Deborah rubs her daughter's back. Ashley stares at her mother's surprisingly youthful face. Maybe there is something to her casual veganism, to the acupuncture, the yoga.

Cheryl laughs. "She was a handful and proud of it. She said Mr. Goldstein had a savior complex. He never tried to understand why she would be anything other than overjoyed to be American. I think he expected more from Helen because she was older, but she had such a hard time leaving her mother. The Goldsteins use to console the children by telling them that their parents' visas would come through, that they would follow. It happened for more of the children than you'd expect, but not Helen. I think she blamed them, in part. And it was worse, since she never found out what happened to Flora."

Deborah's mind drifts to her teenage years when Helen would scold her for being too American, which meant too loose, too loud, too free. It had never occurred to Deborah that Helen did not feel American, that she did not feel free.

Ashley feels a pinging at her temples and realizes she's been furrowing her brow. If she were Helen's mother, she would have made her go, too. No question she would have sacrificed herself for Lydia and Tyler. It was the only choice a mother could make, but that didn't mean it was easy for the child to leave a mother behind.

"Maybe I shouldn't have said all that," Cheryl confesses.

"I'm glad you did," Ashley insists.

Deborah's gaze returns to the picture of Irma and Helen beneath the American flag.

"Do you know why they stopped talking?"

Deborah asks. When Cheryl hesitates, Deborah continues. "My mom didn't let a lot of people in. It was a big deal when Irma and your mom came down, then it just stopped. I should have asked Helen, but I never did a very good job of trying to understand my mother. I'd really like to know now, if you'll tell me."

Ashley remains perfectly still throughout her mother's rambling speech. She wishes Beck were here. Actually, she wishes Jake were here. He hasn't done a good job of trying to understand Deborah, either.

Cheryl crosses and uncrosses her legs. "I know it had to do with a married man Helen had an affair with. Irma was never forthcoming about it, and I didn't dare ask Helen. Let's just say my grandmother didn't approve of what Helen was doing with someone else's husband. Someone's father, too."

Right away, Deborah knows she means the man from the photographs. There's no denying it anymore. He was her father. He was married to another woman with another family. He was not a hero but a traitor. Helen was a traitor, too.

"That ended years before we stopped seeing your mom and grandmother," Deborah argues. She doesn't actually know when

Helen's affair ended, but there are no photographs of the man once Deborah was walking and talking, once she could remember.

Cheryl sucks in her breath. "That's really all I know."

The grandfather clock in the corner ticks loudly, filling the otherwise quiet room with an unsettling countdown.

"Mom says hi, by the way. She's living in Boca now." Cheryl laughs. "She said to tell you she still thinks of you every time she sees Revlon lipstick. I must say, it's an honor to meet the woman who convinced my mother to shoplift. Sheesh, I don't know if she's ever broken another rule. She doesn't even speed up at yellow lights, although that's probably best at her age."

Deborah cannot hide her disdain for this woman who says *sheesh,* who knows more about Helen than she does. This woman, who dresses and acts like she is of a certain age, when she's not even forty, not even deserving of pearls. This woman, who was not in the drugstore when Helen pulled Deborah out by her neck, who is misrepresenting history. "Your mother was the one who convinced me to shoplift. I got hell for it."

As soon as she says this, Deborah realizes

she's wrong. She always speeds up for yellow lights, and late at night, when no one's around, she gets a thrill in running red lights.

Before Cheryl can respond, Ashley's phone buzzes. She has two texts from Lydia. The first, fifteen minutes ago: Where are you? And again, just moments ago: Hello? Earth to Mom? Did you forget about us? Across the room, the grandfather clock says it's 3:15 p.m.

"Shit. We're late." Ashley stands. "I was supposed to pick up my kids fifteen minutes ago."

"Here," Cheryl says, holding out Helen's passport, the photo of her with Flora. "I can make copies of the photos with Irma, too."

Deborah takes the passport. "I'd like that."

At a traffic light, Ashley clenches the wheel, shaking it violently. "Shit. Shit. Shit."

"It's okay. We'll be there soon."

"It's *not* okay. I know that's probably impossible for you to understand, but it's definitely not okay that I left my children waiting for a half hour."

Deborah feels the sting of Ashley's words and fights to keep her tone impassive. "Blame it on me. Tell them I went for a walk, you didn't know where I was and I

270

came back late."

The light turns green and Ashley floods the engine. She glances over at Deborah, trying to understand the emotions behind her stoic face. "I didn't mean that. I just — I have a lot going on right now."

"You're a good mom. Try not to be too hard on yourself." Deborah should have been harder on herself. She should have cursed when she was late.

Ashley reaches out and squeezes Deborah's hand. She cannot lie and say that Deborah was a good mom, too. "You okay?" she asks instead. "Everything Cheryl said about Helen, the married man?"

Deborah looks out the window at the storefronts they race past. "I don't like that woman."

Ashley laughs. "The look on her face when she was, like, *That's really all I know.* Like she just loved knowing something she wasn't telling us."

Deborah laughs, too, until they stop at a light and fall silent. "It's all true. The married man — he must be my father."

"Well, you'll know when you get the birth certificate. We'll know," Ashley corrects. "Whoever he is, we'll get through it together."

By the time they pull up to the school, it

is 3:40 p.m. Tyler comes barreling out of the building, but Lydia lumbers toward the car. As Deborah watches her grandchildren, she's stunned suddenly that she's here with her daughter, that after a few days together, she already knows Lydia and Tyler better than she ever imagined she would. It makes her feel guilty that she's never tried to be part of their lives before, that if it weren't for Helen's death, the fifty children, the Florentine Diamond, she wouldn't be trying now. It makes her think of all the family that came before, the family she's never investigated, not just her father.

"Ash?" Deborah asks. Ashley turns to her, flustered by Lydia's scowl as she approaches the car. "We need to find out what happened to Flora."

The children climb into the backseat, but Ashley remains focused on the pleading across her mother's face. She's right. Finding Deborah's father is one thing, but Flora . . . Flora was Helen's ghost.

"We'll find her, too," Ashley promises.

Beck is expecting a follow-up letter from the Italians, one that will threaten a lawsuit, possibly sweetening the deal with more money. What she does not expect is a knock at her door.

272

When Beck answers, she's wearing her striped terry cloth robe, her hair still wet from the shower. She's not sure who's more startled, the three men outside with a search and seizure warrant or Beck, self-consciously tightening the robe around her waist.

"Can you give me a minute to change?" Beck asks, trying to remain calm. The appearance of the FBI means one thing. Evidence of a crime. And a federal one at that.

They wait, in the foyer, as Beck digs through her closet looking for an outfit that reads innocent. They are here at eight in the morning to catch her off guard, if not in her bathrobe. She wonders who let them inside the building, whether the tenants upstairs realized they were FBI. She wonders if they would be waiting patiently outside her apartment if Beck weren't white, if this was over drugs instead of a centuries-old diamond.

The eyeliner pencil is shaky in her hand, causing her to put it down and stare intently at her face in the mirror. "Relax," she commands. "You have done nothing wrong." Only the guilty tell themselves this.

Somehow, the black pencil rims her eyes, the mascara ends up on her lashes, the scarlet lipstick bloodies her lips. In her collared white shirt and fitted lightweight black pants, it's the closest she'll look to the femme fatale.

The agents follow Beck inside, accepting her offer of coffee.

"I assume this is about my grandmother's brooch?" Beck asks. They look mildly confused, and momentarily she fears they are here to ask her about Ryan.

"Only if your grandmother's brooch had the Florentine Diamond in it."

Beck explains that her grandmother's diamond is in a safe-deposit box at Federalist Bank, careful not to call it the Florentine. There's no proof she knows it's the Florentine Diamond. Sure, the Italians sent her that letter, but she never wrote back. She could argue that she thought it was a practical joke. And the colored diamond report never identified the diamond. How is she supposed to know how rare a 137-carat diamond is? It's not like she's a jewelry expert.

All this rationalizing has the opposite of its intended effect. Her palms grow sweaty. Her knees won't stop shaking. When the men ask for the bank's address, her voice wobbles as she tells them, "The branch on Market Street."

Can they really just swoop in and take the diamond away? Don't they need proof that it was stolen? Do they think *she* stole it? Are they going to arrest her? Everything feels like it's happening too fast and she needs a moment to think, a little time to determine her next step. Then she remembers — "You're going to need a separate warrant to search the safe-deposit box." They cast her a skeptical look. "I'm a paralegal," she explains.

They take another sip of coffee before they leave.

"I trust the diamond will still be in the bank when we get our warrant?" one of them asks her, and she assures him, as steadily as she can, that the diamond isn't going anywhere.

By the time the feds leave, Beck is late for work. Still, she cannot bring herself to get off the couch, to head to the office as though everything is normal. She considers going to the bank to say goodbye to the diamond, certain that the moment the feds seize it, it will never belong to the Millers again. If she does, there will be a record of her visit, which will surely look suspicious. Suspicious of what exactly, she isn't sure, but if the FBI is involved, then the diamond must have been reported as stolen, which leaves her family as the primary culprits.

She needs to be productive, to do something to get ahead of the FBI. Her mother and Ashley have already met with Cheryl Appelbaum, but they haven't called her yet. She's read every article she can find on the Florentine

Diamond, every case and deposition involving the Habsburgs. All dead ends. Still, there must be something she can do, something to keep herself busy. She makes a mental list of all her leads, coming up with two points still unexplored: the maker's mark on the back of the orchid brooch, which Viktor has been looking into for two months, and Kurt Winkler's books on the fall of the empire, equally unpromising.

First, she calls Viktor, who assures her, "My dear, the moment I find it, you'll hear from me. You sound stressed. Do you want to come over for lunch? I'm making coq au vin."

The image of Viktor preparing an elaborate meal for himself makes her impossibly sad, so much so that she almost says yes. "I'd love to, but I have to sort through some work. Thank you, Viktor. For everything, really."

For the first time, it strikes her as odd, how willing he is to help her, until he says, "For the woman who saved my penthouse, I'd do a whole lot more."

After they hang up, Beck still doesn't want to go to work. Peter Winkler, Kurt Winkler's son, never responded to her emails, asking to see his father's private collection. So, she sends another follow-up email, feeling momentarily satiated before the restlessness settles in again. Can the FBI really just take the diamond? Can the Millers lose it that quickly? She checks her phone, hoping Peter Winkler has miraculously written her back. It's evening in Europe. He's not going to return her email today, if ever — if he can even read it. So American of her to assume everyone speaks English, when she can't read a word of German.

German. Suddenly, she remembers something the librarian at the Central Library said when she asked about Winkler's books. He told her they might be at the German Society on Spring Garden Street. "You need to be a member," he'd cautioned about checking out books. Since Beck wasn't certain what she was looking for and had no interest in becoming a member of any society, let alone one dedicated to a language Helen refused to speak, she quickly put it out of her mind. Now, it's the last lead she has. Beck changes into a sundress more appropriate for the humid afternoon and races out of her apartment toward the society's address on Spring Garden Street.

The reading room in the German Society is two stories, with a high ceiling and cherry hardwood floors. A few readers sit at the long, regal tables that line the room. When she walks up to the counter, she expects the librarian to be reading Nietzsche. Instead, he's skimming an Avengers comic.

She hands him the titles of Winkler's books, and he looks up at her with disdain. "You have to be a member of the society to check out books."

"How do you know I'm not one?"

He says something to her in German before returning to his comic.

"Rich, you're going to scare off the natives if you aren't nice to them." Beck turns to see a pale blond guy smiling at her. His eyes are piercingly blue, and his dimples carve crescents into each cheek. She can't help but smile back.

"That's the point," Rich says.

The blond guy takes the piece of paper from Beck and reads the names of Winkler's books aloud. *"Die ungekrönten Habsburger* and *Das Vermächtnis des großen Imperiums."* His eyes grow wide. "Are you studying the Habsburgs?"

"Trying to."

"That's my expertise. Franz Ferdinand, anyway." He hops behind the reference computer to type something, then bounds up to the second floor, returning moments later with the two hardbacks. "The official biographer to Karl," he says, flipping through them. "This Winkler guy is a total sycophant. You can't trust any of this."

278

He reaches into his back pocket for his society identification card and says something to Rich in German. Rich snipes back. Beck tries to decide if she's irritated or charmed — she doesn't need a knight in shining armor, cute as this knight may be.

When he gives her the books, he says, "They're due back in a month. Maybe you should give me your number — you know, just in case I have to track you down."

"Well, if it's just to track me down . . ."

He hands Beck a pen and holds out his palm for her to write her number. It's something she would have done in high school, something she can't believe she's doing now, at thirty-five. His hand is soft, and she fights the urge to rub her cheek against it. Instead, she wraps her fingers around his, closing his fist and locking her number inside. "It's probably best if you give me your number, too. In case I need to renew the books or something."

This comes out clumsy. Beck can feel herself blushing. The dimples in his cheeks deepen as he reaches into his pocket and produces a business card that reads *Christian Fischer, PhD Candidate and Translator.*

As she begins to walk out of the reading room, he calls to her, "I'm Christian."

"I know — it's on your card." She turns back

and smiles, deciding she's indeed charmed. "I'm Beck."

Beck walks into her building to find Tom standing in the hall outside their apartment, his sports coat draped over his arm. Her apartment. Soon to be someone else's. Beck struggles to decipher what his presence means, especially given the frustration on his face.

"You didn't return any of my calls."

Beck reaches into her purse for her phone and sees that she has six missed calls from work. She shrugs as she brushes past him to unlock her door. "I was busy."

She doesn't invite him inside, but he follows her into the apartment, anyway.

"Besides, what's it to you? We aren't working on any cases together right now. It's none of your business if I take the day off." Beck hangs her purse on the coatrack, wondering if he'll follow her into the kitchen as she opens a bottle of wine.

"You didn't take the day off. You just never showed up. Karen was worried. I was worried." Tom hangs his sports coat beside her bag, like he used to when he lived here.

"I don't need you to worry about me," she says as she disappears into the kitchen.

"My apologies for not wanting you to get

fired." Tom sits on the couch with his tie loose, his top two buttons undone, his posture insisting that he's not leaving until she tells him what's going on.

Beck dawdles in the kitchen as she opens a bottle of wine, trying to decide whether she wants him to stay, if she should try to get rid of him. It isn't one of the expensive bottles Tom left. She finished those months ago. When she returns to the living room with two glasses and the cheap bottle, she waits for a snide remark, but he takes it obediently.

"I told Karen you were doing research for me. Please don't make me regret covering for you."

"I didn't ask you to cover for me."

"Jesus, Beck. What the hell is going on? This is shady, even for you."

When they dated, Beck and Tom didn't fight. They had the same neurotically clean living style, no major life changes to navigate. Now, Beck can see that if the fighting had begun, they weren't equipped for it. She was too defensive. He was too self-righteous.

She must be making a wounded face because he immediately looks remorseful. "I didn't mean that. It's just . . . I know Helen's death is hard on you, but your performance at work is lacking. People are starting to notice."

"The FBI were here this morning," Beck admits. She's still not sure she wants to discuss this with Tom, but she needs to defend herself against his accusations on her *performance,* and she's too tired to lie. "About Helen's brooch."

Tom sips his wine as Beck fills him in on everything she knows about the Florentine Diamond.

"So you have no idea how Helen had the diamond?"

"Not even a guess."

Tom reaches for the bottle and pours himself another glass. His legs spread apart as he leans back.

"It's probably a civil forfeiture," Tom decides. "I'll call my friend at the Justice Department tomorrow."

"A civil forfeiture? Like in possession cases?"

"If the government knows a property was involved in a crime but doesn't know who committed the crime, they can seize it, hold on to it until the court determines who it rightly belongs to. It happens with cultural property cases all the time — old coins, paintings, all types of artifacts. You'll get a notice of the complaint, then you can file a claim and answer arguing that it belongs to you."

"Do you think the Italians alerted the feds?"

"Who knows. Whoever did, they must think they have a legitimate claim to the diamond."

"More legitimate than mine." Beck turns away to the corner of the room where Tom used to keep his softball equipment. Tom follows her gaze to the empty corner.

They watch each other until Tom reaches out and tucks a loose piece of hair behind her right ear. As he inches closer, she wants to tell him to stop. When his breath grazes her lips, she cannot find her voice. Her resolve. She shifts toward him until their lips meet and soon they are kissing with more desperation than they ever had before. Tom has always been a measured lover, asking if she's okay so much that she struggles to stay in the moment.

Today, he asks her nothing. He removes his tie, unbuttons his shirt, and pulls off his undershirt, stained with dried sweat. She's forgotten how smooth his chest is, how strong. He holds his body a few inches above hers and searches her face. She waits for him to ask if this is okay, but desire overwhelms him and he pulls her up to undress her. Skin on skin, their bodies meld. It feels less familiar than it should. Already, he has become someone new. But so has she. She pushes him off her and mounts him. This time, it will be on her terms.

ELEVEN

Each evening, Beck checks the mailbox for the notice from the government stating that it has filed its complaint against the Florentine Diamond, even though Tom has told her it can take up to ninety days. She should be thankful for the extra time before the forfeiture case begins. Instead, she's anxious, her patience waning. She hates not knowing what's going to happen.

On the thirteenth day of waiting, she forgets temporarily about the notice. It's a consuming day at work. One of the new associates misses a deadline on discovery and tries to blame it on Beck. It isn't her fault, but it's easier to just apologize and fix his mistake. Besides, the partner on the case knows that Beck would never miss a court deadline. When he thanks Beck, it's obvious the partner understands the situation. This only angers the new associate, and he tells her she better not leave until it's resolved.

The afternoon continues tensely until seven when Beck has finally finished. As she's hurrying toward the elevator, she passes Tom.

"Hey," he says, planting himself in the middle of the hall so she cannot avoid him. "Working late?"

"Yup." Beck tries to squeeze past him. They haven't talked about that night two weeks ago. After they'd finished, they sat back on the couch, panting. It was the best sex they'd had, which made Beck realize how dissatisfying their relationship had been. Tom sighed, satiated, and it disgusted her. The smugness. The assumption that he could sit there for as long as he wanted. Beck found his pants and tossed them to him, saying, "I've got a busy morning tomorrow."

He'd caught his pants, stunned, searching for the right words. "Beck, I —"

"I appreciate you stopping by."

Tom nodded sheepishly and dressed. He probably assumed that she was conflicted over what had happened because she was still in love with him. Normally, this would bother her, but as he darted out, she found she didn't care what he thought.

"Sorry about Steve," Tom says, still blocking the hall to the elevator. He means the new associate, who gave her a hard time about the deadline. "He's a dick."

"He's a lawyer," Beck teases, and Tom laughs too hard. The tension is palpable. They are the only ones in the office and Beck fears he might kiss her.

"Want to grab a drink?" he asks.

"I need to get home. It's been a long day."

He continues to block the hallway, and Beck can feel herself growing irritated. "Any updates on the complaint?"

Beck shakes her head no.

"Get ready," Tom says, awkwardly squeezing her shoulder before heading back to his office.

On the bus, Beck replays their brief encounter in the hall, pleased at how indifferent she was. It wasn't an act. She really is over him. As she gets off at her stop and walks toward her apartment, her mind drifts to Christian, the blond boy from the German Society. He hasn't called her, which surprises her. He'd been so forward. Then again, she hasn't called him, either.

On her stoop, three men dressed sloppily in shorts and T-shirts are discussing the Phillies' pitching staff. She's about to tell them that it's private property when they stand and ask her if she's Rebecca Miller.

Before she can answer, their questions bombard her.

"Ms. Miller, can you tell us about the diamond you found in your grandmother's possessions?"

"Do you know how your grandmother acquired the Florentine Diamond?"

"Is your grandmother a thief?"

"Ms. Miller, how do you feel about your grandmother being one of the world's most elusive jewelry thieves?"

Beck pushes past them and heads inside, checking her mailbox. She's distracted, focused on the three men on her stoop and what they called Helen — a thief. It's their job, this line of inquiry, and she doesn't fault them for it. But Helen was not a thief. Even if Helen didn't come by the diamond honestly, she didn't steal it.

Her attention refocuses when she spots a letter from the government. The notice. That must be how the reporters found out, since it's also published online. Beck slides her finger beneath the adhesive and removes the paper from the envelope.

EASTERN DISTRICT OF PENNSYLVANIA
137.27-carat yellow diamond, valued at $3,000,000, seized by the FBI on May 17 from Rebecca Miller in Philadelphia, PA, for forfeiture pursuant to 18 USC 2254.

Along with a copy of the public notice of the forfeiture, the government has included a copy of the complaint filed with the court. The civil forfeiture case now has a name: *United States of America v. One 137.27-Carat Yellow Diamond Known as the Florentine Diamond.* The details in the complaint surprise Beck. She was expecting to read about a Medici heirloom, belonging to the Italian government. Instead, the complaint mentions the Austrian crown jewels, that the diamond is the national patrimony of Austria, taken unlawfully to the United States. That means the Austrians, not the Italians, alerted the US government to the diamond's whereabouts. Beck curses Ashley and her fair-weathered friend, Georgina. If only her sister had been as tightlipped about the diamond as she had her husband's indiscretions, the FBI might not have seized the diamond.

Not that the FBI physically seized the diamond. It's still in the safe-deposit box at Federalist Bank. It constructively seized it. When Tom called his contact at the Department of Justice, he'd convinced the DOJ to have the bank change the lock on the box and leave the diamond in the vault. Generally, third-party custodians are a bad idea because they end up spending seized money or running away with it, but this is one of the most reputable banks in America. Besides, it's not like the US Marshall Service wants a historic diamond in its possession.

The first thing Beck does is file a claim and answer. She does not need a lawyer for this. It's simple enough.

> *Claim:* The 137.27-carat diamond seized by the federal government belongs to me because I inherited it from my grandmother.
>
> *Answer:* The government's contention that the diamond was illegally taken from Austria is inaccurate because it never belonged to the Austrian government.

Even if it was an Austrian heirloom, that didn't necessarily make it the property of Austria's government. It belonged to the Habsburg Empire, which disbanded. It was debatable whether the diamond subsequently should have been handed over to the first Austrian Republic that rose in its wake. The new government had established a law, mandating all crown property be transferred to the state. But the republic only lasted fifteen years before it was overtaken by fascist leaders, then the Nazis. There's no reason to assume it belongs to the current government. It's the best answer she can come up with, even if it doesn't assert the diamond is hers. For that, she needs more proof. So, she revisits the only viable leads she has, as unpromising as they may be.

Any luck with that maker's mark? she writes to Viktor.

My dear, desperation doesn't suit you.

Embarrassed, she drafts and erases several texts until he writes her again. I'm teasing. It's tedious. But I'll find it.

If Viktor is finding her desperate, Peter Winkler, a total stranger, must think she's a complete lunatic. Still, she writes him again, vowing to herself that if he doesn't respond this time, she'll give up the fruitless quest. Besides, his father's personal Habsburg collection is a long shot at best. Probably just a shoebox of double-headed eagle pins, newspaper clippings, and vanity interviews with the last empress.

With or without the memorabilia, she does have Kurt Winkler's books detailing the fall of the empire, the royal family in exile. They could contain a clue about what happened to the diamond. And she has Christian's business card in her wallet, which lists his services as a translator. She needed to hire a translator, anyway, and it may as well be one with dimples and crisp blue eyes. She dials his number, growing tense as she waits for him to pick up.

He answers like he was expecting her call. It puts her off guard, so she awkwardly dispenses with any small talk and launches into her offer to have him translate the books.

"How soon do you need them?" Christian asks.

"Like yesterday."

She waits for him to ask why, uncertain whether she'll tell him the truth.

"Let's meet for a drink tonight, and you can give me the books. We'll go over the table of contents to see what's most important. If it's only a few chapters and you don't care about things like typos, I can get it to you in a couple of weeks."

"Typos are fine." She cringes. Beck cares deeply about things like typos.

"It's a date," Christian says, and Beck feels a flurry of excitement until she remembers the journalists outside. She'll have to walk past them to meet Christian. She'll have to hear them call Helen a thief. But she has to see Christian, she tells herself. Right now, the books are the only lead she has.

■ ■ ■ ■

Jake rattles the box of chocolates as he sits in the lobby of the Reseda retirement home, waiting for Mr. Frankel. Jake has no idea if Mr. Frankel is lucid and, if he is, how much he remembers from his trip to America. He was only eight when he came over on the SS *President Harding.* But Jake suspects that being relocated to a new country isn't something you forget, regardless of age.

Restless, he grabs a brochure from the table beside him, reading about the Jewish assisted living community. Jake peers down at the chocolates in his lap. They are not kosher. He debates hiding them under the chair when he spots a nurse helping a man with a walker toward the lobby. He's dressed, like old people often are, in clothes too heavy for the warm weather. The man beams at him, and Jake can tell that Mr. Frankel wouldn't care if Jake had brought bacon, he's so happy to have a visitor. This hits Jake with a different sort of guilt. He didn't lie to the nurse about why he wanted to see Mr. Frankel; he didn't divulge any specifics, either.

The nurse suggests Jake take Mr. Frankel to the rose garden, which Mr. Frankel tells him blooms year-round. "I don't know how they do it. My roses were always dormant, even in summer. Somehow —" Mr. Frankel leans against the walker and uses his free hand to gesture across the expanse of yellow, white, pink, and red petals "— it's always a sea of colors here. Are those for me?" Mr. Frankel eyes the box of chocolates Jake is holding.

"They aren't kosher."

"Won't have to share them with the others, then."

They find a bench and Jake helps Mr. Frankel rip the plastic off the box. Mr. Frankel scans the chocolates, debating which one to eat first.

"So, my boy, tell me about yourself," Mr. Frankel says.

"I'm a screenwriter." Jake can't remember the last time he introduced himself this way. "Don't worry, that's not why I'm here."

"Why not? We'd make a good TV show. Half the home is old Hollywood."

"Did you work in the industry?"

Mr. Frankel bites down on a square chocolate, caramel oozing down his chin. "I was a dentist." He wipes the caramel, then licks his fingers. "So, I imagine there's a reason you came to see me, other than to hear about my dental career."

"I think you knew my grandmother, Helen

294

Auerbach."

Mr. Frankel searches his memory for the name, and just before he comes up empty, Jake adds, "From Vienna?"

"I haven't heard that name in a long time." He sighs dramatically. "We were very lucky. Although it didn't always feel that way. I was glad to have my sister with me. I don't know how the others did it, coming alone."

Mr. Frankel reaches into his back pocket for his handkerchief. Jake worries he's about to cry, but the old man uses it to wipe sweat from his brow. "What did Helen tell you about our journey?"

A journey, like it was an adventure. That was probably how the Goldsteins and the children's parents presented it to them.

"Nothing. Helen never even mentioned it," Jake admits. "She told us stories about Vienna but only happy memories."

"It goes one of two ways. My family talked about it. It was easier for us. My sister and I came over together, and my parents were able to emigrate after the war. Helen wasn't so lucky. Talking helped us, but I could see how it wouldn't help everyone."

"I wish she'd told us. I wish we could have helped her."

Mr. Frankel pats Jake's knee. "You're helping her now."

His voice is steady, almost as though he's telling Jake a bedtime story.

"I was one of the younger ones in our group. There was another boy who was five, a girl who was six, then me at eight. Most of the others were around ten. And then there was Helen. She was fourteen, if I remember correctly." Jake nods. "Whew, your grandmother was something. She could put you in your place like that." Mr. Frankel snaps his fingers.

"I'm well acquainted with that." Jake laughs. Being with Mr. Frankel makes Jake wish he'd had a grandfather. His sisters have updated him on Deborah's hunt for her father. Until this moment, he hadn't paid much attention.

"She was always nice to me and my sister, but the other kids, there was this one wiseass on our trip." Mr. Frankel purses his lips as he tries to remember the boy's name.

"Edmund Schneider?" Jake guesses, remembering the name from *My Grandmother and the Other 49 Children.* Edmund had switched the keys to the cabins and stole underwear from the girls' luggage. For the last twenty years of his life, he was imprisoned in North Carolina.

"That's the one. He was always up to something. I guess he got into your grandmother's stuff. She had this doll she always carried with an apron on it, and Edmund slipped a piece

296

of pickled herring into the pocket of the apron. Your grandmother didn't notice until it started to rot, and by then, phew, was she mad. So she gets her hands on two filets of herring and waits until they're good and ripe. She wakes Edmund in the middle of the night, sits on his chest until he's eaten every last bite of that rotten fish. Of course Edmund ran crying to the Goldsteins. They got into it with your grandmother. After that, Edmund didn't play any more tricks on any of us kids again." Mr. Frankel puts the lid on the chocolates and rests the box beside him.

"Is that why the Goldsteins didn't get along with Helen?" Jake remembers Ashley saying something about how Helen clashed with Irvin Goldstein.

Mr. Frankel shakes his head. "That couldn't have helped, but I remember something about a diamond, when we were stopped over in England."

Jake's back straightens.

"I never knew the whole story. Helen had some square diamond that her mother gave her. When we docked in England, she tried to trade it to the father of one of the other kids, who was displaced there. He came aboard to see his son, and she's begging him to help her mother escape. When Mr. Goldstein found out, he was furious."

"How'd she get the diamond past the Nazis?" Jake asks.

Mr. Frankel shrugs. "The inspectors checked our luggage. And the Goldsteins were very clear that we couldn't take anything beyond the pittance the Nazis allowed. One misstep and the Nazis could have changed their mind and not let us leave. I still can't decide if that was very stupid or very brave of her."

"Probably both," Jake says, and Mr. Frankel nods in agreement. "And you're sure it was a square diamond? We have this family heirloom — an egg-shaped yellow diamond. I'm trying to figure out if that's what you mean, if Helen brought it with her from Vienna."

Mr. Frankel reopens the box of chocolates. "I remember it being square. And it wasn't yellow. It looked like a piece of glass. I couldn't figure out why they were making such a fuss over it." Realizing he's already eaten half the chocolates, Mr. Frankel closes the box and pushes it toward the end of the bench.

The diamond Mr. Frankel describes doesn't sound like the Florentine. Besides, if Mr. Goldstein found the Florentine, that would have erupted into a larger scandal. Still, it feels ominous, revelatory. Helen brought a diamond to the US. Where there was one diamond there may have been more.

The nurse finds them in the garden, frowning when she sees the box of chocolates. Mr. Frankel bats his eyes at her.

"Time for dinner. Is your friend joining us?"

Jake is about to refuse, but Mr. Frankel tells him he'd like that very much.

"Like I said. We're good fodder," Mr. Frankel says, holding on to Jake as they walk toward the dining room. "You can't make characters like these up."

"Don't worry," Jake assures him. "I won't write about your friends."

Mr. Frankel stops, still holding Jake's arm. "Oh, you must. If we don't tell stories, they disappear. You must write everything. You must keep us alive."

At his apartment, Jake finds Kristi on the couch. The television is off. Her book lays closed on the coffee table. Light from the table lamp illuminates the profile of her troubled face.

"Sorry I'm so late," he says, kissing her cheek. He left her a message and texted, but he doesn't try to argue his case.

On the coffee table beside her mystery novel, his computer is open, the screen black. Jake doesn't remember leaving it there. He closes it before sitting on the couch next to Kristi. She doesn't look at him, even when he takes her foot and begins rubbing her arch. He racks his brain for what might be wrong. Their next checkup isn't for another two weeks. It's not her birthday or their anniversary.

As he continues to rub her foot, he tries to act normal even though his heart is racing. She must have found out about Trader Joe's, that he's been lying for almost a month and a half. What can he say? He didn't mean to lie, it just happened. It just happened? What kind of bullshit excuse was that? Does it make any difference that he now knows, at least in part, what his script is about? After his conversation with Mr. Frankel, he can picture Helen's voyage to the US, and now that he can envision it, he can commit it to scene. Does it help that, in six months, he's confident he'll have his script completed? That he knows it will sell, and when it does, Trader Joe's and the man in the leather jacket will all be a distant memory, maybe even a funny anecdote?

Kristi winces as he accidentally digs his thumb too deeply into her arch and jerks her foot free of his hand.

"I wasn't trying to snoop," she begins as though she's the one who should apologize.

"Kris, I can explain. I didn't mean to —"

She cuts him off. "My computer died and I really needed to pay my credit card, so I used yours. I wasn't spying on you."

Did Randy email? One of his other co-workers, asking how he was holding up?

"You can use my computer whenever you want, you know that. I'm the one who screwed up, not you."

Something inside Kristi snaps. "I asked you not to, Jake. I asked you not to write about my mother."

It takes Jake a few moments to realize she means the script he started outlining about Mrs. Zhang's escape from China. Jake almost laughs, he's so surprised. All this over some script he didn't even write? A partial outline that would never see the outside of the Bad Ideas folder?

"It's not funny," Kristi says. "What, you can't ruin your family any more than you already have, so you thought you'd have a go at mine?"

Jake's done worse, made stupider, more damaging decisions, but he sees this one cuts to the core of something he doesn't understand.

"Kris, I never wrote it. I outlined a few scenes, then realized it was a bad idea. Look," he says, reaching for his computer. The cursor hovers over the folder that holds the script. "I put it in a folder that's literally called Bad Ideas." He opens the folder and there are more partial scripts than he remembers, at least a dozen PDFs full of fleeting, delusional promise. It embarrasses him to show her this, like he's exposing his browser history or skid marks on his boxers. "There's one about Rico, and another about my boss's grandma, who was a secretary for Al Capone, and this one, that's my old roommate. His dad had two families. They're all stupid, idiotic ideas that will never see the light of day."

She stares at him in disbelief. "That's supposed to make me feel better, that you're mining everyone in your life for stories?"

"That's what being a writer is." Jake is genuinely confused.

"You think Rico wants *you* to write about his mother's immigration? You think your coworker wants *you* to write about her sister's muscular dystrophy?" Jake had never told Kristi about Sadie, and he realizes she's read every abandoned script, all thirteen in the Bad Ideas folder.

"I'm not doing anything with them."

"That's *so* beside the point." Kristi starts pacing and Jake worries the commotion is bad for the baby. "What really gets me is that you actually assumed you understood what my mother went through. *I* don't even understand. But you, you have one conversation over king crab and suddenly you're an expert?"

"I write because I want to understand."

Kristi's laugh is cruel. "I forgot you were the next Steven Spielberg. Do you know what it meant to my mom to share her story with you? Do you know what it meant to me that she trusted you with it?"

Jake hops off the couch and catches Kristi in the middle of the room. "I was trying to honor her."

"She didn't tell you because she wanted you to share it with the world."

"But if we don't tell stories they disappear." These words sounded so right when Mr. Frankel said them. Why do they sound so disingenuous now?

"Getting them wrong is worse."

Jake knows he should be focused on what he can say to make Kristi feel better, but her words drain the energy from his body. *Getting them wrong is worse.* She'd always believed in his writing before.

"Nothing?" Kristi asks when he's been silent too long. "You really have nothing to say?"

"I'm sorry." He is sorry. Sorry for so much more than their current fight. He's sorry for not telling her about his firing from Trader Joe's, the diamond. He's sorry he's stunted, emotionally and professionally. He's sorry he's become the ghost of the man she fell for. He's sorry that she ever fell in love with him, that she feels bound to him when she deserves better.

She shakes her head before she walks down the hall, slamming the bedroom door behind her.

Jake stays on the couch, unsure what just happened. He finds the outline he's begun on Helen and, instead of adding the scenes he'd envisioned while talking to Mr. Frankel, he moves Helen's outline to the Bad Ideas folder. He drags the Bad Ideas folder to the trash, then opens the trash folder, the cursor blinking on Empty. He can hear Kristi stomping around their bedroom. The cursor continues to blink. Instead of clicking to permanently delete the folder, he moves the folder back to his desktop. He isn't ready to have those scripts vanish. Not completely.

"And you're sure it was a different diamond?" Beck asks Jake through the iPad screen. "Mr. Frankel is certain the diamond Helen had on board wasn't the Florentine?"

"I didn't ask him if it was a famous missing diamond, no. He said it was square. And clear. He seemed pretty positive about that."

Jake doesn't want to be on a FaceTime call with his sisters. He has a headache and needs this horrible day to be over. He leans back on the couch, his home for the foreseeable future.

"What's wrong?" Ashley asks from her iPad in her bedroom in Westchester, noticing Jake's despondence. "Did you and Kristi have a fight?"

"I don't want to talk about it."

Ashley hears Ryan banging around in the kitchen below. Since his company banned him from its premises, he has discovered a passion for cooking. In the mornings, he whisks batter for pancakes and Belgian waffles. In the evenings, he dons an apron and roasts chicken, bakes macaroni and cheese. Ashley has never seen Ryan in an apron. She didn't know he was so adept with a whisk. If the children are curious why their father is home to prepare both breakfast and dinner, they do not show it. Each night, they shout requests for the following day's meals.

Earlier that afternoon, Ashley had announced to Ryan that she planned to go back to work. She approached him in the kitchen, while he was blending a marinade for skirt steak. She wasn't asking his permission, and she braced herself for a fight. The

305

children were at school, so she and Ryan could yell as loudly as they wanted, use whatever choice language suited the occasion. Ashley leaned against the kitchen island, preparing for his response, but Ryan had just said, "Okay," as he poured the marinade over the steak. She goaded him, feeding him opportunities to tell her what a challenging job she already had as a mom, that familiar refrain of how it was his mess to clean up. Instead, he told her, "I think that's a great idea. Any company would be lucky to have you," and wandered into the living room to watch baseball. His immediate support didn't quell her desire for a fight. So, she followed him into the living room where his full attention was on the batter at the plate. She stood behind the couch, watching him, waiting for him to say something, anything, so she could pounce. He didn't look back at her, but eventually he said, "You have my full support on this, okay?" She continued to linger, until he reiterated, "Seriously, Ash. I should have encouraged you to go back a long time ago. I'm sorry I didn't. I want this for you." While her anger persisted, it lessened ever so slightly as she realized he was sincere.

The clanging downstairs stops, and Ashley knows that Ryan will soon knock on the door, waiting for permission to enter his own bedroom. He's still sleeping on the pile of blankets on the floor, but as long as they continue to share a room, as long as he supports her decision to work, whatever else happens, they will survive this. Despite her mentioning the D-word, Ashley still isn't ready to give up on him.

"Best advice I can give you is to sort it out before the baby comes. You'll have plenty to fight about then," Ashley tells her brother.

"I said I don't want to talk about it."

"Anyway, Mr. Frankel was just a kid at the time," Beck says, and for once, Jake is thankful for her disinterest in his life. "He wouldn't have known what he saw."

"If it was the Florentine, wouldn't that Goldstein guy have made a big deal about it? It would have gotten out."

"It could mean . . ." Beck turns her attention toward Ashley's side of the screen.

"The hatpin?" Ashley says to Beck.

"It would explain how she had another diamond."

"God, and she was trying to use it to try to save her mother. That's heartbreaking."

Jake's inability to speak in half-thoughts with his sisters appears yet another way he doesn't understand women. "What's a hat-pin?"

"A pin for hats," Beck says deadpan. Jake rolls his eyes. "For a crown, in this instance. When the Florentine disappeared in 1918, it was set in a hatpin with several other diamonds. Helen's brooch wasn't made until the 1950s, so it's possible Helen brought over the whole hatpin and reset the Florentine in the brooch years later."

"The diamond could have been from anywhere, though. Why would you assume it was from the hatpin?"

Beck sighs. "Aren't you supposed to be the storyteller?"

"It's a reach."

"It's a hypothesis. One, obviously, that requires proving. Trust me, I wouldn't jump to conclusions."

"No, Beck Miller would never dare make assumptions."

"Look, just because you're having some issue with your girlfriend, which I'm assuming is your fault, doesn't mean —"

"Did Mr. Frankel have any idea where Helen may have hid the diamond?" Ashley interjects, trying to head off the impending fight.

Jake shrugs. "He said their bags were inspected pretty thoroughly."

"Did he tell you anything else about Helen?" Ashley asks.

"Just that she wouldn't let anyone push her around."

"We already knew that."

"She got into it with Mr. Goldstein and some kid who put rotten fish in her doll."

Ashley laughs. "I bet that kid learned never to mess with Helen."

"Wait, go back," Beck says. "Someone put fish in her doll?"

"In its apron or something," Jake says dismissively.

"The doll," Beck says excitedly to Ashley.

"You think?"

"It's, what, this big?" Jake watches Beck spread her hands about a foot apart. "It'd be big enough to fit the hatpin. And the body was firm, so you wouldn't be able to feel it."

"Can someone please tell me what you're talking about?" Jake asks.

"Helen's doll. The one in her archival box. She used to carry it around everywhere with her," Beck says.

"So you think . . . what?" Jake asks.

"I bet it's hollow inside."

Deborah lies in bed, her birth certificate resting on the pillow beside her. It's only nine o'clock, but her body is fatigued. Sore. It's been months since she's been touched, sexually or medicinally. She needs to start dating again. She needs to find a new acupuncturist, too, preferably one who doesn't have a lustrous ponytail and a mischievous smile. Deborah's always had an active dating life. She likes skin, nakedness, sex. Right now, she'd crave any distraction. The two glasses of wine she's drank have only made her feel more dejected. She needed the first glass to work up the courage to open the envelope from the Pennsylvania Department of Health. The second to grapple with the disappointment that her birth certificate didn't tell her who her father was.

All of the information on the birth certificate she could have filled out herself. Date of birth: February 12, 1952; County of birth: Philadelphia; Mother's maiden name: Helen Auerbach. Deborah's own name: Deborah Flora Auerbach. On the line for father's name: just the cream-colored background of the certificate.

Deborah Flora Auerbach. It had never struck her as odd that she shared her mother's maiden name. Helen always told her daughter that her marriage had been so brief she'd never felt like Helen Klein. She'd wanted to carry on her family's name, so she'd changed their surname back to Auerbach after Joseph died. That, too, was a lie. Helen had always been Helen Auerbach. Deborah had always been Deborah Flora Auerbach until she became Deborah Auerbach Miller. After Kenny left, she'd wanted to change her name back, but the paperwork had been so daunting and, at that time, even getting out of bed was too much for her. Deborah reaches for the birth certificate and rips it in half. For now, she'd rather bear Kenny's surname than Helen's, but she wishes that she'd kept Flora as her middle name, that she could feel more connected to her grandmother.

Her phone rings from across the room. Dazed and a little tipsy, she stumbles toward it.

"You know that doll?" Beck asks as soon as Deborah answers. "Helen's? The one from Austria? I need you to see if it's hollow inside."

The doll rests on the dresser where Deborah has kept it since they found it in the archival box.

"Hollow?" Deborah asks. Hollow like her childhood, like the pit of her stomach, like Helen's lies. Deborah squeezes the doll. "It's firm. I can't tell."

311

"Cut it open."

Deborah really doesn't want to deal with this right now. As she starts to ask if they can do this later, Beck cuts her off. "I need you to do this now, okay?"

She has that Beck Miller bossiness in her voice, a tone that Deborah has always hated. For the moment, however, she likes being told what to do.

In the kitchen, she finds a knife and slices an incision down the back of the doll's soft body. Inside, the cavity is dark and hollow.

"Can you see anything inside?" Beck asks.

Deborah tugs the sides until they spread an inch apart. From the blackness, something catches the overhead light. She tips the doll over and three round diamonds tumble into her palm.

TWELVE

Beck and Deborah step into the elevator and watch the numbers ascend toward Viktor's apartment. Beck hasn't seen Viktor in two and a half months, since he received the IGS color diamond grading report. So much has changed in that time — the weekly FaceTime conversations with her siblings, the dinners with her mother, the details they'd uncovered about Helen's journey with the other children to America, the existence of a secret lover who may have been Deborah's father.

"The penthouse," Deborah says, impressed. Since Deborah found the diamonds in the doll, she hasn't let them out of her sight. While she doesn't fight her children when they tell her they must sell the diamonds to pay a lawyer to represent them in the civil forfeiture, she insists on being involved.

The elevator stops on the top floor. Beck

turns to her mother. "Please don't embarrass me."

"I'll keep all premonitions to myself."

"I'm serious. Don't do anything. Don't say anything. You're silent."

Deborah uses her fingers to lock her lips.

When the apartment door opens, a dapper, white-haired man offers both Miller women glasses of champagne. He's wearing black cashmere, which strikes Deborah as both odd and pretentious. It's eighty degrees outside and drizzling. Who does this guy think he is?

"Beck, you didn't tell me you were bringing your sister," he says before Beck has a chance to introduce her.

Deborah frowns. Flirting this obvious is a form of pity.

"I'm her mother," she tells him as she reaches for a glass of champagne, dismayed when Viktor takes this as an invitation to wink at her.

In his living room, Viktor rests the diamonds on a piece of black velvet. They appear completely translucent against the dark, luscious fabric.

"They're high quality," Viktor confirms. "About three carats each. They look like D quality, but we'd have to send them to the lab to be sure."

314

"That means they're flawless," Beck explains to her mother, who, as promised, hasn't uttered a word since they sat down.

"You're learning." Viktor smiles at Beck. He has perfect teeth. Too perfect. Probably a Scorpio, Deborah decides. Kenny was a Scorpio.

"Can you tell when they're from?" Beck asks Viktor.

"They're definitely vintage." He holds one of the diamonds between his thumb and index finger. "You see how it's a circle with facets? No one cuts diamonds this way anymore."

"We found these in my grandmother's things. Could they have been set in the hatpin?"

It takes Deborah a moment to realize that Beck means the piece that held the Florentine Diamond before the brooch. Viktor holds his breath as he twists the diamonds in his hand. Deborah can see he's drawing it out, gaining authority by making them wait.

"Could be." He pulls a black hardback book on diamonds from the shelves. It falls open to the page with an image of the hatpin. Viktor traces an arc of small circular diamonds along the top of the pin with his pinky. He's wearing a ring with a round diamond at its center, faceted to shimmer in any light. "It's difficult to tell the scale. They could very well be some of the round diamonds here."

"Is there any way to tell for certain?" Deborah hears herself asking. Beck glares at her, but Viktor looks pleased by the interruption.

"I want you to study this diamond very closely," he says, dropping one of the diamonds into her hand. She studies it perfunctorily, then gives it back to him. Along with the other two diamonds, he rolls it onto the velvet like dice. "I will buy you dinner at Le Bec Fin if you can tell me which one is your diamond."

Le Bec Fin hasn't been open for years, not that Deborah ever went there. Deborah lifts one diamond, then another, until all three are resting in her palm, clear as droplets of water against her skin. They are perfectly round, bigger than the diamond she owned years ago. Or thought she owned. When she went to sell her engagement ring, she discovered the diamond Kenny had given her was really cubic zirconia, the white gold in fact silver. "But my husband said it was gold," Deborah had protested to the dealer. "I'll give you thirty-five for it," he said. *"Hundred?"* Deborah asked hopefully.

He looked at her, his face cast in pity as he reached into the register and placed a fifty-dollar bill on the counter. "You aren't the first wife I've had in here," he told her.

The three diamonds in her palm look the same, yet she's positive that the one on the right is the stone she held before. She drops the other two onto the velvet, holding the last diamond in her palm toward Viktor. "This one."

"You're sure?" he asks.

"I'm sure." Its energy feels calmer than the other two, more familiar, but she knows she can't tell them this. "Am I right?"

"I don't know." Viktor smiles coyly. Deborah looks between him and her daughter, irritated.

"He's teasing you. These diamonds are all the same cut and flawless. That means they're absolutely perfect. There's nothing unique or different about them, no imperfections. It's impossible to tell them apart, let alone identify them."

"So, can you sell them or not?" Deborah asks Viktor, embarrassed. Although he is strikingly handsome, she finds him repulsive. Definitely a Scorpio.

"Well." Viktor raises his eyebrows, seemingly calculating a price. Ever the salesman, Deborah thinks. They are about to get swindled. "No one wants this cut anymore, so whomever we sell them to, they'll want to recut them. That will probably scale them down from three carats to two and a half. So we'll have to sell them that way." He keeps pretending to do the math. "Then if we account for the time and cost to cut, plus the fact that you don't have paperwork for them . . . I know a few people who might be interested. Not at market value, of course."

Deborah has to bite the insides of her cheeks to keep from asking what's his cut.

"Whatever you can get," Beck says.

"For my favorite lawyer, I will do my best."

"Viktor, you know I'm not a lawyer," Beck says bashfully.

"Right. You're too trustworthy."

Bile rises in Deborah's throat as her daughter blushes.

In the elevator, Deborah can feel Beck seething. Her stomach drops as the elevator descends, and she wishes she hadn't had that second glass of bubbly.

"What the hell was that?" Beck asks.

"What?" Deborah says defensively.

"Viktor is my friend."

"A man old enough to be your father is your *friend*?"

"Not everyone has an ulterior motive."

318

Oh, but they do.

When they get outside, Beck opens an umbrella even though it's barely raining and motions in the opposite direction of the Red Rabbit. "I've got to go meet the translator."

"Come on, Becca. I didn't mean to cause any trouble."

"You never do."

"What did I do that was so terrible? Explain it to me."

"You didn't trust me."

"I didn't trust Viktor."

"It's the same thing."

Deborah watches her daughter walk away. She wants to chase after her, to wrap her in her arms and ask her why she has to make everything difficult. Beck is a Cancer. Born to be sensitive. She's never learned to tame her emotions. Until she does, she'll never learn to be truly happy.

Ryan pulls up to the train station, double-parking beside the stairs to the platform. He's wearing mesh shorts that Ashley hates and a faded NYU Law T-shirt. The irony is not lost on either of them, not of the provenance of the T-shirt nor the fact that Ashley is about to take the train to the city while Ryan will return home to prepare dinner.

"You're going to do great," Ryan says,

motioning her out of the car. Ever since she told him her plan to put out feelers to her old contacts, he's been wholeheartedly supportive, almost too supportive. It makes her want to instigate a fight, but she resists this instinct. Ryan, for all his faults, has always been straightforward. If he says it's a good idea, it's because he thinks it is. If he assures her she'll do great, it's because he knows she will, even if she isn't so certain herself.

"Let's hope so." Ashley unbuckles her seat belt and steps into the sticky morning. Before she shuts the door, she reminds Ryan, "Tyler has practice at the batting cage today and Lydia's flute lesson starts at four. Oh, and I keep forgetting to pick up your dry cleaning. They have the credit card on file, so you don't need —"

"Ash, I got this. Go kill it." Ryan flashes her his rehearsed smile, and she almost believes it. She wishes she hadn't mentioned his dry cleaning, the suits that he no longer needs to wear.

She leans into the car, grabs a leather tote she hasn't used in ten years, and gives him a quick peck before racing to the train. Her interview isn't until eleven, but Ashley wants to be downtown by ten to review her talking points over a cup of mint tea. She knows her former assistant, Stella, is taking this informational meeting as a courtesy. She also knows that she can walk out of an informational interview with an offer. At least, she used to be able to. Now, only time will tell.

When Ashley rushes out of the building in Tribeca, the embarrassment hits her all at once. She actually thought of Stella as a friend, someone she'd groomed and trusted. Stella had been at her wedding, for crying out loud. And today, today Stella didn't even invite her up to the office. No, they met in the café downstairs where, every few minutes, Stella had glanced at her watch. She didn't tell Ashley it would be an uphill battle, finding a job. She didn't offer her any contacts who might be hiring. Instead, Stella just said, "Good for you, getting back into the work force. But then, you've always been brave." Somehow, brave didn't sound like a compliment.

Ashley stumbles south, unsure where she's headed. She isn't ready to go back to Westchester, to have Ryan pick her up, his eyes sparkling as he asks her how it went, genuinely assuming it couldn't have gone anything less than great. He'll offer her some words of encouragement that will anger her, and they will fight in the car at the train station because Lydia and Tyler are home and they have vowed not to argue in front of the children. She isn't ready for all that, so she just keeps walking until she reaches Battery Park.

It's early June, and her pencil skirt sticks to her thighs. Sweat darkens the satin blouse that she really shouldn't have worn on such a humid day. She leans against the railing where she has a clear view of the Statue of Liberty and Ellis Island in the distance. Was the Statue of Liberty Helen's first sight of America? In all their researching, the Millers haven't bothered to look up where in New York her boat landed. Ashley's feet are killing her, so she removes her right heel to stretch her swollen toes. When she lived in Manhattan, she could have run a marathon in stilettos. When she lived in Manhattan, Stella wouldn't have dared treat her the way she did today. Ashley wouldn't have permitted it. She turns away from the gray water to look at her former city. Now, she allows all sorts of things her past self would have forbidden. She allows her husband to waste his days baking. She allows her daughter to be confused and worried, her son to be blissfully unaware. She allows herself to be defeated.

A few blocks away, a hexagonal granite building stands out from the skyscrapers that surround it. Concrete horizontal louvers comprise the roof, narrowing in a triangular pattern. It's stunning, not that Ashley knows anything about architecture. Still, she finds herself gravitating toward the stoic building.

It feels like fate when she sees the museum's name in white letters across the mirrored entrance: Museum of Jewish Heritage. In the lobby, the metal detector beeps when she tries to walk through. It's the metal in her heels that she can barely walk in. After she passes through the detector without alarm, she takes the elevator to the second floor. The museum isn't a heritage museum so much as a Holocaust memorial, filled with posters in opposition to the Nazis, photographs and videos of survivors. She watches a recording of a woman who describes her time at Dachau as a girl. Helen's family — Ashley's — had been sent to Dachau, too.

A hunched woman with curled white hair approaches. "Do you have any questions?" She introduces herself as a docent. "It's my job to answer your questions. Anything you want to know."

Being a docent isn't a job. Rather, it's the kind of job Ashley always imagined she'd have, one that gave her a sense of worth if not money.

"Why don't we know more?" What Ashley means is, *Why don't I know more?* — more about her family that died at Dachau, more about Helen, more about Judaism. Her children don't even light a menorah at Hanukkah. She knows the candles represent the light that burned for eight days, but she doesn't know who lit those candles, why they didn't have more oil. While the men in Helen's family — her father, Leib, and brother, Martin — were sent to Dachau, Ashley has no idea what happened to Helen's mother, Flora.

The docent smiles at her, evidently used to opaque questions.

"My grandmother escaped Austria," Ashley continues. "Her brother and father were sent to Dachau. We never learned what happened to her mother."

"The Holocaust Memorial Museum in DC has all sorts of records for people who died during the war. Have you tried there?" Ashley admits that she hasn't. "It's alarmingly easy. You just type her name into their database online, and if they have information on her, it will pop up."

From a bench in the park, Ashley pulls up the website for the Holocaust Memorial Museum in DC and follows instructions to

324

its online database. The search form asks for background information she doesn't have on Flora: year of birth, maiden name, prisoner number, death place. She types in Flora's name, then hesitates before clicking the search button. If she finds Flora, she won't be able to un-find her. Once she discovers what happened to her grandmother, she will have to tell the Millers. After that, they will forever know their great-grandmother's fate.

Only one hit for Flora Auerbach appears in the results, and Ashley is surprised she could find her great-grandmother so quickly. Helen had looked for years and never found anything. The website explains that most of the information on survivors and victims wasn't available until the 2000s. By then, Helen must have assumed the window for learning what had happened to her mother had long passed.

Ashley reads the results.

Birth date: 1898
Birth place: Wien
Source: Registry of names of the Lichtenburg Concentration Camp Prisoners List, April 1939
Source: Transport lists to Ravensbrück Concentration Camp, May 1939

Ashley doesn't remember the exact date Helen's train left Vienna for Berlin or when the SS *President Harding* set sail from Hamburg to New York. It was sometime in April 1939. While Helen was traveling to a new life, Flora was traveling toward her death.

First, Ashley clicks on the link to the Lichtenburg Concentration Camp Prisoners List, because Flora could not have died at Lichtenburg if she was transferred to Ravensbrück. She isn't ready to click on the Ravensbrück link where Flora may very well have died. It doesn't matter, anyway. The lists aren't online, only descriptions of the sources and their sponsors. Momentarily, Ashley feels relieved that she cannot discover Flora's death so quickly. Then the relief is replaced with burden: she must find out. She promised Deborah. Helen spent her entire life not knowing what happened to her mother. Ashley owes it to them to discover the truth, no matter how painful. She opens an email and writes to the museum archivist, asking how she can access copies of the records of victims who were transported from Lichtenburg to Ravensbrück.

Two weeks. Jake didn't really believe that

Kristi would stay mad at him, but here he is, two weeks later, waiting alone in the lobby at Good Samaritan while Kristi has her checkup. She's granted him reentry into their bedroom, begrudgingly, always pretending to fall asleep while he's brushing his teeth. He can't remember the last time they cuddled, let alone had sex. He isn't even allowed up to the obstetrician's office. At least he's in the building. Now, it's a matter of finding the right way to make her forgive him.

He drums his thumb against his thigh as he decides what to say to her. He debated printing out the pages of the script, then setting them on fire in the waiting room, but realized this was probably illegal. Or he could have brought his computer and smashed it against the floor, but he can't afford a new computer, and Kristi might consider it another example of how impetuous Jake is. He debates coming clean about being fired and punching the man. It's insanely stupid that he hasn't told her yet. With the civil forfeiture of the diamond, the situation is even more tenuous. There's the very real possibility that the diamond doesn't belong to the Millers, that there won't be ten million dollars, or five hundred thousand even, now that they can't sell to the Italians. Somewhere in the far crevices of Jake's brain, he knows he should get another job, but Helen's script is progressing steadily. A little more time, and he'll know if it's any good. Besides, he's not putting Kristi into debt. He has enough saved for this month's rent. They don't share a credit card.

Jake stands when he sees her approaching, her right palm cradling her near invisible belly. Before she has time to tell him about the appointment, he blurts, "Kris, I'm so sorry. I should have deleted it. I should never have written it. Please, tell me what I can do to make this up to you."

"It's a girl," she says, a smile consuming her face. "We're having a girl."

Without questioning it, Jake pulls Kristi to him. When the small swelling of her stomach brushes against his, he thinks he can feel their daughter inside, tumbling. "A girl."

"I'm sorry, too," Kristi says into his chest. "I overreacted."

"You didn't. It's all me." Jake pulls away so he can look into her eyes. "I'm the one who messed up here."

"That's true. But it's not like you sold the script or anything. And it's nice that you wanted to understand my mom's experience. She'd be flattered —" Kristi hits him playfully. "Don't even think about showing it to her."

Jake crosses his heart and puts his arm around Kristi's shoulders. "Is it still fast, the heartbeat?"

"So fast. I'm sorry I made you wait in the lobby."

Jake shrugs. "There's always next time." She squeezes his waist and, for the moment, Jake decides he's right not to tell her about the firing.

The Golden Girl Thief. That's what the media calls Helen. *Golden* because the Florentine was yellow. *Girl* because she could have been friends with Rose and Dorothy and Blanche. *Thief* because she's not a bandit, an outlaw, a burglar, a kleptomaniac, but an old lady with a diamond that could not possibly be hers. At least, so asserts the press.

Although only Beck's name is listed on the notice of the forfeiture, the press has found the other Millers, the Johnsons, and Kristi Zhang.

Since the last checkup, Jake and Kristi have resumed their intimacy — cuddling and regular sex and Tuesday night movies. They walk to the theater on Vermont Avenue where ticket prices are still at 1990s levels and they splurge on a large bucket of popcorn with extra butter.

During the movie, Kristi gets up twice to pee, then a third time before they trek home.

"I hope I don't have to squat behind a tree," she jokes as they tumble onto the street. It's a cool night, and Kristi snuggles up to Jake as they climb home. They walk slower than usual, Kristi trying to steady her labored breathing as they mount the hill on Franklin Avenue.

"I'm barely showing — how am I this out of breath?" she says, panting.

Jake bends down and motions to his back. "Want me to carry you?" She climbs on and he trudges up to the Shakespeare Bridge, Kristi's laugh trailing them.

They stop on the bridge, looking at the houses below. "Pretty soon we won't be able to do Tuesday night movies," she says, leaning against him.

He squeezes her tight. "We'll just do them at home instead. We can even buy one of those air poppers."

"I don't think anyone uses them anymore."

"Who cares what anyone else does?"

When they walk down Rowena, they spot a crowd of people congregated on the sidewalk near their building. Someone must be having a party. Most of the other tenants are in their twenties, with jobs where they can have keggers on a Tuesday night, but who is he to judge when he hasn't worked in two months?

"Jake —" Kristi slows as the crowd turns toward them. There must be seven people standing outside, some with cameras, others too old to be partying with the twentysomethings that live in the building.

The reporters rush over, encircling Jake and Kristi, asking at once, "Jake Miller, did you know your grandmother stole the world's most valuable diamond?"

"Can you tell us anything about how your grandmother came into contact with the diamond?"

"Care to comment on whether the Florentine belongs to the Millers?"

"Do you know how your grandmother had access to the Florentine?"

"What about your sister Beck? She was kicked out of law school. We're hearing reports that she helped your grandmother steal the Florentine."

He stops trying to push through the crowd. "My sister is not a thief. She's the most moral person I know. And my grandmother isn't a thief, either. She was a Holocaust survivor. Show some respect."

"Then how did she get the diamond?"

"Did she know anyone affiliated with the

Habsburgs?"

"How long has she had the stone?"

"Kristi, do you know anything about Jake's grandmother? How do you feel about having a thief in the family?"

Their questions become a wall of sound. He puts his arm around Kristi and they fight through the reporters like they are braving a strong gust of wind. Once inside the building, the reporters' words are muffled by the thick glass door. Jake hurries Kristi upstairs to their apartment.

Kristi stands in the middle of their living room, chewing her nail. "What was that?"

Jake turns on the TV, and Kristi gives him a look like, *Seriously, dude, you're going to watch* Seinfeld *now*? He flips to the local news. "I guess news of the diamond broke."

Kristi sits beside him on the couch and they watch an image of themselves racing into their apartment, of Jake turning and defending his sister.

"Did you even see a camera crew?" Kristi asks, and Jake shakes his head. "Must be a pretty slow night if we're their lead story."

Jake tries to relax her. "They'll get bored. It's not like we have anything to tell them."

Kristi inches closer to Jake even though their legs are already touching. "I'm glad you're here," she says as though there's anywhere else he might be. Her voice has no reservation in it, but Jake can't shake a lingering wariness that Kristi's forgiveness is provisional. It has nothing to do with Kristi and everything to do with the fact that he hasn't told her about the man he punched, how he spends his days at the library instead of gainfully employed at Trader Joe's. Now isn't the time to tell her, not when she feels comforted by his presence, not when there's a pack of reporters outside.

So, he puts his arms around her and says, "Of course I'm here. Always," willing it to be true.

Once the reporters find the Johnsons, Ashley decides that she and Ryan must tell the children about his crimes. The media doesn't know about his impending criminal charges. The prosecutors have assured them it won't get out until Ryan is sentenced, but reporters have a way of finding information that's supposedly classified. Ashley doesn't want Lydia and Tyler hearing about their father from one of the other kids at school.

They decide to tell the children after dinner, once the reporters have left for the evening and their front yard is dark and quiet again. Ashley sets up an ice cream sundae bar. At first, they let the children go wild, but on the fifth scoop of caramel sauce, Ashley says to Tyler, "Bud, that might be enough."

Lydia sits at the table with her plain vanilla ice cream, no toppings.

"You don't want a little hot fudge?" Ryan asks. "Some whipped cream?"

"I like things simple," Lydia says ominously, although her mother cannot begin to interpret what this means. "So what's the occasion? Why are you trying to bribe us with ice cream?"

"Why would you think we're trying to bribe you?" Ashley asks, making a mental note to be subtler next time they need to break unsettling news to their children.

"When's the last time you bought ice cream instead of frozen yogurt?" Lydia's eyes widen.

"Or whipped cream," Tyler announces, spraying the can onto his index finger and popping his finger into his mouth.

"Is this about the diamond Helen stole?" Before Ashley can protest that Helen didn't steal anything, Lydia continues. "We can read, you know. So now she's a thief, too?"

Ashley hears something in her tone. Is it possible she knows about Ryan? She'd told Beck that she heard them fighting, but Lydia couldn't know that he stole half a million dollars, could she? It still makes her breathless, just how much money he siphoned from his company.

"Are we going to be rich?" Tyler's voice rises an octave. When he smiles, his lips are lined in chocolate.

"We're already rich, dummy," Lydia snipes. When did she get this attitude? When did she start to act like a teenager? "Or we were before Dad messed everything up."

"Lydia!" Ryan chides.

Ashley places her hand on his forearm, trying to calm him. "What is it you think your father did?"

Lydia picks at her cuticles. "I've just heard you guys arguing about money. Is Dad going to jail?" Her voice is so soft she becomes young again.

"Probably," Ashley says. "It's his fault. He's going to do what he can to make it right, but that might mean going away for a while."

Tyler freezes. "For how long?" Melting ice cream drips from his spoon, poised above his bowl.

"We won't know until he pleads guilty and is sentenced."

Tyler wipes his mouth, spreading chocolate across his cheek. "Is he going to come back?"

"Your father will come back," Ashley says. For the first time, this takes no effort. For the first time, she isn't trying to convince herself to forgive Ryan. "It's going to be tough, but we're family. We'll be here for him."

Ryan casts her the first genuine smile he's worn in months. Tight-lipped, not exactly happy, but relieved. When she returns her attention to her children, they do not share his relief. Tyler stabs at the ice cream in his bowl, eyes brimming with tears. Lydia's face has hardened, and Ashley sees a glimpse of Beck in her cold expression, the way everything from their youth had turned her sister angry, secretive.

As Ashley is about to ask her children what she and Ryan can do, what they need from their parents, Ryan cuts in. "I have no excuse for what I did. It was entirely unfair to both of you. To your mom, too. I'm going to do whatever I can to make this right, but it's okay for you to be angry with me. I deserve it. I can only say I'm sorry."

Such a simple expression, *I'm sorry.* To Ashley, there's nothing simple about it. When her husband says this, she believes it.

She reaches for his hand, then reiterates to their children, "We're going to get through this. Together." Her children look up at her, and she holds their gaze until it softens. They trust her. She trusts herself, too. They will get through this. Together.

Soon after news breaks about the diamond, lawyers begin calling Beck, offering their services with reduced hourly fees. Even at a fraction of their normal price, the legal fees will cost more than the diamonds from Helen's doll are worth. More than the few thousand dollars Helen had stashed in her house. More than the brooch is worth, too. No matter how hard up they are for cash, Beck refuses to sell the brooch. While the diamond might not belong to the Millers, the brooch is Helen's. It's a family heirloom, not to be hawked to the highest bidder. Miraculously, her siblings haven't mentioned it, almost as if they've forgotten it exists.

Despite the high-profile nature of the case, this isn't the type of altruistic claim that would entice a firm to represent them pro bono. Representatives of *businessmen* call Beck, too, offering legal services in exchange for a private sale when they win the case. Their certainty worries her almost as much as their cryptic descriptions of their employers. They call Beck on her cell and at work. One sends an associate to her office.

When the receptionist calls Beck to tell her someone is waiting in the lobby, Beck scurries up to the front desk to get rid of the individual. She freezes when she spots a man in khaki shorts and a golf shirt, seated cross-legged in the lobby.

The stranger looks up at her with blue eyes she inherited. Beck has dyed her hair lush colors so it wouldn't resemble his mousy brown, now gray, hair. She'd pierced her nose so the Miller point was less obvious, tattooed her arms to obscure the Miller freckles, but she'd never been able to hide his eyes.

Even though he has shaved his beard, she recognizes him right away.

"Dad," she says automatically. Beck wishes she'd called him something else. Unlike Deborah, who hasn't been Mom for a long time, Kenny has always been Dad.

Beck keeps one step ahead of Kenny as they walk the few short blocks to Library Place. She needed to get him out of her office but doesn't want to be anywhere private with him.

Kenny waits at a table with a cup of coffee while Beck orders fries and a Coke from the burger stand. She isn't hungry, but she needs somewhere to focus her attention while she sits with him.

With every step she takes toward her father's table, she considers dumping her tray and making a run for it. She knows she won't be able to get rid of him that easily. The sooner she sits down and lets him say whatever it is he wants to tell her, the sooner it will be over.

Beck places her tray on the table and settles into the seat across from her father. He takes a sip of his coffee, eyeing her French fries. "You always were a terrible eater," he finally says.

"That was Ashley." Her tone is aggressive, twenty-two years of anger in those three inadequate words.

Kenny continues to drink his coffee. He seems at peace with her anger, which only makes her angrier.

Beck checks the time on her phone. "You've got ten minutes."

"I saw the article in the *Inquirer.* I was worried about you. I wanted to see if you were okay."

"*Okay?* You want to know if I'm *okay?* What about twenty-two years ago, you think I was *okay* then?" She hates that he's reduced her to a predictable script of trite, yet true, emotions. She plans to tell him she's fine, to leave her alone. Instead, what comes out is, "The *Philadelphia Inquirer*?"

The Florentine Diamond made it into all the papers, but her father saw the write-ups in the Philadelphia newspaper.

"Becca, I —"

"*Don't* call me that."

"I live in Atlantic City. For the last few years." His blue eyes search hers imploringly.

Beck checks her phone. "You've got seven minutes."

"I thought you might want to know — Helen, she gave me a diamond." Beck drops the fry she been mashing between her fingers. He has her full attention. "For your mom. Two actually."

"I'm listening."

Helen gave him a two-carat diamond for the ring and another, one carat, to pay for the setting. Kenny was twenty-seven. He'd spent the past several years organizing for Students for a Democratic Society and, with the war over, had no plans for his future. He and Deborah had been dating on and off for a few years, although he doubted Helen knew about the off parts. Before he and Helen met, Deborah had told Kenny that her mother never loved her. When Kenny was finally invited to dinner at the house on Edgehill Road, he realized Deborah was wrong. Helen had guided him into her bedroom, where she took a velvet pouch out of her dresser. She dropped a flower pin with a large yellow stone at its center and several loose diamonds into her hand, then gave Kenny two diamonds.

"If you tell anyone about this, I'll castrate you," Helen said, returning the pin and the other loose diamonds to her dresser. "And don't insult me by asking if they're real."

It was then that Kenny realized Deborah was loved deeply. Helen and Deborah — their love just spoke different languages.

Kenny went to see a jeweler, someone on Jewelers' Row, that Helen had chosen. When he arrived, the man had already designed a ring for Deborah based on Helen's instructions. It felt wrong, having Helen plan their ring, their engagement, especially given Kenny wasn't sure he ever wanted to get married.

"I probably shouldn't tell you that," he says, even though it's hardly a shock to Beck.

"So I told the jeweler I'd consider it, and he seemed pretty surprised." Based on his conversations with Helen, the jeweler had already made the wax for casting. Kenny slipped the diamonds into his pocket and said he would be back in a few days. As he walked out of the store, Kenny decided that he would marry Deborah someday, but not on her mother's terms. A neon sign down the block blinked Diamonds. The dealer didn't ask him where he'd gotten the diamonds, just offered him what sounded like a lot of money.

Helen never mentioned the diamonds she gave Kenny. When Kenny finally placed a ring on Deborah's finger a year later, a half-carat he bought at a pawnshop, Helen stared at the ring, nostrils flaring, and told Deborah that it was beautiful.

"My mother can never be happy for me," Deborah said to Kenny after they left.

"I let her think that. I never told her what I did," Kenny confesses to Beck, staring into his now empty coffee cup.

It's been seventeen minutes. Beck remains seated, trying to determine if her father's story is true. The press doesn't know about the loose diamonds. They don't know about the orchid brooch. The only way he could have known those details was if Helen had actually given him the stones. Helen had never liked Kenny, yet she'd entrusted him with her gravest secret. That seemed an even greater act of love toward Deborah than gifting him the diamonds.

"You know, your mother and I never

divorced," Kenny says as he communes with his disposable coffee cup.

All at once, Beck feels nauseous. Of course this is why he's here. How naive she was to listen to this story, to presume there was any part of Kenny Miller that might be sincere.

Beck grabs her tray. "I have to get back to work."

She dumps the barely eaten food into the bin and feels him at her shoulder, so she walks down the escalator, the corridor toward Seventeenth Street. Despite his large belly, his heavy breathing, he keeps pace.

"I have a legitimate claim to Deborah's share of the diamond," he says, his conviction almost laughable.

"Actually, you don't." Beck tries to match his conviction, but she isn't entirely sure. She didn't study family law in school, and her firm doesn't take on divorces. Plus, Kenny and Deborah have been estranged so long. And Kenny was the one that left. Even if he is still eligible for any alimony, Beck is fairly certain that inheritance falls into a special protected category. "You have no legal right to anything that's ours."

"I'm not trying to upset you," he says when she's forced to stop at a light on

343

Seventeenth. "I didn't want to blindside you."

"This is you not blindsiding me?"

Kenny hands her a business card for some bar and grill in Margate, New Jersey. He's listed as the manager. "I'm trying to do the right thing here."

"Unbelievable." The light changes and the pedestrians create a stream of movement around her. Beck starts to cross the street, then turns to her father. "If you go anywhere near Deborah, *I'll* castrate you."

With that, she storms off, not looking back until she's inside the lobby of her building and is sure Kenny hasn't followed her. She tears his business card in half. As she dangles the card over the trash can, she can't let go. She puts the torn pieces in her coat pocket and hurries upstairs.

Once she's back at her desk, she dials her mother. "You never divorced him," Beck whispers, furious. She should have called her mother from the lobby, away from lurking ears. She knows the gossip that's been floating around about her, even before the story of the diamond broke, since Tom dumped her. Suddenly, she doesn't care.

"It's kind of hard to divorce someone when you don't know where they are."

"Why didn't you tell us?"

"Would it have made things better if I did?"

Beck can't shake that familiar frustration toward her mother for being irresponsible and reckless, for creating a mess where there didn't need to be one. She debates telling Deborah what he said about fighting her for half her assets. While it might make her feel better in this moment, Beck's still pretty sure it's not the law.

"I was afraid," Deborah says softly. "Not of being divorced, but of getting one."

Finally, it clicks. When Deborah used to tell her that Kenny was coming back, she was trying to convince herself as much as she was Beck.

"He told me a story, about Helen." Beck recounts the story of Helen gifting Kenny the diamond, hoping it might make her mother feel better to know what Helen did for her.

Instead, Deborah grows stern. "Don't believe anything that man tells you."

After they hang up, Beck taps on Tom's door. He looks up at her with that mix of desire and suspicion he's taken to giving her. As usual she ignores it and tells him about her father's appearance.

"What an asshole," Tom says. "You're right. Inheritance is outside the scope of

345

alimony. If you do win, he isn't entitled to any of the diamond." Tom taps his index finger on his chin as he contemplates this progression. "What worries me is the story about Helen showing him the Florentine. Hiding the brooch, the dealer on Jewelers' Row, the secrecy. It makes it look like Helen knew the diamond wasn't hers. At least, that's how he could paint it."

"Will paint it," Beck says, leaning against the doorjamb. "So what do I do?"

"For now? Nothing. Don't take the bait."

They both know she's never been good at avoiding a net cast for her.

While Beck vows to ignore Kenny, it proves difficult. The next morning, he's quoted in the papers, not just the *Philadelphia Inquirer,* but the *New York Times,* the *Wall Street Journal.*

Ashley calls Beck, irate. "He's seriously saying Helen paid him in diamonds to leave us?"

"Ash, I'm at work."

"How can they print this? It's slander." Ashley pauses. "That's my other line. It's Jake."

"Please, don't engage. Tell Jake the same thing, okay?"

After they hang up, Beck rests her head on her desk collecting her thoughts. She can

346

picture Kenny, belly-laughing with the press as he tells inflammatory story after inflammatory story. It's always been his greatest attribute, his charisma, some might say his bullshit. Even Beck fell for it, momentarily, when he told her the story about Helen and the diamonds. Had that been a line, too? Only, he'd known details he couldn't have made up. And something about what he said nags Beck. Over the years, the Millers have had several expenditures miraculously paid, not just Deborah's ring, but Ashley's last year of private school — Beck never really believed she'd gotten an alumni scholarship — three sets of braces, supposedly covered by insurance; Beck's freshman year trip to Rome; Deborah's surgery after she broke her arm; Jake's first car. Helen had claimed her friend traded it for a custom suit, but that story, like the others, never sounded right.

There were other costs, too, that Beck can't remember. Is it possible Helen used diamonds from the hatpin to pay for all the gifts of their lives? There wouldn't be records of the sales, at least none she'd be able to find. Still, thinking of all those costs, Beck feels confident that it had all come from Helen, that Kenny's story is true, that where there were five loose diamonds — the three Deborah found in the doll plus the two Helen gave Kenny — there were more. For the first time since the forfeiture, Beck starts to feel her resolve strengthen. The Florentine was Helen's. She'd brought it over in the hatpin. Now, Beck just has to prove it.

THIRTEEN

At the end of June, when the thirty-day deadline is up, over one hundred parties have filed claims on the 137.27-carat diamond, including Kenny Miller. Beck wasn't expecting that. She figured he'd wait until the messy and expensive business of the civil forfeiture was over before trying to take his share. Instead, he's filed his own claim, stating that Helen promised the diamond to him when he and his wife, Deborah, married. It's not the sort of answer the judge will weigh in on, but it weakens the Millers' claim, sullying it with decades-old family drama.

As predicted, several would-be Habsburgs have surfaced in addition to the official heirs. One man claims to be Karl, the last emperor, insisting that he did not die in 1922, and, at the ripe age of 130, is living in Ithaca, NY. Another declares herself the granddaughter of Karl and a reputed mistress. Others pronounce themselves Medicis, even though the Medici line died out centuries before. One man even offers a clear lineage back to Charles the Bold, rumored to have possessed the diamond in the fifteenth century. Another potential claimant alleges that he found the stone on the shores of Lake Michigan. The Star of Michigan is the press's favorite claim, although the press enjoys all the connections to the Austrian royal family and the Medicis that modern-day treasure hunters can concoct.

Beck assures her siblings that the false claims are good for their case because it will slow the prosecutors down. Every claim has to be reviewed by the Department of Justice and dismissed by the court. It will take years for the government to sift through all the files and present them to the court for rejection.

"So you're saying we won't be able to sell the diamond for years?" Ashley asks. The judge in Ryan's case has already ordered the presentencing report and set Ryan's hearing for November. Ryan must return the money before he appears in court. The Johnsons do not have years.

"*If* we win," Beck cautions.

"What if we need the money now?" Jake

tries to keep his voice impassive. He'd been hoping, with the sale of the diamond, he'd be able to pay next month's rent. Either the diamond or Helen's movie, but he's stalled again on that front. There's still a giant hole in his story — how Helen got the hatpin — and without that key plot point, he can't understand why she kept the diamond, what his script is really about.

"Until this is over, there is no money. More time is good, though. We don't have the evidence yet that the diamond is ours."

While Beck is right that the baseless claims will slow down the Department of Justice, they do not delay the District Court from advancing the Millers' claim. With the thirty days passed, four claims move forward: the Austrian government, the Italian government, the Habsburg estate, and the Millers. Not Kenny Miller. Beck wants to celebrate that small victory, but he's still talking to the press, fabricating stories about their family.

Judge Ricci, the district judge hearing their case, is in her forties and wears bright, chunky necklaces over her robe. It gives Beck hope that since the judge is young, female, and fashionable, that together, Judge Ricci and Beck stand out in the sea of silver-haired men in dark suits. The judge, however, appears as indifferent to Beck as she is to the other parties.

"Let me be clear." Judge Ricci looks pointedly at each lawyer, even Beck, who is not a lawyer, but who, for the moment, is representing herself. "I will not tolerate attempts to unnecessarily delay this case. We are here at the taxpayers' expense. It may be in your interest to amass as many hours as possible, but it is not in the interest of this court or the public."

She sets discovery at ninety days, the subsequent deadline to file motions for summary judgment a month later at the end of October. Three months is all they have to collect their evidence, to depose witnesses, to hire experts. And they *will* need experts — on WWI, on Austrian law, specifically the Habsburg Law, which allocated all crown property to the state. On the WWI treaty and reparations that might indebt the Florentine Diamond to the Italians. They will need gemologists and jewelry historians, here and overseas. They will need a lawyer, which in thirty days the Millers have not acquired. Viktor secured a buyer for the diamonds, offering fifteen thousand dollars. Not market price, but more than Beck had feared. Still, it isn't enough to pay for a month of legal fees.

Beck cannot represent her family, not against the big law firms that the Italians and the Austrians have hired as counsel. The Habsburgs have retained an international law firm that specializes in luxury goods. They were involved in a suit over Elizabeth Taylor's diamonds and another involving a quarterback and a blue diamond ring. As much as Beck Miller likes a challenge, this isn't an uphill battle so much as a massacre.

Beck advances the best she can, reading the pages Christian translates and trying to find a lawyer who will be a good fit for her family. Attorneys keep approaching her, but their hourly rates are comical, their plans of attack disconcertingly thin. They're interested in the money, the coverage, not in Helen. Not in the Millers, either. Writers and *businessmen* also contact her, calling the firm, claiming to be Beck's mother, her friend, and, once, her gynecologist. They clog the phone lines and distract the firm's best paralegal. Now, Beck isn't even sure she is the best paralegal. She's preoccupied; even she can admit her work is not up to its usual impeccable standard, which is just another way she feels overwhelmed and disappointed by her own limitations.

Then one day Karen from HR stops Beck in the hall to tell her that the partners would like to see her in the conference room.

"Am I in trouble?" Beck asks, trotting to keep up with Karen.

"I honestly don't know." Karen stops abruptly, causing Beck to almost bang into her. "Whatever happens, I'm here." These words are meant to comfort Beck, who's now positive she's about to be fired.

Of course Tom has to be there. Would it be too much that he recuse himself? Does he really have to bear witness to another humiliating moment in the life of Beck Miller? He keeps his face downturned, focused on the legal pad in front of him, while the partners stand and motion Beck toward an open seat in the middle of the room.

"Beck," one of the name partners begins. "It's no secret that you're facing some mounting legal troubles."

"I'm not being sued," she says defensively, then reconsiders her approach. "They're trying to steal my family heirloom."

"We've read." She waits for the words she's dreading. "We want you to consider taking leave while all of this settles."

"If you are going to fire me, I'd prefer you do it now."

A laugh, and Beck is confused. The name

partner smiles. "Beck, you're the best paralegal we've ever had. We're just concerned this case may be a distraction."

"I can't afford to take unpaid leave. It could be years until this settles." God, years. Years of appeals, whether she wins or loses. This case will go on forever.

"We've considered this, and here's what we propose."

His offer is so absurd Beck has to periodically turn to Karen to confirm she's hearing correctly.

"In addition to our ongoing relationship with you, there are numerous reasons why we're the best firm for your claim," the name partner begins his pitch. "First, we're one of the top firms in Philadelphia. And as you well know, it makes sense to go with a local firm that is familiar with the federal court system in Pennsylvania, the judges, some of whom will be more sympathetic than others. Plus, we have just as much manpower as a firm in New York or DC. We can't offer to do this pro bono. But we'll represent you on contingency and will get reimbursed for expenses only if we win." He doesn't explain to Beck that the expenses will come off the top before the firm takes its third. It goes without saying that, should they win, they will sell the diamond.

"Of course, you should discuss this with your family, but we'd like to put you on the case, full-time. We'll reassign your other work so you can focus your efforts on this. It will be a top priority for our firm."

"I don't need to discuss it with my family," Beck says without hesitating. "This sounds like a great plan."

"Tom tells us he's been helping you with the case? Unless you have any objections, we'd like to keep him on as your representation from the firm."

She looks skeptically at the name partner. Is he trying to screw with her? When he smiles, she realizes that he doesn't know about their relationship. While it's on record, Karen has kept it confidential.

"So we're in agreement?" one of the other partners asks. He doesn't wait for Beck to respond before he says, "Good," and gets up to leave. The other partners fall in line behind him. Within moments, the conference room empties. Only Beck, Karen, and Tom remain at the table.

"You good?" Karen asks Beck, who nods warily. As Karen stands, she shoots Tom a look that Beck would have paid for, it's so perfectly lacquered in disgust.

"I don't want you on my family's case," Beck says as soon as they are alone.

356

Tom acts confused. "I've been helping you so far."

"It means spending a lot of time together, which isn't a good idea."

"Beck, about what happened at the apartment —" Tom begins.

Beck cuts him off. "It was a mistake. Something to get each other out of our systems." As Tom starts to protest, she gestures that she's not finished yet. "I'm over you, but you really hurt me. I opened up to you in a way I hadn't with anyone before." Again, she holds her hand up for him to listen. "Let me finish. I appreciate your help, I do. I just don't trust you with this. There's too much history between us. I don't want you knowing any more of the intimacies of my family."

Tom looks hurt, which evokes a burst of anger in Beck. He does not get to feel bruised by her words. Before she can tell him this, he says, "I don't judge you for what you did. We aren't defined by our mistakes. We're defined by how we respond to them. I didn't care that you *cheated* in high school."

"I didn't cheat —"

Tom wags his index finger to indicate that this is precisely what he means.

"Don't do that with your finger. I'm not a

child," Beck says, feeling childish.

"It took me a while to figure out why your story bothered me so much. I wanted you to open up to me. And it's terrible the way your teacher made you feel."

"He harassed me. Nowadays, he'd be fired for it and blasted all over social media."

"That's just it, Beck. You didn't go to the authorities. You took matters into your own hands."

"You're serious?" Of course he's serious. "It isn't that easy for most people. The principal never would have believed me."

"You don't know that."

"You have no right to judge me," Beck says, careful to keep her voice low. The conference room sits at the center of their office, protected only by plates of glass. Anyone who walks by can hear them.

"That's the thing. I don't judge you. I really don't care what you did. I believe in rehabilitation. If we atone for our mistakes, we can overcome them. That's the thing, though. You still feel aggrieved, like nothing that's happened to you is your fault."

Beck feels the first hot tear, followed by another as he continues to outline his argument, an exhaustive review of her blame on Jake, on her mother, on Molly Stanton from law school, whose name Beck is surprised he remembers, on her high school principal, and on Lizzie Meyers, who had actually thanked Mr. O'Neal for a grade she'd deserved.

"Please stop." While Tom might be right that she distributes blame on everyone but herself, he's wrong about Mr. O'Neal and what happened in high school. The principal never would have believed her over a popular teacher, especially not after she broke into the school computer system. The fact that Tom can't see this proves just how wrong he is to represent her family. "I'm going to ask the partners to put someone else on the case."

Beck stands to leave, then hesitates. If she asks for different representation, she'll have to explain why she doesn't want to work with Tom. The partners don't know that she and Tom dated. Karen kept this secret, even though she should have told them. Beck doesn't want to get Karen in trouble.

Tom walks around the table and stands too close to her. "Let me help you with this."

"Why is it so important to you?"

"Because you deserve someone who will go above and beyond. Helen deserves it. No one else is going to do that."

Beck looks away. When she returns her gaze to his, he's staring insistently at her.

"You don't see why this might be a bad idea?"

"Of course I do, but we're going into this with our eyes open. If it gets to be too much, if for any reason you feel uncomfortable, one word, and we'll put someone else on the case." His eyes implore her, and she wishes she'd asked Karen to stay. It wouldn't be fair, though, putting Karen in the middle of this any more than she already is.

Beck remains unconvinced, but she tells Tom, "Okay. We'll give it a try." She doesn't say yes for him but for Karen, for the Millers. Tom is a good lawyer. Judging from the broad smile on his face, she can tell that he will put up one hell of a fight for her family, even if he didn't fight for her.

Together, they walk down that hall, Beck taking notes as Tom rattles off everything they need to do. First thing, they need to file a motion to suppress the seizure, arguing that there's no proof it's the Florentine. "The IGS report never mentions the Florentine by name. Who's to say it isn't another diamond? Maybe not the Star of Michigan, but there's no definitive proof it's the Florentine."

"The IGS report mentioned a heart-shaped feathering in the diamond. I looked it up, and various documentation of the Florentine noted the same unique inclusion. Charles of Lorraine even mentioned it when he gave the diamond to Marie Antoinette on her wedding day," Beck counters. *With the heart in this diamond,* Charles wrote to his daughter, *so, too, is my heart with you.* "Plus it's the exact weight and dimensions as the Florentine."

"Obviously, we won't win. It's a good place to start, raising doubt about the provenance of the diamond. From there, we'll file motions to delay discovery." He lists off several objections they can raise. "The other parties will want to delay, too."

The longer the delay, the more time they have to prove the diamond is theirs.

Beck continues to walk quietly beside him, jotting down the experts they'll need to find in European law and history, a gemologist — Viktor, but someone else, too, given that he was the first one to identify the diamond and they'll need to call him as a witness — a jewelry historian, past civil forfeiture cases before the Circuit and Supreme Courts that may offer elucidating precedent.

"And keep searching any leads you have on Helen. We don't just need to prove the diamond doesn't belong to one of the other parties. We have to prove it belonged to your grandmother, and now to you."

They stop at her cubicle. "And we need to silence your father. We can file a restraining order if he comes near you or your family again, but it's better if we get rid of him civilly. Try digging up some dirt on him. A guy like that, it shouldn't be too hard."

Beck watches Tom skip down the hall, his gait lighter than she's seen in months. While she still feels wary about working with him, she knows he'll do a good job representing her family. She tells herself that's the most important thing.

"You really think that's a good idea? Tom?" Ashley asks her sister through her iPad screen. Her house is so quiet she can hear the floorboards creaking beneath her feet. Now that Ryan isn't working, it's a rare afternoon that she has the house to herself. Maybe she'll walk around naked. But the press still occasionally stops by, and the last thing she needs is a blurred picture of her nude self on the cover of the *New York Post*. She can only imagine the title, "A Fraud Exposed!"

"I don't trust it. An ex who wants to *help* you." Deborah shakes her head, *tsk*ing.

"I know, Mom. You've made that perfectly clear." Beck rolls her eyes at Deborah, who is sitting beside her on the couch at Edge-hill Road. She's invited herself over for dinner to talk to Deborah about Kenny. If anyone knows his skeletons, it's her mother.

Beck returns her attention to her siblings on the iPad. "He's a good lawyer and he feels guilty. He'll put more of himself into it than some random lawyer."

"Let's just hope he doesn't put too much of himself into it," Ashley snipes.

Deborah laughs until she notices the stricken look on Beck's face.

"I told you that's over."

"So what do we do now?" Jake asks.

"We keep looking for Helen." Beck pulls out a legal pad.

"Uh-oh, Beck made a list," Ashley teases.

Ignoring her sister, Beck outlines the leads they still need to investigate. While the diamonds they found in Helen's doll may have sold for fifteen thousand dollars, they did not produce concrete evidence that Helen brought the hatpin over from Vienna. That's still their operating theory, but they need proof to convince the court.

"But why do we think Helen brought the hatpin with her, just because we found diamonds in a doll from Austria?" Ashley asks.

"The diamonds are from the same era,"

Beck says. Her sister casts her a look: *So?* "Do you have another explanation how Helen could have gotten turn-of-the-century diamonds? Now isn't the time to cast doubt."

"Why not? Isn't that what the other parties will do?" Jake asks.

"That's even more reason to commit to our story. We need to develop a theory, then find evidence that supports it. That's how the law works. There's never 100 percent truth, only competing theories. We need to make sure ours is more convincing than the others."

"And what is our theory, that Helen had the hatpin in Vienna, hid it in her doll, and brought it to the US where fifteen years later she set it in a brooch?" Obviously, Jake knows this is the theory. He's fleshed it out in scene. But it's a story made for fiction, the big screen. Compelling, far-fetched, lacking solid ground.

"If we can find the maker's mark, then yes."

"I still don't understand why that's helpful," Deborah interrupts her daughter.

"It tells us who made the brooch." The clueless expression on Deborah's face persists. Beck flips to a fresh page on her yellow legal pad and writes, *Habsburgs lose*

diamond 1918 → Helen gets diamond →
Diamond set in brooch 1954 or earlier.

"We either need to figure out how the diamond got from the Habsburgs to Helen or the opposite, from the brooch back to Helen."

"And how do we know Helen didn't get the diamond after it was in the brooch? The first photo we have is from 1955," Deborah says.

"Viktor thinks it was made around 1954, so if she was wearing it by New Year's Eve, she's likely the original owner. And even if she wasn't, if we can locate the company that made the brooch, their records should tell us who had it made. From there, we can work backward. Let's just stick to the plan, okay?"

Beck doesn't even bother mentioning Peter Winkler, who after four emails still has not written her back. She doesn't mention Christian, either, dutifully translating Kurt Winkler's books. They've had drinks three times, each ostensibly to discuss the translation. While the flirting continued, it hasn't progressed, and the more Christian smiles at her, the more he casts those dimples, the more she's decided that he's too young for her, too unserious. The flirting is all she needs from him.

"You mean your plan," Jake scoffs.

"Do you have any better ideas?" Beck matches his disdain with her own.

"It just doesn't all add up to me."

"That's why we need more evidence."

Their voices rise, risking a fight. Ashley's own fights exhaust her; she has no interest in sitting through her siblings' futile bickering. So she shares the news she's avoided delivering throughout their conversation. "I found Flora."

It took Ashley days to open the envelope from the Holocaust Museum, and once she did, she wished she'd tossed it into the fireplace unopened. "She was arrested on April 25, 1939," Ashley tentatively begins.

"That was just a few days after Helen left for America," Beck realizes.

"Do you think it was a coincidence that she was arrested so soon after?" Jake asks.

"It's impossible to know," Ashley says.

"If Helen hadn't left . . . If she'd still been with Flora . . ." Deborah stops short of finishing her sentence. These last few weeks, she's been so angry with Helen for lying to her about her father. This doesn't undo that anger, but it burnishes its edges. If Helen hadn't left, if she'd stayed with her mother like she'd wanted to — Deborah can't bear to finish the thought.

366

"Where was she sent?" Beck asks.

"To Lichtenburg. It was one of the first concentration camps. There was this castle the Nazis used. It was only open for another month or so after Flora got there." Ashley keeps her tone dispassionate. It is the only way to get through the details.

"Then where'd she go?" Jake asks.

"Ravensbrück. I couldn't locate her exact files, but she wasn't one of the survivors." Ashley had never heard of Ravensbrück. It was an all-women's camp, a training site for female guards who showed their worth to the SS in their ruthlessness. The majority of the inmates were not Jewish but political prisoners, academics, Romani, *deviants*. Flora probably wasn't one of the "rabbits," who were predominantly Polish, their bodies sliced open, amputated, subjected to gangrene and transplants. It was also statistically unlikely that Flora was one of the few women forced into prostitution or that she was sterilized, a fate inflicted mostly on the Romani. "I don't recommend googling it."

Even if she wasn't one of these populations, if she'd been shot or gassed or fatally malnourished, Flora suffered a horrible death.

"Well," Deborah says, "now we know."

"It's weird. I figured she probably died in

a concentration camp, but knowing for certain . . ." Ashley can't explain why she feels so much worse having her assumptions confirmed, but judging from the expressions on her family's faces, they seem to understand.

"And that Flora was taken away days after she sent Helen to the US," Jake adds. In a script, it's the heartbreaking twist at the end, and Jake curses himself for thinking about narrative at a time like this.

"How does it help us?" Ashley means, *How does it help us heal?* but Beck misinterprets.

"Flora was never going to lead us to the Florentine," Beck adds. "That wasn't the point."

After they hang up, Beck and Deborah sit side by side on Helen's couch, staring into the dark expanse of Helen's dormant television. The air-conditioning that Deborah has put in the window does its best to keep up with July's heat, but the living room remains suffocating. There's something comforting about it, though. Helen never had a window unit. She rarely brought out the fan. The heat makes Beck feel closer to Helen.

"It doesn't change anything," Beck says, wiping a film of sweat from her upper lip.

"Yet, somehow, it changes everything," Deborah counters, wiping her own sweat from her forehead. If they win this case, the first thing she'll do is install central air.

"I need to talk to you about something." Beck feels Deborah stiffen. "It's about Kenny."

"I haven't been in touch with him," Deborah protests. "He's called a few times. I promise, the second he speaks, I hang up on him."

"He called you?" Beck feels the heat rise in her. "I told him I'd castrate him if he came near you."

Deborah laughs. "That's twisted."

"It was what Helen said to him, if he ever told anyone about the diamonds."

"Now that I believe."

Deborah's lightness surprises Beck. "You aren't upset about everything he's been saying?"

Deborah shrugs. "He's a novelty. As soon as the press has a chance, they'll turn on him. It all makes for a good story."

"So let's do it. Let's slaughter him. You must have some dirt on him."

"I do." Deborah pauses. "Isn't there another way? I don't want to go low just because he does." Deborah smiles at the surprise on her daughter's face. "It's that shocking I'd want to take the high road?"

"A bit," Beck teases, then promises, "I'll find another way to get rid of him."

After dinner, Deborah doesn't want Beck to leave, and she feels Beck dawdling, perched at the dining room table after it's cleared. Deborah sits beside her. "Want some tea?"

"Sure."

In the time it takes Deborah to steep a pot of chamomile flowers and fresh mint, Beck has put on reading glasses and turned the dining room table into her evening office. Printed documents cascade around her.

"What's that?" Deborah asks as she places a cup before her daughter.

"The book Christian translated for me. I know Ashley and Jake probably think it's a waste of time. I just . . . I feel like there might be something here. If we can locate when the diamond disappeared, maybe it will help us figure out where it was before Helen had it."

"Can I help?" She waits for Beck to intimate that it is too complicated for her.

Beck removes her glasses and massages her temples. "Sure, I could use a set of fresh eyes."

Beck scans the piles and hands chapter twenty-six, "The Empire's Last Breaths," to her mother.

"There could be something in that chapter about when the royal family fled. I'm reading about later, in Switzerland, then Portugal. So far, I haven't seen anything about any jewels. I know they sold whatever crown jewels they could. They were hard up for cash." Beck slides her glasses up her nose and returns her attention to the page. "I should warn you, Winkler's prose is a bit flowery."

Winkler's prose is flamboyant. Everything is a *valiant travail,* a *noble endeavor* worthy of *myriad generations of intrepid bloodline.* Deborah's eyes start to blur. She rouses herself. She can't appear bored, but Deborah always was a fickle student.

The chapter begins with the relative calm of the royal family's life in Laxenburg, Austria, as their empire crumbled around them. Mass at 6:00 a.m., followed by a breakfast of meat and mineral water before the emperor left for the army headquarters at Baden, returning for lunch with the empress and their — at the time — five children. Winkler continues to describe the emperor's schedule, where someone has written in bolded parenthesis: *(Snooze fest! Blah blah blah . . . I'm glossing over this. If you need something to put you to sleep, give a holler and I'll translate these parts for you!)*

Deborah flips through pages with more bolded parentheses, smiley faces, and jokes *(so this Kaiser walks into a bar . . .).* Deborah grins at Beck.

"What?"

Deborah holds the paper toward her daughter. "Who's Mr. Bold-Parenthesis?"

"Why do you assume it's a he? No one. Christian. The translator. Just keep reading."

And read she does. She reads about Czech independence and the fall of Bulgaria, about the Peoples' Manifesto, which shifted the Austro-Hungarian Empire into a federation of nation-states until she gets to a long section where Winkler quotes the empress's firsthand accounts of the autumn before the empire fell. Unlike Winkler, the empress's words are matter-of-fact. They pull Deborah in.

One section is particularly riveting. The empress, Zita, describes the days after a revolution broke out in Budapest. While she and the emperor traveled to Vienna, they'd left the children behind in Gödöllö, Hungary, not too far from the frontlines in Budapest. They'd been assured that the children would be safer there. Vienna had seemed more dangerous.

On the night the revolutionaries stormed the palace in Gödöllö, Zita woke to a phone call from Budapest. She roused her husband, who sat up in a panic. Before he'd wiped the sleep from his eyes, before he knew that a revolt had started in Hungary, he asked, "Is it the children?" Zita chewed at her knuckle, listening to her husband's side of the conversation as the general filled him in on what was happening in Hungary.

Deborah is about to flip the page, curious to find out whether the children made it out alive, when she notices a footnote: *Four days after the revolution erupted in Budapest, on November 3, the children had to be spirited back to Vienna by their steadfast nurse, a young redheaded beauty who gallantly risked her life to deliver the children safely to their parents in Vienna.*

Deborah squeezes Beck's foot. "Red hair." Beck raises her eyebrows. Deborah reads aloud the footnote about the nurse who saved the children. She pokes the paper for emphasis. "Winkler says the nurse who saved the emperor's children was 'a young redheaded beauty.' " Beck is still looking at her mother like she's wasting their time. "It's Flora."

Beck reaches for the paper and reads the footnote herself.

"Did Helen ever tell you what Flora did before she was born?"

Deborah shakes her head. "But she was known for her red hair. If it was Flora, if she saved future generations of Habsburgs —"

Beck takes off her glasses and smiles. "The emperor might have given her the Florentine as a reward."

FOURTEEN

Before Beck has a chance to tell her siblings about the redheaded nurse, before she pitches her theory to Tom, he stops her in the hallway at work to talk to her about her father.

"This is getting out of control." He thrusts the morning's paper at her. On the front page, Kenny quotes Helen's diary, from which he claims to have proof she promised him the Florentine Diamond.

"Why would they print this? It doesn't even make sense."

"Tell me you've got some info on him."

"Well . . ." Beck hesitates. "Is there another way? It's just . . . things with him and my mom, they were so hard for her. They're not even divorced. I just worry it might escalate."

Tom snaps his fingers. "A divorce. How susceptible is your father to money?"

"I'd say pretty damn susceptible."

"We frame it as a divorce settlement, throw a little money his way, get him to sign an agreement that he won't talk about the case."

"It's worth a shot. We have fifteen thousand dollars from —" Beck pauses. Tom doesn't need to know about the money Viktor procured from the sale of Helen's diamonds. "We can offer him fifteen."

"Is that all you can get?"

Beck thinks of the brooch, still buried in her nightstand, the few thousand still tucked away in coffee cans and potpourri satchels. "I can probably get a bit more, but let's start with fifteen? I think he'll take it. I'll put a call in to him today."

"No." Tom grabs her forearm, then quickly pulls away. "Best if it comes from me."

As always, her first instinct is to fight. She can handle her father. She doesn't need a man, particularly her ex, coming to her rescue. Then she reconsiders, picturing Kenny cowering as Tom lays into him.

Beck doesn't learn what Tom says to Kenny, only that it happens quickly. The following week when he passes her in the hall, Tom casually mentions, "It's been taken care of," and that's the end of the discussion regarding Kenny Miller. That's also the end of the fifteen-thousand-dollar cushion the Millers have from the sale of Helen's diamonds.

In early August, Beck and Tom join the other parties in court to review the numerous motions they've all filed to slow down discovery. As anticipated, Judge Ricci rejects their motion to suppress the seizure. She also rejects the motions from all parties to delay the case. Beck sits beside Tom as the judge issues her rulings.

"Your Honor," one of the Austrians' lawyer protests. "Our witnesses and experts are all overseas. There's simply no way we can bring them over for depositions within a ninety-day period."

"Seems to me a plane ride takes ten hours," the judge says.

"Your Honor." The lawyer for the Italians stands. Beck recognizes his name from the letter she received three months ago. "We insist you grant us access to the diamond so our experts can inspect it."

"Do you doubt the report from the International Gemology Society?" the judge asks.

"We simply feel it's prudent to have our experts confirm that it is indeed the Florentine Diamond before we continue with discovery."

"Us, too," the Habsburgs' lawyer chimes

in. "We have no reason to doubt the grading report, but we need our historians to be able to confirm the diamond in Federalist Bank is the Florentine."

The judge turns to Tom, who has no objections to their request. Before they can protest for more time, the judge announces, "Each party can submit a list of names to access the diamond, and I'll issue an order to the bank to provide limited access upon presentation of satisfactory identification. But the discovery deadline stands. I see no reason why all this cannot be accomplished by the end of September."

The parties agree because they have no other choice. As Beck watches Judge Ricci walk out, she notices the judge's shoulders are slumped, a recognition that try as she might, this case is going to drain resources. Even if she keeps the parties to a speedy trial, there will be appeals upon appeals, possibly all the way up to the Supreme Court. And then there are all the meritless claims, which the paralegals at the Department of Justice must dismiss one by one. That will likely take another year. At least.

En route to their office, Beck and Tom walk through the courtyard in city hall even though it's faster to go around the building. Tourists mill, necks craned for a glimpse of

William Penn towering above them, but Beck loves the outdoor enclave of city hall, the centuries of people who have stood there. Long before their first kiss, on one of their earliest strolls back to the office from the courthouse, Beck told Tom this. Since that first time, they have always walked through city hall.

Tom swings his briefcase like a lawyer in a movie. She knows what he would be saying to her if she was just a client, not a colleague, not his ex-girlfriend. He would be focused on the positives, why a swift case is better. He would highlight the merits of their situation. Instead, he walks quietly beside Beck, a silence that speaks louder than any false hopes. A silence that makes Beck want to prove him wrong. Their position is promising. It has to be.

"I have a lead," Beck hears herself saying.

Having committed the wording to memory, she recites Winkler's footnote verbatim. " 'Four days after the revolution erupted in Budapest, on November 3, the children had to be spirited back to Vienna by their steadfast nurse, a young redheaded beauty who gallantly risked her life to deliver the children safely to their parents in Vienna.'

"We haven't been able to find much, anything really, about our great-

379

grandmother, Flora. One thing we do know is that she had red hair."

They walk out the other side of the courtyard, where the crowd dissipates as they progress across Market. Tom raises his eyebrows. "Red hair?"

"Only 2 percent of the world's population has red hair. I know it's a stretch, but what if the nurse was my great-grandmother? She would have had access to the diamond."

"And you know the nurse's name was Flora?"

Beck shakes her head. For that information, they would need to visit the Haus-, Hof- und Staatarchiv, a branch of the Austrian State archives in the Innere Stadt in Vienna, where the Habsburgs records are stored. The empire kept files on each court employee. A file for the redheaded nurse would be included among the other *die Kammer.*

"Let's say the nurse is your great-grandmother — you think the emperor would have gifted her the Florentine? A diamond that precious to a *nurse?*"

They stop outside their office building. Although they are both going to the eighteenth floor, they remain on the sidewalk amid the smokers and lunchtime amblers.

"We should at least look into it," Beck

implores.

"We'll find someone in Austria to go to the archives," he says, holding the door for her. They step inside the cavernous lobby.

"Maybe I could go," Beck says. Tom laughs, quieting when he realizes she's serious. "The author, Winkler . . . his son lives in Krems an der Donau, near Vienna. In the author's note, it says that Winkler kept extensive notes from his interviews with the empress. She may have mentioned something about the crown jewels. Or the redheaded nurse. I reached out, and he said he'd give me a look." In reality, Beck still hasn't heard from Peter Winkler, despite having sent him a fifth email. With the presence of that essential footnote, however, she's confident that his father's archives must contain something useful. "If I go talk to him, he may open up to me more than some private investigator. And I know stories. From Helen. I'll be able to vet anything we find in a way a stranger won't."

Tom stares at her, before finally saying, "I'll run it by the partners. If they okay it, I want you to bring the translator with you."

"Not a problem," Beck says, trying to hide her excitement at the thought of a week in Vienna with Christian.

■ ■ ■ ■

"Your firm is going to pay for you and Christian to go to Vienna?" Ashley asks Beck through the speaker on her cell phone. "Because of some footnote Deborah found?"

Ashley has traded in her SUV with the moon roof and safety detectors on the mirrors for a used station wagon that does not have Bluetooth. Although she insists to Ryan that the Millers will sell the diamond, that they do not need to put their house on the market, she has agreed to sell off whatever unnecessary luxuries they can, including both their cars. The shocks on the station wagon are worn, and she feels each bump as she drives to pick up her children from day camp, something that has become Ryan's responsibility. Today, Ryan is in the city, meeting with his lawyer, opening an account to hold the money for restitution to his company, and reviewing what he should do over the next two months while he awaits his sentencing.

"What can I say, I have the gift of gab," Beck says. "And the gift of knowing how to make our lawyer feel singularly guilty."

"I guess Tom wasn't a total waste, after

all." Ashley regrets this as soon as she says it.

To her surprise, Beck laughs and says, "I guess not."

"Do we even know Flora was redheaded? Maybe she was, like, auburn. Or maybe Deborah's remembering wrong. That wouldn't be a first."

"It's worth a shot. Plus, I want to get a look at Winkler's archives. His son has them."

"I thought you couldn't get in touch with him."

"Not yet, but I will."

Ashley pulls into the camp parking lot and turns off the engine, staring at the field where children are running in the distance. She hopes Lydia and Tyler are among those playing tag and doing cartwheels, that they are able to tune out their family troubles while they are with their peers. When the counselor blows her whistle announcing pickup, Lydia and Tyler will be surprised to find their mother waiting for them. Tyler will ask, *Where's Dad?* and she will tell him the truth, that he's meeting with his lawyer. They have agreed to answer the children's questions as honestly as possible, without excuses or euphemisms.

"Hey, Beck?" Ashley says as she continues

to stare at the mass of campers playing. "Can I come with you to Vienna?"

As Ashley waits for Beck to say no, she anticipates all Beck's questions because she's asking them of herself: How can she afford it? What about the kids? Can she leave them alone with Ryan? What's going on with Ryan? When is he getting sentenced?

Ashley starts to say never mind, it was a stupid idea, but Beck interrupts, "Of course. You can always come. We still have the money Helen left us in her will. We can use that for a ticket, and maybe Mom can watch Ty and Lydia, give Ryan time to sort everything out."

Jake's request to go on the trip is more surprising. Beck says no on principal, not that it's her decision to make. "Should you be leaving when Kristi's in her second trimester? What if something happens? She'll never forgive you if you're not there."

"She's only twenty-nine weeks. Plus, her mom is with her," Jake says, leaning back on Rico's lumpy couch. The lingering tanginess of frozen pizza bites hangs in the air, making Jake queasy. From the odor to the movie posters tacked to the walls to the dishes littering the room, Rico's apartment is in need of a woman's touch. Even with the water stains and fraying furniture, Jake's apartment is lighter, seemingly more spacious, clean smelling. Assuming it's still his apartment, that is.

"With all the media craziness that's been going on, don't you want to be there for her? I know it's not my place —"

"You're right, it's not your place."

"My firm won't pay for you to come with me."

"I'm not asking for a handout," he says, even though he was. But he's already accrued so much debt since he was fired, what's one more plane ticket? "I'm telling you that I want to go to Vienna and find our family's roots, same as you. This isn't just your mission because you took control of the lawsuit."

Jake can sense Beck wanting to defend herself — she didn't take control of anything; she was served a search and seizure by the FBI. He's about to apologize for coming on too strong when Rico walks in. They chat briefly about plans for the night; it's Rico's weekly poker game, an activity that Jake both can't afford and has never been interested in. He makes enough bad bets on other parts of his life.

"Don't worry," Jake says to Rico. "I'll make myself scarce."

"Who was that?" Beck asks when Jake returns his attention to their conversation. "Where are you?"

The last person Jake wants to tell about his fight with Kristi is Beck. Still, when she asks him, "What happened?" he finds himself admitting, "Everything."

Jake starts with the good, how despite the reporters stalking their building, it brought him and Kristi closer together. It made their home a harbor from the outside world. Then one day, a reporter touched Kristi's arm. He'd only meant to get her attention, but she was late for work, and before she knew what she was doing, she was yelling, and the crowd of reporters slowly stepped away, hushed. She ran to her car, sat behind the wheel, and cried. She needed to talk to Jake. Since he was at work, she knew he wouldn't answer his phone. So she drove over to Trader Joe's to find him.

"Wait, when did you get fired?" Beck asks.

"Like, four months ago. The guy, who was following me . . . I realized he wasn't when I clocked him in the face."

"Jesus, Jake."

"I know, okay. I can pinpoint each wrong turn, starting with the punch." Maybe even earlier when he let the fear creep in and cloud his judgment. One bad decision after

386

the other until he came home from the library, instead of Trader Joe's, and found Kristi sitting cross-legged on the couch, cradling her small stomach. The moment he saw her, he sensed a seismic shift.

Kristi stared into the distance as he kissed her cheek and asked her how her day was. "And how was your day?" she said by way of an answer. "You were at work, right?" He felt an immediate dread as she continued. "Because you can imagine my surprise when I stopped by and discovered you haven't worked there in over four months."

"I can explain."

"Really? I'd love to hear it."

"I was planning on telling you, I swear. The moment I got home, when you asked me what happened to my hand, my brain was telling you what happened and then I just said something different."

"You mean you lied."

"I lied," he admitted. "For what it's worth, I was trying to protect you. I thought we were going to get the money from the Italians, and I didn't want you to worry prematurely. Then when that didn't happen, my script was going so well I thought the best thing was to keep working on it. But I'll get another job. Tomorrow, I'll go out and —"

"To *protect* me?" Her voice raised to

dangerous decibels. "You did this for you. You knew if you told me, you'd have to face all the ways you keep screwing up, and you didn't want to do that, so you lied. For four months."

She was right. Of course she was right.

He sat beside her on the couch. "I'm really sorry, Kris. I don't know what I was thinking." As he reached for her, she jumped up and retreated to the other side of the living room.

Jake and Kristi squabble about dirty dishes, rent. They've never had a big, blowout fight like this. It's something he prided himself on, a sign of a healthy relationship. As he watched Kristi continue to pace, the argument quickly became a catalog of everything that's wrong with him: his lack of follow-through; the death of his ambition; his inability to think any further than five minutes ahead; his insistence that everything will always magically be fine without any effort; the fact that she's drowning in student loan debt, and she still always paid for everything. As he listened, he realized he was wrong. Never fighting wasn't a sign of a healthy relationship.

Jake couldn't get a word in, and he didn't want to. He didn't want to tell Kristi all the things that were wrong with her, because there wasn't anything about her he disliked.

"What's worse is I think you actually like this roll-with-the-punches lifestyle. You think it's romantic or something. See how romantic it is when you're pushing fifty and can't even get a car loan." She shook her head. "You're thirty-seven years old. You can't keep acting like this. Actually, you can keep acting however you want. Go into debt to write your script. Spend the next ten years living in some mold-infested apartment. Do whatever you want."

Jake didn't understand what she was saying, not until she opened the door.

"Please, Kris. I know how bad this is. I can fix it, all right? I'll get a job. We can go to therapy."

Her eyes widened. "With what money? This isn't just about you getting fired, and you know it. You're stuck, Jake. Since I first met you, you've been floundering. I don't know if it was the movie or your fight with Beck, but you can't follow through with anything. It didn't used to bother me, only now, with the baby, all this lying — it's just too much. I can't ignore it anymore." He could see it on her lips. *I'm sorry.* It pained her to have to tell him all this.

"Let me just grab a few things." He walked into their bedroom in a daze. He had no idea what he was putting into the duffel bag. Eventually it was full and he tossed it over his shoulder. In the living room, Kristi resumed her cross-legged position on the couch. The door was still open, revealing the courtyard below. She didn't look up at him as he paused before walking out, waiting, hoping she'd engage.

After he finishes his story, Beck is quiet for so long he wonders if the phone cut off.

"Beck?"

"I'm here." Her tone is colder than he would have expected. Until that moment, he didn't realize he was waiting for her to tell him he could fix this.

"You're always so focused on the what," Beck finally says. "What you did wrong. What you could have done differently. What you can do now to fix it. What about the why? Why did you do it? Not just lying about getting fired or punching the guy. Why didn't you think about the future? You knew Kristi was pregnant. Why didn't that compel you to want to get your life together? It's the why that matters, not the what."

Jake's not sure he understands the difference.

"Take our fight." Jake holds his breath because he has no idea what his sister is going to say. "Sure, I was mad at you because your movie was the impetus for me getting kicked out of law school, but that was my fault. I got kicked out because of my mistakes, not yours. But it was easier to blame you. Plus, I was hurt that you took my experiences without my input or permission and used them for a laugh. Then you just expected us to be excited for you, to support you when you revealed our story to the world. I had to watch like all those other idiots in the theater."

"I didn't consider that. I'm sorry, Beck. I really am."

"I know you are. But forgiveness is a process. You can't force it. And you can't control what forgiveness will look like when it happens. Kristi will forgive you. From everything you've told me about her, she's not going to banish you from your child's life. That doesn't mean she'll get back together with you, though. That's her choice. For now, the best thing you can do is be okay in the in-between."

He isn't clear on what she means — in between what? — but what he hears is persistence. He must not give up. On Beck. On Kristi. On Helen, either.

"Please take me with you, Beck. I'm not running away. This isn't me avoiding my problems. I want to come. I need to. I need to see Vienna and know where Helen came from."

He holds his breath, until finally she says, "Okay."

Such a small word — *okay* — tinged with resignation, like Beck was always going to say that he could come, regardless of whether she wanted him there. Yet Jake decides to hear hope in those four little letters: *Okay, we're done fighting. Okay, you can come to Vienna with us.*

Okay, I forgive you.

■ ■ ■ ■

PART THREE

■ ■ ■ ■

PART THREE

FIFTEEN

At the beginning of September, the Miller children meet at JFK to board an overnight flight to Vienna. Jake has already endured one red-eye and dreads another sleepless night. He didn't tell Kristi he was leaving the country. Until his first plane from LA to New York ascended into the dark sky, it hadn't occurred to him to let her know he was going away. He'll be back in a week. She probably won't notice he's gone. As the plane leveled and the seat belt sign turned off, it hit him: they really were over.

While the Millers wait for their flight to board, Beck receives a text from Viktor, telling her he's found the maker's mark.

Lunch tomorrow? he writes.

Can't, en route to Vienna. Okay if my mom stops by instead?

The dots of Viktor's side of the exchange

thrum until eventually he responds, Sure.

Great! Beck internally apologizes for subjecting Viktor to Deborah.

The flight attendant announces that they'll begin boarding in five minutes, and Beck sneaks away to call her mother.

"Please don't embarrass me," Beck cautions after Deborah agrees to meet with Viktor.

"So you're saying I shouldn't read his tarot cards?"

"Mom —"

"Really, what do you take me for?"

Ashley finds Beck pacing the walkway near their gate and motions to her that their group is boarding.

"I'll send you instructions on what to ask him. And email me the second you're finished talking to him."

"Yes, ma'am," Deborah says, clearly amused.

As they wait in line to board the plane, Beck emails Deborah a list of questions to ask, topics to avoid including acupuncture and the afterlife. Don't make me regret this, Beck writes, then erases. She's not trying to be cruel. Besides, telling Deborah to behave is the surest guarantee that she won't.

Ashley and Beck sit in the aisle and window in front of Jake and Christian. After the dinner course, the flight attendants turn off the lights and the passengers around Jake settle in for a few hours of sleep. Every time he shuts his eyes, he sees Kristi and is reminded that she doesn't know where he is, that it's really over. A piece of Beck's dyed black hair falls behind the headrest, and Jake rubs it between his fingers, gently so it won't wake her. It's brittle from years of dye, like a horse's mane. Kristi's hair is equally black, naturally so, silky and smooth. He took her hair for granted, its softness. It can't be over. Beck was never going to forgive him, yet here he is, on a plane with her to Vienna. Kristi will forgive him, too. She has to. He'll do whatever it takes.

Beck feels her hair fall from Christian's fingers. At least, she assumes it's Christian, playing with her hair. It's surprising that he would reach out so blatantly, given that on each of their four dates he'd flirted intensely without placing a finger on her. At the airport, though, he found all sorts of reasons to make physical contact. A nudge in line as he asked how they were divvying up the rooms. A hand on her back when it was her turn to order at the terminal restaurant, again when he let her step ahead of him onto the plane. An arm squeeze when he'd said he'd try calling Peter Winkler when they arrive in Vienna. "He may be one of those people who doesn't use email. If you'd emailed me instead of called, we might not be here today," Christian said with a wink. She still hasn't decided if she wants anything to happen with him. She's not ready to open up to someone, not that that's what Christian is offering, necessarily. He's too young, for one thing. Too carefree, for another. When he lets go of her hair, she wonders why either of those things matters.

Ashley jolts awake. She's surprised she fell asleep so effortlessly, but she's thousands of feet above Ryan, soon to be thousands of miles away, too. The children hadn't hesitated when Ashley asked them if they'd like to spend a week with Deborah. It's funny how the qualities that made Deborah a terrible mother make her an equally special grandmother. Maybe the same was true of Helen.

Beck tries to sleep beside her. In her sister's pursed mouth, her clenched eyelids, Ashley can see that sleep evades her. Ashley reaches out and laces her fingers through Beck's. Beck opens her eyes and smiles at her sister. Ashley doesn't know what awaits them in Vienna. The redheaded nurse might not be their grandmother. Even if she is, Peter Winkler still hasn't responded to

Beck's emails. If Beck or Christian is able to reach him once they're in Austria, his father's collection of Habsburg keepsakes might not include evidence that the emperor gifted Flora the diamond or any other phantom puzzle pieces that prove the diamond is theirs. Still, they will be in Vienna where Helen grew up, where she lost her family. Ashley understands that's the real reason for this trip. They will walk the streets Flora and Helen walked and will become more connected to them.

The Millers' flight lands too early to check into their hotel, too early to visit the archives, too early for anything except sleep. In the cool early-morning hours, they lumber around the Innere Stadt, Vienna's central district, until they can finally check in at ten. Once in their hotel room, the Millers lay awake, Beck and Ashley in one queen bed, Jake in the other. Despite the jet lag and time difference, their bodies are too animated for slumber, their minds too plagued by home, now very far away. Jake imagines telling Kristi about his first glimpses of Vienna cast in golden light. All the buildings in Vienna are large and varying shades of white. It makes the whole city feel timeless, even though most of the stores

399

sell designer clothing and modern luxury goods. Still, the cleanliness of the city is romantic. If Kristi forgives him, he will bring her to Vienna and together they will discover his homeland.

Keenly aware that none of them is sleeping, Jake finally asks, "Do you think we'll find her?"

"Yes," Beck says too confidently. "There has to be a file for Flora in the archives."

The room returns to silence. Jake and Ashley commune telepathically, worried about Beck. Troubled by her certainty.

Like most buildings in Vienna, the Haus-, Hof- und Staatarchiv branch of the Austrian State archives is massive and off-white, impressively regal. Inside, the collection for the Imperial House and Court is equally massive, comprised of centuries of records. In the dark lobby, the Millers stand beside Christian as he and the archivist speak in hushed voices.

"Flora Auerbach's her married name, right? Do you know if she was married when she worked at the court? If not, what was her maiden name?" Christian asks the Millers.

"Her married name was Auerbach. I couldn't find her marriage license online, so I don't know when she married, what her maiden name was," Ashley tells him.

"How many Floras could there have been in the court in 1918?" Beck poses, noticing a tweak of frustration as Christian returns his attention to the archivist. They continue to speak back and forth, until eventually the archivist waves them along, past a statue of a woman in a voluminous dress, upstairs into the archives. Christian does a little dance routine as he skips up the stairs. Ashley glances over at Beck, who shrugs, feeling herself blush.

"We're going to have to look through all the *die Kammer* files," Christian says. "Even if she did work at the palace, her file might not be here. Apparently, at the end of the empire, a lot of files that didn't seem important were thrown away."

"The file for the nurse who saved the crown prince and the other royal children wouldn't have been considered important?" Beck asks.

Christian shrugs. "It wasn't a monarchy anymore."

"She'll be here," Beck insists. Jake and Ashley flash each other a look but say nothing.

When the archivist brings them the first batch of files, the Millers find so many more positions in the court than they could have imagined: guards and doorkeepers, valets, gun chargers, dresser maids, timekeepers. Instead of being organized by emperor, the employee files are organized alphabetically — papers for Franz Joseph and Sisi's employees, for Ferdinand's, beside Karl and Zita's. Christian has written down a few key words for them: *kinderfrau, kinderpflegerin, kindermädchen, kinder-stubenmädchen,* the various nurses and nannies that took care of the children. After all, Flora may have been a pet name; it may not have been written in her file. Best to check all the files for Karl's children's staff.

Christian hums as he works, singing softly to himself as he flips through the pages.

Ashley squeals when she spots *kinderfrau* in a file, but the nanny, Anna, was caregiver to Franz Joseph's four children, not Karl's.

"This is hopeless," Beck says.

"We just started." Ashley closes the file and reaches for another.

"Two hours and all we've found is one nurse, sixty years too early."

"That's how research goes," Jake reminds her.

"Is that your expert opinion?" Of course he is right. Archival research is like panning for gold, but she doesn't want to hear this from Jake, who has likely never been in an archive before. Beck peers over at Christian, embarrassed that she's lashed out at her brother in front of him, but he smiles at her, seemingly oblivious to her tone. "I'm just frustrated," she says to Jake.

"We all are." Jake stands. "Let's take a break. I'm famished."

They follow Jake to a nearby pub. Along the walk, Christian continues to nudge Beck, to graze her arm, to do a little hop-step to get her to laugh. Beck nudges him back when he stumbles on an uneven stone, telling him to watch where he's walking, keenly aware that Ashley is monitoring their interactions.

The bar Jake selects is dark and smoky, but the back room is nonsmoking, bright with lace tablecloths and red booths. They file into a booth, and Jake orders a *bier* for everyone, one of the few German words he knows. Beck can hear the soft pop of Christian's jaw as he chews his Wiener schnitzel. Beck doesn't eat veal and orders chicken, smothered in paprika sauce.

She drops her fork to her plate where it clangs against the ceramic. "I can't believe I listened to Deborah. This is insane. A redheaded nurse?"

Ashley and Jake eye each other in a way that has become routine. It's a key moment

403

that could go one of two ways: they can bond over blaming Deborah, or they can fight. This isn't Deborah's fault. Beck persuaded her law firm to send her here. Even if Deborah planted the seed, Beck had watered it and allowed it to flourish. Her siblings let Beck's comment linger as they finish their Wiener schnitzel. Christian continues to eat, unfazed, singing one of his little ditties. Ashley doesn't know if it's a real song or one he makes up on the spot.

After lunch, they start to walk toward the archive, past long buildings that are all the same height, five or six stories. Stone with careful detail. Their uniformity unnerves Beck, despite their beauty; she isn't sure why.

"I think we should call it quits for today," Beck says.

Christian checks his watch. "The archive's open for another ninety minutes."

When Beck starts to speak, no words come out. How can she explain that, while it was her idea to bring them to Vienna, suddenly the prospect of digging through records feels like a waste of time. There are simply too many files for them to sift through. They could have a year and they still might not locate Flora's file, if it's there, if it wasn't thrown out one hundred years ago, if Flora was even the redheaded nurse. Besides, they are in the city where Helen grew up, where her mother taught her to sew, where her brother took her to cafés to watch the men play chess and debate, where her father brought her to the opera. They should be visiting the opera house, the Danube, the Ferris wheel. They shouldn't be wasting their few days in Vienna in the archives where the prospects of finding a file on Flora are so slim.

"Maybe you can finish off the afternoon without us?" Ashley suggests.

"I can," Christian says. "But it'll decrease our chances of finding anything."

"What if you hire a couple of the archivists? They'll be more productive than we are," Jake adds, looking to Beck for confirmation.

"I think the firm would pay for that," Beck agrees.

Christian shrugs. It isn't really up to him, and Jake spots relief on his face. Christian waves goodbye as he plods toward Herrengasse.

"Strange man you've found," Ashley tells her sister. "Oh, my God, you're blushing."

Beck's cheeks are indeed warm. She likes Christian's strangeness, the way he's unimposing, the way he skips instead of walks,

405

the way he's always singing. She likes that he didn't get awkward when she snapped at her siblings. She's finding she likes all sorts of things about him.

"So." Ashley weaves her arms through her siblings. "Where are we headed?"

"I have an idea." Beck whips out her phone and looks up directions to the Israelitische Kultusgemeinde Wein, where the Goldsteins borrowed a spare office to hold interviews with hundreds of children and their parents to fill the fifty visas.

The Millers walk toward the river until they reach the building, set back on a cobblestone street that's chained off from cars. They stare at the gold Hebrew letters above the door, characters they cannot read. In this building, Flora had convinced the Goldsteins to take Helen abroad.

Ashley digs into her purse for her phone and finds a copy of the black-and-white photograph from *My Grandmother and the 49 Children*, where the line of families snakes this very building. The windows are different, as are the signs above distinct wooden doors. In the photo, the sign is in German, equally indecipherable to Jake as the Hebrew today. Nazi officers inspect the families' documentation, their faces hidden in shadow. Helen is not in this photograph, or if she is, Jake can't locate her.

"Why do you think the Goldsteins chose her?" Jake asks his sisters. Helen was older than the other forty-nine children. Why, out of hundreds of Viennese Jewish children, did she stand out as a candidate for a good American?

"Why did they choose any of them?" Beck poses.

No one responds. They've read that the Goldsteins chose families they believed had a greater chance of reuniting, but beyond that it must have been arbitrary. Maybe Mrs. Goldstein liked Helen's smile or her dress. Maybe she wanted an older girl and saw something nurturing in Helen. All the Millers know is that here, in this building, whatever their reasons, the Goldsteins had selected their grandmother and brought her to America.

The next morning at breakfast, there's no discussion of the Millers joining Christian at the archives. With a flourish, Christian butters his bread and asks Beck, "Shall I hire two more archivists for the day?"

"Whatever you need," Beck tells him.

"I'll try that Peter Winkler guy, too."

"That would be great." Beck pretends to be pleased, but she feels as pessimistic about

Peter Winkler and his father's memorabilia as she does the royal archives.

After breakfast, the Millers take the U to Brigittenau, the Twentieth District where Helen grew up. From Brigittenau they follow the Danube toward Leopoldstadt, where Helen and her mother were relocated. Leopoldstadt has become the hip part of Vienna with vegan ice cream parlors and locally designed clothing boutiques. Jake feels a pang of guilt — this is the part of Vienna he would want to live in while Helen was moved here against her will.

Day two blends into day three, and Christian has not found the nurse to the last emperor's children. He did, however, manage to get in touch with Peter Winkler, who seemed only vaguely aware of Beck's emails. When Christian explained that he was a PhD student studying the Habsburgs, Peter enthusiastically offered access to his father's files. Together, they made a plan to visit Krems an der Donau on the Millers' second to last day in Austria. Until then, day three becomes day four, and Christian hasn't uncovered any documents on Karl and Zita's nurse. The Millers have not returned to the archives to help him. They have not been able to escape the shape of Helen and Flora's Vienna grafted onto their own.

They visit Schönbrunn Palace, the summer residence of the Habsburgs, and tour the few domicile rooms open to the public. Most are Franz Joseph's quarters, but at the end of the tour, there's a bathroom that Zita was updating with modern plumbing and a flushing toilet. It wasn't completed until after the empire fell. Zita never got to use it.

"Do you think Flora lived here?" Ashley asks her siblings. There's no way for them to know.

At the treasury, they wander through dark cool rooms of crown jewels, case upon case of bejeweled swords, crowns, chain mail, and religious iconography. Among these treasures, a few cases are empty. Beck assumes the jewels are on loan. When she asks the guard, he explains that those are the jewels the Habsburgs stole at the fall of the empire. The cases will remain empty until the jewels are returned to the homeland.

Beck reads the descriptions on each case, searching for the Florentine, until she remembers that the diamond was on display at the Kunsthistorisches Museum, not the treasury. Surely, if the Austrians win the forfeiture case, the Florentine will be returned here, made public with the other Habsburg treasures. Beck walks around the dark rooms of crowns, crosses, and slippers, imagining where, if she were the curator, she would put the Florentine. It would be the premier jewel of the collection, like the Hope Diamond at the Smithsonian, the crown jewels at the Tower of London. Each day, thousands of tourists would come to see the Florentine Diamond. She thinks of Helen's dresser, now filled with Deborah's clothes, the space behind it where the Florentine was lodged, seemingly missing. No one, other than Helen, had seen the Florentine in years. No one else will as long as it remains in a safe-deposit box in Federalist Bank in Philadelphia.

For a moment, Beck hopes the Millers lose their case. Then her phone buzzes with a message from Christian.

I found Flora.

"Ah, Beck's sister," Viktor says when he finds Deborah in the hall outside his apartment. He holds out his signature flute of bubbly.

"Do you greet all your guests with champagne or just me and my daughter?"

"So Beck really is your daughter?" he exclaims with mock surprise. "Come, I have good news for you."

Deborah follows Viktor into the living room

410

where a manila envelope rests on the glass coffee table.

"It took a while, but eventually I located the right catalog." Viktor reaches into the envelope and pulls out a glossy black-and-white magazine that says *Brand Name and Trademark Guide, 1956.* He flips through and stops on the *S* brands, where he points to *SJ.* The company's name is printed below: *Spiegel's Jewelers.*

"This is the maker's mark that was on the back of the orchid brooch," Viktor explains as he lays out black-and-white photos of a modest storefront, Spiegel's Jewelers etched onto the picture window. "Spiegel's Jewelers started as a one-man operation on Sansom Street."

"So this is who made the brooch?"

Viktor nods and reaches into the manila envelope for an obituary from the *Philadelphia Inquirer,* which he hands to Deborah. "Joseph Spiegel set up his business in a tiny office space in 1920 after he immigrated to America. By 1930, he had his own storefront and managed to stay open during the war. He passed away in 1960, then the business was handed down from his son to grandson. Now, it's called Spiegel and Sons and is on the Main Line, in downtown Wayne."

Her heart pounds so intensely she suspects

411

Viktor can hear it thumping. The obituary includes a photo of Joseph Spiegel. Although she hasn't seen the photograph before, she recognizes his broad forehead, his square jawline, his slender nose so similar to her own.

The paper falls from her hand to the floor. She leans back, shuts her eyes, and steadies her breath.

"You okay?" Viktor leans toward her but knows better than to touch her. "Let me get you a glass of water."

It seems like Viktor is gone for longer than necessary, and Deborah is grateful for the moments alone. This obituary has stripped her of any lingering doubt. The married man from Helen's photographs — Joseph Spiegel, not Joseph Klein — was indeed her father. He had a family, a business, a jewelry shop where Helen had the brooch made. Her father had not died in 1953 in Korea when Deborah was one. He died in 1960 in Philadelphia when she was eight and could have known him.

Deborah reaches down to retrieve the obituary. A heart attack, at age sixty-four, survived by his wife and two children. The obituary says nothing of a third child nor the mistress who bore her. As she scans the article, Deborah remembers that, in the late '50s, Helen cut her hair into a bouffant. She maintained the hairdo through the '60s until her mane

412

turned white. Then Helen let it grow past her shoulders and started wearing it in a braided crown, her signature hairstyle until her death. In the photographs Helen had kept of her and Joseph picnicking, dancing, dining hand in hand, Helen didn't have the bouffant. The fact that she had no photographs from the bouffant era didn't necessarily mean Helen had stopped seeing him, but it marked a change in their relationship from one that was memorialized in photographs to something more furtive.

Viktor returns with a glass of water. Its coldness soothes her throat. She finishes the glass and rests it beside the obituary. Her eyes skim the newspaper, returning to that same thought: 1960, eight years old, she could have known her father. Helen didn't want her to have a relationship with him. Then in the third paragraph she sees a detail she'd overlooked: *Before immigrating to America, Spiegel was the timekeeper to the last emperor of Austria.*

"He knew the emperor?"

Viktor's eyes flit across the text. "Quite well, I'd suspect. He probably would have been in meetings with the emperor."

Suddenly, it's all too clear. Flora was not the nursemaid. Despite the diamonds they found in Helen's doll, Helen did not bring the Floren-

413

tine to America. Joseph Spiegel, royal time-keeper, a man with access to the emperor, must have brought it with him to America. He must have given the Florentine Diamond to Helen. Her children are in Austria, pursuing a false lead that she instigated.

Deborah looks around the library with its floor-to-ceiling bookshelves, its glass doors that lead to a colonial dining room. Viktor is watching her, likely arriving at the same conclusion she does: this is the story of how Helen got the Florentine Diamond.

She turns to him. "Why are you helping us?"

"Your daughter helped me immeasurably a few years ago. I can never repay her, but anything I can do, I'll try." He says this so straightforwardly that Deborah struggles to remember why her first instinct was to distrust him.

"Are you a Scorpio?" He looks confused. "Your sign."

"A Taurus. Is that good or bad for me?"

She tells him about the Taurus, its stubbornness, its creativity. "I thought you were a Scorpio when I first met you," she confesses, although this means nothing to him.

"I'm sorry about the trick I played on you, with the diamond guessing game."

Deborah shrugs. "I picked the right diamond. It had a calmer energy than the other two."

"Well, I suppose I owe you dinner, then." Viktor is unable to contain his smile and she sees that his teeth, while straight, are not perfect. On the bottom they crowd each other. She fights the urge to run her finger across those crooked teeth. If she tried, she has the feeling he would let her.

"I suppose you do," she says.

When the elevator opens on the nineteenth floor, Tyler and Lydia walk casually to the hostess stand, knowing exactly what to do. If Deborah were their age, she would have raced over to the floor-to-ceiling windows and greedily inhaled the view, but her grandchildren are indifferent to the novelty of sky-high dining.

Viktor is waiting at the table, dressed as he has been the two previous times she's seen him in a black cashmere turtleneck and khaki pants, seemingly immune to the heat that lingers into September.

He stands when he sees them approaching, and Deborah is struck by how handsome he is, how unhappy Beck would be if she knew he was smiling at her like that. Ashley gave Deborah a generous budget for watching the kids — one Deborah could have lived off for a month. She could have hired a babysitter, but as long as the children

415

are with her, this isn't a date. She doesn't have to tell Beck.

Viktor has already ordered chicken fingers and French fries, which arrive as soon as Deborah and the children sit. As Viktor watches the kids eat, Deborah catches a glimmer in his eye, perhaps envy. Something about that look tells her Viktor has no children in his life.

When he pours her a glass of champagne, she asks, "Is that the only thing you drink?"

He laughs. "What else would I have?"

Deborah motions to the waiter and orders two Rob Roys. "I always like something stronger on a first date."

"This is a date, then?" he asks, and it takes her a moment to realize he's teasing.

Viktor really doesn't drink anything besides bubbly, and the effects of the rye are instantaneous. Shoulders relaxing, he tells her about his apprenticeship on Jewelers' Row, how it was the old-style European way of learning the trade, starting with a broom and ending with a blowtorch. When he begins to talk about diamonds, the children grow interested.

"My mom has a diamond," Tyler tells Viktor. "Dad gave it to her."

As he asks the children if they know how diamonds are formed, the waiter drops off their entrées. Viktor requests four pieces of paper and crayons.

"First, I want you to draw a volcano," he instructs. Eager students, Lydia and Tyler draw ragged-topped mountains. Tyler's spews hot green lava.

"Lava isn't green, dummy," Lydia says.

"You're right," Viktor says, prompting a smug look from Lydia. "But Tyler is right, too." Tyler sticks his tongue at his sister. Deborah debates admonishing the children, then decides their bickering is healthy. They shouldn't be taught to always get along. "If a volcano has olivine in it, it will rain tiny green gems. In fact, this is what happens with diamonds."

Together, they sketch the earth's mantle beneath the volcano, and Viktor documents the diamond's journey from the diamond stability zones to the earth's surface. Deborah feels a smile spread across her face as Viktor tells the children to ball up the paper into asteroids and throw it at the table. Tyler aims his at the darkening puddle of ketchup on his plate.

"Why do you always have to be so gross," Lydia says as Tyler smooshes the paper into the ketchup. When he picks it up, the paper asteroid has left indentations in the puddle, and Viktor, ever the elegant mediator, agrees that while ketchup might not be the most hygienic of samples, the markings the paper-asteroid left in the ketchup are like the scars real asteroids etched into the surface of the earth. He points to the crevices in the ketchup. "Diamonds can be made in those indentations. The impact is hot enough to create the right conditions."

The science lesson is quickly replaced by ice cream headaches and sugar crashes, and Deborah sees the signs of a meltdown across Tyler's yawning face.

"I'd better get them back," she says. Viktor insists on walking them to the garage and paying for her parking. With the Red Rabbit in sight, Deborah is embarrassed suddenly by the rust stains on her car's hood, the dents and scratches on the bumpers.

As she is about to apologize, he says, "I had a Rabbit in the '70s. It was my favorite car."

The children file into the backseat and Deborah feels a tightness in her chest as Viktor comes close, then closer. At the last moment, he kisses her on the cheek, and her stomach drops with disappointment.

"Your grandchildren are delightful," he tells her as he opens the driver's side door.

"I'm afraid I can't take much credit for that."

He closes the door behind her, taps the hood of the car as a parting gesture. He doesn't tell her that he had a nice time or that he'll see her soon. He mentions nothing about the maker's mark. He doesn't ask her if she's told Beck about Joseph Spiegel, his access to the emperor. She pulls onto the street, winding her way toward I-76. First Chester, now Viktor. Has she lost her touch?

The following morning, a bouquet of wildflowers appears on the porch, fashioned with a piece of twine. Not a rose or lily in sight, just delphinium, blue thistle, snapdragon, daffodils, and chamomile — of course Deborah can name them all — with a white card that simply reads *V.* in navy calligraphy.

"Who gave you weeds?" Tyler asks, finding his grandmother standing in the open doorway. By the time she turns to answer, he has disappeared into the kitchen, opening and closing all of the cupboards, concocting a game out of Helen's dishware.

"You break it, you buy it," she calls to Tyler, rushing into the kitchen before any bowls find their way to the unforgiving floor. It's only hours later, once the wildflowers have been placed in a vase and Deborah is hustling the children out of the house for an afternoon in Old City, that she realizes she never told Viktor where she lives.

Although Deborah had promised to email Beck as soon as she spoke to Viktor, she doesn't write her daughter. It's still too raw, this news of Joseph Spiegel, her father, likely the real diamond thief. She's not ready to accept any of it. As long as she doesn't check in with her daughter, Beck won't have to know that she's seeing Viktor, either. Besides, it's not like Beck has written her.

Over pasta at Vetri, Deborah tells Viktor about Flora. Since the wildflowers arrived, they've gone to the Academy of Natural Science with the children, but this is their first one-on-one date. Deborah uses some of the funds Ashley left to hire a babysitter. She insists on meeting Viktor at the restaurant, despite his offer to pick her up. This thing with Viktor, she wants to take it slow, something she's never done before, not even with Kenny.

Viktor agrees that she was right not to say anything to her children. "They're already in Vienna. Besides, who knows? Your theory on Flora may turn out to be right." He doesn't tell her it was crazy to assume from one small detail — red hair — that this mysterious nursemaid might have been her grandmother, even though she's been berating herself ever since she found out about Joseph Spiegel. "Stranger things have happened."

"It wasn't Flora," she tells him. "It was Joseph."

"Either way, it can't hurt to stop by Spiegel and Sons to see if they have any paperwork on Helen's brooch," Viktor suggests. "Family businesses like that, they tend to keep meticulous records. If Helen brought the diamond for him to set, there's probably a record of it. Then you'd know whether or not he gave it to her."

"I can't go there," Deborah admits. "It's complicated."

It gives her whiplash, how quickly she takes him as a confidant. She tells Viktor about the photographs she found of Helen and Joseph, of herself on his knee when she was a baby, of her birth certificate with the father's name left blank. She can't recall the last time she's spoken at such length, talking through the entrée and dessert courses.

"Assuming Joseph is your father, it may have been his decision to leave his name off your birth certificate," Viktor says. "As a single woman, Helen would have had to get a signed agreement from him, acknowledging paternity. If he was married, he might not have wanted to do that. Or she may have been trying to protect you. If he was on the birth certificate, he could have fought for custody, tried to take you away."

That would have been terrifying to Helen. She would have done anything not to lose her daughter.

Viktor places his hand on Deborah's. His skin is warm. "You okay?"

"I've been so busy thinking she betrayed me I didn't stop to consider that she may have been protecting me."

"It's funny how similar they seem, betrayal and protection."

Deborah casts him a funny look. She doesn't quite understand what he means. Then again, she knows little about him.

"I've been talking too much. I want to know more about *you*." Deborah coats *you* with innuendo, rubbing his arm.

Viktor downs a glass of red wine, forgoing his signature bubbly when she mentioned that she prefers a bold Italian red. Already, she's changing him. He explains how his career evolved from apprenticing with a jeweler to getting certified by the International Gemology Society to designing for Tiffany's to his side gig of fabricating knockoff engagement rings, which was how he met Beck.

"Tiffany's was very good to me." He refills his glass, and Deborah realizes that the prospect of her judging him makes him nervous. "It's difficult to explain. I didn't feel wronged or unappreciated. They trusted me, I guess too much. It was easy. I couldn't fight the temptation. And as your daughter proved, it didn't violate any trademark copyright laws." He studies her, trying to intuit her thoughts. "I knew it was wrong, even if it wasn't illegal. I wish I could tell you some noble story about sticking it to capitalist society, but I saw an opportunity, and I took it."

Deborah hesitates, stunned by his honesty. It makes her want to be honest, too. "I've started thirty-seven companies over the last thirty years," she admits. "Not one of them has been profitable." She didn't realize she knew the number. There it was, thirty-seven bakeries and dog-walking and wellness companies, all failures. This should embarrass her, but she knows she'll come up another idea. It's like a Rubik's cube — the perfect fit is there. She simply hasn't found it yet.

"Here's to your thirty-eighth idea," Viktor says, raising his refilled glass. It's all she can do to not leap across the table and kiss him.

Instead, she asks, "Will you come with me,

to visit the store?"

His response, "There's nothing I'd like more," is almost as perfect as the kiss that follows.

The next afternoon, Deborah parks the Red Rabbit on Lancaster Avenue and together she and Viktor stare at the store's sign: Spiegel and Sons.

"Do you think they'll be upset when they find out who I am? What if I'm wrong and he was just a friend, a fellow Austrian?"

"Don't worry about them. You need to do this for you," Viktor says, kissing her knuckles.

The brass bell rings as Viktor pushes open the door. With its patterned carpeting and taupe walls, Spiegel's Jewelers resembles a bank lobby. She's been to banks that look like this. They've laughed her out before she finished her business pitch.

There are no price tags on the jewelry. The cases, while full, are not cramped. Deborah immediately understands that everything in the store is exceedingly expensive.

Viktor takes the lead in a way that would normally annoy her, asking the man at the counter if he's Daniel Spiegel, the shop owner and grandson of Joseph Spiegel. But Viktor is merely her liaison into this world she doesn't understand. When Daniel Spiegel takes off his glasses and tells him that he is, Viktor nods for Deborah to proceed.

"My name is Deborah Miller," she begins. "Your grandfather may have known my mother, Helen Auerbach?"

At the sound of her name, Daniel stiffens. "What do you want?"

A woman nearby, whom Deborah assumes is Daniel's wife, casts him a confused look.

"She was my grandfather's . . ." Daniel begins to explain to his wife. He doesn't finish his statement, but she grows visibly uncomfortable.

In those angry, unadorned words, Deborah hears that it's all true — Helen's relationship with Joseph, his gifting her the Florentine Diamond. The air-conditioned store becomes hot. Her knees buckle, and Viktor grabs her elbow.

"Maybe we should sit down," he says, guiding her to a chair.

"You should leave," Daniel says to Viktor. The two men stare at each other until Daniel looks away. "Please."

"Dan," his wife says softly, "it's not her fault."

"Do you know what your mother did to our family?" Daniel's voice rises. "My grandmother had to be institutionalized when she found out about the affair, about you. It ruined —"

"Dan," his wife repeats sternly. "It's not her fault." She turns her attention to Deborah. "Why are you here? What do you want to know?"

Three sets of eyes rest on Deborah, making her skin itch. She's never liked being the center of attention. Viktor begins to speak, but she cuts him off. This is her story to tell. Her truth to uncover.

"My mother told me my father died in Korea," Deborah explains. Viktor squeezes her shoulder for encouragement. "I never questioned that story, not until a few months ago when we found a brooch in Helen's bedroom after she died. An orchid brooch that your father designed for her."

Deborah details the photographs she found of Helen and Joseph, photographs of herself with Joseph, too. She explains the story she's pieced together, the maker's mark on the back of the brooch. "I'm assuming you've heard about the court case involving the Florentine Diamond?" Daniel's eyes spark. "It's my family. We're the Millers. I think your grandfather may have fashioned the Florentine into a brooch for my mother."

Daniel studies her more intently than he

did before, pursing his lips. "That's impossible. Other jewelers may have been willing to look the other way, but my grandfather was known for his honesty, in business at least. He wouldn't have designed a piece of jewelry to hide a stolen diamond. Especially not one that had belonged to the empire. He loved his country."

Deborah asks to borrow Viktor's phone, where photos of the orchid brooch are stored. Deborah's flip phone is too old for things like the cloud and quality cameras.

When Deborah shows him the brooch, Daniel shakes his head insistently. "My grandfather never would have made something so *gaudy.*"

Deborah flips to another photograph of the back of the brooch, where *SJ* is engraved on the finding.

Now, it's Daniel turn to go weak. He leans against the counter, rubs his hand across his face, as if trying to wake himself up.

"He must have records," Viktor inserts. "If he designed the brooch, there must be some documentation of it in your archives."

"Our records are kept in storage. Off-site. It would take weeks to locate them."

"We don't have weeks," Deborah says.

"I'm sorry, it's impossible." Daniel disappears into his office, and his wife follows him.

"Is that it?" Deborah asks as Viktor reaches out to help her stand.

"For now." She follows him onto Lancaster Avenue, confident that Viktor's calmness is the right response.

As they're unlocking the Red Rabbit, Daniel's wife runs out of the store, furtively checking behind her shoulder. She spots Deborah and Viktor standing beside the car and holds out a slip of paper to Deborah. "The off-site location my husband mentioned — it's our attic. It's completely disorganized, but you're welcome to take a look. I'll be home all day tomorrow."

Deborah stares at an address in Berwyn. "What about your husband?"

She bats the thought away. "He's so tightly wound you could grow a diamond in his ass."

Daniel's wife introduces herself as Heidi, and they make a plan to meet at her house the following afternoon when Daniel will be golfing at the country club. As Deborah and Viktor watch Heidi scurry into the store, Deborah asks, "Do you think they'll have a record of the brooch? Whatever the particulars, it was a shady deal."

Viktor shrugs, immune to the shadiness of

his industry. "People keep records of illegal deals all the time. That's why they often get caught. It's worth a look at least."

Sixteen

The Millers meet Christian in their hotel lobby and walk to a wine bar the concierge recommends. Evenings in Vienna are perfectly cool, bordering on chilly, and the Millers savor the respite from the heat that plagues both the east and west coasts of home. They button their fall coats — winter coat for Jake — and traverse Stephansplatz Square. Christian has traded his typical uniform of a gray T-shirt and faded, ripped jeans for a blazer over a button-up plaid shirt tucked into black pants. The outfit makes him look older, and Beck can picture him at thirty, at forty, the professor of students' fantasies.

As they walk past St. Stephen's Cathedral into the maze of streets that comprises the central shopping district, Christian swings a leather folder. Whatever is in that folder will shape their next move, but Christian doesn't hint at what information rests inside.

The wine bar sits across the street from the premier Wiener schnitzel restaurant in Vienna, its long line wrapping around the corner, tourists dressed to varying degrees of appropriateness for the evening's dropping temperature. Behind the bar, an older blonde woman fixes them a platter of meat and cheese, bringing it to the table with a bottle of Grüner Veltliner. Christian waits until she pours everyone a glass before unhooking his leather envelope and pulling out a file.

"I didn't find Flora Auerbach, but I did find Flora Tepper, who was the nursemaid to Emperor Karl's five eldest children from 1913 to 1918."

"That's got to be her, right?" Ashley says excitedly.

Beck studies Christian's handsome face, which doesn't mirror her sister's enthusiasm.

"It would be a pretty major coincidence if it wasn't." Jake turns his attention to Beck. "You said Flora wasn't a common name, right?"

Beck keeps her eyes on Christian, who casts her a look she can't decipher.

"To know for sure, we can always go to the Jewish archives to locate her marriage certificate." Christian explains that, until

431

1938, records were kept by a person's parish or synagogue. "Here's the thing —" Christian lays a photocopy of Flora Tepper's *grundbuchblatt,* the official employee record, on the table. He translates the categories of information on Flora: office, name, date and place of birth, religion, marital status and children, educational background, languages spoken. Christian's finger stops on a phrase and date typed at the bottom of the page: *wurde aus dem Hofdienst entlassen, 10 November 1918.*

"It means she was fired from court service."

The Millers stare at that indecipherable phrase, their giddiness abating. A fired employee was an employee spurned. An employee who might steal. An employee unlikely to be gifted something as valuable as a priceless yellow diamond.

Christian clears his throat for emphasis. "When the republic took power, there was the question of what to do with all the court employees. Most became civil servants or were forced to retire. Other posts were canceled. I haven't heard of many being fired, especially not someone from the personal household." Christian signals to the date at the bottom of the page. "What troubles me is the date. On the night of

November 11, the royal family fled to their hunting home in Eckartsau. On the tenth, they didn't know they were going to have to leave so soon, and at that time, they weren't strapped for cash. Karl withdrew tons from the treasury, and that was before the *krone* lost most of its value. There's no reason they couldn't have afforded to take her with them."

"So why do you think she was fired?" Ashley asks.

Christian points to Flora's religion: *katholisch.*

"Flora wasn't Catholic," Ashley insists, then reconsiders. "Was she?"

"Wouldn't Helen have mentioned that?" Jake asks. "And wouldn't that have saved her from the camps?"

"Well —" Christian has his professorial voice on, and Beck wishes she didn't like the sound of it so much. "It's possible she converted to Judaism later. Interfaith marriage wasn't allowed at the time. So, if she was Catholic, she would have had to convert to marry your great-grandfather. On the other hand, if she lied, Zita was extremely devout. Everyone in the household had to go to mass twice a day and make daily confessions. Everyone who worked in her private household had to be Catholic."

Jake strokes his stubbled chin. "So, if she lied, and the empress found out . . ."

Christian nods.

"How did she even get a job with the royal family?" Ashley asks. "That must have been a prime job in those days."

"She'd have needed a personal connection. That's how those positions were filled. Family or friend," Christian explains.

"We're getting sidetracked," Beck asserts, her disappointment masked in authority. "It doesn't matter how she was hired, if she was Catholic. What matters is she was fired. Fired employees don't get lavish parting gifts."

"*If* it's your great-grandmother," Christian reminds her. While Beck appreciates his efforts to maintain some fragment of hope, it doesn't change their fate. If it isn't their great-grandmother, they have no other leads. If it is, she was a thief.

No one has touched the piles of meat and cheese that crowd their table, glistening with sweat from the heat of the stuffy bar. Beck reaches for a piece of salami and tears it into strips. Christian orders a second bottle of wine.

"If she did steal the diamond after she was fired," Jake poses, "wouldn't the emperor have gone looking for her? When he noticed the diamond was missing, why wouldn't he have sent someone to find her?"

Beck wants to say, *Who cares?* Christian interjects. "Karl had an aide send the jewels ahead to Switzerland while the royal family went to the countryside in Austria. He may not have known it was missing until they arrived in Switzerland. By then, there were so many people who'd betrayed them. He might not have considered Flora a suspect."

Ashley shakes her head, and a strand of hair falls loose from her ponytail and into her face. "This doesn't add up. How would she even have had access to the crown jewels? She worked with the children. I don't see how —"

"Ash." Beck is surprised by her sister's distressed face, by how much she needs Flora to be the heroine. This isn't just about money for Ashley. If they lose the diamond, if Ryan goes to prison, if Ashley loses hope, how will she survive? Not if — when. These are all inevitabilities now.

"I'm sorry the answers I found aren't helpful," Christian says.

Ashley blows her hair from her face, her expression turning cold. "If only we'd sold to the Italians."

"So it's my fault." Beck tries to remain calm. She knows her sister is confronting more than the loss of the diamond.

"This all could have been over four months ago. The reporters, the articles, the lawsuit, the people following us. None of it needed to happen and we would be $500,000 richer."

"Come on, Ash," Jake says. "Let's not do this."

"Sure, take her side. Even though she refused to talk to you for years for something that was her fault, sidle up to Beck like you always do."

Anger is acidic on Ashley's tongue, metallic in her nostrils. She can feel the Miller-style blowout building inside her, but she surprises everyone, herself included, by starting to sob. Christian rubs his arms and looks away. The woman behind the bar busies herself with the cheese and meat display, pretending not to notice.

"Hey." Beck walks around the small table and hugs her sister. Jake stands, too, and clutches them both.

When they part, Ashley laughs self-consciously and wipes the tears from her cheeks. Her siblings laugh, too. Jake punches her arm. Christian watches, bewildered, and Beck figures he's an only child, that this sort of instant anger coupled with instant forgiveness is foreign to him. Either that, or he's the rare breed of human that simply gets along with his family.

Ashley waves to the woman behind the counter and leaves a bundle of twenty-euro bills on the table. Jake has noticed that Ashley always pays with cash these days, something she's never done before.

They step into the brisk night and head toward the hotel. Ashley and Jake linger behind Beck and Christian.

"She might not have stolen it," Christian says.

"It doesn't matter. The firing casts reasonable doubt."

Christian gazes sideways at Beck. "Do you still want to go to Krems an der Donau tomorrow?"

She shrugs. "Peter Winkler's expecting us. It was so hard to get in touch with him. I feel bad canceling."

"I'm sorry this trip was a waste."

"It's not a waste."

Christian smiles and reaches for her hand. His palm is slightly clammy in hers.

Just then, Ashley looks up from kicking at the stone beneath her feet and grabs Jake's arm, motioning to where Christian and Beck walk ahead, holding hands, melding into an anonymous couple along the cobblestone streets of Vienna.

■ ■ ■ ■

In the morning, everyone is quiet as the train pulls away from Heiligenstadt Station toward Krems an der Donau where Peter Winkler lives. The strong sun pierces the windows, warming Beck's face as she watches Vienna recede. The landscape shifts from thatched roofs to colorful houses to vineyards in various stages of harvest.

When the Millers arrive in Krems, the medieval town is as quaint as they imagined. Peter Winkler owns a gallery on Wichnerstraße, but invites them to meet him at his home in the hills above town. They traverse the main street — one long strip of cafés, apothecaries, outdoor clothing stores, and art galleries — and climb toward a stone church at the top of the hill. The street narrows, and they squeeze through a series of tunnels burrowed into the buildings. At the top of the hill, the street circumvents the church, and they wind their way around to the other side of the hill where they begin their descent. Here, the streets grow wider, the houses larger. They stop at a yellow house covered in vines. It looks older than the other stucco houses on the street, not only because of the vines. The house itself is gothic while everything around it has clearly been rebuilt.

The Millers have never been in a house this old. Even Philadelphia is young by comparison. The floors creak with every step. The stone walls produce a tangy and cool must that makes the Millers feel like they are in a museum, not someone's living room.

Peter Winkler has a potbelly and thinning white hair. He looks like Santa Claus, and his willingness to gift them his father's belongings strikes Beck as equally unbelievable. Of course he speaks perfect English, but Beck is glad to have Christian with them, even if they won't need his translation services. Whenever she catches his eye, Christian blushes, and she wonders if he's remembering how she screamed when she came or how he'd giggled when she first touched him. Beck has never been the older woman before. With less than a decade between them, their age gap might not be wide enough to claim that role. Still, it was obvious that she had more experience, which was exciting, uninhibiting. She likes having him here, knowing that it could happen again if she allows it to. That power is arousing.

Peter sits back, waiting for them to say

something. Beck begins by thanking him, to which he shrugs.

"I'm sorry it was so hard to get in touch." Winkler has already brought his father's boxes from the attic to the living room. He places one beside the coffee table and lifts the top off. "My father wanted to restore the monarchy until the day he died."

They pass around photos of the Habsburgs with dates and descriptions on the back. The photographs are disordered, not protected by archival materials that would keep them in mint condition. The photo of Karl and Zita's wedding has patinaed, the white of Zita's floor-length veil yellowed from neglect.

"That's Franz Joseph, the emperor," Peter says, pointing to a man with a Victorian handlebar mustache standing beside the newlyweds. The Millers file through more photographs of the happy couple with Franz Joseph: one from a dinner at the Schönbrunn Palace, another where a smiling boy with wispy blond hair stands beside the seated emperor.

"That's Otto, my father's best friend," Peter says.

The only other pictures of Franz Joseph are of his coffin, with Karl and his family following the dark wooden box. The empress is cloaked in a black veil. The emperor, baby-faced, dons a mustache thinner and shorter than his uncle's had been. Crowds of saluting men flank them as they walk behind the coffin. The photograph is labeled *30 November 1916.* The end of one era, the start of another one, short-lived, destined to fall.

Christian passes around a photograph from *30 Dezember 1916,* Karl's coronation in Budapest as the Hungarian king. He holds a scepter and wears a crown smaller than the one on Zita's head. On the bust of Zita's embroidered dress, Beck spots two brooches. They are out of focus, the diamonds an overexposed white. Neither resembles the hatpin that housed the Florentine.

The Millers continue to mine the box, spotting dozens more photographs of the family from their various stages of power and exile. In several, Zita is praying. In other photographs, boys appear with hunting rifles. The pictures extend beyond the empire to Switzerland and Madeira, dinners at mansions in Tuxedo Park and Quebec, where the royal family lived during WWII. The photos extend beyond Zita, too, to subsequent generations of Habsburgs, young girls and boys in fluorescent ski clothes and satin formal wear.

"Look," Jake exclaims, holding a photograph toward his sisters. In it, a woman is seated on the floor with four children. She holds a fifth in her arms. It is clearly their great-grandmother, Flora. On the back, the description reads, *Kindermädchen mit den Kindern. September 1916.*

That's it, then, Beck thinks. Flora stole the Florentine Diamond.

The next box is less helpful than the first. A few framed portraits of various Habsburg emperors lavished in red velvet. A postcard of Schönbrunn Palace. A tin box filled with bronze pins of the empire's double-headed eagle. The third box harbors coins and buttons. Beck returns everything to the box, feeling embarrassed that she ever believed the diamond might legally be theirs, that these boxes would be filled with recorded interviews, documenting the fall of the empire, that the emperor would have gifted the Florentine to anyone, let alone a servant.

Beck feels the weight of a hand on her back. "We still have one more box," Ashley reminds her. "You're not saving the best for last?" she asks Peter.

Whether he'd intended to or not, the last box is indeed the best. A collective gasp echoes through the room. The box is filled with VHS tapes. The white label along the side of the first tape reads, *Kaiserin Zita, Vol. 1, 1978.*

"Do you have a VCR?" Jake asks.

Winkler calls to his wife, who emerges from the kitchen, and asks her something in German before she disappears upstairs.

"They might have one in the attic," Christian explains to the Millers.

While Winkler's wife opens and closes drawers and closets upstairs in her quest for a forgotten VCR, the Millers continue to dig through the box. There are also volumes two, three, and four of interviews with Zita, as well as a fifth VHS, labeled *Otto.*

"She gave all these to your father?" Ashley asked.

"Otto did. After Zita died, he urged my father to write a book on her. He'd interviewed her for his earlier books on Karl, and Otto wanted him to write another book about his mother. He gave my dad whatever he had that might be helpful. I thought there was more, but this was all I could find."

Mrs. Winkler reappears with a bulky, ancient-looking VCR, and Peter flips through the channels until he finds the right one to connect the VCR. The screen fills with static before a white-haired Zita mate-

443

rializes on the television. She is seated in what looks to be a library, dressed in a black turtleneck, long pearls dangling down her bust. Zita's hair is cropped short around her wrinkled face, the beauty of her youth calcified with age. When she speaks, her voice croaks, hoarse as though she hasn't used it in a long time. Kurt Winkler bellows offscreen to announce the date — *18 Oktober 1978* — and introduces the Kaiserin.

"They are in her apartment in the convent in Switzerland," Christian tells the Millers.

Beck likes watching the interview without understanding Zita's words. It allows her to know the empress at a more primal level. The first tape documents when she met Karl, how they fell in love. Peter's wife wraps her arms around her husband's bicep as she leans toward the television.

"Have you watched these before?" Beck asks the Winklers.

"Never," Peter says softly.

Age has not faded Zita's memory. Her story is chronological and precise.

"She's describing the coronation," Christian whispers as Zita's voice turns lofty, singsong. Midsentence, the video cuts to static and Winkler stands to hit Eject. Ashley and Jake eye each other but say nothing, settling in for a long afternoon.

The second tape is a continuation of the same interview. Christian has forgotten that he is supposed to translate and, like the Winklers, is entranced by the story unfolding. Zita's face remains stoic, other than the occasional indulgence of a smile or laugh. Still, it's obvious she's describing happier times, those halcyon days before they were losing the war and their brief hold on the empire.

Like the first video, the second tape contains nothing relevant. The third one is inserted into the VCR and Jake wants to remain optimistic, but he isn't. Not about these tapes. Not about Kristi, either.

When the third tape only reveals a confusing chronology of failed peace attempts and Karl losing his grip on the empire, Jake's stomach grumbles audibly. Beck glares at him, as though he should be able to keep his hunger in check.

"Why don't we take a break?" Ashley stretches her arms exaggeratedly. "Go grab a bite."

"You two go," Beck says. "I'm not hungry."

Not wanting to fight, Ashley and Jake leave without protest. As they amble toward town, Jake walks without bending his knees, his hip cracking audibly. "Getting old sucks," Jake says, but Ashley insists it's just the hangover, lodged into their joints like poison.

"Hey, Ash," Jake asks. "How do you do it, keep a relationship going for so long?"

Ashley freezes, then remembers he doesn't know about Ryan. The timing was never right. Also, she didn't want him to know. As a man, Jake would judge Ryan, even if he was in no position to judge anyone.

"Kristi," Jake continues. "I've ruined everything."

Suddenly, Ashley feels like she might vomit even though her stomach is empty. When Ryan had said the same thing, curled on their bathroom floor, it had been pathetic, like he hoped she'd find some way of making it not true. When Jake repeats those words now — *I've ruined everything* — they are fatal, predetermined.

"No," Ashley says. "You haven't." And Ryan hadn't, either — not entirely.

The timing is right, so she tells Jake everything that's happening with Ryan, starting with the FBI agent. "I was being followed," she admits to her brother. "But not because of the diamond." She explains the target letter, Ryan's subsequent guilty plea, the $500,000 they still need to collect before his sentencing hearing in a month.

On the steep and narrow streets of Krems an der Donau, it strikes her as ironic that Ryan owes the exact amount the Italians had offered the Millers.

"We're going to have to sell the house."

"Shit, Ash." Jake throws his arm around his sister's shoulders as they turn onto the promenade. After a pause, he asks, "So you forgive him?"

Forgiveness is like training for a marathon. Ashley tracks each day, gauging her progress, but she won't know what shape they're in until his case goes before the sentencing judge.

"It's touch and go," she tells her brother. "Some days, I feel like I've forgiven him, and other days I'm still so mad. I don't want to sell our house. I don't want my kids to have everyone at school know their father is in prison. I don't want to be married to a criminal, either. But I'm not ready to give up on him."

That's it, Jake realizes. Ashley doesn't want to lose hope that they can work it out. Jake doesn't need to make Kristi forgive him. He needs to make her want to believe in him again.

Along the promenade, tourists lounge beneath café awnings. Ashley checks her phone. It's 8:00 a.m. on the east coast. Ryan

447

is probably fixing the kids breakfast, something elaborate that he whips up from scratch. Her children will miss this Ryan more than the one who was always at the office.

I miss you, Ashley texts her husband. It's the closest she's ready to come to *I forgive you.*

Christian and Beck continue to sit side by side on the Winklers' dark wood floor, listening to Zita's interview. As she drones on, Beck tries to determine what will happen when they return with no helpful evidence. Will the firm force them to withdraw their claim? Will they submit a halfhearted motion for summary judgment, knowing they will not convince the court that the diamond belongs to the Millers?

Abruptly, Zita's inflection turns cold. Nothing changes in her posture, yet she's visibly stiffer.

Christian grabs Beck's forearm and whispers, "She's talking about Flora, when they left the children in Gödöllö." The words drip down her eardrums into every vein, coursing through her body.

Zita clenches the arms of her chair and leans forward, teeth bared. Christian holds his breath. "She says they never should have

448

left the kids with that whore of a nurse-maid." He blushes at *whore*. "And she keeps going."

Never mind that Flora smuggled the kids to Vienna, back to their parents and safety and the rest of their lives. *Did you know she was pregnant?* Zita asks Winkler, who could not have known. He's never heard of Flora before. *Unwed and with child?*

"Pregnant?" Beck turns to Christian. "How could she be pregnant? Helen wasn't born until 1925." Then she remembers Martin, Helen's older brother. Is it possible that he was conceived while she worked at the palace? If so, was Leib his father?

"There wasn't anything in the papers," Christian says apologetically. "Tomorrow, we can check the archives for a birth certificate, know for sure."

Fear creeps into Beck's voice. "Was it the emperor's?"

Pregnant, the empress continues. *No husband. A bastard child.* The expression on Zita's face turns contemplative, guilt-stricken. *I found her diary after we fired her. The father was our chauffeur, who had been with them in Gödöllö. The one who died when the children fled. I had no idea they were involved, otherwise I never would have left him with them.*

Beck's body relaxes. The child wasn't the emperor's.

Winkler's says something offscreen, and Christian whispers, "He's asking what happened to her journal."

The guilt on Zita's face morphs into anger as Christian translates. *I burned it.*

"Why would she burn it?" Beck asks, but before Christian can respond, Beck hears the word she's been craving since she got here. It sounds more graceful in German than it does in English. Mellifluous.

"Florentiner."

The following afternoon, when Deborah arrives at the Spiegels' home, she doesn't bring Viktor. She needs to do this alone. Viktor has given her instructions on what types of documents to look for, renderings of the brooch that would prove Joseph made the pin, any records that detailed the cost of a sale, anything that conveyed it was free, which would almost certainly mean he gifted it to his lover.

The Spiegels live in a rural part of Berwyn, in a small farmhouse between large parcels of land. Deborah has a bad feeling as she knocks on the door. What will any of these records prove, really? Even if he made the brooch for free, does that mean he gave

450

Helen the diamond, too? And if her search comes up empty, does that suggest that the whole story is speculation, the diamond, the affair, the genealogy?

Heidi invites Deborah into the living room while she brews a pot of coffee. Deborah surveys the photographs on the mantel as she waits. The Spiegels have two children. There's a photograph of their son behind the counter of Spiegel and Sons, another of their daughter in a graduation cap, waving outside the International Gemology Society campus. Deborah wonders what that must be like, inheriting not just a house or a diamond but a family trade, a vocation. A purpose.

On the end of the mantel, Deborah spots a photograph of Joseph and a man who must be Daniel's father outside their former storefront on Jewelers' Row. Another of Joseph and a woman, heads angled toward each other, against a solid backdrop. It takes Deborah a moment to realize this is their wedding portrait. They look comfortable together, at ease, not necessarily in love. She lifts the photo off the mantel and stares at Joseph's wife's plain but appealing face. Through the image, Deborah can sense her aura, dependable and stable. It's difficult to imagine a woman like that coming undone.

A throat clears, and Deborah turns to find

451

Heidi holding two cups of coffee. She returns the photograph to the mantel and, before she can apologize for snooping, Heidi motions her toward the attic.

"We don't have much time," she says as they mount the stairs.

The attic, smelling strongly of mildew, is unfinished and over one hundred degrees on this early-fall day. In the far corner, several boxes are stacked with the Spiegel's Jewelers logo printed on the side. If the paperwork is in one of these boxes, there's no promising it hasn't been gnawed by a squirrel or hasn't disintegrated to dust.

Heidi sets her coffee cup on the ground and opens the first box. "I'm afraid our filing system isn't the most organized."

Calling it a system is generous. While the boxes have decades inscribed on the tops, they are filled haphazardly with notebooks, receipts, ledgers, orders, and appointment books.

Viktor told Deborah that the brooch was mid-century, post war. By 1960, Joseph Spiegel was dead. She decides to start with a box from the 1950s.

Only the paperwork inside doesn't match the dates on the box. Decades of ledgers and sketchbooks are intermixed, until the '80s when Daniel took over and implemented a recordkeeping system, organized not just by date but by type of sale and document. Then the twenty-first century hit and all records were stored on hard drives, even renderings, which were no longer drawn by hand. This would be so much easier today, typing Helen's name into a computer and accessing every exchange she had with Spiegel's Jewelers.

"Ooh, is this it?" Heidi asks, holding up a sketch of a bouquet of violets, set in yellow burnished leaves.

"Those are violets. We're looking for an orchid." Deborah wishes she'd brought a photograph of the brooch. Heidi holds out another sketch. "Those are buttercups . . . That's a rose . . . That's a sunflower . . . Those are poppies . . . That's a pansy . . . Those are grapevines." Deborah didn't realize flower pins were such a trend.

Heidi hums as she flips the pages of a sketchbook, narrating everything she inspects. "This ring was three thousand dollars in 1952. Can you imagine? This must be three carats . . . Huh, this guy never paid for his cuff links. I wonder if there's a statute of limitations on unpaid bills." She laughs, calculating over sixty years of interest. "Cal-ee-bray sapphires," Heidi says. "I've never heard of those before . . . Oh, look, a duck!"

In her head, Deborah chants *Om,* trying to summon her inner peace. It's difficult for Deborah, who's never been particularly gifted at attention to detail, to focus on the faded calligraphy of Joseph's ledgers, while Heidi is quacking like a duck.

"This is it!" she squeals. "An orchid."

Deborah's heart races as she looks at the sketchbook. The drawing is indeed an orchid, but a dendrobium not a cattleya. Deborah shakes her head, and Heidi looks annoyed. A landline rings downstairs, and Heidi leaves to answer it.

Deborah flips through page after page of sales and repair jobs, scrap metal purchases, renderings for custom pieces. Heidi does not return. The flower pieces are her favorite, not just because of the orchid brooch. Deborah loves flowers, how their beauty is fleeting, the way their smell turns from sweet to putrid. Maybe that should be Deborah's next business, flower arrangements. With his connections, Viktor could get her into jewelry shops, engagements parties, weddings. Viktor. She wonders what he and the children are doing. He's agreed to watch them in exchange for a home-cooked vegan dinner, which the children will scrunch their faces at, pleading for pizza.

Preoccupied with Viktor's square jawline and crisp blue eyes that look aqua against his white hair, she's flipped through an entire ledger without reading the names and dollar amounts. As she turns back to review the pages she's glossed over, she glimpses a few letters — *Auer* — and then it is gone.

Which page was it? She files through slowly and at last she sees it. Helen Auerbach, a receipt of payment for the sale of two four-carat diamonds to Joseph Spiegel. The date is March 17, 1949. Deborah flips through the book just to be sure, but that's the first notation she finds for Helen.

Helen's name doesn't appear again until May, when she sold another diamond and then another the following month. The largest sale was in February 1952. Eight diamonds. That was a few months before Deborah was born, around the time that her mother bought the house on Edgehill Road.

Deborah finds Helen's name for the last time in 1954, in October, the diamonds listed not as a sale but as a trade for a custom job. In addition to the diamonds, Helen also traded scrap metal. Silver. Deborah remembers that the hatpin was made of sterling. At the bottom of the page, it reads, *Transaction for custom work, paid in full. Diamonds and emeralds used in design, supplied by jeweler at cost. Large yellow diamond provided by customer. No additional monetary payment required.*

Deborah reads that sentence, over and over again. *Large yellow diamond* — he must mean the Florentine. *Provided by customer* — he must mean Helen. If Helen had traded for the custom job, if she'd paid in full with sterling and white diamonds, if she'd supplied her own stone, then the Florentine wasn't a mistress's gift, after all. Maybe Helen wasn't even a mistress, but Deborah remembers Daniel's words, his tone when he accused Helen of ruining his family, of driving his grandmother to the asylum, the emptiness Deborah felt when she first saw that photograph of Joseph holding her as a child. Deborah continues to mine the box for sketchbooks. A drawing of the orchid brooch must be here somewhere. Partly, she wants to see it, the careful lines creating the perfect curve of the sepals, the fine points of the petals. Mostly, she knows those few sentences are insufficient. She needs to be able to show the rendering alongside the ledger to prove he's talking about the Florentine Diamond. If she can find a drawing, maybe the diamond really has been the Millers' all this time.

For the next hour, Deborah continues to dig through the archival boxes, working her way into the '70s. During that time, Heidi does not return to the attic. Deborah gives one box a perfunctory look, open and shut, until a red leather-bound notebook catches her eye. She believes deeply in energy. Not just of diamonds and people, but land, objects, notebooks. Even before she opens it, she knows the drawing of the cattleya orchid is inside.

In the pages of that red leather-bound notebook, Deborah finds dozens of sketches dedicated to Helen's brooch. Renderings for several potential designs for the Florentine Diamond, birds and leopards, bib necklaces and simple pendants, all drawn to scale, complete with the measurements of the yellow diamond featured in each piece. Then the last quarter of the book is dedicated to detailed drawings of the different petals, variations in sapphires and emeralds, different orchestrations for the two pins on the back of the brooch, coupled with endless notes about how to situate the lopsided, shield-shaped diamond into the finding. Deborah holds the notebook and shuts her eyes. She feels Joseph. She feels Helen. She feels Flora, right here in this sketchbook. Then she feels a hand tapping her on the shoulder and sees Daniel hovering above her.

Deborah makes it down the long driveway before she pulls over beside a field. She steps out of the car and breathes in the invigorating fresh air. Daniel Spiegel rushed her out so quickly she didn't have a chance to thank Heidi, didn't get to make a pitch for taking the drawings with her. She doesn't need a physical copy. She's committed all the drawings to memory — the studded leaves, the gilded findings, the perfect cattleya orchid, that essential sentence, too: *large yellow diamond provided by customer.*

Beck jumps up and down. "Florentine. She just mentioned the Florentine."

From here Zita continues to discuss Flora's lover, the chauffeur, who died in the revolt. *If they wanted a child together, they should have married first. That's God's way. Could I have had more compassion after he died saving our children? Probably. That doesn't change their sin. And it does not make it right that my husband gave her our diamond.*

And Zita keeps going, divulging a story beyond Beck's wildest imagination. Zita says that her kind, devout, generous, and foolish — yes, she called the emperor foolish — husband was overcome with gratitude to the nursemaid who saved his children's lives, overwrought with anxiety at having to flee his land. He didn't challenge Zita when she announced that Flora would be fired. He did not

458

beg the case for the woman who rescued their children. Instead of trying to change his wife's mind, he gave Flora the hatpin. Sure, it was a sin that she was unwed and pregnant, but to leave her destitute? The Habsburgs had plenty of other gemstones, loads of cash. Besides, the Florentine Diamond was unlucky. They didn't need that kind of bad omen following them into the unknown. Flora's life already promised to be unlucky. Maybe the Florentine would have the opposite effect on her. The emperor hoped this was true. Even after they left Switzerland, when their money was worthless, the bulk of their jewels stolen by untrustworthy confidants, when they were penniless in Madeira and he was on his deathbed, Karl never regretted giving the Florentine to their nursemaid Flora.

"She said before they left Austria? The emperor gave the Florentine to Flora as a gift? *Before* they left Austria?" This is the first time Beck has said their names together: Florentine, Flora. So effortlessly, they belong together.

Christian repeats her speech in German, then translates. " 'My kind and foolish husband felt guilty that we were leaving her behind, when she was with child and had just risked her life to save our children. Before we left, he apologized to her that she could not come

459

and gave her our Florentine. And that sinful girl, she accepted his extravagant gift. Even if the emperor never regretted the kindness he showed to her, it was too much. The sin wasn't in the giving. It was in the taking, the keeping.' "

If the emperor gave the Florentine Diamond to Flora before they fled, then he also gave it to her before the empire fell, before the Habsburg Law was enacted, before everything that had belonged to the crown automatically belonged to the republic. It meant that, at the start of the republic, the diamond was Flora's, not the throne's.

On the couch, the Winklers whisper, growing wary of Christian and Beck crouched on the floor in the front of their television. They're beginning to realize that this is not merely a trip of Austrian decedents nostalgic for their roots.

Peter stands, looming over Christian and Beck. He ejects the video, returns it to the box, and piles the boxes on top of each other.

When Peter bends down to lift the boxes, Christian asks if he can help. Peter responds in German, then careens with their weight as he carries them upstairs.

"We should go," Christian whispers to Beck.

The street is empty as they scurry away from the house toward town. Once they've rounded a corner, Christian lets go of her arm and leans against a stone building, catching his breath. "Is he chasing after us?"

"I don't think Peter is capable of chasing after much."

"He could have called the police."

"And said what? Christian —" When they lock eyes, Christian leans forward to kiss her. His kiss is relentless. She shuts her eyes and leans into him, gripped by an urgency she doesn't entirely understand.

When Beck hears her name, she's still leaning against Christian. Her brother waves. Her sister smiles, bemused. Beck wipes her mouth and tries to hide Christian even though her siblings have seen their bodies curved toward each other on a secluded corner, their stolen moment on a medieval road.

Beck fills her siblings in on the sections of the story they missed, Christian occasionally inserting details Beck overlooks in her haste.

"Wait, she burned Flora's diary? Why would she do that?" Jake asks, imagining all the details that filled the pages, the minutiae of her daily life that he could never make up, the quality of her love for the chauffeur that sacrificed his life for her.

"I think she felt guilty," Christian offers. "Firing her like that was pretty cold. Plus, with the emperor gifting Flora the diamond, she probably didn't want any evidence around that would suggest he did so willingly."

"I would have loved to see her journal," Jake presses.

"Well, it's gone," Beck snipes. "So get over it." She leans against the wall and sighs. "It's all on those tapes. Everything we need to prove that the emperor gifted Flora the stone before the empire fell, before the Habsburg Law was in effect, is in Winkler's living room and we can't use it." Although her siblings trust the story Beck has told them, a court, the other parties, won't. Not without proof.

Jake starts walking in the direction of the Winklers' home.

"Where are you going?" Ashley calls to him.

"To get the tapes," he calls back as he disappears around the corner. They scurry to follow him.

"He kicked us out," Christian says as he catches up.

"He didn't kick me out." Jake leads them back to the familiar gothic house. He signals for them to stay behind so he can approach alone. They see Peter's wife open the door but are too far away to hear the conversation that unfolds when a nonplussed Peter materializes beside his wife. Beck sways anxiously as she watches Jake and Peter converse, springing into action when Peter opens the

462

door wider, and Jake motions for everyone to follow him inside.

As Beck passes Jake on the way in, she asks him, "What did you say to him?"

"I told him the truth."

The truth is that, whether or not the Florentine was cursed, Flora's life was riddled with pain. Her husband and son were taken to Dachau. She and her daughter were relocated to Leopoldstadt. The truth is that she managed to get her daughter on a boat to America, promising to follow but never did. Mere days later, the Nazis caught up with her. She never saw her daughter again. She never saw her husband or son, either. The truth is that Flora was a savior. First, she saved the emperor's children, rescuing them from danger in Hungary. Then, twenty years later, she saved her own child, sending her across the Atlantic, with no family, no one waiting for her on the other side. Only a hatpin with over a hundred diamonds, including the Florentine, to keep her safe. The truth is that the Florentine is the last piece of Flora. The last piece of Helen's childhood. The last piece of their Austria. The truth is that in the century since the emperor gave Flora the diamond, Helen never sold it. It was worth millions of dollars, and Helen set it in a brooch. Even if they lose the stone to the Austrians or the Habsburgs or the Italians, all of this will still be true. This is no longer about keeping the Florentine; it's about setting the record straight. Flora Tepper was not a thief. Helen Auerbach was not a thief, either. They were brave women who did what they needed to survive, to save their children.

Jake was persuasive enough to get them inside, to have the tea replaced in the living room, but the box of tapes remains upstairs. A fan churns audibly as the Winklers wait for the Millers to convince them to bring the tapes down again.

"We aren't trying to steal Austrian national heritage," Beck insists. "We just want to present the truth as we've gathered it to the court and let the judge decide. If the judge still thinks it belongs to Austria, we'll give up."

"Willingly," Ashley inserts.

"We won't appeal."

Jake raises his right arm. "Hand to God." Where's this come from? He's never done this before. "We deserve a chance, though, to present the stories we've learned. If the diamond returns to Austria, Flora's story should be part of the Florentine's history."

The Millers watch as Mrs. Winkler whispers to her husband. They quip back and forth. It's unclear if they are agreeing or arguing. Eventually, Mrs. Winkler stands. Halfway up the stairs, she shouts for her husband to follow.

The Millers don't risk moving or speaking until the Winklers return with the tapes.

They watch the tape again, *"Florentiner"* just as sublime as it was minutes before. There's a foreboding silence in the room, when Beck digs her phone out of her purse and asks if she can record. Peter's face turns a decipherable shade of red, but his wife interjects, "Of course. Tape. Gather what you need."

The tape continues past where Zita discusses the Florentine Diamond.

"As soon as the emperor died, Zita started searching for Flora to get the Florentine back," Christian paraphrases. "Only, she was looking for a Catholic girl. At the time, she didn't know Flora was Jewish, that she should add liar to her list of sins. Zita stresses that it didn't bother her that Flora was Jewish. The Jewish community was important to the empire."

To Zita, it was that Flora had lied about religion, that she'd gone to church every day and prayed as though it meant something to her. As she continues to speak, Zi-

465

ta's tone grows less venomous. Christian's voice turns deliberate, careful with the words he translates.

There were few she could trust with a mission as valuable as finding the *"Florentiner."* She solicited the services of one of Karl's childhood friends, a man who had helped them escape to Switzerland, who aided Karl in his ill-fated attempt to take back Hungary. She told him only that she was looking for a former nursemaid. For years, he searched futilely for the Catholic Flora Tepper. Zita wasn't clear how thorough his search was. So she promised him a reward. The girl had the *"Florentiner."* If he found her, Zita would split the sale with him. His search intensified. Still, he didn't find the unwed Catholic mother. Then the Nazis arrived, absorbing what was left of her homeland into Germany. Zita didn't hear from Karl's adviser again. By 1940, when she fled to the US, she assumed he was dead and she would never see the *"Florentiner"* again.

Flora's death wasn't her fault, Zita insisted. How could she have known what Karl's friend would do? Her words grow desperate as she seemingly pleads for forgiveness. Christian glances warily at Beck. She nods for him to continue.

Karl's friend became a Nazi officer. Early

to the party, he grew powerful under Eich-mann. How did this happen? How could someone who had loved the empire turn to a hateful party that despised everything the Habsburgs had stood for? He was in the records department. That's where he found her. Something to do with an American couple that was taking her daughter to America. The exit paperwork included the mother's maiden name, Flora Tepper. A Jewish woman. That was when he sent his men to look for her and the Florentine.

"They never found the diamond," Christian relays forlornly. "Zita never learned the details, just that they searched her small apartment and then the soldiers took Flora away. It was one of her greatest regrets, the fate of her nursemaid."

On the TV, Zita grows quiet, looking down at her withered hands. She squeezes them together until her swollen fingers turn red. She looks like she wants to say more, but there's nothing left to say. The tape ends there, with Zita's downturned face, her private communion.

Christian looks as pained as Zita. The Winklers grow forlorn, too. Jake lies on the floor, staring up at the off-white ceiling. He can't parse through his thoughts. They are muddy, clouded, confused. He feels compelled to do something, only what is there to do? There's no way to change events that happened eight decades ago.

Beck locks eyes with Christian. *You okay?* he mouths, and she nods even though she's far from okay. It's not like she could have prevented what happened, but she feels responsible for Flora's death, as though knowing how the pieces fit together in a terribly perfect puzzle makes it her fault. After all, she found the brooch. She wore it to work. She brought the diamond to Viktor. She is the reason they are here, uncovering a past that would otherwise still remain hidden.

Ashley feels strangely empowered. Zita *should* feel guilty. It helps Ashley to know that Zita carried that regret with her, that forty years after Flora's death, when the interview was recorded, she still felt culpable.

On the next tape, Zita is wearing the same pearls with a different blouse, blue instead of black. Her face is freshly made. Her voice is loftier, almost nostalgic.

"She's talking about their life in New York," Christian says. The tape plays for a few minutes, watching a different Zita detail her time in the gated community of Tuxedo Park.

"We can stop there," Beck says.

The room grows tense as Beck asks Peter Winkler to put into writing that he has agreed to copy the tapes, that he's voluntarily giving the Millers his father's memorabilia.

"We need to be able to tell the court that we acquired all of this lawfully," Beck explains.

Jake taps his foot, annoyed at his sister's tone. She's trying to be gentle but comes off condescending. Still, Peter signs the note that Beck drafts.

As Peter walks them out, he asks, "What will you do with the diamond if you win?"

They have to sell it. Once its worth is established, they will not be able to pay the state inheritance and capital gains taxes. They will have to put it on the market, forced into the choice their grandmother never made.

Beck begins to explain to Peter that they have no choice. What she says instead is, "I don't know."

By the time they walk the cobblestoned streets toward the train station, the day has receded into dusk. The sky is red as they wait on the platform for their train to arrive, all four of them squished onto a bench designed for three.

469

"If we hadn't come, if we hadn't found those tapes, we'd think she was a thief," Ashley says.

Beck studies her sister. She has so much more depth than Beck gives her credit for. There's no good way to say this, so instead she hugs Ashley.

Jake stares vacantly in the direction of the approaching train. His brain has been numb since they watched Zita's video. It's difficult to remember why he felt so invigorated after his speech to the Winklers, the right he assumed he had to Flora's story. And what now? It feels wrong that he knows more about Flora than Helen did.

"It's not enough," Jake says. This trip has changed him. He can feel his bones resetting, but the change is not enough to win Kristi back. Zita's guilt is not enough to diminish the unjustness of Flora's death.

The train pulls up. They step onto it, single file, and settle into two rows that face each other. It is not enough. Ashley feels it, too. No monetary value for the diamond will suffice, no court settlement will feel like a win. Even if Zita's story persuades the judge, even if they're awarded the diamond, even if she can use the money to save her house, it is not enough to redress what happened to Flora.

Only Beck feels satisfied. "You're right," she says to her siblings as she nuzzles into Christian. "It might not be enough to compel the court, but everything Zita said is true. Whatever the judge decides. Her story is still true. That's enough for me."

SEVENTEEN

When the Millers return with their army of records and hours of interviews, the real battle begins. They have Zita's tapes, detailing how the emperor gifted Flora the hatpin. They have an affidavit from Peter Winkler, stating that the taped interviews were his father's, recorded to assist in writing the empress's biography. They have Helen's hollow doll, photographs of her carrying it on the SS *President Harding,* Deborah's sworn testimony that she located three round diamonds inside. They have Viktor's testimony, explaining how he sent the shield-shaped yellow diamond from Helen's brooch to the International Gemology Society for grading that confirmed it was the Florentine and why he suspects the three round diamonds Deborah found came from the hatpin. They have additional testimony from another gemologist, confirming Viktor's assessment that the diamond in Helen's brooch is the Florentine and that the three round diamonds likely originated from the hatpin. They have Joseph Spiegel's ledgers and renderings, which Tom convinced Daniel Spiegel to provide to the Millers, proving the shield-shaped yellow diamond was removed from the hatpin and reset in the orchid brooch. They have Helen's will, allocating the brooch to Beck, the Family Settlement Agreement where the Millers agreed to share the diamond evenly. Combined, it's a plausible story, a convincing argument for why the court should let them keep the diamond.

Before Deborah's deposition, Beck had warned Tom that he should stay clear of any questions about Joseph Spiegel's relationship with Helen. It would only make her mother appear evasive and flighty before the other parties. Deborah had enough trouble sharing the story with her children. Besides, it wasn't relevant to their case.

Plausible story or not, compelling argument notwithstanding, the other parties object. They focus on Zita's tapes, the linchpin of the Millers' argument. Zita was not under oath, they protest. The tapes were not recorded as testimony. She is not alive to stand for cross-examination. Plus, Zita was in her eighties at the time of the inter-view. Her memory cannot be trusted, and even if it can, how can they know whether the emperor was in his right mind when he gave Flora the Florentine? Few things are as stressful as the fall of an empire. The Ital-ians even propose that Zita may have been demented at the end, to which the Austrians vehemently object. Zita may have been a deposed empress, but she was an Austrian treasure. Still, they concur with the Italians and the Habsburgs that interviews are hearsay, inadmissible as evidence.

Judge Ricci appears more convinced by these arguments than Tom and Beck would like. She agrees that the videotapes cannot be classified as recorded recollections under the exceptions to hearsay, as those pertain specifically to recorded recollections of wit-nesses who are alive and fit to be deposed. Many of Zita's statements in the videos require clarification and would necessitate cross-examination. Tom argues that Zita's recordings are ancient documents, thus admissible, but it depends on how one defines "documents," whether "documents" should be interpreted broadly to include a video recording.

In the end, however, the judge reasons that Zita's statements were against her own self-interest.

"Her interviews reveal that she knew her husband had willfully gifted Flora Tepper, later known as Flora Auerbach, the Florentine Diamond," Judge Ricci reads to the four parties. "Although Emperor Karl von Habsburg may have been under exceeding pressure at the time, his wife, Empress Zita of Bourbon-Parma, admitted that he never regretted giving the Florentine Diamond to Flora Tepper, later known as Flora Auerbach, not even on his deathbed. As such an admission was against Zita's own interest in the diamond, I find her statements credible and admissible as evidence."

When the other parties begin to object to the judge's finding, she continues. "This is my final decision. I will accept the video interviews into evidence. If you oppose, you can take it up upon appeal."

The other parties race out of the courtroom, while Beck and Tom linger.

"Did that really just happen?" Beck asks.

"It really just did," Tom responds, equally stupefied.

The next morning, the Habsburgs pull their claim. Their lawyers make a statement to the press: "While the Florentine Diamond will always be a Habsburg heirloom, the family has decided to focus on more pressing concerns. Whoever wins the claim, the family hopes that they will make the sensible decision to put it on display at a museum where the public can treasure the diamond as much as generations of the royal family did."

Immediately, the Italians and the Austrians file procedural motions to try to slow down the discovery process, insisting that they need to call new expert witnesses to evaluate whether the emperor could legally gift Flora the diamond before the Habsburg Law was enacted. Even if he could, Flora had kept the diamond in Vienna for twenty years before Helen took it to America, twenty years where she may have been legally obligated to return the diamond to the Austrian government, twenty years where the Austrian government in turn may have been required to pay it in reparations to the Italians.

But good old Judge Ricci is steadfast. "Each party has conducted hours of deposition testimony from numerous experts regarding the Habsburg Law and the Treaties of Peace, 1920. Are you really trying to tell me that these experts' opinions are insufficient?" Before the lawyers can respond, she answers her own question. "I see no need to call new witnesses only to ask them questions other experts have already answered. The discovery deadline remains set at the end of the month." Then the parties will have thirty days to file their motions for summary judgment, so the judge can decide if any of them has a rightful claim to the Florentine.

Before the clock on the thirty days to draft their argument starts ticking, the Italians pull their claim. Their lawyers offer a cryptic statement to the press about prioritizing investigations into other cultural property.

It is a rare instance, Tom admits to Beck, where he doesn't know why they've withdrawn. "Maybe they discovered something we didn't? It was pretty obvious the judge wasn't going to side with them over the Austrians. She'd have to be crazy to weigh in on European law. They must have realized that whatever dispute they have with Austria would have to play out in European court. But why they wouldn't stick with it and appeal, you've got me."

"Words everyone wants to hear from their lawyer," Beck says to him over celebratory whiskeys at the Continental.

"Two down, one to go. Just us against the Austrian government now," Tom says, lifting his tumbler toward Beck.

Beck rests the glass on her bottom lip.

"What do you think it means, that the judge didn't extend discovery? It's good, right? She's already decided how she's going to rule?"

"Given she let us admit some pretty hefty evidence — I'm not a betting man, but let's just say if I were representing the Austrians, I'd be furious."

"But you're not. You're representing me." Beck doesn't mean this flirtatiously, but her voice has its own agenda.

"And as your lawyer, it's worth toasting with more whiskey." Tom downs the remains of his glass and motions to the waitress for another round, even though Beck has barely touched her old-fashioned. "I've been thinking," he begins, which immediately ties Beck's stomach in knots. "We should probably revisit the possibility of a settlement."

"Would the Austrians even be interested?" Beck asks, relieved that they are still on the familiar footing of the law. "*Can* we settle? What about the pending claims?" The Department of Justice still has over sixty claims left to review and dismiss before the case can officially close.

"They're baseless," Tom says, taking their drinks from the waitress's tray.

"How can we settle on a case that's still open?"

Tom smiles approvingly at Beck. "Most lawyers don't think to ask that. You have a good legal mind, Beck. I've always known this about you."

Beck pats her hair self-consciously, simultaneously flattered by his recognition of her intellect and irked by his condescension. This is the mix of emotions Tom has always brought out in her, she realizes, even when she was falling in love with him.

"The deal would have to be provisional," he continues. "But we could argue to the judge that having the diamond on display in Vienna wouldn't negatively impact the DOJ's evaluation of the other claims."

"And we could still get the money now?" Beck imagines telling Ashley that she won't have to sell her house.

"It would probably be kept in escrow until all the claims are settled, but we can try to convince the judge to release it now, if you really need it and can guarantee you'd pay it back if somehow one of the other claims is more convincing than yours or the Austrians. I think it's best to keep it in escrow."

As long as the money is waiting for them, Beck thinks, Ashley can get a bridge loan or borrow against the settlement. If they can reach an agreement with the Austrians, Ashley won't have to sell her house.

"And my father, that's taken care of?" she asks, and Tom nods. "All right, let's reach out to the Austrians' lawyers, then."

Tom appears to have heard some other agreement in Beck's words, and before she knows it, he's finished his drink and inches his chair toward hers. Dread courses through her as he caresses her hair. "I've missed you."

"You see me every day." Beck shakes her hair free from his touch.

He strokes her cheek and she can tell from his unfocused eyes that alcohol has emboldened him. He runs his finger down her nose to her lips. "I miss this."

It feels good to be touched. Almost good enough to let Tom continue. After she returned from Austria, she and Christian saw each other a few times. Something shifted almost immediately. Outside the City of Dreams, their encounters became part of that dream, infused with the romance of Vienna's narrow streets. Quickly, she discovered that Christian liked to go out every night to dive bars where he would order watery beer and well shots, staying until he was either kicked out for falling asleep or sent home at closing. As she helped him home, he talked dirty to her in slurred German. Frankly, it bored Beck.

The binge drinking, the putrid smell of bars that clung to her clothes, Christian's vulgar requests. Spending time with Christian showed her that, somehow, without acquiring any of the things she'd expected from her thirties — a partner, a family, a home, even a career — somewhere along the way, she'd become an adult. And, as an adult, she doesn't want the fraught embrace of her ex-boyfriend, either.

As Tom's face approaches hers, she turns away. "Don't. I told you, it was a mistake. I don't want to repeat it again." As Tom starts to apologize, she stops him. "Let's be clear. Friends, okay?"

Tom's face is red from embarrassment as much as from the alcohol but he agrees, "Friends," and glances at his watch. "I didn't realize how late it is."

Beck remembers the last time he used his watch trick on her, at Helen's shiva, when Tom told her family about the yellow diamond brooch. She's calm now, more collected than he is, and Beck hasn't become so much of an adult that she doesn't get the tiniest pleasure in ultimately rejecting him.

When Jake returns to LA, he solicits Rico's help in purchasing a ring. Together, they visit a jewelry store on Vermont Boulevard in Los Feliz.

"I don't know," Rico says as they survey a tray of turquoise rings. "These don't look like engagement rings to me."

"That's the point." Jake signals to the woman at the other end of the counter. She reluctantly puts down her phone and walks toward them. "Kris wouldn't want anything that looks expensive. She'd want something sentimental."

Jake asks the saleswoman if she has any topaz rings. She guides them toward a case farther into the store. "Topaz is the birthstone for November." When Rico doesn't understand, Jake adds, "Kristi's due on November 2."

"What if she's early?"

As the saleswoman places a tray of silver rings with yellow faceted stones on the counter, Jake googles *October birthstone*. "Do you have tourmaline, too?"

The saleswoman rolls her eyes and retrieves another tray of multicolored stones. "Do you know her size?"

"Small? Maybe extra-small? She's pregnant, so she might be wearing a bigger size?"

"Her *ring* size." The saleswoman holds up her ring finger, and she may as well be giving Jake the middle finger. Rico stifles a laugh.

"Is there a common size? She's petite."

"Probably a five or six," the saleswoman says. "But just because she's small doesn't mean her hands are small."

Jake settles on four rings. Two size-five rings — one tourmaline, the other topaz — and two size-six, each under fifty dollars.

As they are walking onto Vermont, Rico asks, "Are you sure about this? It doesn't seem totally thought out."

"Trust me, I know Kristi. In fact, four rings are even better than one."

When Jake arrives at her apartment with the four small boxes, Kristi answers the door, startled to see him.

"Jake?" Kristi leans back to bear the weight of her stomach. It's significantly larger than a few weeks before, perfectly round, and Jake wants to spread his fingers across it, to feel their child inside. "What are you doing here?"

The unctuous smell of sesame, soy, and oyster sauces wafts out of the apartment, which can only mean one thing. Mrs. Zhang is here, cooking for her daughter. He wonders if Kristi told her mother about the script, about Jake being fired. The thought of Mrs. Zhang seeing him with the four ring boxes makes him want to retreat, but he keeps his feet planted firmly, waiting for

Kristi to let him inside.

As Kristi looks between him and the ring boxes, terror consumes her pretty face.

"I know I've been a disappointment. I lied to you. And kept secrets. Made bad decisions that affected both of us. I have no excuse. I'm not here to make one. It was stupid of me. And weak. And immature." Jake waits for her to counter any of his statements. When she doesn't, he keeps listing his shortcomings. "Selfish. Reckless. I think I've been waiting, since we first started dating, to mess it all up. Then, when everything was falling into place with you and the baby —"

"So you're saying it's my fault?"

"No, Kris." Jake tries to take her hand, but she pulls it away. "It's my fault. All of it. Always. You were right when you said I was stuck. I was so stuck I couldn't see it. I'm not stuck anymore. At least, I'm trying to get unstuck." He begins to open one of the boxes.

"Jake." She shakes her head. She doesn't even ask him why he has four rings instead of one. "You'll always be a part of our family, but we're done. I'm sorry. I can't get into this again with you."

Kristi continues to block the door, looking tormented at having to ask him to leave.

If it's this difficult for her, she must still love him. Part of her must still want to work it out. He recalls what Beck said about the in-between, how he can't force forgiveness. This is where they are, and he has to be okay with it, for now. But he's not going to give up on her.

As he turns to leave, Mrs. Zhang walks into the living room. "Jake," she calls, walking toward him with open arms. "I thought I heard you. Are you staying for dinner?"

"Jake was just leaving."

"No," Mrs. Zhang protests. "There's plenty of food. Come." She takes Jake by the arm and guides him into the kitchen where plates of noodles, dumplings, and stir-fry rest on the modest kitchen table. "She's just scared," Mrs. Zhang whispers to Jake, motioning for him to sit in one of the mismatched wooden chairs.

For most of dinner, they eat without speaking, delighting in Mrs. Zhang's cooking. Jake piles enormous quantities onto his plate. He's not particularly hungry, but Mrs. Zhang appreciates when he eats a lot, and he's happy to be able to please someone in the room. Plus, as long as his mouth is stuffed with food, he doesn't have to speak, doesn't need to ask Kristi what happens now.

Finally, Mrs. Zhang asks, "So what's this I read about your grandmother being a thief?"

Jake waits for Kristi to admonish her mother, to tell her she shouldn't listen to gossip. She, too, stares intently at Jake.

"Well," Jake begins. "My grandmother didn't talk about it, but she came over from Austria during the Holocaust with forty-nine other children. She brought the Florentine Diamond with her. My sisters and I just got back from Vienna where we were investigating her past."

"You were in Vienna?" Is that hurt he detects in Kristi's voice? Or surprise?

Jake tells them about his trip, about Flora's life as a nurse to the emperor's children and as a mother in Nazi-occupied Vienna. In both roles, she did what she had to to keep the children alive, first the emperor's, then her own daughter. He omitted the deaths that had occurred along the way to keeping Helen safe, but Mrs. Zhang seemed to understand what happened to the family that stayed behind.

Mrs. Zhang rests her chopsticks across her plate. "I left alone, too. My mother made me. I didn't want to abandon my family, but she promised they would follow. My sister and I were the only ones who made it out, though."

Jake turns to Kristi, whose eyes water. His eyes sting, too.

"I'm very lucky to have my sister, but I think about my parents every day. For them, I had to look forward, not back. I had to learn to be happy, to have my own family. If not, it was a waste."

Mrs. Zhang lifts her chopsticks and Jake watches her continue to eat, seeing no conflict on her face. She has learned to be happy. It was not a waste. Flora, Helen — their deaths were not a waste, either. At last, Jake knows what his movie has to be about.

After dinner, Mrs. Zhang shoos Jake and Kristi into the living room under the guise of needing to clean the kitchen. Jake wants to sit on the couch with Kristi, but she heads straight to the door.

"So things with you and Beck are better?" she asks, holding the door open for Jake. She makes a pained expression as she rubs her belly. "She's been poking me like crazy. Usually she submits if I push her back. I hope that's a sign she'll be docile as a teenager." Once she's visibly relaxed, she asks again, "So, you and Beck?"

Jake shoves his hands in his pockets, knowing they will otherwise reach for her. "I finally understand why she felt so betrayed. I'm trying to be more careful. I think she's starting to trust me again."

"I knew you two would figure it out."

Jake braves a step toward her. "Our case is good, Kris. Like, really good. I'm going to put the money in a trust, for our daughter. If you'll let me, I'd like to use some of it to get you a bigger apartment, maybe even vet school, if you still want to go."

Instead of responding, Kristi tells him, "I have another appointment, next week. Nothing big — just a checkup."

Jake wants to lift her into the air and kiss her like it's the end of a romantic movie, then he remembers the in-between and keeps his hands burrowed in his pockets as he promises, "I'll be there."

Ashley knows her time is running out. Since her meeting with Stella in June, she's had informational meetings with former teammates at a health food company, lifestyle brands, and ad agencies, none of which is looking for a publicity director, ten years delinquent. In a month, Beck will submit Flora's story to the court and the judge will decide whether the Florentine Diamond belongs to the Millers. A few weeks later, Ryan will have to return the money he stole, a half million dollars that they currently do not have. Still, Ashley isn't ready to sell the house.

"Ash." Ryan tries to keep his voice down so the children will not hear. He and Ashley are in their bedroom, Ashley protected under the covers while Ryan stands in his boxers. "We have to put the house on the market."

"Just give me a few weeks," she says, trying to control the volume of her voice, too. Although Beck has cautioned that Zita's testimony might not be enough to persuade the court that the diamond belongs to the Millers, Ashley feels optimistic for the first time in months.

"My sentencing is in a month. We need to return the money then."

"*You* need to return the money." Ashley crosses her arms protectively over her chest as Ryan casts her a wounded look. When Ryan is out of prison, they will be *we* again. "My case is airtight. I'll win, then I'll give you the money to pay back your company."

"No case is airtight." Ryan sits down beside her on the bed, trying a different approach. "Look, even if you do win —"

"*When* I win."

"When you win, it could take months to find a buyer for the diamond. We're out of time. I'm out of time. We can use the

489

diamond money to buy a new house. A bigger house."

"I don't want a bigger house. I want this house where our children learned to walk and lost their first teeth."

"Maybe it's better if we start somewhere new."

Ashley considers that, a new life in a new town. They could move north, to Maine, buy an old farmhouse and live quietly off the land. But Ashley and Ryan are not gardeners. They are not fixer-uppers. They wouldn't know how to live a quieter life. "I want things to go back to the way they were."

She knows how naive this sounds, but when Ashley finds a job, when Ryan completes his sentence, they can have a modified version of this life, one where they haven't lost everything.

"Just give me a few weeks? Beck has to file our claim in the next month. We'll know more then, and you'll still have a few weeks before you need to return the money. This house won't take long to sell. Or I can always take a loan out against it. Please, Ry."

This is a terrible plan. There isn't enough time. Still, Ryan reaches over to stroke his wife's face.

"Okay," he says, kissing her forehead. "We'll wait a few weeks."

Tom and Beck spend late nights at the office, poring over drafts of their motion. They fret over the Habsburg Law. Even if Karl gifted Flora the diamond before the law went into effect, the Florentine Diamond was property of the crown and not the emperor himself. It may not have been his to give. In response, Flora may have been legally obligated to return the Florentine Diamond to the republic. Plus, if she kept it hidden in Vienna for twenty years, doesn't that suggest that she knew it might not lawfully be hers? It's the hairline fracture that threatens to shatter their argument. There's always one, no matter how good the case, something for the other side to exploit, something that prevents any scenario in the law from being a slam dunk.

They proceed with their argument as best they can, eyes bloodshot and twitching from lack of sleep, until time seems to fold in on itself and Beck isn't certain what day it is, only that the deadline is close. At three the next afternoon, Tom taps on the partition of Beck's cubicle. Beck knows it's afternoon because she heard her coworkers return from lunch.

491

"You'll never guess whom I just got a call from," Tom says, almost giddy.

Beck bolts up, realizing she'd been sleeping with her eyes open. "The Austrians want to settle?" This is a ridiculous guess. They've been so adamant.

"They want to talk at least. I know, I wasn't expecting it, either. After Judge Ricci let us admit the tapes, maybe they realized she's more likely to side with us and figured a settlement is better than a long road of appeals. Cheaper, probably."

Beck sets something up with a magistrate judge who will oversee the settlement talks. He insists that all parties be present during the negotiations, a tactic he hopes will help them reach an agreement.

The night before everyone arrives, Deborah and Viktor lay in bed, sharing one pillow, bodies angled toward each other.

"Do you think they'll actually settle?" Deborah closes the sliver of space between them. She likes feeling his breath on her face as he talks. It's warm and minty.

"It's more a matter of whether you're willing to take whatever money they offer."

"Will they offer enough?"

"Do you want them to offer enough?"

"I don't know." She inches even closer

until the tips of their noses touch. "I wish I could see it again. The Florentine. I never got to hold it. I think if I did, I'd know how to feel. Not just about the diamond, about my mother, too."

By now, Viktor is familiar with Deborah's logic, the way she trusts energies more than words, objects more than people. The diamond knows Helen's story better than anyone.

Deborah has accepted that Joseph Spiegel was her father but remains unable to shake a lingering resentment that Helen never trusted her with the truth. Sure, Joseph was married. Sure, the affair erodes the romantic image she had of her father, the war hero. Of all people, though, Deborah wasn't one to judge. In fact, it may have helped their relationship, knowing that Helen made mistakes, too.

Viktor runs his hand through Deborah's ear-length hair. She's growing it out, dying it a new shade of red, less purple, closer to the auburn hue of her childhood. Viktor sees her youth and encourages her to show it to the world. He sees all sorts of things in Deborah that she's never seen in herself. He believes in her thirty-eighth business idea — the organic flower arrangements — and rents space in the greenhouse on his roof so

493

she can grow flowers before the last frost. He knows her mistakes yet insists she's a good mother. She's open to change. That's a sign of a role model, of someone who will never grow old. With every aching joint and muscle spasm, Deborah's body is painfully aware of just how old it is. Still, when Viktor tells her she's beautiful, brave, capable, she believes him.

He kisses her eyelids after she shuts them. "Let's see it, then. Let's have you hold the diamond."

She laughs. "That's impossible."

Viktor looks hurt. "You're the one who taught me that nothing is impossible."

Did she teach him that? She taught him to believe in powers he couldn't see, in yoga and acupuncture, in veganism, and in red wine, but she hadn't realized this amounted to an ideology.

"It's in a vault."

Viktor wiggles his nose against hers. "It just so happens that I'm on the list of individuals allowed access to the diamond, and your family is in need of a final evaluation of the Florentine in advance of the settlement negotiations."

"We are, are we?" Deborah tenses as Viktor wraps his arm around her. "Beck wouldn't like it."

"Beck doesn't need to know everything." He squeezes her close. "You need to say goodbye to Helen."

"Okay," she whispers, and kisses him.

In the morning, Deborah puts on her nicest dress, which is purple velvet and hardly professional. Still, Viktor tells her she looks perfect.

"Eccentrically old money," he says as she places half a grapefruit before him, the other half in her bowl. Deborah thinks they can share grapefruits for the rest of their lives, two halves of the same whole.

Deborah straightens his tie, which is already perfectly straight. "And you, Mr. Castanza, dapper as always."

Once they arrive at the bank, Deborah waits in the lobby as Viktor approaches the manager's desk. Occasionally they turn toward her and she smiles, but the bank manager does not smile back. After they've been talking awhile, Viktor waves her over and together they sign their names to gain access to the vault.

Deborah has never been inside a vault before. The sourness of all that metal and cement burns her nostrils. The silence rings in her eardrums. It takes her the entire hall to realize she's emotionally unprepared to hold her mother's most secret possession.

After the manager leaves them alone in the vault, making them promise to return the owner's key to her when they sign out, Viktor places the safe-deposit box on the table with a clang. "You ready?"

No, she thinks.

"Ready as ever," she says instead.

He drops the diamond into her hand. It's heavy and cool against her skin. At first she feels no energy, good or bad — just a piece of carbon against her palm. As she shuts her eyes and squeezes the diamond, her palm begins to tingle. Quickly, the stone grows hot, searing her skin. She keeps a firm grip on it, despite the burning, trying to locate her mother's energy amid that heat. The stone sends an electric shock down her forearm, but she breathes through the pain, searching for Helen, for Flora, beneath that violent energy. Her heart pounds too fast. Sweat gathers at her hairline. When the current seizes her arm, she feels like all the death she's unleashing from the stone might actually kill her. She drops the diamond, hears it hit the floor as she races into the cool, empty hall.

Deborah leans against the cement wall, catching her breath. Everything about this is wrong. Their being here. The diamond in the vault. Her trying to reconcile with her mother through the stone. The diamond belonging to the Millers, spreading its bad luck like a virus. It's all wrong.

Viktor finds her in the hall. "You okay?"

He rubs her arms, and she pulls him to her. His energy is so much warmer than the diamond's. Softer. Right in every way that stone was wrong. Despite his calming effect, she still feels the aftershock of that stone buzzing through her.

He kisses her head. Strokes her youthful red hair. "What happened?"

"That stone is evil." She waits for him to laugh, and although he stiffens, he does not tease her.

"I'm sorry. I thought it was a good idea."

"It's not your fault. You couldn't have known." They start walking out of the vault. "I didn't break it, did I?"

"It takes a lot more than a spill on a cement floor to crack a diamond." For some reason, she knows he's talking about them.

"I love you." This is the first time she's said this to him. She doesn't mean to say it now, but it's true. It feels good to divulge something she knows is true.

"I love you, too." There's a strange reservation in his voice. As he looks down at her, he seems nervous. Deborah wonders if this is the first time he's ever said those words to someone, and she feels the last of the manic current leave her body. This was a good idea, she decides. Coming here was the most perfect idea Deborah has ever had.

EIGHTEEN

On the morning of the settlement conference, Deborah wakes up early to make her children a lucky breakfast: vegan pancakes with bananas and walnuts. When they lived in Mt. Airy, she used to make the nonvegan version for them on the first day of school, before big tests, games, and concerts. She hopes the breakfast will remind her children of the times they were together in the past, all the times they can be together in the future, too.

When the Millers bound downstairs with more energy than they usually have at eight in the morning, they say nothing about the symbolism of the meal.

"These look great," Ashley tells her mother.

"I'm starving," Jake says, lifting a pancake from the platter.

Deborah feels a slight disappointment, but they are all here, eating together. Maybe they don't need to recall happier days. Maybe they need to focus on the ones ahead. Deborah wishes Viktor was here to eat pancakes with the Millers, to be part of this morning. He had an early meeting in the city and stayed at his apartment for the night. It's the first night in weeks that they haven't shared a bed. Part of her likes it, getting to miss him.

As they eat, Beck gives everyone a rundown of how the day will go. The settlement conference will take place at Beck's firm, since the Austrians' lawyers are coming from DC. Tom will meet with the Austrians' lawyers and the magistrate judge before the Millers and the Austrian representatives arrive. They'll be ushered into separate rooms for the negotiations, and the magistrate judge will zip back and forth between the parties. If all goes well, it should be over in a few hours. Then the Millers can go to the bank to say goodbye to the Florentine.

"And if it doesn't go well?" Ashley asks, picking a banana slice out of the pancake, too nervous to eat.

"It will," Beck vows. "We're not going to get ten million for the diamond, but Tom will make sure we get enough to settle. It's in everyone's best interest."

"What will they do with the Florentine?" Jake asks.

"It will probably be on display in the treasury with the other crown jewels," Beck says.

Deborah cuts her pancakes into pieces, thinking that's the best place for the Florentine, behind glass where it can't impart its bad luck on anyone else.

"And will anyone know?" Jake presses. "When it's in a museum, will the display say anything about how the diamond got there?"

"That isn't up to us," Beck says.

"It should be," Jake insists. "We should have a say in how the story of the diamond is told."

"Jake," Ashley warns. "It's not the time."

"What, to care about my family legacy?"

"I'm just saying, don't fuck this up."

"Like I fuck everything else up?"

"I didn't say that."

"You didn't need to."

"Millers," Beck snaps. "Pull it together — we're on the same team. Let's focus on getting an agreement. After, we can contact a newspaper in Vienna or something, okay?"

Her siblings reluctantly agree. Deborah thinks if Viktor could see Beck, he'd be as proud of her as Deborah is.

■ ■ ■ ■

The magistrate judge visits the Austrians first, giving Tom time to reiterate everything Beck has already told her family. This settlement is about money. It isn't about whom the diamond rightfully belongs to, whether Flora should have turned it over to the Austrians in 1919, whether it was even Karl's to give. It's about how much cash it will take for the Millers to rescind their claim, to allow the Austrians and the US government to reach an agreement to return the diamond to its homeland.

The Austrians' initial offer is alarmingly low, lower than the Italians' a year ago.

"We weren't going take that from the Italians. Why would we take that now?" Ashley asks.

"And it's even less because we have to give him a third." Jake gestures toward Tom. Despite Beck's truce with Tom, her insistence that he's been invaluable to their case, Jake cannot shake his dislike of this boring, predictable man who broke his sister's heart.

Ignoring the dig, Tom says, "It's a starting point. They know we're not going to take it."

The Millers return with a counteroffer

that is equally outlandish. The Austrians inch up, the Millers down. Still, their sums are millions apart.

"Do we have a magic number?" Tom asks the Millers.

"Eight million," Ashley blurts out, then calculates her share, whether it would be enough to avoid selling the house. "Actually, six."

"Four," Beck says. "If we can get them up to four, we'll take it." That's three for the value of the Florentine as a diamond, plus one million for its history.

"I just want some promise that it will be on public display and that they'll mention Flora," Jake says.

"That isn't something we can force them to agree to," Tom cautions.

"Jake, we've been over this," Beck reminds him.

"It just doesn't feel right, the world not knowing about Flora."

"I know." Beck glances at Tom, whose eyes are wide with worry. "I promise we'll find a way to honor her, just not right now."

In the end, the Austrians will go no higher than three and a half million dollars. It's been four hours of back and forth and takes another hour to hammer out the agreement. After five hours of negotiating, the magistrate judge is visibly exhausted and leaves Tom and the Austrians' lawyers to present the offer to Judge Ricci. They need her to agree, since there are still outstanding claims on the diamond.

While they wait, the Millers walk to Rittenhouse Square. They sit on two side-by-side benches and fantasize about their individual shares of the settlement — about $550,000 after expenses and the firm's fee.

Ashley pictures the overjoyed expression on Ryan's face when she tells him they won't have to sell the house. Sure, they'll have to take out a bridge loan until all the claims are settled, but they'll get to keep their family home. The children will spot them embracing in the kitchen, ask what happened, and Ashley will reach for them and say, *Nothing. Everything.* They won't understand, but they'll know they're safe.

Jake imagines walking into a bank with Kristi, holding her elbow as she cradles their child. When the teller asks, he'll hand her the check for $550,000, written over to his daughter. They'll exit the way they entered, as a family. He'll brave a kiss, and the pressure of Kristi's lips against his will feel like a homecoming.

Beck realizes that she'll be able to afford the rent on her apartment without Tom's help. She envisions sitting at her dining room table, a stack of loans and bills beside her, writing checks for each one. She tastes the sour adhesive of the envelopes as she licks them shut, feels the rush of wind as she walks onto Twenty-Fifth Street toward the mailbox. Since she was sixteen and Deborah took out those credit cards in her name, she's been in debt. It's foreign to her, not having to worry about the interest that mounts each month, about a credit score so abysmal she'll never be eligible for a loan. Beck watches her mother, who looks unprecedentedly calm, and Beck knows that she, too, is overwhelmed by the money, the love, the family that she never dreamed she'd have again. She wonders whether they will hear from Kenny, despite the agreement he signed, now that there's money. If he tries anything that threatens her mother's chance at happiness, Beck might really deliver on her promise to emasculate him.

Deborah is indeed feeling a profound sense of rightness she's never experienced before, not even in the house in Mt. Airy. The first thing she is going to do is take Viktor on vacation — maybe Venice, where they can lounge on a gondola and stay in a suite that overlooks one of the canals, making love in a king-size bed with the windows open.

By the time Beck gets the call from Tom that the judge has agreed to their arrangement, the afternoon light is fading. The days are starting to get shorter again, the darkening sky reminding them that it will soon be winter. Tom tells Beck that the FBI has approved a final visit to the vault.

"Do we have time to get to the bank before it closes?" Jake asks, stretching his legs and appearing in no great rush.

Beck checks her phone. It's after four. "I think we can just make it."

As the Millers hurry through the park, Deborah texts Viktor to meet them at the bank.

"Can we give him a few minutes?" Deborah asks when they arrive at Federalist Bank and Viktor hasn't texted back. "He promised to bring champagne."

"We don't need champagne."

"It doesn't seem right, celebrating without him."

The Millers fidget as the minutes tick by. Deborah checks her phone again. Still no word from Viktor. "He'll be here."

Beck gently guides her mother toward the door. "He can meet us inside."

Deborah gives the street one final scan in

each direction before stepping into the lobby. As the Millers follow the manager into the vault, her phone buzzes.

I'm sorry, Viktor writes. Something about his text feels off.

You still have time to make it. If not, we'll see you later? she responds, willing away the nagging discomfort that settles in her stomach.

"You ready?" Beck asks once the Millers are alone in the vault.

You ready? Those were Viktor's words when Deborah stood beside him in this very room and bore the violent energies of the diamond. Suddenly, Deborah wants to shout, *Don't open it. Don't let this be the end.* She balls her fists to restrain her outburst. It's irrational, her response. For so long, she's trained herself to distrust anything that feels this right. Nothing has changed with Viktor, she tells herself. He simply couldn't come today. He was apologizing because he wanted to be there. Everything is fine.

This isn't the end. She unclenches her fists, but her neck remains tight. She's as ready as she'll ever be.

The Millers are giddy as Beck places the safe-deposit box on the table and opens the lid. Everyone leans over her to see inside the box.

There's nothing there.

"It's supposed to be here, right?" Jake asks.

"Of course it's supposed to be here." Ashley glances at Beck for confirmation. Her sister stares, dumbfounded, at the empty box.

When Deborah sees the empty cavity, she lets out a gasp. Jake turns toward her and sees a truth on her frozen face that she hasn't fully admitted to herself.

"What did you do?"

The room grows airless, and Deborah leans against the table, breathing the deep, long breaths of Shavasana. Aware that her children are staring at her, she doesn't turn toward them. She can't see the accusation that hardens their faces, can't endure their simmering questions, can't defend herself because, once she does, it will all be true. Viktor will be gone.

"Please tell me this isn't happening," Ashley says. "This can't be happening."

"Deborah," Jake breathes. "What the hell did you do?"

Only Beck remains quiet, paralyzed by the story taking shape before her.

"Let me have a moment. I need to think." Deborah stares at the scratches etched into the top of the metal table. "Viktor and I stopped by yesterday to see the diamond, but —"

"What do you mean you *stopped by*? You can't just stop by." Jake clenches his fists, trying to control his anger. "This is property of the FBI. Do you know how many laws you broke?"

"I didn't do anything." Deborah looks up to see over twenty years of hatred on her son's face. Her daughters' expressions are no more sympathetic. "It was here when I left, I swear. It was right here in this box. This isn't my fault."

"That's always the case, isn't it?" Ashley doesn't wait for her mother to respond, just keeps going. "Nothing's ever your fault. You're always the victim."

"I don't know what you want me to say. We came, saw the diamond, and left. End of story." She knows better than to tell them about the electric shock the diamond ignited inside her, all that death compacted into one stone. She knows better than to tell them about Viktor's proclamation of love, too. "I mean, I may have left the vault a few moments before Viktor did."

By now, Jake is mumbling about how stupid Deborah is, how reckless, but why should that surprise him? It's not like she's ever been responsible a single moment in her life. "Did you stop to think how this might affect us? What am I saying, of course you didn't. You've *never* thought about us."

"That's not true. I know I wasn't the most reliable mother in the world, but I thought about you three all the time."

"I guess that puts you in the running for mother of the year," Jake snipes.

"Not the most reliable? Is that what you tell yourself?" Ashley laughs cruelly.

"Please don't gang up on me. I didn't mean for this to happen."

Ashley shakes her head in disbelief. "Here we go again with the victim card."

"Stop saying that," Deborah says, feeling as victimized by her children as she does by Viktor.

"Victim, victim, victim," Ashley chants.

Beck watches her family fight, too hollowed for words. Her eyes drift toward the ceiling where a camera is mounted in the corner. Whatever happened to the diamond, the truth has been recorded, right there on that camera. The FBI will watch the tape. They will discover what happened. They will see this moment, too, when the Millers unravel, acting like petulant children. It will all be documented.

Jake paces, taking long strides across the room. This is how the second act of a script about the forfeiture would end — *family loses diamond.* "Your story makes no sense. Why would Viktor steal the diamond? He's been helping us from the start. If he was going to steal it, wouldn't he have done it as soon as he knew what the diamond was?"

"Ask Beck. She's the one who got him involved." Deborah regrets the words as soon as she says them.

Beck momentarily forgets about the camera in the corner, the record it keeps. Shaking, she turns to her mother. "Don't you *dare* blame this on me."

Deborah feels small as she faces her children, desperate to scream, *Can't you see I'm heartbroken?* Her eyes sting, but crying will only inspire more ire, more hatred. Part of her craves their cruelty, any feeling besides the complete emptiness that consumes her at the thought of Viktor, the room in Venice they will never inhabit, the love she still believes is true.

To her surprise, Jake shifts his attention to Beck. "Why *did* you go to Viktor?"

"Why would you trust him?" Ashley asks.

"You really want to have a conversation about trusting the wrong men, Ash?"

"Don't," she warns.

Ashley has goaded Beck and there's no stopping her now. "I'm not the one who

511

turned a blind eye while my husband stole half a million dollars."

"Ryan stole half a million dollars?" Deborah asks, aghast. When she'd listened to Ashley and Beck talking about Ryan's legal troubles, she hadn't heard a dollar amount. Deborah had no idea it was so much.

"His six-figure salary apparently wasn't enough for him," Beck says.

"Stop," Ashley pleads.

The sinister pleasure on Beck's face sends a chill through Deborah.

"What's the matter, Ash? Can't take everyone knowing your perfect family is a lie? And why *did* he steal that money? What was missing from your life? What was he trying to fix with cars and jewelry and fancy dinners?"

"Please, just stop."

"No, I'm curious now. What are you really so upset about — is it that your husband's going to prison, or that you won't get to drive a Mercedes anymore?"

Ashley holds Beck's gaze for a moment, but her sister's expression is impossibly callous. She can see more insults building in Beck's brain. As the tears form in Ashley eyes, she runs out of the vault before Beck can say anything else cruel.

"Real nice," Jake says to Beck. "You've

always had a way with words."

"That's your department. I can't wait to see how all of this plays out on the big screen, how you'll mine this for your own gain."

"My own gain? You have *no idea* what I've been through."

"So now it's all poor Jake?" Beck can't control the nasty comments she spouts at Jake, how it's his own fault that Kristi left him. It's laughable, really, that he, Jake Miller, is going to be a father.

Jake slumps to the floor. Everything she says rings true. It *is* laughable. He's laughable. "I've lost everything."

"And that's supposed to be my fault?" There's no warmth in Beck's eyes, no empathy in her tone.

"If you hadn't gone to Viktor, none of this would have happened. You can say whatever nasty things you want to me, to Ash. That won't change the fact that this is your fault."

Beck recoils like he's punched her. Typical. Beck can dish it out but can't take it.

"All of this is your fault," he repeats, taking another jab.

Deborah rushes over to Beck and pulls her daughter toward her, casting Jake a look so disapproving it almost makes him feel guilty. But who is Deborah to suddenly be

513

the arbiter of bad behavior?

Momentarily, Beck lets her mother embrace her, then pushes her away. "I asked you not to date him," she says before storming out.

"Was that really necessary?" Deborah shakes her head at her son.

Jake laughs. "Congratulations, Deborah. You've really fucked it all up this time."

He leaves Deborah alone in the vault. Deborah checks her phone one last time, hoping that she'll have a text from Viktor, that he'll say he fell asleep and is on his way, praying that this has all been a misunderstanding, something they can laugh about when they reconvene at the house on Edgehill Road.

The gray safe-deposit box rests on the table, open and empty. Deborah hears Ashley's accusation, *You're always the victim,* and it's true. She was the victim. Kenny made her that way. She loved him and he left her penniless. But Ashley's words are true in another way — she's always made a bad situation worse. Things with Viktor had felt different. She had been different. He taught her to believe in herself. She won't let him take that away from her, won't let herself be victimized again.

She reaches for her phone. Still no text

from Viktor. His silence only strengthens her resolve. She calls Tom to tell him what's happened.

from Vicar. His silence only strengthens
her resolve. She calls Tom to tell him what's
happened.

NINETEEN

The house is dark when Tom drops Deborah at Edgehill Road. Her car is still downtown, parked where it will be ticketed, possibly towed, but when Tom had asked her if she'd needed a ride, she'd said she did.

Deborah has no idea what time it is. Everything happened so slowly, the police and FBI questioning her, then making her wait as they tried to locate her children. Tom sat with her, reassuring her that everything would be okay. She did the right thing, calling him. Eventually, he convinced the FBI to let her go home for the night.

As Tom walked her out, an agent said, "I trust you won't be disappearing on us?"

"I'm not going anywhere," Deborah told them. What she meant was, *I don't have anywhere to go.*

"Are you going to be okay?" Tom asks, putting the car in Park.

"I'll be fine." She unbuckles her seat belt. "Do you think Beck is okay?"

"She's tougher than she seems." Tom leans against the steering wheel, and Deborah feels a motherly pride in his words. Beck *is* tough. Tom didn't break her. This won't, either.

"What about the settlement?"

"The FBI will find Viktor. He can't just disappear."

Oh, but he can. Viktor is capable of anything. Deborah wants to hate him for this, but it's what she loves most about him.

For two days, Deborah does not leave Helen's bed. Tom calls with updates on the FBI's search for Viktor, with regrets that he hasn't been able to find Beck. He stopped by her apartment, waited for an hour on the stoop. She never arrived. He's called her friends, the few she has. None of them has heard from her, either. Deborah is charmed by his attentiveness, even if she doesn't trust it. While Viktor may not have robbed her of her conviction in herself, their love, he's stripped her of her ability to trust other people, especially men. Maybe she should have learned this years ago, but it feels like a bleak way to live, knowing that you can't believe people are who they present themselves to be. She thanks Tom for his updates, promises to call him the moment she hears from Beck and stays in bed, not sleeping, not eating. She watches her ghostly image in the mirror above Helen's dresser, thinking about Viktor, now gone, about her mother, now gone, too, about how she'll never have closure with either of them.

It's after nine by the time Ashley arrives in Westchester. Her children are still up, watching a James Bond movie with Ryan in the living room, his arms around their shoulders. Tyler's eyes bulge as he watches a car chase, and Lydia kicks her legs in anticipation. Ryan looks up and spots her spying on them from the hall. He smiles, then quickly grows concerned. He begins to stand, but Ashley walks over to the couch and sits beside Tyler, kissing the mop of hair on her son's head. Engrossed in the movie, her children barely notice her. She leans back against the couch. Tomorrow, she can tell Ryan about Viktor and the diamond. For now, all she wants to do is watch the rest of the movie with her family.

From the bank, Jake heads straight to the airport and waits standby for an open seat back to LA. Flight after flight takes off full. He has a flight booked for the following afternoon, but he can't return to the house on Edgehill Road. Can't afford a hotel room, either, now that there is no $550,000, now that he's still just an out of work screenwriter, sleeping on his friend's couch. $550,000. Enough for his daughter's college, for rent on a sizable two-bedroom apartment for Kristi, enough to float him while he finishes his script. It's useless, these fantasies. The money is gone. All because of Deborah and Beck. Reckless Deborah, who will never change. And self-righteous, stubborn Beck, who never should have brought Viktor into their lives. If Kristi were here, she would remind Jake that they're hurting, but he doesn't care. They are responsible for their fates born out of bad judgment and selfishness. He knows he's right to blame them.

Another flight boards with no empty seats. Jake is going to have to camp out in the terminal until morning. The airport grows emptier, and Jake lies down on a row of seats, angling his body beneath the rigid armrests. He continues to replay his fight with Beck, how he'd told her he lost everything. And he has — Kristi, his writing career, his job at Trader Joe's, his chance at a family, all gone thanks to the Florentine Diamond. But Beck had no compassion for him. She had no compassion for Ashley, either.

He checks his phone. It's after ten. He has no idea where Ashley has settled for the night. Of his numerous missed calls, none are from his siblings. He finds Ashley's number and listens as her line rings. She picks up on the fifth ring, like she was debating whether to answer his call.

"Jake." Her voice is cautious.

"Hey, Ash —" he starts, but doesn't know how to continue. "Are you okay?"

"Not really. You?"

"Not at all."

"Sorry I ran out like that. I just couldn't face her. Either of them."

"It wasn't fair, how she treated you."

Ashley pauses. "So this is it, then."

"Who knows."

"I'm going to have to sell the house. Ryan's sentencing hearing is in three weeks. He has to return the money then. If we can't sell, I don't know what's going to happen to him."

Jake sits up, cracks his aching back. "I can come up, take a train and be there in a few hours."

"You're still in Philly? Did you go to the house?"

"I'm at the airport. Been waiting standby.

I'm serious, Ash. Say the word and I'm there."

"No, you need to go back to LA. Deal with your own life."

"You'll keep me posted about anything that happens with Ryan?"

"You'll be my first call." Jake hears what she's really saying — she isn't prepared to talk to Beck, either.

Jake listens to the soft snoring of the other passengers, settling in until morning. He is one of them, just another stranger in the airport, with nowhere to go. No fiancée, no family, no money. He has his unborn daughter, but who is he to her? For the first time in his life, he thinks he's no better than his own father.

When Beck walks out of the bank, she doesn't know where she's headed, only that she can't spend another second with her family. She can't bring herself to go to the house on Edgehill Road or her apartment in Fairmount, which in a few weeks will belong to someone else. She should call Tom, the FBI, but all she can think about is Viktor. It had been so easy for her to trust him when it was never easy for her to trust anyone. She isn't ready to confront his betrayal, so she starts walking. Her thoughts turn to the terrible things she said to her siblings. It isn't their fault that Viktor proved deceitful. She was wrong to lash out at them, but they'd turned on her so quickly their abandonment felt as cruel as Viktor's. And worse, Deborah had instigated it, shifting the blame from herself to Beck. After all the times Beck has forgiven her, after she's defended her mother to her siblings, to Kenny, to have her turn on Beck like that. It felt unfathomably cruel. At least she won't have to protect her mother from Kenny anymore. Now that there is no money, they definitely won't be hearing from him again.

As she walks by her office building, she realizes Tom is probably upstairs, wrapping up some paperwork on their futile settlement. She can hear him saying, *Viktor, really?* Her body guides her past the building, through city hall, and while she tells herself that she isn't walking anywhere in particular, she knows she's headed to Christian's.

He doesn't ask her what she is doing at his studio or if she is okay, only opens the door and lets her inside. Wordlessly, she takes off his T-shirt and jeans, then her suit, which she's still wearing from the settlement negotiation that afternoon. He lies down on an area rug that smells of spilled beer and Doritos, and she straddles him.

Afterward, they sit naked on his couch. He snaps open a beer for her.

"Can I have something stronger?"

He finds a bottle of whiskey in the cabinet, and she swigs directly from the bottle.

For two days, Christian supplies her with cheap beer and whiskey washed down with morning sex and afternoon fucking and pizza. During those forty-eight hours, news of the diamond's disappearance reaches the media. If Christian hears of it, he doesn't let on, just keeps buying more beer, more pizza, more condoms. For two days, they barely speak. They do not mention the Florentine Diamond, Helen, Flora, or Vienna. They do not turn on the television or the stereo. On the third morning she wakes at Christian's, she hears her phone buzzing on his kitchen counter. He charged it for her, and she's charmed by this. She strokes Christian's smooth back, watching him sleep. One day, he might become someone she could fall in love with, but he isn't there yet.

Her voicemail box is full. A news update sits between thirty-seven unopened texts and twenty-three missed calls: "The Florentine Diamond, Missing Again." Despite herself, she opens the link and reads about Helen, the Millers, the settlement with the Austrians gone awry, Viktor. The article ends, *Authorities are trying to determine if Viktor Castanza acted alone or if Deborah Miller was an accomplice.*

Of all the mischaracterizations of her family the press has drawn, this one lands with Beck. Despite the mistakes she's inflicted on her children, Deborah would never steal from them.

Beck finds her clothes in a ball beside the front door where she left them three days earlier, feeling an almost animalistic need to see her mother. She slips on her black skirt, her white blouse, her blazer. Christian stirs awake when Beck sits beside him on the bed.

"I need to go." She kisses his forehead. "Thank you."

"Anytime." He casts her his boyish smile.

On Edgehill Road, the sidewalk is swarming with camera crews, who turn when they see Beck, their feet crunching the vibrant leaves that have fallen from the trees that line the street. Instinctively, Beck hides her face and fights the current of people up the walkway to her family's house. When she enters, the television blares in the empty living room. The morning news is on, and a young reporter stands outside Viktor's building, her dark hair blowing in the wind as she tells viewers, "I'm standing at the site of Mr. Viktor Castanza's apartment, the last known whereabouts of the diamond. The building manager reports video coverage of Mr. Castanza entering and leaving the building on October 16, just hours after he was seen exiting Federalist Bank. The FBI has an APB out on Mr. Castanza, but he hasn't been spotted since. We're going to switch over now to Edgehill Road in Bala Cynwyd, where reporters tell me Beck Miller, who works for Mr. Castanza's former counsel and was the first individual to discover the Florentine Diamond, has reportedly returned home after also disappearing for the last forty-eight hours."

The TV switches over to a moment ago when Beck was darting through reporters, her face shielded by her arm. She can hear them outside, still calling to her, can see their shadows through the window's thin curtains.

Footsteps drumroll as Deborah barrels down the stairs. "Becca, is that you?"

Deborah's hair is a nest around her pale face. In two days, she looks like she's lost five pounds and aged ten years.

"Oh, thank God," Deborah says, and races

down the last few steps, nearly pouncing on Beck. Her body has a faint, musty odor, her breath thick with morning, but Beck holds her tighter.

When they hear their names, they release each other and turn toward the television.

"The FBI is investigating whether the Millers have been in contact with Mr. Castanza or if he was working alone."

A close-up of Viktor fills the screen. On the television, he's even more dapper than in life, his eyes an impossible blue, his lush hair so white it shines like platinum.

"I'm sorry," Beck says to her mother. "I never should have brought Viktor into our lives."

Deborah places both hands on her daughter's cheeks, something she's never done before. "There's nothing wrong with trusting people. Don't stop because of this."

The intensity makes Beck uncomfortable, but her mother's hands remain on her cheeks, holding her there, until she agrees.

When she lets go, Beck asks, "Have you heard from Ashley and Jake?"

Beck is always the quickest to anger, the cruelest. She's also the most resilient, Deborah realizes. For Beck, the words she and her siblings spat at each other in the vault are just that: words. Released and forgotten.

"They're gone," Deborah says. She stares vacantly at the image of Viktor as it disappears from the screen, fearing she will never understand this time in her life.

TWENTY

Viktor did take the diamond. Of that much, the FBI is certain. They question Deborah, alone and with Tom. Her story never changes. Zoomed in, the security camera footage caught him dropping the diamond into his pocket as he pretended to return it to the safe-deposit box. They announce to Tom and to the media that Deborah Miller is no longer a suspect, that Viktor Castanza was working alone.

Like kidnapping cases, the first forty-eight hours are the most critical. The FBI checks airline records, Amtrak, SEPTA, Greyhound, gas station cameras along I-95, tollbooths on the Pennsylvania Turnpike. Viktor has vanished as completely as the Florentine. Beck continues to stay on Edgehill Road with her mother. The FBI checks in with them daily, but they do not hear from Viktor again. Each day the number of news crews decreases until, by the following week, they've all moved on.

Jake knocks on what used to be his apartment door.

"I need one minute," Kristi says as she opens the door, then rushes back to her room. As he waits, Jake braves a step inside. Preparations for their daughter's arrival litter the space — a stroller, boxes of bottles and diapers beside the couch, a changing table against the window.

Jake helps Kristi down the apartment complex's stairs. Her stomach is so large he's surprised she can walk.

"If this baby doesn't come out soon, I'm going to reach in there and pull her out myself," she tells Jake as she situates herself in the passenger seat.

At the doctor's, Kristi lets Jake follow her into the observation room.

"You're sure?"

"We're getting down to the wire. It's important you know what's going on," Kristi says, plopping onto the bed.

While the doctor checks Kristi's cervix, Jake remains completely still, trying to draw as little attention to himself as possible.

"Everything looks good," the doctor tells Kristi. "She turned, so we don't have to do an external cephalic version."

Jake has no idea what an external cephalic version is, but it sounds terrifying. Kristi says, "Thank God."

The doctor removes her gloves and tosses them into the trash. "We'll see you next week."

With that, she leaves, and Jake averts his eyes as Kristi changes into her pants. As they walk toward reception, Jake asks what an external cephalic version is.

"It's where they push and twist on your stomach to turn the baby around," Kristi explains. "It's supposed to be really painful."

"Well, it's good it worked out on its own." This is a stupid, Jake Miller thing to say. Of course he would be relieved that everything just magically turned out okay.

To his surprise, Kristi smiles and weaves her arm through Jake's. "What would you say to a walk around the reservoir? I'm supposed to be getting exercise. I should warn you, it's more of a waddle than a walk."

"I'll waddle with you anywhere," Jake says.

It's just a walk, Jake reminds himself as they stroll past the meadow where families are flying kites and childless couples are lounging in the sun. They are just getting some exercise, even if it feels more like a first date. All the things he wants to say but knows he shouldn't make him awkwardly quiet, like he was the first time they went out.

Kristi is talking ceaselessly, just like she did on their early outings. She tells Jake how everyone at the vet has been treating her better since her pregnancy became obvious. She describes her freezer, overflowing with meals her mother has made, even though her mother plans to drive down as soon as she goes into labor and stay with her for the first month.

Their steps grow smaller as they wind their way around the final bend of the reservoir, toward Jake's car.

"How's the script going?" Kristi asks.

"Good." And it is going well. Jake knows the whole arc of the story now: Helen's motivation for keeping the diamond, what happened to her family in Vienna. "I've still got a lot of work to do. Maybe you'll read it when I'm done?" His heart races like he's asked her to marry him again.

"I'd be honored," Kristi says, causing them both to blush.

Twelve days have passed, and still there are no sightings of Viktor. Ashley removes all the family photographs from the living room mantel, placing them in a box Tyler will run up to the attic. The house smells of chocolate chip cookies that Ryan is baking for the open house that afternoon. They've decided to sell the house without a real estate agent to save on the commission. Ashley has cleaned, pared down their furniture to streamline the rooms, and bought Prosecco. It feels odd, creating the fantasy of a perfect family by packing up the memories the Johnsons have built in this house. As Ashley places the lid on the cardboard box of framed photographs, she spots a picture of her family from Lydia's dance recital. Ashley has always loved this photo, even though there are better snapshots from trips to Martha's Vineyard and Rome. But this is the only one where they are looking at each other rather than the camera. She lifts it out of the box and returns it to the mantel.

At three, Ryan takes the kids miniature golfing while Ashley stays behind to manage the open house. The children have grown attached to Ryan while Ashley was gone, competing to show him their drawings, to regale him with tales of prisoners taken during capture the flag, anecdotes they would normally race to tell Ashley. Ryan's sentencing hearing is just a week and a half away. While the children don't know the exact date, they know to consume as much of their father as possible, before it's too late.

By 3:15, no one has shown up to the house, and Ashley starts to panic. Did they find out about Ryan? The prosecutors had promised the case would stay out of the papers. Maybe it's because of the Florentine Diamond? Ashley was never considered a suspect in its robbery. Still, something is keeping the people away. Ashley bites her nails, then catches herself. She messes the pamphlets by the front door to look like others have already sifted through them. She hides three cookies in the cupboard, leaving an obvious space on the tray in the kitchen, and downs a glass of Prosecco. The driveway remains empty.

For the first time since she ran out of the vault, Ashley wants to call Beck. Her sister would know how to quell her anxieties, fears of what will happen when Ryan does not have the money by his sentencing hearing. Then she remembers what Beck said in the vault. If Ashley calls, she doesn't know which Beck she'll get — the one who promised they'd get through this together, or the one that made her feel so alone.

By 3:45, she's drunk one more glass of Prosecco. The house looks perfect. It *is* perfect. How is no one here? Without the sale, what's going to happen to her husband? His sentence was going to be reduced on account of returning the money. She doesn't want to know how much jail time a half million dollars buys, so she wanders into the kitchen for a third glass of Prosecco.

A little after four, tires crackle in the driveway. She wasn't expecting Ryan and the kids for another half hour. She quickly dumps the rest of the glass down the drain and dries her eyes with the back of her palm. As she plasters a smile on her face, ready to tell her family it went great, two strangers walk in, followed soon after by another couple.

While Deborah insists that the first rule to moving is to only take what fits in the Red Rabbit, Beck hires movers with a truck. Deborah objects until she sees the sleek gray couch Tom had purchased for the Fairmount apartment, the flat-screen television, the midcentury bar cart being carried into the house by three burly men.

"Tom didn't want any of this?" Deborah asks Beck as two men navigate the stairs with an antique dresser.

"I didn't ask."

"Atta girl," Deborah says, plopping onto their new couch.

It's been two weeks since Viktor disappeared, and Beck can't believe that she's moving back into the house on Edgehill Road. She's been living on her own for fifteen years. Now, at thirty-six, she's returned. Somehow, this doesn't feel like defeat. Despite her closeness to Helen, she hadn't considered Edgehill Road a harbor, somewhere she could always return. It wasn't until Deborah moved in and filled the house with color that Beck felt like this house could be her home again.

"I'm thinking of quitting," Beck tells her mom. She doesn't mean to say this. In fact, she hasn't even fully admitted it to herself. After Viktor disappeared with the diamond, something at work changed. It has been seven years since Beck was expelled from law school. Seven years of licking her wounds. Seven years where she could have made a plea to the school for reentry, in which she could have proved she was sorry and had been rehabilitated. Instead, she spent the last seven years becoming the best paralegal at her firm, caring only about winning regardless of whether her clients were in the right. Now that the diamond is gone and she isn't speaking to either of her siblings, winning doesn't feel so important anymore.

"I'm starting a new business," Deborah says. "Flower arrangements. Want to help me?"

Beck has never shared her mother's love of flowers, and she certainly knows better than to go into business with Deborah. Still, Beck says, "Sure, until I figure out what's next."

The taller, thicker mover knocks on the wall to get their attention.

"That's everything." He holds a clipboard in one hand, a padded envelope in the other. Beck crosses the living room to complete the paperwork. As she signs the agreement, he reads the name on the package. "One of you Deborah Miller?"

Confused, Deborah takes the envelope from him and sees it has no return address. She tears it open and peeks inside. It's filled with packets of seeds. Delphinium, blue thistle, snapdragon, daffodils, and chamomile. Deborah gasps, rushes upstairs, shutting the bedroom door behind her. She leans against the closed door and hugs the package to her chest.

Weeds, Tyler had called the bouquet when it arrived after her first date with Viktor.

The Johnsons have to take out a loan against the sale of the house, but they have the money to pay back Ryan's company plus enough for three months' rent on a new place. It's significantly smaller than the home they owned but in the same school district. The children have to share a room. At first, they both adamantly refuse, but despite their initial complaints, Lydia and Tyler enjoy the shared space. Ashley lets them have a TV, and they play video games late into the night, stumbling downstairs in the morning with glazy eyes.

On the morning of Ryan's sentencing, Ashley is dressed in one of her old skirt suits. Ryan's lawyer thinks it's a good idea, Ashley accompanying Ryan to the hearing, a reminder to the judge of the family he's leaving behind. When the children tumble into the kitchen where Ryan is packing lunches, Lydia looks at her mother's formal clothes, worried. The kids know that today is the day. Lydia's troubled gaze forces Ashley to consider how today will be for her children, taking the bus home, returning to this empty, foreign house. Ryan's lawyer assured him that the judge will give him two weeks to turn himself in, that he won't be incarcerated on the spot. As the kids eat their pancakes, Ashley pulls Ryan aside.

"I can't come with you today."

"Ash —"

"I need to be here, for the kids. I don't know what I was thinking, that we'd let them return home alone."

Ryan nods. He hadn't considered this, either. "You'll drop me at the train after we drive the kids to school?"

The image of Ryan taking the train home alone breaks her heart, too, but this is part of his punishment; it isn't a debt his children can pay for him.

"So, this is it," Ryan says to his wife when she pulls into the train station's parking lot. Together, they watch the crowd waiting on the platform. "I'm sorry. I don't know if I've said that enough. I'm really sorry. Sorry for everything I've —" Ryan continues to list everything he's put her through. Ashley can't listen. He has apologized so much that it's starting to have the opposite effect on her, stirring the anger that otherwise lays dormant.

She doesn't want to fight, so she points toward the platform and tells her husband he doesn't want to be late.

Driving home, Ashley cannot fight the tears. Her eyes become so blurry that she has to pull over. Before she convinces herself otherwise, she dials her sister, who still hasn't apologized. The line continues to ring, and Ashley fights every impulse to hang up, until Beck's voicemail picks up and all she can manage to say is, "I need you."

She dries her eyes, blows her nose, and pulls into traffic. A few moments later, her phone rings. She feels a flurry through her chest. But it isn't Beck. It's a 212 number she doesn't have saved.

"Ash, it's Georgina."

"Hi," Ashley says, confused. Why is Georgina calling her? There's no diamond. No promise of a commission.

"Listen, I only have a sec. I wanted to call you right away. I heard you're looking for work." Ashley grips the steering wheel, embarrassed. All those informational interviews. Of course old friends talk. And this is just the beginning of the talk about Ashley Johnson. "There's an opening in Bartley's publicity department you'd be perfect for."

It's an associate position rather than the head of a department, but a foot in, with solid pay and long-term possibilities.

"And they want me?"

"You'll have to interview, of course. With my recommendation, it's yours if you want it. Won't it be fun, working together?"

Immediately, Ashley plans to say yes. Instead, she asks, "Can you give me a few days to think about it?"

"Sure," Georgina says, unable to mask her surprise. "But I'll need to know soon. This is a personal favor. They won't hold the job forever."

Perhaps Georgina feels guilty for alerting the Italians — an act she'll never admit — or maybe she pities Ashley now that her family lost the diamond. Either way, Ashley does not want a job as a personal favor. She wants a position because she's good at what she does.

"I'll let you know early next week," she says.

She decides not to mention the position to Ryan. As soon as she tells him, she'll have to take it. It would be crazy not to accept. Still, her gut tells her to pass. She decides if she does not come up with a logical reason to say no by the following week, she'll interview for the opening.

That evening the Johnsons have more pressing concerns. Their new house is two miles from the train station, and Ryan texts to say he'll walk back. He arrives forty minutes later, jacket dangling over his arm, tie loose, shirt and hair wet with sweat despite the brisk weather.

"What's for dinner?" he says as he walks in. "I'm starving." His voice is upbeat, but his face is forlorn. Ashley can't decipher his expression, so she takes his jacket and tells him there's a pizza in the oven.

Lydia and Tyler are disturbingly well behaved as they nibble on their crust, waiting for their father to declare his fate. Ryan inhales a piece of pizza. When he reaches for another, Ashley intervenes. "Ry, what happened?"

"The judge followed the recommendations in the presentencing report. Eighteen months. It could have been worse."

"Could have been worse? That's a year and a half." Lydia throws her half-eaten pizza onto her plate and races down the hall. Her door slams. Ryan stands, but Ashley stops him.

"Leave her be. She needs to be mad right now." *I need to be mad, too,* Ashley thinks. It makes no difference that Ryan could have gotten a longer sentence. She just hopes he won't start apologizing again because if he does she'll explode.

Ryan sits back down, and Tyler walks over to hug his father. As Ryan strokes his son's hair, neither of them speaks. Ashley watches Tyler be vulnerable. Maybe, if Ryan had learned this, too, the Johnsons wouldn't be here, with their patriarch about to turn himself into federal prison.

The next morning Ashley's phone rings,

and again she assumes it's Beck. Again, she's disappointed by another number she doesn't recognize, this time from her local area code. Why hasn't Beck returned her message? She knew the date of Ryan's sentencing. Ashley hadn't asked for an apology; she'd asked for something Beck could give. As she hits the call button to answer her buzzing phone, the anger returns.

"Is this Ashley? This is Mrs. Whitmore. We bought your house."

Immediately, the frustration turns to panic. The papers have been signed. The money paid, all cash. Why is she calling?

"I'm so glad I reached you. We've been having trouble selling our old house and realized we should probably hire a stager. The person who staged your house did such a good job — I'm hoping you might share the company's number?"

"The stager? I didn't hire anyone. I did it myself."

Mrs. Whitmore laughs. "You wouldn't be available, would you?"

Although Ashley knows she's joking, she says, "Actually, I would."

When they hang up, her phone buzzes almost instantaneously. Only, it isn't Mrs. Whitmore, sending her the address to her old home. I'm here, Beck's text reads. Tell me what I can do.

Twenty-four days after Viktor and the diamond disappeared, the baby is four days late. Kristi has scoured the internet for ways to self-induce. She tries acupuncture, Szechuan stews, ghost pepper hot sauce, castor oil. She twists her nipples and does squats. Nothing has an effect on the baby, curled up and stubborn in Kristi's womb. The only thing she does not try, for obvious reasons, is sex. The doctors have scheduled an induction in three days.

Since Jake returned to LA, he's settled into a new routine. He checks in with Kristi each morning before he sits down to write, then calls her again in the afternoon as he walks to work. He got a job as a barback at a mixology bar designed to look like a tree house. The line outside makes him feel old, and more people light up cigarettes than he thought still smoked in LA. But the pay is good, the shifts so busy that the hours pass quickly. He returns to Rico's exhausted enough to pass out on the couch, only to begin the cycle again the next morning.

He has to do more research than he anticipated, but he works on the script at a steady clip, chipping away scene by scene, writing with a sense of clarity he's never had before.

The script makes him think of the Millers, even though they aren't in it. Jake used the photograph Beck and Deborah found, of Helen in her fur stole with Joseph's arm around her shoulders, as inspiration for his story. In the script, this is Helen's wedding night, the first time she wears the orchid brooch. In the script, Joseph is not married. He does not have another family. He does not die and leave Helen alone. It reads so right that Jake begins to believe it's true.

In a few weeks, he'll have enough money saved from his new job to rent his own apartment. For now, he heads to Rico's, relieved to find the living room dark so they won't have to hang out. Jake is so tired he falls asleep in jeans that smell of beer and cigarettes, his teeth unbrushed. A sleep too heavy for dreams, too heavy for ringing phones.

Rico shakes him. "Jake? Jake?" Jake mumbles and rolls over. The shaking becomes more forceful, and he blinks one eye open. Rico holds out his phone.

"What time is it?" Jake asks, scratching the back of his head. He darts up when he sees it's four thirty and has seven missed calls from Kristi. His fingers fumble as he tries to call her back. Mrs. Zhang picks up on the first ring.

"Is everything okay?"

"Kristi went into labor a few hours ago but it was too dangerous. She had a C-section. She's recovering now."

"Is she okay? The baby?"

"Yes." He can't tell if there's accusation or worry in her voice.

"I'm on my way."

Jake throws on his shoes without tying them, grabs a sweatshirt, and races toward the door, but Rico stops Jake. "You smell like an alcoholic."

Jake begins to protest that he doesn't have time to change, but Rico is right. He can't turn up at the hospital in the middle of the night smelling like he's been at the bar, even if it's the bar where he works. He mines a T-shirt and jeans from the pile of clothing in Rico's corner. While not exactly clean, they're pristine in comparison to the clothes he was sleeping in.

The twenty-minute drive to the hospital feels interminable as he curses at himself for sleeping through his daughter's birth. He manages to hit every red light, or so it seems, making the drive that much more painful. He and Kristi have been in a good place. Not where he wants to be, but companions, teammates. And now — now he flakes the one moment she actually needs him. Everything she's said about him, every reason she doesn't want him as a partner, it's all true. Even when he tries to be better, he still manages to fuck it all up.

Mrs. Zhang meets him in the hallway and rushes him into the room. When they enter, Kristi's sleeping. Her eyes drift open when she hears them. She's hooked up to an IV and a catheter. Her skin is blotchy, hair oily and wispy around her face. She's never looked more beautiful.

He rushes to her side as she futilely tries to sit up. "Kris, I'm so sorry I wasn't here."

"Oh, Jake." She strokes his hair.

"I'm so sorry I missed it, Kris. Our daughter's birth."

She shushes him. "You're here now." She motions toward the corner of the room where somehow he's missed the bassinet. Jake walks over and sees the baby, his daughter, swaddled in pink. Her eyes are crusted shut, her head somewhat misshapen. They say children come out looking like their fathers, but Jake just sees Kristi across his daughter's face.

He lets his daughter sleep and returns to Kristi's bed. Without being detected, Mrs. Zhang has tiptoed out of the room. They are alone, and Kristi lets him embrace her.

"Helen," Kristi says as Jake pulls away. "We should call her Helen."

Jake Miller is not a crier. He didn't cry when his father left, on those nights in high school where Beck had crawled into his bed and snuggled with him, softly sniffling and asking if it was her fault their dad was gone. He didn't even cry when Helen died, when he sprinkled dirt onto her casket. Today, as he says his daughter's name for the first time, "Helen," his eyes overflow.

Once Kristi has fallen back to sleep, Jake steps into the hall to call his sister. It's been almost a month since the diamond went missing, since he's spoken to Deborah or Beck.

"It's perfect," Ashley says when Jake tells her his daughter's name.

"Can you come out to meet her, our Helen?" He's finding every excuse to say her name. Helen, his daughter. Helen Zhang Miller. Helen, finally a Miller.

"I want to. It sounds like the best escape. We have so little time left with Ryan, though. And I know it probably sounds like a line, but I don't have the money."

"Sure," Jake says, unable to fight the disappointment. Mr. Zhang is driving down from San Jose. Kristi's cousin, who lives in

Santa Monica, is visiting in the morning. He wants his family here, too. Ashley, Lydia, and Tyler.

"You're coming home in March, right?" Ashley asks. "Maybe you can bring Kristi and Helen Jr.?" Helen Jr. rolls so effortlessly off Ashley's tongue that Jake realizes that's what they will call her, as unconventional as it may be.

"March?"

"For the unveiling. Beck is planning it around the kids' spring break, so they don't have to miss school."

Jake forgot all about the Jewish tradition of unveiling the gravestone, that March will mark one year since Helen's death. One year of mourning. Of searching. Of finding. Of losing. Helen, Kristi, the Florentine Diamond, Beck, even Deborah. The cycle seems complete; lost, found, lost again. A closed circuit.

"Jake, you have to come. Please. It's up to you to fix this."

"They have phones, too. They could call me."

"You know them. They won't. They're embarrassed. It's their fault, everything with Viktor."

"You're in touch with them, then?"

"Starting to be. We're going to go down

for Thanksgiving. They aren't perfect, none of us are. But we're the only family we have."

Jake knows she's right. He's working on being a better person, for Kristi, for Helen Jr., but there are only so many relationships he can work on at one time.

"I'll think about it," he tells her, and they both know that he's made up his mind.

By March, the Florentine Diamond has been missing for five months, and still, no one has seen or heard from Viktor. No one other than Deborah, who gets a new package of seeds every Monday. Tulips, lilies, sunflowers. All organic, non-GMO. Their sprouts have over-taken the third bedroom, Helen's former sewing shop now a greenhouse. Soon, Deborah will plant them outside. She's told no one about the seeds — not the FBI, not Beck, either.

On the week of Helen's unveiling, Viktor sends Deborah orchid seeds. Orchids are notoriously fickle. Deborah will not be able to grow them from seed. Still, he remembered the anniversary of Helen's death. Despite his betrayal, Viktor still loves her.

The morning the Millers unveil Helen's tombstone is balmy. No jackets are needed to fight the wind. No boots to wade through patches of snow. Just bare earth where the grass begins its regrowth and green buds that pock the tree branches.

Ashley and Beck weave their arms through their mother's, steadying her across the uneven incline. Lydia and Tyler race ahead toward Helen's grave where the rabbi waits beside the tombstone covered with a white sheet.

"So Jake really isn't coming?" Deborah asks.

"We've been over this," Ashley says. "He's got a lot going on with the script and Helen Jr."

"That's bullshit," Beck says.

"It's Helen's unveiling," Deborah protests.

"I don't know what you want me to say. I tried. He's not coming."

They arrive at the graveside where Beck nods to the rabbi that she can begin. Before she does, Beck asks Ashley, "Is it any good, the script?" She knows Ashley has been in regular touch with Jake, that she gets weekly pictures of Helen Jr., that she's read drafts of his script.

"It's excellent."

The rabbi begins with a psalm in Hebrew, one that Beck selected.

As the rabbi translates, "Happy is he whose transgression is forgiven, whose sin is pardoned," Deborah thinks Beck chose this psalm for Viktor, that, like Deborah, she misses him.

She feels Beck move beside her, stepping toward the tombstone to place a small round rock on its top. It's been stripped of its white cloth. Beneath a Star of David, beneath Helen's name, her date of birth and death, the gravestone reads:

> Beloved Grandmother,
> Mother, and Daughter
> One of the Fifty Children
> Survivor

As Beck steps away from the grave, she reaches into her coat pocket and fingers the pointed leaves of Helen's brooch. It seems vital that the brooch is here to say goodbye to Helen, too.

Deborah is the next to leave a rock on Helen's headstone. Resting her hand on the curve of stone, she shuts her eyes and says goodbye to her mother. The granite is cool against her skin, but it sends a warm wave of energy through her body. It's Helen's energy, grounded and sensible. Dependable. Nothing like the violence she'd felt when she held the Florentine Diamond. Viktor was right; Helen had done everything she could not to let Joseph Spiegel come between them. Beside

Survivor on the gravestone, Deborah wishes she'd thought to add *Protector*.

The children and Ashley place their stones beside Deborah's until there are five small stones lining the top. Tyler is the first to cry, and Lydia hugs her brother. Deborah embraces them both, her cheeks wet with tears, and she reaches for Ashley and Beck to join them. They stand there graveside, sobbing, for Helen, for the end of a year of mourning, for the engraving that memorializes Helen's past, for the five stones resting on top of the headstone, for the sixth stone that should be there, too.

Jake tells himself that he was too busy to fly east for Helen's unveiling. Between Helen Jr., notes on his script, shifts at the bar, he simply can't get away. It's just a gravestone. It will still be there whenever he wants to visit Helen. He tells this to Ashley, to Kristi, too. They both say they understand but warn that it's a decision he can't take back.

By April, when Viktor's case is still open but no longer active, Jake has enough money saved for a deposit on a studio in Kristi's building. He furnishes it with a bed and nightstand, a small table, not even a television. Some might find it depressing, the barrenness of the space, but Jake doesn't want to get comfortable here.

His apartment is out of range for a baby monitor, so Kristi texts him whenever Helen Jr. wakes up. He keeps waiting for her to offer him the couch, but the living room is Helen Jr.'s — if he sleeps there, he will wake her. So he retreats to his studio to sleep. He stays in Kristi's apartment all day while Kristi is at work, finishing edits when Helen rests, taking her to the park and the reservoir when she needs a distraction. It's a routine, a family life. Not exactly the one he wants, but the one he accepts.

When he and Kristi's days off align, they bring Helen Jr. to the beach, to Huntington Gardens where she marvels at the flora from all over the world. In Santa Monica, they sit beneath an umbrella that Jake has hammered into the sand. Jake wipes the sand from Helen Jr.'s hand before she can shovel it into her mouth. It becomes a game, and she repeatedly tries to thwart Jake, laughing as he says, "No. Helen, no."

Kristi looks up and smiles at them before returning to Jake's pages. It's uncomfortable, pretending not to watch her read. Kristi is a slow reader. Methodical. It takes her more than a minute to read each page, even though it's a script, not a novel, the bulk of the page blank space. He can't watch anymore so he lifts Helen and charges into the ocean. She laughs as waves hit her calves. It's a perfect moment until salt water splashes in her eyes and she starts to cry. She wails and rubs her eyes, the telltale sign that she's crashing. Jake carries her, thrashing and screaming, back to the umbrella.

"Kris, we should get going," he says, trying to keep hold of Helen Jr. as she writhes in his arms. The sounds of her cries wreck him, even though he knows she's not in pain.

Kristi looks up at him with a strange mix of pride and longing. She rests the last page of the script on the pile by her side. "It's perfect."

That night, when they put Helen to bed, Kristi leads Jake into her bedroom.

"You're sure?" he asks.

"Don't ruin it," she says. It's been eight months since he's kissed her. She opens her mouth and he slips his tongue between her teeth. Right away, it becomes wondrously familiar.

While Jake keeps his apartment, two floors down, he spends his nights in Kristi's bed, their bed. If Helen Jr. notices the change, nothing in her behavior conveys it. She's the same happy child whose cry continues to break her father even when he knows it's just tiredness or hunger.

In June, when they have all begun to lose count of how many months it's been since the diamond has disappeared, Jake sells his script. It isn't a life-altering amount of money. It isn't $550,000. But it's enough for a deposit on a two-bedroom apartment in Frogtown.

He arrives at Kristi's with a bottle of champagne and the four ring boxes he bought when he got home from Vienna. So much has changed since last September when the Millers returned victoriously from the City of Dreams. Briefly, it seemed so promising, their lives flush with money, their relationships better than ever, but he didn't have any of the things then that he has now.

"Babe," he calls when he enters the apartment, warm from the kitchen where Kristi is cooking her mother's eggplant recipe. She barrels into the living room, holding Helen Jr. against one hip. Helen Jr. has recently started to crawl, and she fights for her freedom.

Kristi notices the champagne. "So, it's official?"

"They want to start shooting in the fall."

Kristi lets Helen Jr. free and runs over to Jake, embracing him.

"It could still go south," Jake reminds her

to prevent her from getting her hopes up. That's Hollywood — a project too big to fail one minute, abandoned the next.

"Shh," Kristi says, pulling him toward her. The boxes bulge in his pockets, creating awkward space between them. He takes them out, waiting for her to say, *Oh, Jake,* and start to cry, but she appears as wary of those boxes as she was the last time he tried to give them to her.

"Kris —" Jake begins.

"Don't." She forces him to meet her eye. "We're together. You, me, Helen. We're in this, but I can't marry you, not while you still aren't speaking to your family."

"I talked to Ashley and the kids yesterday," he protests, even though he knows this isn't what she means. "I can't, Kris. I'm afraid to let them into our lives, into Helen Jr.'s life. They're destined to disappoint."

"I can't tell you what to do. If we marry, I want it to be a merging of our families. I don't want to start off with any more people missing." Jake knows she means her mother's family, Helen's. "And that script you wrote, the one we're celebrating? It belongs to them, too. You should let them share it with you."

Kristi takes the champagne bottle and disappears into the kitchen, leaving him standing alone with the four ring boxes. He returns them to his pockets, feels a gentle tugging at his leg, and sees his daughter trying to stand against him. She's not strong enough yet, not that that diminishes her effort. Jake bends down and lifts her into the air.

In the kitchen, a cork pops and Kristi returns with the champagne. They clink glasses, but the moment isn't as celebratory as he wants it to be. He knows Kristi is right about the script, the story it bears. Part of him wants to share it with Beck, to have her be proud of him. In the eight months since she ran out of the vault, she hasn't contacted him. Ashley keeps reminding him that he needs to be the bigger person. Something holds him back, though. Stubbornness, perhaps, or the lingering anger over the $550,000, which still rattles him at random moments. It isn't the money exactly. He wants to be a bigger person — he just doesn't know how.

TWENTY-ONE

A year and a half later

When Jake learns that his new film will premiere at Sundance, he only invites Ashley. He hasn't seen Beck or Deborah since the diamond's disappearance two years ago. Kristi has stayed true to her promise not to marry him so long as he remains estranged from the Millers. Even this is not enough to compel him to let his mother and sister back into his life, into Helen Jr.'s life. Besides, Jake and Kristi are living as partners, as mother and father to their daughter. It's easy for him to forget that their union isn't legally recognized. He still thinks of Beck at times — whenever he hears a Nirvana song on the oldies station or sees a bird tattoo that resembles the one on his sister's forearm — but thinking about her is like poking a fading bruise. It doesn't hurt unless he prods it, and eventually the pain becomes more familiar than the injury itself.

As he's packing for the weekend in Park City, his mind drifts to Helen. When he was writing his script, he didn't have to miss her. She was with him while he crafted her dialogue, while he experienced the moments of her life previously unavailable to him. While he got to know Flora, too. Leib. Martin. Now that he has finished the film, he feels her absence more acutely than he has in the years since she's been gone. He only could have written this movie after she died, but he can't imagine watching it without her now. It reminds him of *My Summer of Women,* when she'd declined his invitation to the premiere, nudging him to invite Deborah in her place. Despite the fraught relationship she had with Deborah, Helen had wanted them to be family, all of them. Suddenly, it doesn't seem right, honoring Helen while forsaking the Millers.

Beck is in her second week of the semester when she receives the letter from Jake. In the fall, she'd enrolled in a master's program for school counseling. Unlike her law school application, where she'd omitted her expulsion, she shaped her personal essay around her misdeeds in high school, explaining how they compelled her to want to help others. In class, with her peers, she's open about

Mr. O'Neal. Together, they plot what they would do as counselors if a similar situation arose.

Beck is cooking dinner when the delivery-man knocks on the door of Edgehill Road. Right away, she recognizes Jake's nearly illegible handwriting on the envelope. It's been the same since high school, slanted, almost hieroglyphic. He'd trained himself to write this way, thinking it looked edgy, then had never been able to simplify his script. When she was in college, Beck had gotten Jake to transcribe a Simone de Beauvoir quote in his unique hand, then had it inked onto her lower back. As she takes the envelope from the deliveryman she unconsciously rubs her right side where her brother is permanently branded onto her.

The envelope is addressed to her and her mother. A letter, she assumes, but whether it's to make amends or to fortify their estrangement, she can't begin to guess. She wonders whether this is what it felt like for Jake, those years after *My Summer of Women* premiered when he was waiting for her to forgive him. Although she's dying to open it, she rests it on the dining table, so she and Deborah can look at it together when her mother returns from the flower shop.

Unsurprisingly, Deborah's flower business

never took off, not simply because she decided to grow flowers people other than her grandson associated with weeds. She simply didn't have enough output. The weather was too erratic, the summer too hot, the competition from established florists too steep. Despite her lack of business prowess, she has an eye, a knack for putting together the perfect bouquet. Recognizing her talent, a local florist offered her a job as an arranger. It's nothing fancy, but it's consistent, and she likes the work. For the first time in as long as she can remember, she isn't looking for the next idea. Sometimes, she thinks about the diamond. Mostly, she misses Viktor. Every Monday, his seeds arrive like clockwork. She plants them, mourns the death of each seed that doesn't sprout like she's losing Viktor all over again, but the packages keep coming, reminding her that someday he might return, too.

By seven, when her mother walks in the door, Beck has set the table and dished out two bowls of vegetable chili for their dinner. While her mother has not turned her vegan, Beck has agreed to keep all meat and dairy out of the house. They both pretend it's to prevent contaminating Deborah's daiya cheese with the cooties of Swiss or Muenster. Really, it's so Deborah doesn't have to test her willpower. She feels better about herself when she follows her vegan diet, so Beck supports her mother, however much she wishes she could slip a little beef into their chili.

"What's this?" Deborah shouts as she walks into the dining room. From the kitchen, Beck hears her mother tear open the envelope. In the past, Beck would have screamed at her mother for opening it without asking Beck first, especially since Beck has been resisting the urge to read Jake's letter for the last hour. Today, she finds it funny. Typical Deborah. There's something comforting in her predictability.

"Beck," she shouts, and Beck runs into the dining room. Deborah holds up a reservation for two plane tickets. "Guess who's going to Sundance?"

Beck takes the envelope from her mother and unearths a short note from Jake: *I hope you'll come.*

"That's it?" Deborah asks. "That's all he has to say to us?"

"It's plenty," Beck insists.

"I don't understand why I can't go, too." Lydia pouts, leaning against the doorframe as she watches her mother pack. "Jake

562

invited me, you know. It's not fair that you just said no."

Lydia is a teenager now and every inch of her acts the part. Toward Ashley at least. Ryan is insulated from her attitude, her wrath, her scheming. After an early release for good time, he's been home for eight months. In prison, he'd lost his middle-aged bloat and returned to his family taut, something of a stranger. He's quieter now, not exactly broken, but humbled. Rather, he's become more of the man Ashley had met in her early twenties, always complimenting her and making small gestures like having a glass of wine waiting when she walks in the door or folding her eye mask on her nightstand so she's able find it when she's ready for bed. When he was away, almost every meal was takeout. Now that he's returned, the kitchen is once again his domain. He's expanded his cooking repertoire from the ham and baked fish his mom used to make to chicken Kiev, beef Stroganoff, goulash. Ashley and Ryan agree that this family arrangement works best for them, one where women work and men stay home, keeping themselves out of trouble.

After Ashley staged the Whitmores' house, it had sold in a weekend. Their agent asked her to stage two other houses, then offered her a position. Ashley didn't explain to Georgina why she decided to turn down the job at Bartley's. If Georgina were to find out what Ashley is doing instead, she'd tell their old friends, *I offered her a real job. I feel sorry for her, I do, but thank God she didn't take it. I mean, could you imagine? Tragic.* Ashley's life isn't tragic. She has a job she loves, one on a schedule she sets around her family.

For the first month after Ryan returned home, her children were stiff and overly polite with their father, not quite trusting that he was back. Quickly, they began requesting meals, and it became a game, seeing if their father could make baked Alaska, if he had the audacity to cook rabbit. He became a regular at their soccer tournaments and dance recitals. Ashley was relieved that her children weren't embarrassed to have him on the sidelines and in the audience, cheering them on like any other proud father. Eventually, their acceptance gave her the courage to let him in, too.

"We've been over this," Ashley says to her daughter. "You and Ty are going to have a nice weekend with your father."

"All they ever want to do is watch James Bond movies." Lydia holds her pointer finger to her temple and pretends to shoot. "It's so boring."

There are several reasons Ashley needs to go to the premiere alone. First, there's Ryan. She can't bring Lydia and not bring Tyler, and Ryan can only exit the state with permission. She's not ready to leave him alone for a weekend. Whether it's because she doesn't quite trust him or because she feels guilty, she isn't sure.

Second, there's Ashley herself. While Ryan was away, she acted as a single parent. There were weekends where she and the kids drove down to Philadelphia, others where Deborah or Beck came to visit, but even when Deborah watched the kids so Ashley could have a glass of wine with a friend, she was constantly distracted, waiting for a call that the kitchen had caught on fire or that Tyler had broken his arm, doing some sort of séance with his grandmother. This is the first time she can get away in as long as she can remember.

Finally, there's the Millers. She doesn't trust the four of them together again for the first time since they lost the diamond. Whatever's been left unsaid, they need the freedom to say it, to be able to have a Miller-style blowout if the weekend calls for it. That can't happen if Lydia and Tyler are

565

with them.

Ashley stares at her daughter from across the room. Lydia is wearing her uniform of black leggings and a hand-cut T-shirt that is about two inches shorter than Ashley would prefer. She simultaneously looks her age and so much older.

"I need to go alone," Ashley says as she places a camel V-neck sweater in her suitcase.

"Whatever. Besides, it's not like there's anyone famous in Jake's movie, anyway. And, like, half of it's in German." Walking away, she adds, "Also, that's an old lady sweater. Not in a good way."

Ashley surveys the sweater before deciding her daughter is right. All the clothes in her bag are earth-toned as though she's hoping that, if she dresses understatedly, the Millers will behave understatedly, too. As she reconsiders her wardrobe, she realizes she's more than a little nervous about this weekend.

Again, the Miller women meet in Salt Lake City, where a driver takes them to that small, usually quiet town in the mountains. This time, they're familiar with the dress code — boots and sweater jackets, simple makeup and hair. The Millers know a lot more about *The Wom-*

en's Empire than they did *My Summer of Women.* They know it starts with Flora and ends with Helen, that the film is, as one critic wrote, "a heart-wrenching tale of one woman's courage and the lasting impact it had on her daughter." They know they are not a part of this movie, not directly, which makes them more connected to it than the previous film that had tried to capture their lives.

When they arrive at the theater, they can't find Jake. Helen Jr. is in LA with Kristi, which reaffirms Ashley's decision not to bring her children. The Millers must do this alone.

"I guess he's doing some sort of interview," Ashley says, reading a text. "He says he'll find us after."

As the Millers file into a row in the middle of theater, Beck whispers to Ashley, "You know he's not doing an interview."

"Let him have this," Ashley whispers back.

The film begins at night in a taxi on the way to Westbahnhof Station. It's 1939. Helen is the first to speak, begging her mother in German, *Please don't make me go.* Flora does her best to remain upbeat, reminding her daughter that she will have a good life in America, that she is one of the lucky ones. They drive through the rain, Helen muffling her sobs, Flora stroking the hair of a doll in her lap, staring out the window as she tries not to cry. Neither character mentions the doll, but the camera focuses on it momentarily.

Ashley finds a travel pack of tissues at the bottom of her purse, takes one to dab her eyes, and passes the package to her mother and sister.

When Helen and Flora arrive at the station, many of the other children and their families are already waiting. Around them, dogs sniff their bags, ready to attack at the Storm Troopers' sign. When the Goldsteins arrive, the families follow the Americans to the platform. Flora pulls Helen aside as the others continue to walk ahead.

I need you to listen very carefully, Flora whispers, eyeing the guards that circle. *Take this.* She presses the doll into Helen's chest. *Once you're in America and you know it's safe, you can look inside the body of the doll. Do you remember how to cut open a seam?* Helen nods. *Until then, do not let this doll out of your sight. When you sleep, it's with you. Anywhere you go, it goes, too. Don't let anyone touch it. It is your favorite doll. Your papa gave it to you. You cannot be without it.*

A guard approaches them, and Flora motions her daughter to catch up with the others. Flora turns to look at him. He's too young for the uniform he wears, for the hate that hardens his boyish features.

The Goldsteins count the children to make sure they're all there. Once they've reached fifty, they begin to board their car. The good-byes are restrained. Only the youngest, who cannot help themselves, wail, and their parents rush them aboard the train before they cause a scene.

Flora gives her daughter one last hug and says, *I will see you soon. Until then, be good.*

She steps back to join the other parents, watching Helen climb onto the train. The children lean out the windows of their car. They do not blow kisses. They know better than to wave goodbye, to make any gesture that looks like a salute. Helen continues to watch her mother as the train pulls away.

Deborah reaches for her daughters. They cling to each other for the duration of the movie.

After the opening scenes, *The Women's Empire* splits into two storylines, one that flashes back to 1918, the other that moves forward from the train station, following Helen to America.

In 1918, Flora's narrative begins as a romance between a young nurse and the chauffeur who accompanies her to Hungary with the emperor's children. In the early scenes, the camera lingers on Flora and Istvan, a clandestine graze of hands, a stolen kiss. He teaches her to drive. She teaches him the nursery rhymes she sings to the children. The lighting is moody. Classical music plays in the background. They are so young, so beautiful, but quickly their love grows complicated when Flora discovers she's pregnant and they must rush to marry. Before they have a plan in place, revolutionaries storm the palace. Istvan instructs Flora to take the children to the car as he fends off the mob. Flora pleads that she won't leave him, but he insists. As she runs with the children, gunshots echo around them. She puts the car into gear like he's taught her, and pulls away from the palace, her vision blurry from tears.

Her return to the summer palace in Vienna is short-lived, not as welcomed as one might expect, given she's just saved the heirs to the empire. Pregnant and unwed, Flora is banished from her post and must return to Vienna where she has no one. But she's not entirely alone. Before the emperor ships her off, he gives her a parting gift, a precious hatpin, as a thank-you for saving his children.

Flashing forward to 1939, Helen's story is tonally distinct from Flora's, with darker lighting and marked silence. The boat makes her seasick. She fights with the Goldsteins, who find her ungrateful. Privately, they argue whether bringing her was a mistake. There are several shots of Helen staring out to sea, clutching the doll. She disobeys her mother and slices it open to find the hatpin with the Florentine Diamond. When she arrives in Philadelphia, she boards with a family who also finds her sullen. At first, she makes few friends. Each night, she removes the hatpin from its hiding place in her dresser and stares at it before going to bed.

The film leaps to Helen's twentieth birthday, when she's old enough to leave the boarding-house. In order to rent an apartment on Broad Street, she sells a few of the smaller diamonds from the hatpin to a jeweler, Joseph, an Austrian widower who runs a tiny shop on Jewelers' Row. In Vienna, Joseph made watches and jewelry for the emperor. He didn't know Flora, but he knew life in the empire, the crown jewels, the Florentine Diamond. The connection between him and Helen is instantaneous, passionate.

As Helen learns to love, so, too, does Flora. In the 1920s, when Vienna is a liberal para-dise, Flora meets Leib, the second love of her life, at the street market while she and her son, Martin, are buying vegetables. Martin is a naughty child, endearingly so, and Flora scolds him for trying to steal a piece of candy. Not watching where she's going, she bumps into a handsome stranger, scattering the flowers he's carrying. She helps him pick them up, and when he asks her name and she says Flora, he looks at the flowers and thinks she's lying. Leib is so different from Istvan. Muscular where her former lover was lean, playful rather than serious. Like Helen, she's initially resistant to love, and the film cuts between the women learning to let down their guard and embrace the happiness they don't think they deserve.

From there, the film quickly progresses through Vienna in the '30s as the republic becomes a fascist state, then is annexed into Nazi Germany. Again, Flora's life comes crashing down around her. Her husband and son are taken away. She and Helen are relocated to a small, dingy apartment. Meanwhile, in the future, postwar, Joseph wines and dines Helen. As a wedding present, Joseph sets the Florentine in a flower brooch to honor Flora.

The film ends where it begins, at the station in Vienna. Flora watches the train disappear down the tracks, her daughter vanishing into a new life. The camera zooms in on Flora's resolute face, fraught with everything the audience knows that she doesn't. When the screen turns black, there isn't a dry eye in the theater.

Once the applause dies down and everyone

shuffles into the lobby, the Miller women remain seated, unable to put their feelings into words.

When Jake returns, bounding down the aisle to collect his family, he startles. He doesn't know how to interpret his mother and sisters, frozen in their seats watching the dark screen. A familiar dread rises in him as he approaches. He'd checked with Kristi, Ashley. This film honors Helen and Flora. Yet his family sits as quietly as they did after *My Summer of Women.*

Jake inches toward them, bracing himself for another Millerstyle blowout. When his family turns to face him, they aren't angry like he fears but overcome with pride.

"Oh, Jake," Ashley says, running up to hug him.

Beck and Deborah follow Ashley and form a huddle around Jake. His body relaxes. He inhales their scents, the patchouli of his mother, the lavender of Beck's shampoo, the piquancy of Ashley's designer perfume. A bouquet of Millers, enveloping him.

As they walk out of the theater, Beck asks him, "Why'd you decide not to include Zita?"

"I thought about it, but I didn't want to vilify her."

Beck nods. "And Ravensbrück?"

"I didn't want it to become another sadistic

Nazi film, either. That wasn't the point." Despite himself, Jake asks his sister, "So, you liked it?"

Beck nudges her brother with her shoulder. "It was perfect."

She hasn't said she's sorry, and Jake knows they won't talk about their fight in the vault, Viktor, the Florentine Diamond. This is what an apology looks like from Beck, from all of them, Jake included. A Miller-style apology, and as Jake walks into the lobby, flanked by his sisters and mother, off to celebrate Helen and Flora, they all know this is enough.

AUTHOR'S NOTE

This novel came together somewhat seren-
dipitously. For years, I'd had a vague idea
for a novel about a diamond. I love gemstones and how they are a harmony of
geological history, personal history, and, in
the case of a stone like the Florentine
Diamond, international history, too. When I
initially set out to tell a story about a
diamond, I'd never heard of the Florentine
and wasn't planning on writing about the
fall of the Austro-Hungarian Empire. I just
knew I wanted to craft a story centering on
a diamond that had gone missing and followed the bread crumbs of research until
they landed at the Florentine.

This began, as most modern searches do,
with Google. On lists of missing jewels the
Florentine Diamond kept popping up.
There are other famous missing stones —
the Irish crown jewels, the Great Mogul
Diamond, and the Eagle Diamond, to name

a few — but what intrigued me about the Florentine was that every account of its disappearance was slightly different. The articles I read contradicted each other on how the diamond arrived in Italy with the Medicis. They conflicted on who had stolen it in 1918 and the likely whereabouts of the diamond today. Many experts think it was recut into a brilliant round diamond that was sold in Geneva in 1981, but that theory cannot be substantiated and the current whereabouts of that stone are unknown. While such uncertainty isn't promising for relocating the diamond, it's good for a writer of fiction. It afforded me the freedom to create an alternate history for the Florentine that was entirely of my making.

Still, I wanted to tie my narrative as closely to history as I could. I've done my best to be faithful to the past where it's known. This starts with the Medicis. The first confirmed documentation of the diamond was in 1657 — although I've seen that date contested, too — by John Baptiste Tavernier when he toured the Grand Duke of Tuscany's collection. From there, after the Medicis stopped producing male heirs and Francis of Lorraine took over Tuscany, he renamed the diamond the Florentine and brought it to Austria upon his marriage to

Maria Theresa of Austria in 1736. It remained with the Habsburgs until the fall of the empire in 1918.

From these confirmable facts about the diamond I had the starting date for my novel: 1918. After reading *Danubia* by Simon Winder to gain a general appreciation for the massive scope of the Habsburg Empire, I focused my research on the last emperor and empress, Karl and Zita. They were the last proprietors of the diamond, the ones to send the crown jewels ahead to Switzerland when they fled Vienna, those at least tangentially responsible for the disappearance of the Florentine. Despite their legacy, little has been written about them in English. After all, they were in power for only two years. I was quickly drawn to the writings of journalist Gordon Brook-Shepherd, whose biographies on Karl, Zita, and their eldest son, Otto, established the bulk of my knowledge on the royal family. Brook-Shepherd was friendly with Otto, which provided him access to the family's personal archives. It also loaded his writings about the family with bias, as his praise of Karl and Zita contradicted other less flattering descriptions I read of the royal couple. Again, this allowed me to take liberties, particularly when it came to Zita, whose character I largely fabricated on the page. From all accounts I've read, Zita was a strong-willed, deeply religious, and devoted woman, determined to modernize Schönbrunn Palace before the empire so quickly fell. After her husband died, she was equally committed to beatifying him and to having the crown restored to her son Otto. What she was not, was the downfall of Flora Auerbach.

Flora Auerbach is a work of fiction that started with a footnote. In Brook-Shepherd's *The Last Habsburg,* he details the royal couple's decision to leave their children in Gödöllö, Hungary, when they returned to Vienna in October 1918. Beneath a brief description of the revolution in Hungary, Shepherd had written a one-sentence footnote about the mission to rescue the children. It said nothing about who saved them, only that they had a lively drive back to Vienna by way of Pressburg. And that was it. All mention of the harrowing affair.

From my conversations with art lawyer Sarah Odenkirk, I knew that if I wanted to craft a backstory that would convince a court the diamond was lawfully the Millers', I needed a courageous act that might warrant the emperor voluntarily gifting such a valuable stone. In this brief footnote I'd found it. It led me to a series of important questions: Whom would the royal couple have trusted with their children? Who might have snuck the royal children to safety? In turn, why would the emperor have felt compelled to give away such a prized diamond? Thus, Flora the nursemaid was born.

Like my vague instincts of wanting to write about a diamond, I also knew I wanted to set my second novel in Philadelphia. I was feeling a tad homesick when I began this project, and setting the story in Philadelphia enabled me to feel a little closer to home. Then, when I began doing events for my debut novel, *The Bookshop of Yesterdays,* and several of them were in the Philadelphia area, Philly readers were so excited when I told them my next book was set around the city. This committed me to my setting, but once I began researching Helen's past, I realized that Philadelphia was the perfect setting for more significant historical reasons.

As quickly as I decided to set the novel in Philadelphia, I also knew that I wanted the Millers to be Jewish. Much of the community I grew up in outside Philadelphia was comprised of Reform Jews, and I've always been interested in the question of what it means to be Jewish when you aren't religious. At the time, I hadn't planned on writing about the Holocaust. In fact, I was pretty desperate to avoid it. My Jewish ancestors had all immigrated to the US by the early twentieth century, so I wasn't sure it was my history to tell. Plus, so many authors have written so eloquently about the Holocaust that I didn't know what I could contribute. But when I began to think about the link between Austria after WWI and modern-day United States, it felt like I was circumventing a giant hole by trying to write around the Holocaust. Then I discovered the fifty children and that changed everything.

As I began plotting Helen's path to the US, I decided pretty quickly that she emigrated alone. At the time, I didn't know much about Jewish refugee children during WWII, but as soon as I began researching, the scholarship was overwhelming. Judith Tydor Baumel has written extensively about the children who immigrated to Britain and the US. In *Unfulfilled Promise,* she briefly mentions a scheme by a Jewish organization in Philadelphia to bring fifty children to the US from Germany. And as research so often goes, from those two paragraphs, I did some digging in ship records on Ancestry.com and in newspapers only to discover that the children were brought over from Vienna — part of Nazi Germany at the time — by Gilbert and Eleanor Kraus, who personally traveled to Austria to rescue the children. From there, the Goldsteins and Helen's journey to the US started to take shape.

I'd be remiss not to mention both the HBO documentary *50 Children: The Rescue Mission of Mr. and Mrs. Kraus,* directed by Steven Pressman, and his subsequent book, *50 Children,* which together offer an exhaustive overview of the Kraus's heroic journey to Nazi-controlled Vienna and the American lives of the children they saved. While my characters are a work of fiction and Helen's guilt over leaving her mother behind is uniquely her own, these works were instrumental in helping me understand the scope of such a mission.

The main thing I've learned from writing this book is to follow the research. It can lead you to unexpected corners of history you'd otherwise never know. When I started writing this novel, I had no idea what it would become. Somehow, through inquisitiveness and discovery, it evolved more into the book I wanted to write than I ever could have anticipated.

FURTHER READING

The Habsburgs

Brook-Shepherd, Gordon. *The Last Empress: The Life and Times of Zita of Austria-Hungary, 1892–1989.* New York: Harper-Collins Publishers, 1991.

Brook-Shepherd, Gordon. *The Last Habsburg.* New York: Weybright and Talley, 1968.

Brook-Shepherd, Gordon. *Uncrowned Emperor: The Life and Times of Otto von Habsburg.* London: Hambledon and London, 2003.

Winder, Simon. *Danubia: A Personal History of Habsburg Europe.* New York: Farrar, Straus and Giroux, 2014.

Diamonds

Balfour, Ian. *Famous Diamonds.* London: William Collins Sons and Co, 1987.

Everitt, Sally, and David Lancaster. *Christie's Twentieth-Century Jewelry.* New York: Watson-Guptill, 2002.

Falls, Susan. *Clarity, Cut, and Culture: The Many Meanings of Diamonds.* New York: New York University Press, 2014.

Raulet, Sylvie. *Jewelry of the 1940s and 1950s*. New York: Rizzoli, 1988.

Cultural Property and the Law

Donovan, Jim, ed. "Cultural Property Law." *United States Attorneys' Bulletin* 64, no.2 (March 2016), www.justice.gov/usao/resources/journal-of-federal-law-and-practice.

Gerstenblith, Patty. *Art, Cultural Heritage, and the Law: Cases and Materials*. Durham, NC: Carolina Academic Press, 2004.

Goodman, Simon. *The Orpheus Clock: The Search for My Family's Art Treasures Stolen by the Nazis*. New York: Scribner, 2015.

O'Connor, Anne-Marie. *The Lady in Gold: The Extraordinary Tale of Gustav Klimt's Masterpiece, Portrait of Adele Bloch-Bauer*. New York: Knopf, 2012.

Wittman, Robert K., and John Shiffman. *Priceless: How I Went Undercover to Rescue the World's Stolen Treasures*. New York: Crown Publishers, 2010.

Jewish Children Refugees

Baumel, Judith Tydor. *Unfulfilled Promise: Rescue and Resettlement of Jewish Refugee Children in the United States, 1934–*

1945. Juneau, Alaska: Denali Press, 1990.

Jason, Philip K., and Iris Posner, eds. *Don't Wave Goodbye: The Children's Flight from Nazi Persecution to American Freedom.* Westport, CT: Praeger, 2004.

Pressman, Steven, and Paul A. Shapiro. *50 Children: One Ordinary American Couple's Extraordinary Rescue Mission into the Heart of Nazi Germany.* New York: Harper, 2014.

ACKNOWLEDGMENTS

As I sit here, compiling a list of everyone who deserves more praise and gratitude than I can possibly offer in these acknowledgments, I'm amazed at just how many people it's taken to bring this book into being. First, to my publishing family: my always-supportive agent, Stephanie Cabot, her wonderful assistant, Ellen Coughtrey, and Rebecca Gardner, Will Roberts, Anna Worrall, and everyone at The Gernert Company; to the team at Park Row Books, especially Erika Imranyi, Emer Flounders, and my editor, Natalie Hallak, whose enthusiasm for the book has rivaled my own and whose diligence continues to astound me. Additionally, I'd like to thank all the amazing booksellers and librarians I got to meet while promoting my first novel, *The Bookshop of Yesterdays.* Your enthusiasm for my work and for the fiction world more generally made me excited to get back to the page, so I could share this book with you. Also, to all the readers who provided me with much-needed motivation to write another novel. Your emails and letters have been an unexpected joy in the publishing process.

Every writing project teaches you some essential truth, and with this novel, I discovered the tremendous generosity of strangers. This project involved a considerable amount of research, more than I hope is obvious on the page. Thank you to Sarah Odenkirk for explaining the basics of cultural property and art law to me and for planting the seed that helped me craft Flora's backstory. To Ann Flores for explaining diamond grading, educating me on jewelry houses, and introducing me to Elizabeth Taylor's diamonds.

To everyone at the Gemological Institute of America who donated their time to teaching me about gemstones and your incredible institution: to Amanda Luke, who fortuitously showed up at my reading at Northshire Bookstore in Saratoga Springs and put me in touch with her colleagues at GIA; to Stephen Morisseau for hosting me on an unforgettable tour; to Nellie Barnett and Kelly Bennett for showing me around; to McKenzie Santimer for illustrating how gemstones are made; and so many others. A special thanks to Al Gilbertson for explaining the nuances of midcentury jewelry and to Cathy Jonathan for helping me explore countless designs for Helen's brooch before landing on the perfect cattleya orchid.

Quig Bruning at Sotheby's was also instrumental in teaching me about historic diamonds. Thanks for showing me the Magnificent Jewels Collection and pointing me toward other mysteries in the gemological world that helped me with my story about the Florentine.

Thank you to Bob Raymar for putting me in touch with Bob Wittman, whose career with the FBI's Art Crime Team I wish I could have in another life. Bob not only shared his stories of recovering stolen art but was the first to explain the role civil forfeitures play in cultural property cases. This led me to Stef Cassella, whom I blindly emailed after reading his essay on forfeiture laws to protect cultural heritage. Stef, I still can't believe how much time you donated to explaining the mechanics of cultural property law and civil forfeitures to a complete stranger.

Equally unbelievable was the assistance of Martin Mutschlechner, a historian at Schönbrunn Palace in Vienna. Your vast knowledge of the Habsburgs is astonishing. Thank you for answering my often peculiar and idiosyncratic questions about Karl and Zita. You provided me with so many details on their lives that I otherwise never could have uncovered.

For other facets of research, thank you to Rebecca Rosenberger Smolen, who detailed the probate process in Pennsylvania. To Candice Gray, who shared her stories of working as a vet tech. While much of what you two taught me didn't make it into the final draft, it gave me the necessary background to feel confident about what did. To Mara Fein, professional genealogist, who in teaching me how to conduct ancestral research helped me work backward to plant genealogical clues for the Millers to find. Thank you to Rita Durant for helping correct mistakes in my use of German and to Susan Greenbaum and Debbie Poul for helping with details about Philadelphia.

Every writer needs trusted readers, and I'm fortunate to have many. Thank you to Emily Baker, Antonio Elefano, Tatiana Uschakow, Alexandra D'Italia, Amanda Treyz, Debra Poul, Lindsay Perrotta, and Jess Cantiello for reading various drafts and providing invaluable input. A special additional thanks to Amanda Treyz for trekking through the snow in Krems an der Donau with me until I found the perfect yellow house for my book and for instilling a love of Grüner Veltliner in me.

I'm equally lucky to have such a supportive and inspiring community of friends. There are too many of you to name here, but I hope you know that your companionship means so much to me.

Before my first novel, my parents had never read any of my writing, but this time, I let them in from the earliest drafts. Thanks to my dad, Jack Meyerson, for answering all the legal questions I was too embarrassed to ask my other contacts. To my mom, Pam Meyerson, for her attention to detail in reading my final draft. To my brother, Jeff, for his encouragement and calming presence. To my adorable niece, Alice, for providing me with much-needed distractions and for posing in countless photos with my first novel. I hope there will be many more with this book. To my sister-in-law, Jen Chan, for sending said pictures when I needed a smile and for always being so encouraging of this and every project. To Linda Chan for sharing her courageous past with me. To Jessica Chan for answering my random and somewhat morbid questions about childbirth yet again with this novel.

To the Perrottas for their support and for providing me with another home in Saratoga Springs.

Finally, to Adam and the little family we're starting together. I don't think I'll ever fully accept your limitless belief in me, but I require it nonetheless. I can't wait to start this next stage of our lives together. And to our son, who as I write this is still inside me. Thank you for reminding me with your painful kicks and elbows that I'd better get moving if I want to finish this book before you arrive. It's impossible to think that right now I don't know you, but soon you'll be the center of our world.

ABOUT THE AUTHOR

Amy Meyerson is the author of the international bestseller, *The Bookshop of Yesterdays*. She teaches in the writing department at the University of Southern California, where she completed her graduate work in creative writing. She has been published in numerous literary magazines and currently lives in Los Angeles.

The employees of Thorndike Press hope you have enjoyed this Large Print book. All our Thorndike, Wheeler, and Kennebec Large Print titles are designed for easy reading, and all our books are made to last. Other Thorndike Press Large Print books are available at your library, through selected bookstores, or directly from us.

For information about titles, please call:

(800) 223-1244

or visit our website at:

gale.com/thorndike

To share your comments, please write:

Publisher
Thorndike Press
10 Water St., Suite 310
Waterville, ME 04901